# UNWIND

*Also by Neal Shusterman*

Unwind
Unwholly
Unstrung (an e-novella)
Unsouled


Everlost
Everwild
Everfound

# UNWIND
## NEAL SHUSTERMAN

SIMON AND SCHUSTER

First published in Great Britain in 2008 by Simon & Schuster UK Ltd
1st Floor, 222 Gray's Inn Road, London WC1X 8HB
A CBS COMPANY

www.simonandschuster.co.uk

This edition published in 2012

Originally published in 2007 by Simon & Schuster Books for Young Readers,
An imprint of Simon & Schuster Children's Publishing Division, New York

Copyright © 2007 by Neal Shusterman

A CIP catalogue record for this book is available
from the British Library.

ISBN: 978-0-85707-997-8

3  5  7  9  10  8  6  4

Printed and bound by CPI Group (UK) Ltd, Croydon, CR0 4YY.

Dedicated to the memory
of Barbara Seranella

*"If more people had been organ donors*
*Unwinding never would have happened."*
—THE ADMIRAL

# Acknowledgments

When it comes to a novel, the sum of the parts are sometimes greater than the whole. This book could not have been possible without my editor, David Gale, who challenged me to make this book the best it could be. In fact, I owe a debt of gratitude to everyone at Simon & Schuster, not just for their support of this book, but for being so supportive of all my work.

Thanks to my kids, Brendan, Jarrod, Joelle, and Erin, for being the kind of wonderful kids no one would ever unwind—and a special thanks to Jarrod, who not only created my MySpace page, but pre-read *Unwind* and gave me a set of brilliant editorial notes that substantially helped me with early drafts even before the manuscript went to the publisher.

Thanks to Haidy Fisher and her son, Cyrus, who came up with the name CyFi, and let me borrow it for one of my favorite characters.

To my writing group, the Fictionaires, for their constant insight, as well as Trumanell Maples and Leigh Ann Jones, media specialists extraordinaire, who helped immensely as I was working through my second draft.

To Steve Layne, who, when I told him this idea, sat me down and said "You MUST write this book."

Thanks to my assistant, Brandi Lomeli, for being my brain.

I'd like to thank Justin Sewell of despair.com (one of the funniest websites I've ever seen) for allowing me to reference their "demotivational" poster on "Ambition."

I'd also like to thank Charles Pamment of the BBC, Jim Bremner and Joe Zentner of desertusa.com, and Dave Finn, for their help with the factual info between sections. The soul for sale on eBay, and the response is real. The airplane graveyard exists—and the chilling story of the Ukrainian babies taken for their parts is true, proving that fiction is all too often one rationalization away from reality.

# The Bill of Life

The Second Civil War, also known as "The Heartland War," was a long
and bloody conflict fought over a single issue.

To end the war, a set of constitutional amendments known as
"The Bill of Life" was passed.

It satisfied both the Pro-life and the Pro-choice armies.

The Bill of Life states that human life may not be touched
from the moment of conception until a child reaches
the age of thirteen.

However, between the ages of thirteen and eighteen, a parent may
choose to retroactively "abort" a child . . .

. . . on the condition that the child's life doesn't "technically" end.

The process by which a child is both terminated and yet kept alive
is called "unwinding."

Unwinding is now a common, and accepted practice in society.

## Part One

# Triplicate

*"I was never going to amount to much anyway, but now, statistically speaking, there's a better chance that some part of me will go on to greatness somewhere in the world. I'd rather be partly great than entirely useless."*

—SAMSON WARD

# 1 · Connor

"There are places you can go," Ariana tells him, "and a guy as smart as you has a decent chance of surviving to eighteen."

Connor isn't so sure, but looking into Ariana's eyes makes his doubts go away, if only for a moment. Her eyes are sweet violet with streaks of gray. She's such a slave to fashion— always getting the newest pigment injection the second it's in style. Connor was never into that. He's always kept his eyes the color they came in. Brown. He never even got tattoos, like so many kids get these days when they're little. The only color on his skin is the tan it takes during the summer, but now, in November, that tan has long faded. He tries not to think about the fact that he'll never see the summer again. At least not as Connor Lassiter. He still can't believe that his life is being stolen from him at sixteen.

Ariana's violet eyes begin to shine as they fill with tears that flow down her cheeks when she blinks. "Connor, I'm so sorry." She holds him, and for a moment it seems as if everything is okay, as if they are the only two people on Earth. For that instant, Connor feels invincible, untouchable . . . but she lets go, the moment passes, and the world around him returns. Once more he can feel the rumble of the freeway beneath them, as cars pass by, not knowing or caring that he's here. Once more he is just a marked kid, a week short of unwinding.

The soft, hopeful things Ariana tells him don't help now. He can barely hear her over the rush of traffic. This place where they hide from the world is one of those dangerous places that

3

make adults shake their heads, grateful that their own kids aren't stupid enough to hang out on the ledge of a freeway overpass. For Connor it's not about stupidity, or even rebellion—it's about feeling life. Sitting on this ledge, hidden behind an exit sign is where he feels most comfortable. Sure, one false step and he's roadkill. Yet for Connor, life on the edge is home.

There have been no other girls he's brought here, although he hasn't told Ariana that. He closes his eyes, feeling the vibration of the traffic as if it's pulsing through his veins, a part of him. This has always been a good place to get away from fights with his parents, or when he just feels generally boiled. But now Connor's beyond boiled—even beyond fighting with his mom and dad. There's nothing more to fight about. His parents signed the order—it's a done deal.

"We should run away," Ariana says. "I'm fed up with everything, too. My family, school, everything. I could kick-AWOL, and never look back."

Connor hangs on the thought. The idea of kicking-AWOL by himself terrifies him. He might put up a tough front, he might act like the bad boy at school—but running away on his own? He doesn't even know if he has the guts. But if Ariana comes, that's different. That's not alone. "Do you mean it?"

Ariana looks at him with her magical eyes. "Sure. Sure I do. I could leave here. If you asked me."

Connor knows this is major. Running away with an Unwind—*that's* commitment. The fact that she would do it moves him beyond words. He kisses her, and in spite of everything going on in his life Connor suddenly feels like the luckiest guy in the world. He holds her—maybe a little too tightly, because she starts to squirm. It just makes him want to hold her even more tightly, but he fights that urge and lets go. She smiles at him.

4

"AWOL . . ." she says. "What does that mean, anyway?"

"It's an old military term or something," Connor says. "It means 'absent without leave.'"

Ariana thinks about it, and grins. "Hmm. More like 'alive without lectures.'"

Connor takes her hand, trying hard not to squeeze it too tightly. She said she'd go if he asked her. Only now does he realize he hasn't actually asked yet.

"Will you come with me, Ariana?"

Ariana smiles and nods. "Sure," she says. "Sure I will."

Ariana's parents don't like Connor. "We always knew he'd be an Unwind," he can just hear them saying. "You should have stayed away from that Lassiter boy." He was never "Connor" to them. He was always "that Lassiter boy." They think that just because he's been in and out of disciplinary school they have a right to judge him.

Still, when he walks her home that afternoon, he stops short of her door, hiding behind a tree as she goes inside. Before he heads home, he thinks how hiding is now going to be a way of life for both of them.

Home.

Connor wonders how he can call the place he lives home, when he's about to be evicted—not just from the place he sleeps, but from the hearts of those who are supposed to love him.

His father sits in a chair, watching the news as Connor enters.

"Hi, Dad."

His father points at some random carnage on the news. "Clappers again."

"What did they hit this time?"

"They blew up an Old Navy in the North Akron mall."

5

"Hmm," says Connor. "You'd think they'd have better taste."

"I don't find that funny."

Connor's parents don't know that Connor knows he's being unwound. He wasn't supposed to find out, but Connor has always been good at ferreting out secrets. Three weeks ago, while looking for a stapler in his dad's home office, he found airplane tickets to the Bahamas. They were going on a family vacation over Thanksgiving. One problem, though: There were only three tickets. His mother, his father, his younger brother. No ticket for him. At first he just figured the ticket was somewhere else, but the more he thought about it, the more it seemed wrong. So Connor went looking a little deeper when his parents were out, and he found it. The Unwind order. It had been signed in old-fashioned triplicate. The white copy was already gone—off with the authorities. The yellow copy would accompany Connor to his end, and the pink would stay with his parents, as evidence of what they'd done. Perhaps they would frame it and hang it alongside his first-grade picture.

The date on the order was the day before the Bahamas trip. He was going off to be unwound, and they were going on vacation to make themselves feel better about it. The unfairness of it had made Connor want to break something. It had made him want to break a lot of things—but he hadn't. For once he had held his temper, and aside from a few fights in school that weren't his fault, he kept his emotions hidden. He kept what he knew to himself. Everyone knew that an unwind order was irreversible, so screaming and fighting wouldn't change a thing. Besides, he found a certain power in knowing his parents' secret. Now the blows he could deal them were so much more effective. Like the day he brought flowers home for his mother and she cried for hours. Like the B-plus he brought home on a science test. Best grade he ever got in science. He handed it to his father, who looked at it, the color draining from his face. "See, Dad, my grades are getting better. I could even bring my science grade up to an A by the end of the semester." An hour later his father was sitting in a chair, still clutching the test in his hand, and staring blankly at the wall.

Connor's motivation was simple: Make them suffer. Let them know for the rest of their lives what a horrible mistake they made.

But there was no sweetness to this revenge, and now, three weeks of rubbing it in their faces has made him feel no better. In spite of himself he's starting to feel bad for his parents, and he hates that he feels that way.

"Did I miss dinner?"

His father doesn't look away from the TV. "Your mother left a plate for you."

Connor heads off toward the kitchen, but halfway there he hears:

"Connor?"

He turns to see his father looking at him. Not just looking, but staring. *He's going to tell me now,* Connor thinks. *He's going to tell me they're unwinding me, and then break down in tears, going on and on about how sorry sorry sorry he is about it all.* If he does, Connor just might accept the apology. He might even forgive him, and then tell him that he doesn't plan to be here when the Juvey-cops come to take him away. But in the end all his father says is, "Did you lock the door when you came in?"

"I'll do it now."

Connor locks the door, then goes to his room, no longer hungry for whatever it is his mother saved for him.

\* \* \*

7

At two in the morning Connor dresses in black and fills a backpack with the things that really matter to him. He still has room for three changes of clothes. He finds it amazing, when it comes down to it, how few things are worth taking. Memories, mostly. Reminders of a time before things went so wrong between him and his parents. Between him and the rest of the world.

Connor peeks in on his brother, thinks about waking him to say good-bye, then decides it's not a good idea. He silently slips out into the night. He can't take his bike, because he had installed an antitheft tracking device. Connor never considered that he might be the one stealing it. Ariana has bikes for both of them though.

Ariana's house is a twenty-minute walk, if you take the conventional route. Suburban Ohio neighborhoods never have streets that go in straight lines, so instead he takes the more direct route, through the woods, and makes it there in ten.

The lights in Ariana's house are off. He expected this. It would have been suspicious if she had stayed awake all night. Better to pretend she's sleeping, so she won't alert any suspicion. He keeps his distance from the house. Ariana's yard and front porch are equipped with motion-sensor lights that come on whenever anything moves into range. They're meant to scare off wild animals and criminals. Ariana's parents are convinced that Connor is both.

He pulls out his phone and dials the familiar number. From where he stands in the shadows at the edge of the backyard he can hear it ring in her room upstairs. Connor disconnects quickly and ducks farther back into the shadows, for fear that Ariana's parents might be looking out from their windows. What is she thinking? Ariana was supposed to leave her phone on vibrate.

He makes a wide arc around the edge of the backyard,

wide enough not to set off the lights, and although a light comes on when he steps onto the front porch, only Ariana's bedroom faces that way. She comes to the door a few moments later, opening it not quite wide enough for her to come out or for him to go in.

"Hi, are you ready?" asks Connor. Clearly she's not; she wears a robe over satin pajamas. "You didn't forget, did you?"

"No, no, I didn't forget. . . ."

"So hurry up! The sooner we get out of here, the more of a lead we'll get before anyone knows we're gone."

"Connor," she says, "here's the thing . . ."

And the truth is right there in her voice, in the way it's such a strain for her to even say his name, the quiver of apology lingering in the air like an echo. She doesn't have to say anything after that, because he knows, but he lets her say it anyway. Because he sees how hard it is for her, and he wants it to be. He wants it to be the hardest thing she's ever done in her life.

"Connor, I really want to go, I do . . . but it's just a really bad time for me. My sister's getting married, and you know she picked me to be the maid of honor. And then there's school."

"You hate school. You said you'd be dropping out when you turn sixteen."

"*Testing* out," she says. "There's a difference."

"So you're not coming?"

"I want to, I really, *really* want to . . . but I can't."

"So everything we talked about was just a lie."

"No," says Ariana. "It was a dream. Reality got in the way, that's all. And running away doesn't solve anything."

"Running away is the only way to save my life," Connor hisses. "I'm about to be unwound, in case you forgot."

She gently touches his face. "I know," she says. "But I'm not."

9

Then a light comes on at the top of the stairs, and reflexively Ariana closes the door a few inches.

"Ari?" Connor hears her mother say. "What is it? What are you doing at the door?"

Connor backs up out of view, and Ariana turns to look up the stairs. "Nothing, Mom. I thought I saw a coyote from my window and I just wanted to make sure the cats weren't out."

"The cats are upstairs, honey. Close the door and go back to bed."

"So, I'm a coyote," says Connor.

"Shush," says Ariana, closing the door until there's just a tiny slit and all he can see is the edge of her face and a single violet eye. "You'll get away, I know you will. Call me once you're somewhere safe." Then she closes the door.

Connor stands there for the longest time, until the motion sensor light goes out. Being alone had not been part of his plan, but he realizes it should have been. From the moment his parents signed those papers, Connor was alone.

He can't take a train; he can't take a bus. Sure, he has enough money, but nothing's leaving until morning, and by then they'll be looking for him in all the obvious places. Unwinds on the run are so common these days, they have whole teams of Juvey-cops dedicated to finding them. The police have it down to an art.

He knows he'd be able to disappear in a city, because there are so many faces, you never see the same one twice. He knows he can also disappear in the country, where people are so few and far between; he could set up house in an old barn and no one would think to look. But then, Connor figures the police probably thought of that. They probably have every old barn set up to spring like a rat trap, snaring kids like him. Or maybe he's just being paranoid. No, Connor knows his situation

10

calls for justified caution—not just tonight, but for the next two years. Then once he turns eighteen, he's home free. After that, sure, they can throw him in jail, they can put him on trial—but they can't unwind him. Surviving that long is the trick.

Down by the interstate there's a rest stop where truckers pull off the road for the night. This is where Connor goes. He figures he can slip in the back of an eighteen-wheeler, but he quickly learns that truckers keep their cargo locked. He curses himself for not having forethought enough to consider that. Thinking ahead has never been one of Connor's strong points. If it was, he might not have gotten into the various situations that have plagued him over these past few years. Situations that got him labels like "troubled" and "at risk," and finally this last label, "unwind."

There are about twenty parked trucks, and a brightly lit diner where half a dozen truckers eat. It's 3:30 in the morning. Apparently truckers have their own biological clocks. Connor watches and waits. Then, at about a quarter to four, a police cruiser pulls silently into the truck stop. No lights, no siren. It slowly circles the lot like a shark. Connor thinks he can hide, until he sees a second police car pulling in. There are too many lights over the lot for Connor to hide in shadows, and he can't bolt without being seen in the bright moonlight. A patrol car comes around the far end of the lot. In a second its head- lights will be on him, so he rolls beneath a truck and prays the cops haven't seen him.

He watches as the patrol car's wheels slowly roll past. On the other side of the eighteen-wheeler the second patrol car passes in the opposite direction. *Maybe this is just a routine check,* he thinks. *Maybe they're not looking for me.* The more he thinks about it, the more he convinces himself that's the case. They can't know he's gone yet. His father sleeps like a log, and his mother never checks on Connor during the night anymore.

Still, the police cars circle.

From his spot beneath the truck Connor sees the driver's door of another eighteen-wheeler open. No—it's not the driver's door, it's the door to the little bedroom behind the cab. A trucker emerges, stretches, and heads toward the truckstop bathrooms, leaving the door ajar.

In the hairbreadth of a moment, Connor makes a decision and bolts from his hiding spot, racing across the lot to that truck. Loose gravel skids out from under his feet as he runs. He doesn't know where the cop cars are anymore, but it doesn't matter. He has committed himself to this course of action and he has to see it through. As he nears the door he sees head-lights arcing around, about to turn toward him. He pulls open the door to the truck's sleeper, hurls himself inside, and pulls the door closed behind him.

He sits on a bed not much bigger than a cot, catching his breath. What's his next move? The trucker will be back. Connor has about five minutes if he's lucky, one minute if he's not. He peers beneath the bed. There's space down there where he can hide, but it's blocked by two duffle bags full of clothes. He could pull them out, squeeze in, and pull the duffle bags back in front of him. The trucker would never know he's there. But even before he can get the first duffle bag out, the door swings open. Connor just stands there, unable to react as the trucker reaches in to grab his jacket and sees him.

"Whoa! Who are you? What the hell you doin' in my truck?"

A police car cruises slowly past behind him.

"Please," Connor says, his voice suddenly squeaky like it was before his voice changed. "Please, don't tell anyone. I've got to get out of this place." He reaches into his backpack, fumbling, and pulls out a wad of bills from his wallet. "You want money? I've got money. I'll give you all I've got."

"I don't want your money," the trucker says.

"All right, then, what?"

Even in the dim light the trucker must see the panic in Connor's eyes, but he doesn't say a thing.

"Please," says Connor again. "I'll do anything you want. . . ."

The trucker looks at him in silence for a moment more. "Is that so?" he finally says. Then he steps inside and closes the door behind him.

Connor shuts his eyes, not daring to consider what he's just gotten himself into.

The trucker sits beside him. "What's your name?"

"Connor." Then he realizes a moment too late he should have given a fake name.

The trucker scratches his beard stubble and thinks for a moment. "Let me show you something, Connor." He reaches over Connor and grabs, of all things, a deck of cards from a little pouch hanging next to the bed. "Did ya ever see this?" The trucker takes the deck of cards in one hand and does a skillful one-handed shuffle. "Pretty good, huh?"

Connor, not knowing what to say, just nods.

"How about this?" Then the trucker takes a single card and with sleight of hand makes the card vanish into thin air. Then he reaches over and pulls the card right out of Connor's shirt pocket. "You like that?"

Connor lets out a nervous laugh.

"Well, those tricks you just saw?" The trucker says, "I didn't do 'em."

"I . . . don't know what you mean."

The trucker rolls up his sleeve to reveal that the arm, which had done the tricks, had been grafted on at the elbow.

"Ten years ago I fell asleep at the wheel," the trucker tells him. "Big accident. I lost an arm, a kidney, and a few other things. I got new ones, though, and I pulled through." He looks at his hands, and now Connor can see that the trick-card hand is a little different from the other one. The trucker's other hand has thicker fingers, and the skin is a bit more olive in tone.

"So," says Connor, "you got dealt a new hand."

The trucker laughs at that, then he becomes quiet for a moment, looking at his replacement hand. "These fingers here knew things the rest of me didn't. Muscle memory, they call it. And there's not a day that goes by that I don't wonder what other incredible things that kid who owned this arm knew, before he was unwound . . . whoever he was."

The trucker stands up. "You're lucky you came to me," he says. "There are truckers out there who'll take whatever you offer, then turn you in anyway."

"And you're not like that?"

"No, I'm not." He puts out his hand—his *other* hand—and Connor shakes it. "Josias Aldridge," he says. "I'm heading north from here. You can ride with me till morning."

Connor's relief is so great, it takes the wind right out of him. He can't even offer a thank-you.

"That bed there's not the most comfortable in the world," says Aldridge, "but it does the job. Get yourself some rest. I just gotta go take a dump, and then we'll be on our way." Then he closes the door, and Connor listens to his footsteps heading off toward the bathroom. Connor finally lets his guard down and begins to feel his own exhaustion. The trucker didn't give him a destination, just a direction, and that's fine. North, south, east, west—it doesn't matter as long as it's away from here. As for his next move, well, first he's got to get through this one before he can think about what comes next.

A minute later Connor's already beginning to doze when he hears the shout from outside.

"We know you're in there! Come out now and you won't get hurt!"

Connor's heart sinks. Josias Aldridge has apparently pulled another sleight of hand. He's made Connor appear for the police. Abracadabra. With his journey over before it even began, Connor swings the door open to see three Juvey-cops aiming weapons.

But they're not aiming at him.

In fact, their backs are to him.

Across the way, the cab door swings open of the truck he had hidden under just a few minutes before, and a kid comes out from behind the empty driver's seat, his hands in the air. Connor recognizes him right away. It's a kid he knows from school. Andy Jameson.

*My God, is Andy being unwound too?*

There's a look of fear on Andy's face, but beyond it is something worse. A look of utter defeat. That's when Connor realizes his own folly. He'd been so surprised by this turn of events that he's still just standing there, exposed for anyone to see. Well, the policemen don't see him. But Andy does. He catches sight of Connor, holds his gaze, only for a moment . . .

. . . and in that moment something remarkable happens.

The look of despair on Andy's face is suddenly replaced by a steely resolve bordering on triumph. He quickly looks away from Connor and takes a few steps before the police grab him—steps *away* from Connor, so that the police still have their backs to him.

Andy had seen him and had not given him away! If Andy has nothing else after this day, at least he'll have this small victory.

Connor leans back into the shadows of the truck and slowly

15

pulls the door closed. Outside, as the police take Andy away, Connor lies back down, and his tears come as sudden as a summer downpour. He's not sure who he's crying for—for Andy, for himself, for Ariana—and not knowing makes his tears flow all the more. Instead of wiping the tears away he lets them dry on his face like he used to when he was a little boy and the things he cried about were so insignificant that they'd be forgotten by morning.

The trucker never comes to check on him. Instead Connor hears the engine start and feels the truck pulling out. The gentle motion of the road rocks him to sleep.

The ring of Connor's cell phone wakes him out of a deep sleep. He fights consciousness. He wants to go back to the dream he was having. It was about a place he was sure he had been to, although he couldn't quite remember when. He was at a cabin on a beach with his parents, before his brother was born. Connor's leg had fallen through a rotted board on the porch into spiderwebs so thick, they felt like cotton. Connor had screamed and screamed from the pain, and the fear of the giant spiders that he was convinced would eat his leg off. And yet, this was a good dream—a good memory—because his father was there to pull him free, and carry him inside, where they bandaged his leg and sat him by the fire with some kind of cider so flavorful, he could still taste it when he thought about it. His father told him a story that he can no longer remember, but that's all right. It wasn't the story but the tone of his voice that mattered, a gentle baritone rumble as calming as waves breaking on a shore. Little-boy-Connor drank his cider and leaned back against his mother pretending to fall asleep, but what he was really doing was trying to dissolve into the moment and make it last forever. In the dream he did dissolve. His whole being flowed into the cider cup, and his parents placed it gently on the table, close enough to the fire to keep it warm forever and always.

Stupid dreams. Even the good ones are bad, because they remind you how poorly reality measures up.

His cell phone rings again, chasing away the last of the dream. Connor almost answers it. The sleeper room of the truck is so dark, he doesn't realize at first that he's not in his own bed. The only thing that saves him is that he can't find his phone and he must turn on a light. When he finds a wall where his nightstand should be, he realizes that this isn't his room. The phone rings again. That's when it all comes back to him, and he remembers where he is. Connor finds his phone in his backpack. The phone ID says the call is from his father.

So now his parents know he's gone. Do they really think he'll answer his phone? He waits until voicemail takes the call, then he turns off the power. His watch says 7:30 a.m. He rubs the sleep out of his eyes, trying to calculate how far they've come. The truck isn't moving anymore, but they must have traveled at least two hundred miles while he slept. It's a good start.

There's a knock on the door. "Come on out, kid. Your ride's over."

Connor's not complaining—it was outrageously generous of this truck driver to do what he did. Connor won't ask any more of him. He swings open the door and steps out to thank the man, but it's not Josias Aldridge at the door. Aldridge is a few yards away being handcuffed, and in front of Connor is a policeman: a Juvey-cop wearing a smile as big as all outdoors. Standing ten yards away is Connor's father, still holding the cell phone he had just called from.

"It's over, son," his father says.

It makes Connor furious. *I'm not your son!* He wants to shout. *I stopped being your son when you signed the unwind*

17

*order!* But the shock of the moment leaves him speechless.

It had been so stupid of Connor to leave his cell phone on—that's how they tracked him—and he wonders how many other kids are caught by their own blind trust of technology. Well, Connor's not going the way Andy Jameson did. He quickly assesses the situation. The truck has been pulled over to the side of the interstate by two highway patrol cars and a Juvey-cop unit. Traffic barrels past at seventy miles per hour, oblivious to the little drama unfolding on the shoulder. Connor makes a split-second decision and bolts, pushing the officer against the truck and racing across the busy highway. Would they shoot an unarmed kid in the back, he wonders, or would they shoot him in the legs and spare his vital organs? As he races onto the interstate, cars swerve around him, but he keeps on going.

"Connor, stop!" he hears his father yell. Then he hears a gun fire.

He feels the impact, but not in his skin. The bullet embeds in his backpack. He doesn't look behind him. Then, as he reaches the highway median, he hears another gunshot, and a small blue splotch appears on the center divider. They're firing tranquilizer bullets. They're not taking him out, they're trying to take him down—and they're much more likely to fire tranq bullets at will, than regular bullets.

Connor climbs over the center divider, and finds himself in the path of a Cadillac that's not stopping for anything. The car swerves to avoid him, and by sheer luck Connor's momentum takes him just a few inches out of the Caddy's path. Its side mirror smacks him painfully in the ribs before the car screeches to a halt, sending the acrid stench of burned rubber up his nostrils. Holding his aching side, Connor sees someone looking at him from an open window of the backseat. It's another kid, dressed all in white. The kid is terrified.

18

With the police already reaching the center divider, Connor looks into the eyes of this frightened kid, and knows what he has to do. It's time for another split-second decision. He reaches through the window, pulls up the lock, and opens the door.

# 2 · Risa

Risa paces backstage, waiting for her turn at the piano.

She knows she could play the sonata in her sleep—in fact, she often does. So many nights she would wake up to feel her fingers playing on the bed sheets. She would hear the music in her head, and it would still play for a few moments after she awoke, but then it would dissolve into the night, leaving nothing but her fingers drumming against the covers.

She *has* to know the Sonata. It *has* to come to her as easily as breathing.

"It's not a competition," Mr. Durkin always tells her. "There are no winners or losers at a recital."

Well, Risa knows better.

"Risa Ward," the stage manager calls. "You're up."

She rolls her shoulders, adjusts the barrette in her long brown hair, then she takes the stage. The applause from the audience is polite, nothing more. Some of it is genuine, for she does have friends out there, and teachers who want her to succeed. But mostly it's the obligatory applause from an audience waiting to be impressed.

Mr. Durkin is out there. He has been her piano teacher for five years. He's the closest thing Risa has to a parent. She's lucky. Not every kid at Ohio State Home 23 has a teacher they can say that about. Most StaHo kids hate their teachers, because they see them as jailers.

Ignoring the stiff formality of her recital dress, she sits at the piano; it's a concert Steinway as ebony as the night, and just as long.

Focus.

She keeps her eyes on the piano, forcing the audience to recede into darkness. The audience doesn't matter. All that matters is the piano and the glorious sounds she's about to charm out of it.

She holds her fingers above the keys for a moment, then begins with perfect passion. Soon her fingers dance across the keys making the flawless seem facile. She makes the instrument sing . . . and then her left ring finger stumbles on a B-flat, slipping awkwardly onto B-natural.

A mistake.

It happens so quickly, it could go unnoticed—but not by Risa. She holds the wrong note in her mind, and even as she continues playing, that note reverberates within her, growing to a crescendo, stealing her focus until she slips again, into a second wrong note, and then, two minutes later, blows an entire chord. Tears begin to fill her eyes, and she can't see clearly.

*You don't need to see,* she tells herself. *You just need to feel the music.* She can still pull out of this nosedive, can't she? Her mistakes, which sound so awful to her, are barely noticeable.

"Relax," Mr. Durkin would tell her. "No one is judging you."

Perhaps he truly believes that—but then, he can afford to believe it. He's not fifteen, and he's never been a ward of the state.

Five mistakes.

Every one of them is small, subtle, but they are mistakes nonetheless. It would have been fine if any of the other kids' performances were less than stellar, but the others shined.

Still, Mr. Durkin is all smiles when he greets Risa at the reception. "You were marvelous!" he says. "I'm proud of you."

"I stunk up the stage."

"Nonsense. You chose one of Chopin's most difficult pieces. Professionals can't get through it without an error or two. You did it justice!"

"I need more than justice."

Mr. Durkin sighs, but he doesn't deny it. "You're coming along nicely. I look forward to the day I see those hands playing in Carnegie Hall." His smile is warm and genuine, as are the congratulations from the other girls in her dorm. It's enough warmth to ease her sleep that night, and to give her hope that maybe, just maybe, she's making too much of it and being unnecessarily hard on herself. She falls asleep thinking of what she might choose to play next.

One week later she's called into the headmaster's office.

There are three people there. *A tribunal,* thinks Risa. Three adults sitting in judgment, like the three monkeys: hear-no-evil, see-no-evil, speak-no-evil.

"Please sit down, Risa," says the headmaster.

She tries to sit gracefully but her knees, now unsteady, won't allow it. She slaps awkwardly down into a chair far too plush for an inquisition.

Risa doesn't know the other two people sitting beside the headmaster, but they both look very official. Their demeanor is relaxed, as if this is business as usual for them.

The woman to the headmaster's left identifies herself as the social worker assigned to Risa's "case." Until that moment, Risa didn't know she had a case. She says her name. Ms. Something-or-other. The name never even makes it into Risa's memory. She flips through the pages of Risa's fifteen years of life as casually as if she were reading a newspaper.

"Let's see . . . you've been a ward of the state from birth. It looks like your behavior has been exemplary. Your grades have been respectable, but not excellent." Then the social worker looks up and smiles. "I saw your performance the other night. You were very good."

*Good*, thinks Risa, *but not excellent*.

Ms. Something-or-other leafs through the folder for a few seconds more, but Risa can tell she's not really looking. Whatever's going on here was decided long before Risa walked through the door.

"Why am I here?"

Ms. Something-or-other closes her folder and glances at the headmaster and the man beside him in an expensive suit. The suit nods, and the social worker turns back to Risa with a warm smile. "We feel you've reached your potential here," she says. "Headmaster Thomas and Mr. Paulson are in agreement with me."

Risa glances at the suit. "Who's Mr. Paulson?"

The suit clears his throat and says, almost as an apology, "I'm the school's legal counsel."

"A lawyer? Why is there a lawyer here?"

"Just procedure," Headmaster Thomas tells her. He puts a finger into his collar, stretching it, as if his tie has suddenly become a noose. "It's school policy to have a lawyer present at these kinds of proceedings."

"And what kind of proceeding is this?"

The three look at one another, none of them wanting to take the lead. Finally Ms. Something-or-other speaks up. "You must know that space in state homes are at a premium these days, and with budget cuts, every StaHo is impacted—ours included."

Risa holds cold eye contact with her. "Wards of the state are guaranteed a place in state homes."

"Very true—but the guarantee only holds until thirteen."

Then all of a sudden everyone has something to say.

"The money only stretches so far," says the headmaster.

"Educational standards could be compromised," says the lawyer.

"We only want what's best for you, and all the other children here," says the social worker.

And back and forth it goes like a three-way Ping-Pong match. Risa says nothing, only listens.

"You're a good musician, but . . ."

"As I said, you've reached your potential."

"As far as you can go."

"Perhaps if you had chosen a less competitive course of study."

"Well, that's all water under the bridge."

"Our hands are tied."

"There are unwanted babies born every day—and not all of them get storked."

"We're obliged to take the ones that don't."

"We have to make room for every new ward."

"Which means cutting 5 percent of our teenage population."

"You do understand, don't you?"

Risa can't listen anymore, so she shuts them up by saying what they don't have the courage to say themselves.

"I'm being unwound?"

Silence. It's more of an answer than if they had said "yes."

The social worker reaches over to take Risa's hand, but Risa pulls it back before she can. "It's all right to be frightened. Change is always scary."

"Change?" yells Risa, "What do you mean 'change'? Dying is a little bit more than a 'change.'"

The headmaster's tie turns into a noose again, preventing

blood from getting to his face. The lawyer opens his briefcase. "Please, Miss Ward. It's not dying, and I'm sure everyone here would be more comfortable if you didn't suggest something so blatantly inflammatory. The fact is, 100 percent of you will still be alive, just in a divided state." Then he reaches into his briefcase and hands her a colorful pamphlet. "This is a brochure from Twin Lakes Harvest Camp."

"It's a fine place," the headmaster says. "It's our facility of choice for all our Unwinds. In fact, my own nephew was unwound there."

"Goody for him."

"Change," repeated the social worker, "that's all. The way ice becomes water, the way water becomes clouds. *You will live,* Risa. Only in a different form."

But Risa's not hearing anymore. Panic has already started to set in. "I don't have to be a musician. I can do something else."

Headmaster Thomas sadly shakes his head. "Too late for that, I'm afraid."

"No, it's not. I could work out. I could become a boeuf. The military always needs more boeufs!"

The lawyer sighs in exasperation and looks at his watch. The social worker leans forward. "Risa, please," she says. "It takes a certain body type for a girl to be an Army boeuf, and many years of physical training."

"Don't I have a choice in this?" But when she looks behind her, the answer is clear. There are two guards waiting to make sure that she has no choice at all. And as they lead her away, she thinks of Mr. Durkin. With a bitter laugh, Risa realizes that he may get his wish after all. Someday he may see her hands playing in Carnegie Hall. Unfortunately, the rest of Risa won't be there.

\* \* \*

24

She is not allowed to return to her dormitory. She will take nothing with her, because there's nothing she needs. That's the way it is with unwinds. Just a handful of her friends sneak down to the school's transportation center, stealing quick hugs and shedding quick tears, all the while looking over their shoulders, afraid of getting caught.

Mr. Durkin does not come. This hurts Risa most of all.

She sleeps in a guest room in the home's welcome center, then, at dawn, she's loaded onto a bus full of kids being transferred from the huge StaHo complex to other places. She recognizes some faces, but doesn't actually know any of her travel companions.

Across the aisle, a fairly nice-looking boy—a military boeuf by the look of him—gives her a smile. "Hey," he says, flirting in a way only boeufs can.

"Hey," Risa says back.

"I'm being transferred to the state naval academy," he says. "How about you?"

"Oh, me?" She quickly sifts through the air for something impressive. "Miss Marple's Academy for the Highly Gifted."

"She's lying," says a scrawny, pale boy sitting on Risa's other side. "She's an Unwind."

Suddenly the boeuf boy leans away, as if unwinding is contagious. "Oh," he says. "Well . . . uh . . . that's too bad. See ya!" And he leaves to sit with some other boeufs in the back.

"Thanks," snaps Risa at the scrawny kid.

The kid just shrugs. "It doesn't matter, anyway." Then he holds out his hand to shake. "I'm Samson," he says. "I'm an Unwind too."

Risa almost laughs. Samson. Such a strong name for such a mealy boy. She doesn't shake his hand, still annoyed at having been exposed to the handsome boeuf.

"So, what did you do to get yourself unwound?" Risa asks.

"It's not what I did, it's what I *didn't* do."

"What didn't you do?"

"Anything," Samson answers.

It makes sense to Risa. Not doing anything is an easy path to unwinding.

"I was never going to amount to much anyway," Samson says, "but now, statistically speaking, there's a better chance that some part of me will go on to greatness somewhere in the world. I'd rather be partly great than entirely useless."

The fact that his twisted logic almost makes sense just makes her angrier. "Hope you enjoy harvest camp, Samson." Then she leaves to find another seat.

"Please sit down!" calls the chaperone from the front, but no one's listening to her. The bus is full of kids moving from seat to seat, trying to find kindred spirits or trying to escape them. Risa finds herself a window seat, with no one beside her.

This bus trip will be only the first leg of her journey. They explained to her—to all the kids after they boarded the bus— that they would first be taken to a central transportation center, where kids from dozens of state homes would be sorted onto buses that would take them to wherever they were going. Risa's next bus would be a bus full of Samsons. Wonderful. She had already considered the possibility of sneaking onto another bus, but the bar codes on their waistbands make that an impossibility. It's all perfectly organized, and foolproof. Still, Risa occupies her mind with all the scenarios that could lead to escape.

That's when she sees the commotion out of her window. It's farther up the road. Squad cars are on the other side of the freeway, and as the bus changes lanes, she sees two figures in the road: two kids racing across traffic. One kid has the other in a chokehold and is practically dragging him. And both of them have run right in front of the bus.

Risa's head is slammed against the window as the bus suddenly pulls to the right to avoid the two kids. The bus fills with gasps and screams, and Risa is thrown forward, down the aisle, as the bus comes to a sudden, jarring stop. Her hip is hurt, but not bad. It's just a bruise. She gets up, quickly taking stock of the situation. The bus leans sideways. It's off the road, in a ditch. The windshield is smashed, and it's covered with blood. Lots of it.

Kids around her all check themselves. Like her, no one is badly hurt, although some are making more of a fuss than others. The chaperone tries to calm down one girl who's hysterical.

And in this chaos, Risa has a sudden realization.

This is not part of the plan.

The system might have a million contingencies for state wards trying to screw with things, but they don't have a plan of action for dealing with an accident. For the next few seconds, all bets are off.

Risa fixes her eyes on the front door of the bus, holds her breath, and races toward that door.

# 3 · Lev

The party is big, the party is expensive, the party has been planned for years.

There are at least two hundred people in the country club's grand ballroom. Lev got to pick the band, he got to choose the food—he even got to select the color of the linens: red and white—for the Cincinnati Reds—and his name, Levi Jedediah Calder, is stamped in gold on the silk napkins for people to take home as a remembrance.

This party is all for him. It's all *about* him. And he's determined to have the best time of his life.

The adults at the party are relatives, friends of the family, his parents' business associates—but at least eighty of the guests are Lev's friends. There are kids from school, from church, and from the various sports teams he's been on. Some of his friends had felt funny about coming of course.

"I don't know, Lev," they had said, "it's kind of weird. I mean, what kind of present am I supposed to bring?"

"You don't have to bring anything," Lev had told them. "There *are* no presents at a tithing party. Just come and have a good time. I know *I* will."

And he does.

He asks every girl he invited to dance, and not a single one turns him down. He even has people lift him up in a chair and dance with him around the room, because he had seen them do that at a Jewish friend's bar mitzvah. True, this is a very different kind of party, but it's also a celebration of him turning thirteen, so he deserves to get lifted up in a chair too, doesn't he?

Lev finds that the dinner is served far too soon. He looks at his watch to see that two hours have already gone by. How could it have gone so quickly?

Soon people grab the microphone and, holding up glasses of champagne, they start making toasts to Lev. His parents give a toast. His grandmother gives a toast. An uncle he doesn't even know gives a toast.

"To Lev: It's been a joy to watch you grow into the fine young man you are, and I know in my heart that you'll do great things for everyone you touch in this world."

It feels wonderful and weird for so many people to say so many kind things about him. It's all too much, but in some strange way it's not enough. There's got to be more. More food. More dancing. More time. They're already bringing out the birthday cake. Everyone knows the party ends once the cake is served. Why are they bringing out the cake? Can it really be three hours into the party?

Then comes one more toast. It's the toast that almost ruins the evening.

Of Lev's many brothers and sisters, Marcus has been the quietest all evening. It's unlike him. Lev should have known something was going to happen. Lev, at thirteen, is the youngest of ten. Marcus, at twenty-eight, is the oldest. He flew halfway across the country to be here at Lev's tithing party, and yet he's barely danced, or spoken, or been a part of any of the festivities. He's also drunk. Lev has never seen Marcus drunk.

It happens after the formal toasts are given, when Lev's cake is being cut and distributed. It doesn't start as a toast; it starts as just a moment between brothers.

"Congrats, little bro," Marcus says, giving him a powerful hug. Lev can smell the alcohol on Marcus's breath. "Today you're a man. Sort of."

Their father, sitting at the head table just a few feet away, lets out a nervous chuckle.

"Thanks . . . sort of," Lev responds. He glances at his parents. His father waits to see what's coming next. His mother's pinched expression makes Lev feel tense.

Marcus stares at Lev with a smile that doesn't hold any of the emotion a smile usually comes with. "What do you think of all this?" he asks Lev.

"It's great."

"Of course it is! All these people here for you? It's an amazing night. Amazing!"

"Yeah," says Lev. He's not sure where this is going, but he knows it's going somewhere. "I'm having the time of my life."

"Damn right! The time of your life! Gotta wrap up all those life events, all those parties, into one—birthdays, wedding, funeral." Then he turns to their father. "Very efficient, right, Dad?"

29

"That's enough," their father says quietly, but it only makes Marcus get louder.

"What? I'm not allowed to talk about it? Oh, that's right—this is a celebration. I almost forgot."

Lev wants Marcus to stop, but at the same time he doesn't.

Mom stands up and says in a voice more forceful than Dad's, "Marcus, sit down. You're embarrassing yourself."

By now everyone in the banquet hall has stopped whatever they were doing and are tuned in to the unfolding family drama. Marcus, seeing he has the room's attention, picks up someone's half-empty glass of champagne, and holds it high. "Here's to my brother, Lev," Marcus says. "And to our parents! Who have always done the right thing. The *appropriate* thing. Who have always given generously to charity. Who have always given 10 percent of everything to our church. Hey, Mom—we're lucky you had ten kids instead of five, otherwise we'd end up having to cut Lev off at the waist!"

Gasps from all those assembled. People shaking their heads. Such disappointing behavior from an eldest son.

Now Dad comes up and grabs Marcus's arm tightly. "You're done!" Dad says. "Sit down."

Marcus shakes Dad's arm off. "Oh, I'll do better than sit down." Now there are tears in Marcus's eyes as he turns to Lev. "I love you, bro . . . and I know this is your special day. But I can't be a part of this." He hurls the champagne glass against the wall, where it shatters, spraying fragments of crystal all over the buffet table. Then he turns and storms out with such steady confidence in his stride that Lev realizes he's not drunk at all.

Lev's father signals the band and they kick into a dance number even before Marcus is gone from the huge room. People begin to fill the void of the dance floor, doing their best to make the awkward moment go away.

"I'm sorry about that, Lev," his father tells him. "Why don't you . . . why don't you go dance?"

But Lev finds he doesn't want to dance anymore. The desire he had to be the center of attention left along with his brother. "I'd like to talk to Pastor Dan, if that's all right."

"Of course it is."

Pastor Dan has been a family friend since before Lev was born, and he has always been much easier to talk to than his parents about any subject that required patience and wisdom.

The banquet hall is too loud, too crowded, so they go outside to the patio overlooking the country club's golf course.

"Are you getting scared?" Pastor Dan asks. He's always able to figure out what's on Lev's mind.

Lev nods. "I thought I was ready. I thought I was prepared."

"It's natural. Don't worry about it,"

But it doesn't ease the disappointment Lev feels in himself. He's had his entire life to prepare for this—it should have been enough. He knew he was a tithe from the time he was little. "You're special," his parents had always told him. "Your life will be to serve God, and mankind." He doesn't remember how old he was when he found out exactly what that meant for him.

"Have kids in school been giving you a hard time?"

"No more than usual," Lev tells him. It's true. All his life he's had to deal with kids who resented him, because grown-ups treated him as if he was special. There were kids who were kind, and kids who were cruel. That was life. It did bother him, though, when kids called him things like "dirty Unwind." As if he was like those *other* kids, whose parents signed the unwind order to get rid of them. That couldn't be further from the truth for Lev. He is his family's pride and joy. Straight As in school, MVP in little league. Just because he's to be unwound does NOT means he's an Unwind.

There are, of course, a few other tithes at his school, but they're all from other religions, so Lev has never felt a real sense of camaraderie with them. The huge turnout at tonight's party testifies to how many friends Lev has—but they're not *like* him: Their lives will be lived in an undivided state. Their bodies and their futures are their own. Lev has always felt closer to God than to his friends, or even his family. He often wonders if being chosen always leaves a person so isolated. Or is there something wrong with him?

"I've been having lots of wrong thoughts," Lev tells Pastor Dan.

"There are no wrong thoughts, only thoughts that need to be worked through and overcome."

"Well . . . I've just been feeling jealous of my brothers and sisters. I keep thinking of how the baseball team is going to miss me. I know it's an honor and a blessing to be a tithe, but I can't stop wondering why it has to be me."

Pastor Dan, who was always so good at looking people in the eye, now looks away. "It was decided before you were born. It's not anything you did, or didn't do."

"The thing is, I know tons of people with big families . . ."

Pastor Dan nodded. "Yes, it's very common these days."

"But lots of those people don't tithe at all—even families in our church—and nobody blames them."

"There are also people who tithe their first, second, or third child. Every family must make the decision for itself. Your parents waited a long time before making the decision to have you."

Lev reluctantly nods, knowing it's true. He was a "true tithe." With five natural siblings, plus one adopted, and three that arrived "by stork," Lev was exactly one-tenth. His parents had always told him that made him all the more special.

"I'll tell you something, Lev," Pastor Dan says, finally

meeting his eye. Like Marcus, his eyes are moist, just one step short of tears. "I've watched all your brothers and sisters grow and, although I don't like playing favorites, I think you are the finest of all of them in so many ways, I wouldn't even know where to start. That's what God asks for, you know. Not first fruits but best fruits."

"Thank you, sir." Pastor Dan always knows what to say to make Lev feel better. "I'm ready for this," and saying it makes him realize that, in spite of his fears and misgivings, he truly is ready. This is everything he has lived for. Even so, his tithing party ends much too soon.

In the morning the Calders have to eat breakfast in the dining room, with all the leaves in the table. All of Lev's brothers and sisters are there. Only a few of them still live at home, but today they've all come over for breakfast. All of them, that is, except Marcus.

Yet, for such a large family it's unusually quiet, and the clatter of silverware on china makes the lack of conversation even more conspicuous.

Lev, dressed in his silk tithing whites, eats carefully, so as not to leave any stains on his clothes. After breakfast, the good-byes are long, full of hugs and kisses. It's the worst part. Lev wishes they would all just let him go and get the good-byes over with.

Pastor Dan arrives—he's come at Lev's request—and once he's there, the good-byes move more quickly. Nobody wants to waste the pastor's valuable time. Lev is the first one out in his Dad's Cadillac, and although he tries not to look back as his father starts the car and drives away, he can't help it. He watches as his home disappears behind them.

*I will never see that home again,* he thinks, but he pushes the thought out of his mind. It's unproductive, unhelpful, selfish.

33

He looks at Pastor Dan, who sits beside him in the backseat watching him, and the pastor smiles.

"It's all right, Lev," he says. Just hearing him say it makes it so.

"How far is the harvest camp?" Lev asks to whoever cares to answer.

"It's about an hour from here," his Mom says.

"And . . . will they do it right away?"

His parents look to each other. "I'm sure there'll be an orientation," says his father.

That short answer makes it clear to Lev that they don't know any more than he does.

As they pull onto the interstate, Lev rolls down the window to feel the wind on his face, and closes his eyes to prepare himself.

*This is what I was born for. It's what I've lived my life for. I am chosen. I am blessed. And I am happy.*

Suddenly his father slams on the brakes.

With his eyes closed, Lev doesn't see the reason for their unexpected stop. He just feels the sharp deceleration of the Cadillac and the pull of the seat belt on his shoulder. He opens his eyes to see they have stopped on the interstate. Police lights flash. And—was that a gunshot he just heard?

"What's going on?"

Then, just outside his window is another kid, a few years older than him. He looks scared. He looks dangerous. Lev reaches over to quickly put up his window, but before he can this kid reaches in, pulls up the lock on the door, and tugs the door open. Lev is frozen. He doesn't know what to do.

"Mom? Dad?" he calls.

The boy with murder in his eyes tugs on Lev's white silk shirt, trying to pull him out of the car, but the seat belt holds him tight.

"What are you doing? Leave me alone!"

Lev's mom screams for his father to do something, but he's fumbling with his own seat belt.

The maniac reaches over and in one swift motion unclips Lev's seat belt. Pastor Dan grabs at the intruder, who responds with a quick powerful punch—a jab right at Pastor Dan's jaw. The shock of seeing such violence distracts Lev at a crucial moment. The maniac tugs on him again, and this time Lev falls out of the car, hitting his head on the pavement. When he looks up he sees his father finally getting out of the car, but the crazy kid swings the car door hard against him, sending him flying.

"Dad!" His father lands in the path of an oncoming car. The car swerves and, thank God, it misses him—but it cuts off another car, hitting it, that car spins out of control, and the sound of crashes fills the air. Lev is pulled to his feet again by the kid, who grabs Lev's arm and drags him off. Lev is small for his age. This kid is a couple of years older, and much bigger. Lev can't break free.

"Stop!" yells Lev. "You can have whatever you want. Take my wallet," he says, even though he has no wallet. "Take the car. Just don't hurt anyone."

The kid considers the car, but only for an instant. Bullets now fly past them. On the southbound roadway are policemen who have finally stopped traffic on their side of the interstate, and have made it to the median dividing the north and southbound lanes. The closest officer fires again. A tranq bullet hits the Cadillac and splatters.

The crazy kid now puts Lev into a choke hold, holding Lev between himself and the officers. Lev realizes that he doesn't want a car, or money: He wants a hostage.

"Stop struggling—I've got a gun!" And Lev feels the kid poke him in the side. Lev knows it's not a gun—he knows it's just the kid's finger, but this is clearly an unstable individual, and he doesn't want to set him off.

"I'm worthless as a human shield," Lev says, trying to reason with him. "Those are tranq bullets they're shooting, which means the cops don't care if they hit me—they'll just knock me out."

"Better you than me."

Bullets fly past them as they wind around swerving traffic. "Please—you don't understand—you can't take me now, I'm being tithed. I'll miss my harvest! You'll ruin everything!"

And finally, a hint of humanity comes to the maniac's eyes. *"You're an Unwind?"*

There are a million more things to be furious about, but Lev finds himself incensed by what he's just been called. "I'm a *tithe*!"

A blaring horn, and Lev turns to see a bus bearing down on them. Before either of them has a chance to scream, the bus careens off the road to avoid them and smashes head-on against the fat trunk of a huge oak, stopping the bus cold.

There's blood all over the smashed windshield. It's the bus driver's blood. He hangs halfway through, and he's not moving.

"Oh, crap!" says the maniac, a creepy whine in his voice.

A girl has just stepped out of the bus. The crazy kid looks at her, and Lev realizes that now, while he's distracted, is the last chance he's going to have to get away. This kid is an animal. The only way to deal with him is for Lev to become an animal himself. So Lev grabs the arm that's locked around his neck and sinks his teeth in with the full force of his jaws until he tastes blood. The kid screams, letting go, and Lev bolts away, racing toward his father's car.

As he nears it, a back door opens. It's Pastor Dan opening the door to receive him, yet the expression on the man's face is anything but happy.

With his face already swelling from the crazy kid's brutal punch, Pastor Dan says with a hiss and strange warble to his voice, "Run, Lev!"

Lev wasn't expecting this. "What?"

"Run! Run as fast and as far as you can. RUN!"

Lev stands there, impotent, unable to move, unable to process this. Why is Pastor Dan telling him to run? Then comes a sudden pain in his shoulder, and everything starts spinning round and round and down a drain into darkness.

# 4 · Connor

The pain in Connor's arm is unbearable. That little monster actually bit him—practically took a chunk out of his forearm. Another car slams the brakes to avoid hitting him, and gets rear-ended. The tranq bullets have stopped flying, but he knows that's temporary. The accidents have gotten the Juvey-cops momentarily distracted, but they won't stay that way for long.

Just then, he makes eye contact with the girl who got off the bus. He thinks she's going to go stumbling toward all the people who are running from their cars to help, but instead she turns and runs into the woods. Has the whole world gone insane?

Still holding his stinging, bleeding arm, he turns to run into the woods as well, but stops. He turns back to see the kid in white just reaching his car. Connor doesn't know where the Juvey-cops are. They're lurking, no doubt, somewhere in the tangle of vehicles. That's when Connor makes a split-second decision. He knows it's a stupid decision, but he can't help himself. All he knows is that he's caused death today. The bus driver's, maybe more. Even if it risks everything, he's got to balance it somehow. He's got to do something decent, something good to make up for the awful consequence of his kicking-AWOL. And so, battling his own instinct for self-preservation, he races toward the kid in white who was so happily going to his own unwinding.

It's as Connor gets close that he sees the cop twenty yards away, raising his weapon, and firing. He shouldn't have risked this! He should have gotten away when he could. Connor waits for the telltale sting of the tranq bullet but it never comes, because the moment the bullet is fired, the boy in white takes a step back, and he's hit in the shoulder. Two seconds, and his knees buckle. The kid hits the ground, out cold, unwittingly taking the bullet meant for Connor.

Connor wastes no time. He picks the kid up off the ground and flips him over his shoulder. Tranq bullets fly, but no others connect. In a few seconds Connor's past the bus, where a gaggle of shell-shocked teens are getting off. He pushes past them and into the woods.

The woods are dense, not just with trees but with tall shrubs and vines, yet there's already a path of broken branches and parted shrubs made by the girl who ran from the bus. They might as well have arrows pointing the police in their direction. He sees the girl up ahead and calls out to her. "Stop!" She turns, but only for an instant, then renews her battle with the dense growth all around her.

Connor gently puts down the boy in white and hurries forward, catching up with her. He grabs her arm gently, yet firmly enough so that she can't pull away. "Whatever you're running from, you won't get away unless we work together," he tells her. He glances behind him to make sure that no Juvey-cops are in sight yet. There aren't. "Please—we don't have much time."

The girl stops fighting the bushes and looks at him.

"What do you have in mind?"

# 5 · Cop

Officer J. T. Nelson has spent twelve years working Juvenile. He knows AWOL Unwinds will not give up as long as there's an ounce of consciousness left in them. They are high on adrenaline, and often high on illegal substances as well. Nicotine, caffeine, or worse. He wishes his bullets were the real thing. He wishes he could truly take these wastes-of-life out rather than just taking them down. Maybe then they wouldn't be so quick to run—and if they did, well, no great loss.

The officer follows the path made through the woods by the AWOL Unwind, until he comes to a lump on the ground. It's the hostage, just dumped in the path, his white clothes smudged green from the foliage, and brown from the muddy earth. *Good,* thinks the officer. It was a good thing this boy took that bullet after all. Being unconscious probably saved this kid's life. No telling where the Unwind would have taken him, or what he'd have done to him.

"Help me!" says a voice just ahead of him. It's the voice of a girl. The officer isn't expecting this.

"Help me, please, I'm hurt!"

Deeper in the woods a girl sits up against a tree, holding her arm, grimacing in pain. He doesn't have time for this, but "Protect and Serve" is more than just a motto to him. He sometimes wishes he didn't have such moral integrity.

He goes over to the girl. "What are you doing here?"

"I was on the bus. I got off and ran away because I was scared it would explode. I think my arm's broken."

He looks at the girl's arm. It's not even bruised. This should be his first clue, but his mind is already too far ahead of him to catch it. "Stay here, I'll be right back." He turns, ready to pick up his pursuit, when something drops on him from above. Not some*thing*, some*one*. The AWOL Unwind! The officer is knocked to the ground, and suddenly there are two figures attacking him—the Unwind and the girl. They're in this together. How could he have been so stupid? He reaches for his tranq pistol, but it's not there. Instead he feels its muzzle against his left thigh, and he sees triumph in the Unwind's dark, vicious eyes.

"Nighty-night," the Unwind says.

A sharp pain in the officer's leg, and the world goes away.

# 6 · Lev

Lev wakes up to a dull ache in his shoulder. He thinks maybe he slept funny, but he quickly realizes the ache is from an injury. His left shoulder was the entry point of a tranq bullet, though he doesn't realize that just yet. All the things that had happened to him twelve hours before are like faint clouds in his mind that have lost their shape. All he knows for sure is that he was on his way to his tithing, he was kidnapped by a murderous teenager, and for some strange reason the image of Pastor Dan keeps coming back to him.

Pastor Dan was telling him to run.

He's sure that it must be a false memory, because he can't believe Pastor Dan would do such a thing.

Everything's blurry as Lev opens his eyes. He doesn't know where he is, only that it's night and he's not where he should be. The insane teen who took him sits across a small fire. There's a girl there, too.

That's when he realizes he'd been hit by a tranq bullet. His head hurts, he feels like he might puke, and his brain is still only at half power. He tries to get up, but can't. At first he thinks that's also because of the tranquilizers, but then he realizes he's tied to a tree by thick vines.

He tries to speak, but his voice comes out as a little groan and a lot of drool. The boy and girl look at him, and he's sure they're going to kill him now. They kept him alive just so he'd be awake when they killed him. Maniacs are like that.

"Look who's back from Tranqville," says the boy with wild eyes. Only his eyes aren't wild now, just his hair—it's all sticking up like he slept on it.

Although Lev's tongue feels like rubber, he manages to get out a single word. "Where . . ."

"Not sure," says the boy.

Then the girl adds, "But at least you're safe."

*Safe?* thinks Lev. *What could possibly be safe about this?*

"H. . . h. . . hostage?" Lev gets out.

The boy looks to the girl, then back to Lev. "Kind of. I guess." These two talk in an easy tone of voice, like they're all friends. *They're trying to lull me into a false sense of security,* thinks Lev. *They're trying to get me on their side, so I'll take part in whatever criminal activities they have planned.* There's an expression for that, isn't there? When a hostage joins the kidnappers' cause? The *Something* syndrome.

The crazy kid looks to a pile of berries and nuts obviously foraged from the woods. "You hungry?"

Lev nods, but the act of nodding makes his head spin so much, he realizes that no matter how hungry he is, he'd better not eat, because it'll come right back up. "No," he says.

"You sound confused," says the girl. "Don't worry, it's just the tranqs. They should wear off pretty soon."

*Stockholm syndrome!* That's it! Well, Lev won't be won over by this pair of kidnappers. He'll never be on their side.

*Pastor Dan told me to run.*

What had he meant? Did he mean run from the kidnappers?

41

Maybe, but he seemed to be saying something else entirely. Lev closes his eyes and chases the thought away.

"My parents will look for me," Lev says, his mouth finally able to put together whole sentences.

The kids don't answer because they probably know it's true.

"How much is the ransom?" Lev asks.

"Ransom? There's no ransom," says the crazy kid. "I took you to save you, idiot!"

To save him? Lev just stares at him in disbelief. "But . . . but my tithing . . ."

The crazy kid looks at him and shakes his head. "I've never seen a kid in such a hurry to be unwound."

It's no use trying to explain to this godless pair what tithing is all about. How giving of one's self is the ultimate blessing. They'd never understand or care. Save him? They haven't saved him, they've damned him.

Then Lev realizes something. He realizes that he can use this entire situation to his advantage. "My name's Lev," he says, trying to play it as cool as he can.

"Pleased to meet you, Lev," says the girl. "I'm Risa, and this is Connor."

Connor throws her a dirty look, making it clear that she gave him their real names. Not a good idea for hostage-takers, but then most criminals are stupid like that.

"Didn't mean for you to take the tranq bullet," Connor tells him. "But the cop was a bad shot."

"Not your fault," says Lev, even though every bit of it is Connor's fault. Lev thinks about what happened, and says,"I would never have run from my own tithing." That much, Lev knows, is true.

"Good thing I was around, then," says Connor.

"Yeah," says Risa. "If it wasn't for Connor running across

that highway, I'd probably be unwound by now too."

There's a moment of silence, then Lev, biting back his anger and revulsion, says, "Thank you. Thank you for saving me."

"Don't mention it," says Connor.

Good. Let them think he's grateful. Let them think they're earning his trust. And once they're lulled into their own false sense of security, he'll make sure they both get exactly what they deserve.

# 7 · Connor

Connor should have kept the Juvey-cop's gun, but he wasn't thinking. He was so freaked out at having tranq'd a cop with his own weapon, he just dropped it and ran—just as he dropped his backpack on the interstate so he could carry Lev. His wallet with all his money was in that pack. Now he has nothing but pocket lint.

It's late now—or, more accurately, early—almost dawn. He and Risa had kept moving through the woods all day, as best they could with Connor having to carry an unconscious tithe. Once night fell, he and Risa had taken turns keeping watch while the other slept.

Connor knows that Lev can't be trusted, that's why Connor tied him to the tree—but there's no reason to trust this girl who had come running out of a bus either. It's only their common goal of staying alive that binds them.

The moon has left the sky now, but there's a faint glow promising a quick arrival of dawn. By now their faces would be everywhere. *Have you seen these teens? Do not approach. Considered extremely dangerous. Call the police immediately.* Funny how Connor had wasted so much time in school trying to convince people he was dangerous, but when it came down to it, he was never sure if he was all that dangerous at all. A danger to himself, maybe.

All the while, Lev watches him. At first the boy's eyes had been lazy and his head lolling to one side, but now those eyes are sharp. Even in the dimness of the dying fire Connor can see them. Chilly blue. Calculating. This kid is an odd bird. Connor's not quite sure what's going on on Planet Lev, and not quite sure he wants to know.

"That bite's gonna get infected if you don't take care of it," Lev says.

Connor looks to the spot on his arm where Lev bit him, still puffy and red. He had tuned the pain out until Lev reminded him. "I'll deal with it."

Lev continues to study him. "Why are you being unwound?"

Connor doesn't like the question for a whole lot of reasons. "You mean why WAS I being unwound—because, as you can see, I'm not being unwound anymore."

"They will if they catch you."

Connor feels like punching that smug look off the kid's face, but he restrains himself. He didn't rescue the kid just to beat him up.

"So, what's it like," Connor asks, "knowing all your life you're going to be sacrificed?" He meant it as a jab, but Lev takes the question seriously.

"It's better than going through life without knowing your purpose."

Connor's not sure if that was intentionally meant to make him squirm—as if his life has no purpose. It makes him feel like *he's* the one tied to a tree, not Lev. "I guess it could be worse," says Connor. "We could have all ended up like Humphrey Dunfee."

Lev seems surprised by the mention of the name. "You know

that story? I thought they only told it in my neighborhood."

"Nah," says Connor. "Kids tell it everywhere."

"It's made up," says Risa, having just woken up.

"Maybe," says Connor. "But there was this one time a friend and I tried to find out about it while surfing one of the school's computers. We hit this one website that talked about it, and how his parents went all psycho. Then the computer crashed. It turns out we were hit by a virus that wiped out the entire district server. Coincidence? I don't think so."

Lev's taken in, but Risa, fairly disgusted, says, "Well, *I'll* never end up like Humphrey Dunfee, because you have to have parents for them to go psycho—and I don't." She stands up. Connor looks away from the dying fire to see that dawn has arrived.

"If we're going to keep from being caught, then we should change direction again," Risa says. "We should also think about disguising ourselves."

"Like how?" asks Connor.

"I don't know. Change our clothes first. Haircuts maybe. They'll be looking for two boys and a girl. Maybe I can disguise myself as a boy."

Connor takes a good look at her and smiles. Risa's pretty. Not in the way Ariana was pretty—in a better way. Ariana's prettiness was all about makeup and pigment injections and stuff. Risa has a natural kind of beauty. Without thinking, Connor reaches out to touch her hair, and gently says, "I don't think you could ever pass for a guy—"

Then suddenly, he finds his hand tugged behind him, his whole body spins around, and she painfully wrenches his arm up the small of his back. It hurts so much, he can't even say "Ouch." All he can say is, "Eh-eh-eh!"

"Touch me again and your arm gets ripped off," Risa tells him. "Got that?"

"Yeah. Yeah. Fine. Hands off. Got it."

Over at the oak tree, Lev laughs, apparently pleased to see Connor in pain.

She lets him go, but his shoulder still throbs. "You didn't have to do that," Connor says, trying not to show how much it still hurts. "It's not like I was going to hurt you or anything."

"Yeah, well, now you won't for sure," says Risa, maybe sounding a bit guilty for being so harsh. "Don't forget I lived in a state home."

Connor nods. He knows about StaHo kids. They have to learn to take care of themselves real young, or their lives are not very pleasant. He should have realized she was a touch-me-not.

"Excuse me," says Lev, "but we can't go anywhere if I'm tied to a tree."

Still, Connor doesn't like that judgmental look in Lev's eyes. "How do we know you won't run?"

"You don't, but until you untie me, I'm a hostage," Lev says. "Once I'm free, I'm a fugitive, like you. Tied up, I'm the enemy. Cut loose, I'm a friend."

"If you don't run," says Connor.

Risa impatiently begins untying the vines. "Unless we want to leave him here, we'll have to take that chance." Connor kneels to help, and in a few moments, Lev is free. He stands and stretches, rubbing his shoulder where the tranq bullet had hit him. Lev's eyes are still blue ice and hard for Connor to read, but he's not running. *Maybe*, thinks Connor, *he's over the "duty" of being tithed. Maybe he's finally starting to see the sense of staying alive.*

# 8 · Risa

Risa finds herself unsettled by the food wrappers and broken bits of plastic they start coming across in the woods, because the first sign of civilization is always trash. Civilization means people who could recognize them if their faces have been smeared on the newsnet.

Risa knows that staying completely clear of human contact is an impossibility. She has no illusion about their chances, or their ability to remain unseen. As much as they need to remain anonymous, they cannot get by entirely alone. They need the help of others.

"No, we don't," Connor is quick to argue as the signs of civilization grow around them. It's not just trash now, but the mossy remnants of a knee-high stone wall, and the rusty remains of an old electrical tower from the days when electricity was transmitted by wires. "We don't need anyone. We'll take what we need."

Risa sighs, trying to hold together a patience that has already worn through. "I'm sure you're very good at stealing, but I don't think it's a good idea."

Connor appears insulted by the insinuation. "What do you think—people are just going to give us food and whatever else we need out of the goodness of their hearts?"

"No," says Risa, "but if we're clever about it instead of rushing into this blind, we'll have a better chance."

Her words or maybe just her intentionally condescending tone makes Connor storm off.

Risa notices Lev watching the argument from a distance. *If he's going to run, thinks Risa, now's the time for him to do it, while Connor and I are busy fighting.* And then it occurs to her that this is an excellent opportunity to test Lev, and see if he really is standing by them now, or biding his time until he can escape.

"Don't you walk away from me!" she growls at Connor, doing her best to keep the argument alive, all the while keeping an eye on Lev to see if he bolts. "I'm still talking to you!"

Connor turns toward her. "Who says I have to listen?"

"You would if you had half a brain, but obviously you don't!"

Connor moves closer until he's deeper into her airspace than she likes anyone to get. "If it wasn't for me you'd be on your way to harvest camp!" he says. Risa raises a hand to push him back, but his hand shoots up faster, and he grabs her wrist before she can shove him. This is the moment Risa realizes she's gone too far. What does she really know about this boy? He was going to be unwound. Maybe there's a reason for it. Maybe a good reason.

Risa is careful not to struggle because struggling gives him the advantage. She lets her tone of voice convey all the weight. "Let go of me."

"Why? Exactly what do you think I'll do to you?"

"This is the second time you've touched me without permission," Risa says. Still, he does not let go—yet she does notice his grip isn't all that threatening. It isn't tight, it's loose. It isn't rough, it's gentle. She could easily pull out of it with a simple flick of her wrist. So why doesn't she?

Risa knows he's doing this to make a point, but what the point is, Risa isn't sure. Is he warning her that he can hurt her if he wants to? Or maybe his message is in the gentle nature of his grip—a way of saying he's not the hurting type.

*Well, it doesn't matter,* thinks Risa. Even a gentle violation is a violation.

She looks at his knee. A well-placed kick could break his kneecap.

"I could take you out in a second," she threatens.

If he's concerned, he doesn't show it. "I know."

Somehow he also knows that she won't do it—that the first

time was just a reflex. If she were to hurt him a second time, though, it would be a conscious act. It would be by choice.

"Step off," she says. Her voice now lacks the force it had only moments before.

This time he listens and lets go, moving back to a respectable distance. They both could have hurt one another, but neither of them did. Risa isn't quite sure what that means, all she knows is that she feels angry at him for such a mixture of reasons, she can't sort them out.

Then suddenly a voice calls to them from the right. "This is very entertaining and all, but I don't think fighting is going to help much."

It's Lev—and Risa realizes that her little ruse has backfired. She had set out to test him with a fake argument but the argument turned real, and in the process she completely forgot about Lev. He could have taken off, and they would not have known until he was long gone.

Risa throws Connor an evil look for good measure and the three of them continue on. It isn't until ten minutes later, when Lev goes off to relieve himself in private, that Connor talks to Risa again.

"Good one," Connor says. "It worked."

"What?"

Connor leans closer and whispers, "The argument. You put it on to see if Lev would run when we weren't paying attention, right?"

Risa is bowled over. "You knew that?"

Connor looks at her, a bit amused. "Well . . . yeah."

If Risa felt uncertain about him before, it's even worse now. She has no idea what to think. "So . . . everything that happened back there was all a show?"

Now it's Connor's turn to be unsure. "I guess. Sort of. Wasn't it?"

Risa has to hold back a smile. Suddenly she's feeling strangely at ease with Connor. She marvels at how that could be. If their argument had been entirely real, she'd be on her guard against him. If it had been entirely a show she'd be on guard too, because if he could lie so convincingly, she'd never be able to trust him. But this was a mixture of both. It was real, it was pretend, and that combination made it all right—it made it safe, like performing death-defying acrobatic tricks above a safety net.

She holds on to that unexpected feeling as the two of them catch up with Lev, and move toward the frightening prospect of civilization.

# Part Two

# Storked

*"You can't change laws without first changing human nature."*

—NURSE GRETA

*"You can't change human nature without first changing the law."*

—NURSE YVONNE

# 9 · Mother

The mother is nineteen, but she doesn't feel that old. She feels no wiser, no more capable of dealing with this situation, than a little girl. When, she wonders, did she stop being a child? The law says it was when she turned eighteen, but the law doesn't know her.

Still aching from the trauma of delivery, she holds her newborn close. It's just after dawn on a chilly morning. She moves now through back alleys. Not a soul around. Dumpsters cast angular black shadows. Broken bottles everywhere. This she knows is the perfect time of day to do this. There's less of a chance that coyotes and other scavengers would be out. She couldn't bear the thought of the baby suffering needlessly.

A large green Dumpster looms before her, listing crookedly on the uneven pavement of the alley. She holds the baby tight, as if the Dumpster might grow hands and pull the baby into its filthy depths. Maneuvering around it, she continues down the alley.

There was a time, shortly after the Bill of Life was passed, that Dumpsters such as that would be tempting to girls like her. Desperate girls who would leave unwanted newborns in the trash. It had become so common that it wasn't even deemed newsworthy anymore—it had become just a part of life.

Funny, but the Bill of Life was supposed to protect the sanctity of life. Instead it just made life cheap. Thank goodness for the Storking Initiative, that wonderful law that allows girls like her a far better alternative.

As dawn becomes early morning, she leaves the alleys and

enters a neighborhood that gets better with each street she crosses. The homes are large and inviting. This is the right neighborhood for storking.

She chooses the home shrewdly. The house she decides on isn't the largest, but it's not the smallest, either. It has a very short walkway to the street, so she can get away quickly, and it's overgrown with trees, so no one either inside or out will be able to see her as she storks the newborn.

She carefully approaches the front door. No lights are on in the home yet, that's good. There's a car in the driveway—hopefully that means they're home. She gingerly climbs the porch steps, careful not to make a sound, then kneels down, placing the sleeping baby on the welcome mat. There are two blankets wrapped around the baby, and a wool cap covers its head. She makes the blankets nice and tight. It's the only thing she's learned to do as a mother.

She considers ringing the bell and running, but she realizes that would not be a good idea. If they catch her, she's obliged to keep the baby—that's part of the Storking Initiative too—but if they open the door and find nothing but the child, it's "finder's keepers" in the eyes of the law. Whether they want it or not, the baby is legally theirs.

From the time she learned she was pregnant she knew she would end up storking this baby. She had hoped that when she finally saw it, looking up at her so helplessly, she might change her mind—but who was she kidding? With neither the skill nor the desire to be a mother at this point in her life, storking had always been her best option.

She realizes she's lingered longer than is wise. There's an upstairs light on now, so she forces herself to look away from the sleeping newborn, and leaves. With the burden now lifted from her, she has sudden strength. She now has a second chance in life, and this time she'll be smarter—she's sure of it.

As she hurries down the street, she thinks how wonderful it is that she can get a second chance. How wonderful it is that she can dismiss her responsibility so easily.

# 10 · Risa

Several streets away from the storked newborn, at the edge of a dense wood, Risa stands at the door of a home. She rings the bell, and a woman answers in her bathrobe.

Risa offers the woman a big smile. "Hi, my name is Didi? And I'm collecting clothes and food for our school? We're, like, giving them to the homeless? And it's like this competition—whoever gets the most wins a trip to Florida or something? So it would be really, really great if you could help out?"

The sleepy woman tries to get her brain up to speed with "Didi," airhead for the homeless. The woman can't get a word in edgewise because Didi talks way too fast. If Risa had had a piece of chewing gum, she would have popped a bubble somewhere in there to add more authenticity.

"Please-please-pretty-please? I'm, like, in second place right now?"

The woman at the door sighs, resigned to the fact that "Didi" isn't going away empty-handed, and sometimes the best way to get rid of girls like this is just to give them something. "I'll be right back," the woman says.

Three minutes later, Risa walks away from the house with a bag full of clothes and canned food.

"That was amazing," says Connor, who had been watching with Lev from the edge of the woods.

"What can I say? I'm an artist," she says. "It's like playing the piano; you just have to know which keys to strike in people."

Connor smiles. "You're right, this is way better than stealing."

"Actually," says Lev, "scamming IS stealing."

Risa feels a bit prickly and uncomfortable at the thought, but tries not to show it.

"Maybe so," says Connor, "but it's stealing with style."

The woods have ended at a tract community. Manicured lawns have turned yellow along with the leaves. Autumn has truly taken hold. The homes here are almost identical, but not quite, full of people almost identical, but not quite. It's a world Risa knows about only through magazines and TV. To her, suburbia is a magical kingdom. Perhaps that's why Risa was the one who had the nerve to approach the house and pretend to be Didi. The neighborhood drew her like the smell of fresh bread baking in the industrial ovens of Ohio State Home 23.

Back in the woods where they can't be seen from anyone's window, they check their goody bag, as if it's full of Halloween candy.

There's a pair of pants and a blue button-down shirt that fits Connor. There's a jacket that fits Lev. There are no clothes for Risa, but that's okay. She can play Didi again at a different house.

"I still don't know how changing our clothes is going to make a difference." Connor asks.

"Don't you ever watch TV?" says Risa. "On the cop shows they always describe what perps were last wearing when they put out an APB."

"We're not perps," says Connor, "we're AWOLs."

"We're felons," says Lev. "Because what you're doing—I mean, what we're doing—is a federal crime."

"What, stealing clothes?" asks Connor.

"No, stealing ourselves. Once the unwind orders were

56

signed, we all became government property. Kicking-AWOL makes us federal criminals."

It doesn't sit well with Risa, or for that matter with Connor, but they both shake it off.

This excursion into a populated area is dangerous but necessary. Perhaps as the morning goes on they can find a library where they can download maps and find themselves a wilderness large enough to get lost in for good. There are rumors of hidden communities of AWOL Unwinds. Maybe they can find one.

As they move cautiously through the neighborhood, a woman approaches them—just a girl, really, maybe nineteen or twenty. She walks fast, but she's walking funny, like she's got some injury or is recovering from one. Risa's certain she's going to see them and recognize them, but the girl passes without even making eye contact and hurries around a corner.

# 11 · Connor

Exposed. Vulnerable. Connor wishes they could have stayed in the woods, but there are only so many acorns and berries he can eat. They'll find food in town. Food, and information.

"This is the best time not to be noticed," Connor tells the others. "Everyone's in a hurry in the morning. Late to work, or whatever."

Connor finds a newspaper in the bushes, misthrown by a delivery boy. "Look at this!" says Lev. "A newspaper. How retro is that?"

"Does it talk about us?" asks Lev. He says it like it's a good thing. The three of them scan the front page. The war in Australia, lying politicians—the same old stuff. Connor turns the page clumsily. Its pages are large and awkward. They tear easily and catch the breeze like a kite, making it hard to read.

No mention of them on page two, or page three.

"Maybe it's an old newspaper," suggests Risa.

Connor checks the date on top. "No, it's today's." He fights against the breeze to turn the page. "Ah—there it is."

The headline reads, PILEUP ON INTERSTATE. It's a very small article. A morning car accident, *blah-blah-blah*, traffic snarled for hours, *blah-blah-blah*. The article mentions the dead bus driver, the fact that the road was closed for three hours. But nothing about them. Connor reads the last line of the article aloud.

"It is believed that police activity in the area may have distracted drivers, leading to the accident."

They're all dumbfounded. For Connor, there's a sense of relief—a sense of having gotten away with something huge.

"That can't be right," says Lev, "I was kidnapped, or . . . uh . . . at least they *think* I was. That should be in the news."

"Lev's right," says Risa. "They always have incidents with Unwinds in the news. If we're not in there, there's a reason."

Connor can't believe these two are looking this gift horse in the mouth! He speaks slowly as if to idiots. "No news report means no pictures—and that means people won't recognize us. I don't see why that's a problem."

Risa folds her arms. "*Why* are there no pictures?"

"I don't know—maybe the police are keeping it quiet because they don't want people to know they screwed up."

Risa shakes her head. "It doesn't feel right. . . ."

"Who cares how it feels!"

"Keep your voice down!" Risa says in an angry whisper. Connor fights to keep his temper under control. He doesn't say anything for fear he's going to start yelling again and draw attention to them. He can see Risa puzzling over the situation and Lev looking back and forth between the two of them. *Risa's not stupid,* thinks Connor. *She's going to figure out that this is a good thing, and that she's worrying for nothing.*

But instead, Risa says, "If we're never in the news, then who's going to know if we live or die? See—if it's all over the news that they're tracking us, then when they find us, they have to take us down with tranquilizer bullets and take us to be harvested, right?"

Connor has no idea why she's stating the obvious. "So, what's your point?"

"What if they don't want to take us to be unwound. What if they want us dead?"

Connor opens his mouth to tell her how stupid that is, but stops himself. Because it's not stupid at all.

"Lev," says Risa, "your family's pretty rich, right?"

Lev shrugs modestly. "I guess."

"What if they paid off the police to get you back by killing the kidnappers . . . and to do it quietly, so no one ever knew it happened?"

Connor looks to Lev, hoping the kid will laugh at the very suggestion, telling them that his parents would never, ever do such a terrible thing. Lev, however, is curiously silent about it as he considers the possibility.

And at that moment two things happen. A police car turns onto the street, and somewhere very close by, a baby begins to cry.

*Run!*

This is the first thought in Connor's mind, his first instinct, but Risa grabs his arm tightly the moment she sees the police car, and it makes him hesitate. Connor knows hesitation can mean the difference between life and death in dire situations. But not today. Today it gives him enough time to do something Connor rarely does in an emergency. He goes beyond his first thought, and processes his *second* thought:

*Running will attract attention.*

He forces his feet to stay in one place, and takes a quick moment to assess their surroundings. Cars are starting in driveways as people head off to work. Somewhere a baby is crying. High-school-aged kids are gathered on a corner across the street, talking, pushing each other, laughing. As he looks to Risa, he can tell they're both of one mind, even before she says, "Bus stop!"

The patrol car rolls leisurely down the street. Leisurely, that is, to someone who has nothing to hide, but to Connor its slow pace is menacing. There's no way of telling if these officers are looking for them or just on a routine patrol. Again, he fights down the urge to run.

He and Risa turn their backs to the police car, ready to stride off inconspicuously toward the bus stop, but Lev is not with the program. He faces the wrong way, staring straight at the approaching cop car.

"What, are you nuts?" Connor grabs his shoulder and forces him around. "Just do what we do, and act natural."

A school bus approaches from the other direction. The kids at the corner begin gathering their things. Now, at last, there's permission to run without looking out of place. Connor begins it, taking a few strides ahead of Risa and Lev, then turns back, calling with a calculated whine, "C'mon, you guys— we're gonna miss the bus again!"

The cop car's right beside them now. Connor keeps his back to it and doesn't turn to see if the officers inside are watching them. If they are, hopefully they'll just hear the conversation and assume this is normal morning mayhem, and not think twice. Lev's version of "acting natural" is walking with wide eyes and arms stiff by his side like he's crossing a minefield. So much for being inconspicuous. "Do you have to walk so slow?" Connor yells. "If I get another tardy, I'll get detention."

The squad car rolls past them. Up ahead, the bus nears the stop. Connor, Risa, and Lev hurry across the street toward it—all part of the charade, just in case the cops are watching them through their rearview mirror. Of course, thinks Connor, it could backfire on them, and the cops could cite them for jaywalking.

"Are we really going to get on the bus?" asks Lev.

"Of course not," says Risa.

Now Connor dares to glance at the cop car. Its blinker is on. It's going to turn the corner, and once it does, they'll be safe. . . . But then the school bus stops and turns on its blinking red lights as it opens its door—and anyone who's ever ridden a school bus knows that when those red lights start blinking, all traffic around them must stop and wait until the bus moves on.

The cop car comes to a halt a dozen yards short of the corner, waiting until the bus is finished loading. That means that the cop car will still be sitting right there when the bus pulls away. "We're screwed," Connor says. "Now we *have* to get on the bus."

It's as they reach the sidewalk that a sound which has been too faint and too low-priority to care about suddenly snares Connor's attention. The crying baby.

At the house in front of them, there's a bundle on the porch. The bundle is moving.

Connor instantly knows what this is. He's seen it before. He's seen a storked baby twice on his own doorstep. Even though it's not the same baby, he stops in his tracks as if it is.

"C'mon, Billy, you'll miss the bus!"

"Huh?"

It's Risa. She and Lev are a few yards ahead of him. She speaks to Connor through gritted teeth. "C'mon, 'Billy.' Don't be an idiot."

Kids have already started piling onto the bus. The police

61

car sits motionless behind the blinking red lights.

Connor tries to make himself move, but can't. It's because of the baby. Because of the way it wails. *This is not the same baby!* Connor tells himself. *Don't be stupid. Not now!*

"Connor," whispers Risa, "what's wrong with you?"

Then the door of the house opens. There's a fat little kid at the door—six, maybe seven. He stares down at the baby. "Aw, no way!" Then he turns and calls back into the house, "Mom! We've been storked again!"

Most people have two emergency modes. Fight and Flight. But Connor always knew he had three: Fight, Flight, and Screw Up Royally. It was a dangerous mental short circuit. The same short circuit that made him race back toward armed Juvey-cops to rescue Lev instead of just saving himself. He could feel it kicking in again right now. He could feel his brain starting to fry. "We've been storked again," the fat kid had said. Why did he have to say "again"? Connor might have been all right if he hadn't said "again."

*Don't do it!* Connor tells himself. *This is not the same baby!*

But to some deep, unreasoning part of his brain, they're all the same baby.

Going against all sense of self-preservation, Connor bolts straight for the porch. He approaches the door so quickly, the kid looks up at him with terrified eyes and backs into his mother, an equally plump woman who has just arrived at the door. Her face wears an unwelcoming scowl. She stares at Connor, then spares a quick glance down at the crying baby, but she makes no move toward it.

"Who are you?" she demands. The little boy now hides behind her like a cub behind a mother grizzly. "Did you put this here? Answer me!" The baby continues to cry.

"No . . . No, I—"

"Don't lie to me!"

He doesn't know what he hoped to accomplish coming here. This is none of his business, not his problem. But now he's made it his problem.

And behind him the bus is still loading kids. The police car is still there, waiting. Connor could have very well just ended his life by coming to this house.

Then there's a voice behind him. "He didn't put it there. I did."

Connor turns to see Risa. Her face is stony. She won't even look at Connor. She just glares at the woman, whose beady eyes shift from Connor to Risa.

"You got caught in the act, little dearie," she says. The words "little dearie" come out like a curse. "The law might let you stork, but only if you don't get caught. So take your baby and go, before I call those cops over."

Connor tries desperately to unfry his brain. "But . . . but . . ."

"Just shut up!" says Risa, her voice full of venom and accusation.

This makes the woman at the door smile, but it's not a pleasant thing. "Daddy here ruined it for you, didn't he? He came back instead of just running away." The woman spares a quick dismissive look at Connor. "First rule of motherhood, dearie: Men are screwups. Learn it now and you'll be a whole lot happier."

Between them, the baby still cries. It's like a game of steal the bacon, where no one wants to take the bacon. Finally, Risa bends down and lifts the baby from the welcome mat, holding it close to her. It still cries, but much more softly now.

"Now get out of here," says the fat woman, "or you'll be talking to those cops."

Connor turns to see the cop car partially blocked by the school bus. Lev stands halfway in and halfway out of the bus, keeping the door from closing, a look of utter desperation on his face. The irritated bus driver peers out at him. "C'mon, I don't have all day!"

Connor and Risa turn away from the woman at the door and hurry for the bus.

"Risa, I—"

"Don't," she snaps. "I don't want to hear it."

Connor feels as broken as he did the moment he found out his parents had signed the order to unwind him. Back then, however, he had anger to help dilute the fear and the shock. But there's no anger in him now, except for anger at himself. He feels helpless, hopeless. All of his self-confidence has imploded like a dying star. Three fugitives running from the law. And now, thanks to his short-circuit stupidity, they are three fugitives with a baby.

# 12 · Risa

She can't even begin to guess what possessed Connor.

Now Risa realizes he doesn't just make bad decisions, he makes dangerous ones. The school bus only has a few kids on it as they step on, and the driver angrily closes the door behind them, making no comment about the baby. Perhaps because it's not the only baby on the bus. Risa pushes past Lev and leads the three of them to the back. They pass another girl with her own little bundle of joy, which couldn't be any older than six months. The young mother curiously eyes them, and Risa tries not to make eye contact.

After they're sitting in the back, a few rows away from the nearest riders, Lev looks at Risa, almost afraid to ask the obvious question. Finally he says. "Uh . . . why do we have a baby?"

"Ask *him*," says Risa.

Stone-faced, Connor looks out the window. "They're look-ing for two boys and a girl. Having a baby will throw them off."

"Great," snaps Risa. "Maybe we should all pick up a baby along the way."

Connor goes visibly red. He turns toward her and holds out his hands. "I'll hold it," he says, but Risa keeps it away from him.

"You'll make it cry."

Risa is no stranger to babies. At the state home she occa-sionally got to work with the infants. This one probably would have ended up at a state home too. She could tell that the woman at the door had no intention of keeping it.

She looks at Connor. Still red, he intentionally avoids her gaze. The reason Connor gave was a lie. Something else drove him to run to that porch. But whatever the real reason was, Connor's keeping it to himself.

The bus comes to a jarring halt and more kids get on. The girl at the front of the bus—the one with the baby—makes her way to the back and sits right in front of Risa, turning around and looking at her over the seat back.

"Hi, you must be new! I'm Alexis, and this is Chase." Her baby looks at Risa curiously, and drools over the seat back. Alexis picks up the baby's limp hand, and makes it wave like she might wave the hand of a toy doll. "Say hello, Chase!" Alexis seems even younger than Risa.

Alexis peers around to get a look at the sleeping baby's face. "A newborn! Oh, wow! That's so brave of you, coming back to school so soon!" She turns to Connor. "Are you the father?"

"Me?" Connor looks flustered and cornered for a moment before he comes to his senses and says, "Yeah. Yeah, I am."

"That's *sooooo* great that you're still seeing each other. Chaz—that's Chase's father—doesn't even go to our school anymore. He got sent to military school. His parents were so mad when they found out that I was, you know, 'uploaded,' he was afraid they might actually have him unwound. Can you believe it?"

Risa could strangle this girl if it weren't for the fact that it would leave drooling Chase motherless.

"So, is yours a boy, or a girl?"

The pause before answering is awkward and uncomfortable. Risa wonders whether or not there's a discreet way to check without Alexis seeing, but realizes there isn't. "Girl," Risa says. At least there's a 50 percent chance she's right.

"What's her name?"

This time Connor pipes up. "Didi," he says. "Her name's Didi." This brings forth a little grin from Risa in spite of how angry she is at him.

"Yeah," says Risa. "Same as me. Family tradition."

Clearly Connor has recovered at least a portion of his senses. He seems a bit more relaxed and natural, playing the role as best he can. The redness in his face has receded until it's only his ears that are red.

"Well, you're going to love Center-North High," Alexis says. "They've got a great day care center, and really take care of student-mothers. Some teachers even let us nurse in class."

Connor puts his hand over Risa's shoulder. "Do fathers get to watch?"

Risa shrugs off his arm, and quietly stomps on his foot. He winces, but says nothing. If he thought he was out of the doghouse, he's dead wrong. As far as she's concerned, his name is Fido.

"It looks like your brother is making friends," says Alexis. She looks to where Lev was sitting, but he's moved a seat ahead and is talking to boy sitting next to him. She tries to hear what they're talking about but can't hear anything beyond Alexis's blathering.

"Or is it *your* brother?" Alexis says to Connor.

"No, he's mine," says Risa.

Alexis grins and rolls her shoulders a bit. "He's kind of cute."

Risa didn't think it was possible to like Alexis any less than she already did. Apparently she was wrong. Alexis must see the look in Risa's eyes, because she says, "Well, I mean cute for a *freshman*."

"He's thirteen. He skipped a grade," Risa says, burning Alexis an even meaner warning gaze that says, *Keep your claws away from my little brother*. She has to remind herself that Lev really isn't her little brother. Now it's Connor's turn to stomp on her foot—and he's right to do it. Too much information. Lev's real age was more than Alexis needed to know. And besides, making an enemy is not in their best interests.

"Sorry," says Risa, softening her gaze. "Long night with the baby. It's made me cranky."

"Oh, believe me, I've totally been there."

It looks as if the Alexis Inquisition might continue until they reach the school, but the bus comes to another sudden stop, making little Chase bump his chin on the seat back, and he begins to cry. Suddenly Alexis goes into mother mode, and the conversation ends.

Risa heaves a deep sigh, and Connor says, "I really am sorry about this." Although he sounds sincere, she's not accepting any apologies.

# 13 · Lev

This day has not gone according to plan.

The plan was to get away as soon as they reached civilization. Lev could have run the moment they broke out of the woods. He could have, but he didn't. *There'll be a better time,* he had thought. A perfect time would present itself if he had patience, and kept watchful.

Pretending to be one of them—pretending to be *like* them had taken every ounce of Lev's will. The only thing that kept him going was the knowledge that very soon everything would be as it should be.

When the police car had turned onto the street, Lev was fully prepared to throw himself at the car and turn himself in. He would have done it if it weren't for one thing.

Their pictures weren't in the paper.

That bothered Lev even more than the others. His family was influential. They were not to be trifled with. He felt certain that his face would be the biggest thing on the front page. When it wasn't, he didn't know what to think. Even Risa's theory that his parents wanted her and Connor killed seemed a possibility.

If he gave himself up to the police, what if they turned and fired real bullets at Risa and Connor? Would the police do that? He wanted them brought to justice, but he couldn't bear the thought of their deaths on his head, so he had let the squad car go past.

And now things are worse. Now there's this baby. Stealing a storked baby! These two Unwinds are out of control. He no longer fears that they'll kill him, but that doesn't make them any less dangerous. They need to be protected from themselves. They need . . . they need . . . they need to be unwound. Yes. That's the best solution for these two. They're of no use to anyone in their current state, least of all themselves. It would probably be a relief for them, for now they're all broken up on the inside. Better to be broken up on the outside instead. That way their divided spirits could rest, knowing that their living flesh was spread around the world, saving lives, making other people whole. Just as his own spirit would soon rest.

He ponders this as he sits on the bus, trying to deny how mixed his feelings about it are.

While Risa and Connor talk to a painfully perky girl and her baby, Lev moves one seat forward in the bus, putting more distance between them. A boy gets on the bus and sits down next to him, wearing headphones and singing to music that Lev can't hear. The kid slips his backpack in between them on the seat, practically wedging Lev in, and returns his full attention to his tunes.

That's when Lev gets an idea. He looks behind him to see Connor and Risa still involved with the other girl and her baby. Carefully Lev reaches into the kid's backpack and pulls out a dog-eared notebook. Written on it in big black letters is DEATH BY ALGEBRA, with little skulls and crossbones. Inside are messy math equations and homework graded down for sloppiness. Lev quietly turns to a blank page, then he reaches into the kid's pack again, pulling out a pen. All the while, the kid is so absorbed in his music, he doesn't notice. Lev begins to write:

HELP! I'M BEING HELD HOSTAGE
BY TWO AWOL UNWINDS.
NOD IF YOU UNDERSTAND . . .

When he's done, he tugs the boy's shoulder. It takes two tugs to get his attention.

"Yeah?"

Lev holds out the notebook, making sure he does it in such a way that it's not too obvious. The boy looks at him and says:

"Hey, that's my notebook."

Lev takes a deep breath. Connor's looking at him now. He's got to be careful. "I know it's your notebook," Lev says, trying to say as much as he can with his eyes. "I just . . . needed . . . one . . . page. . . ."

He holds the notebook a little higher for the kid to read, but the kid's not even looking at it. "No! You should have asked first." Then he rips out the page without even looking at it, crumples the paper, and to Lev's horror hurls it toward the front of the bus. The paper wad bounces off the head of another kid, who ignores it, and it falls to the floor. The bus comes to a stop, and Lev feels his hope trampled beneath thirty pairs of scuffed shoes.

# 14 · Connor

Dozens of buses pull up to the school. Kids mob every doorway. As Connor gets off the bus with Risa and Lev, he scans for a way to escape, but there is none. There are campus security guards and teachers on patrol. Anyone seen walking away from school would draw the attention of everyone watching.

"We can't actually go in," says Risa.

"I say we do," says Lev, acting more squirrelly than usual.

A teacher has already taken notice of them. Even though the school has a day care center for student mothers, the baby is very conspicuous.

"We'll go in," says Connor. "We'll hide in a place where there aren't any security cameras. The boys' bathroom."

"Girls'," says Risa. "It'll be cleaner, and there'll be more stalls to hide in."

Connor considers it, and figures she's probably right on both counts. "Fine. We'll hide until lunch, then slip out with the rest of the kids going off campus."

"You're assuming this baby wants to cooperate," says Risa. "Eventually it's going to want to be fed—and I don't exactly have the materials, if you know what I mean. If it starts crying in the bathroom, it will probably echo throughout the whole school."

It's another accusation. Connor can hear it in her voice. It says: *Do you have any idea how much harder you've made things on us?*

"Let's just hope it doesn't cry," says Connor. "And if it does, you can blame me all the way to harvest camp."

Connor is no stranger to hiding in school bathrooms. Of course, before today, the reason was simply to get out of class. Today, however, there's no class where he's expected, and if he's caught, the consequences are a little bit more severe than Saturday school.

They slip in after the first period bell rings and Connor coaches them on the finer points of bathroom stealth. How to tell the difference between kids' footsteps and adults'. When to lift your feet up so no one can see you, and when to just announce that the stall is occupied. The latter would work for both Risa and Lev, since his voice is still somewhat high, but Connor doesn't dare pretend to be a girl.

They stay together yet alone, each in their own stall. Mercifully, the bathroom door squeals like a pig whenever it's opened, so they have warning when anyone comes in. There are a few girls at the beginning of first period but then it quiets down and they are left with no sound but the echoing drizzle of a leaky flush handle.

"We won't make it in here until lunch," Risa announces from the stall to Connor's left. "Even if the baby stays asleep."

"You'd be surprised how long you can hide in a bathroom."

"You mean you've done this often?" asks Lev, in the stall to his right.

Connor knows this fits right into Lev's image of Connor as a bad seed. Fine, let him think that. He's probably right.

The bathroom door squeals. They fall silent. Dull, rapid footsteps—it's a student in sneakers. Lev and Connor raise their feet and Risa keeps hers down, as they had planned. The baby gurgles, and Risa clears her throat, masking the noise perfectly. The girl is in and out in less than a minute.

After the bathroom door squeaks closed, the baby coughs. Connor notices that it's a quick, clean sound. Not sickly at all. Good.

"By the way," says Risa, "it *is* a girl."

Connor thinks to offer to hold it once more, but figures right now that would be more trouble than it's worth. He doesn't know how to hold a baby to keep it from crying. Connor decides he has to tell them why he went temporarily insane and took the baby. He owes them that much.

"It was because of what the kid said," Connor says gently.

"What?"

"Back at that house—the fat kid at the door. He said they'd been storked *again*."

"So what?" says Risa. "Lots of people get storked more than once."

Then, from his other side, Connor hears, "That happened to my family. I have two brothers and a sister who were brought by the stork before I was born. It was never a problem."

Connor wonders if Lev actually thinks the stork brought them, or if he's just using it as an expression. He decides he'd rather not know. "What a wonderful family. They take in storked babies, and send their own flesh and blood to be unwound. Oh, sorry—*tithed*."

Clearly offended, Lev says, "Tithing's in the Bible; you're supposed to give 10 percent of everything. And storking's in the Bible too."

"No, it isn't!"

"Moses," says Lev. "Moses was put in a basket in the Nile and was found by Pharaoh's daughter. He was the first storked baby, and look what happened to him!"

"Yeah," says Connor, "but what happened to the next baby she found in the Nile?"

"Will you keep your voices down?" says Risa. "People could hear you in the hall, and anyway, you might wake Didi."

Connor takes a moment to collect his thoughts. When he speaks again, it's a whisper, but in a tiled room there are no whispers. "We got storked when I was seven."

"Big deal," says Risa.

"No, this *was* a big deal. For a whole lot of reasons. See, there were already two natural kids in the family. My parents weren't planning on any more. Anyway, this baby shows up at our door, my parents start freaking out . . . and then they have an idea."

"Do I want to hear this?" Risa asks.

"Probably not." But Connor's not about to stop. He knows if he doesn't spill this now, he's never going to. "It was early in the morning, and my parents figured no one saw the baby left at the door, right? So the next morning, before the rest of us got up, my dad put the baby on a doorstep across the street."

"That's illegal," announces Lev. "Once you get storked, that baby's yours."

"Yeah, but my parents figured, who's gonna know? My parents swore us to secrecy, and we waited to hear the news from across the street about their new, unexpected arrival . . . but it never came. They never talked about getting storked and we couldn't ask them about it, because it would be a dead give-away that we'd dumped the baby on them."

As Connor speaks, the stall, as small as it is, seems to shrink around him. He knows the others are there on either side, but he can't help but feel desperately alone.

"Things go on like it never happened. Everything was quiet for a while, and then two weeks later, I open the door, and there on that stupid welcome mat, is another baby in a basket . . . and I remember . . . I remember I almost laughed. Can you believe it? I thought it was funny, and I turned back to my mother, and I say 'Mom, we got storked again'—just like that little kid this morning said. My Mom, all frustrated, brought the baby in . . . and that's when she realizes—"

"Oh, no!" says Risa, figuring it out even before Connor says:

"It's the same baby!" Connor tries to remember the baby's face, but he can't. All he sees in his mind's eye is the face of the baby Risa now holds. "It turns out that the baby had been passed around the neighborhood for two whole weeks—each morning, left on someone else's doorstep . . . only now it's not looking too good."

The bathroom door squeals, and Connor falls silent. A flurry of footsteps. Two girls. They chat a bit about boys and dates and parties with no parents around. They don't even use the toilets. Another flurry of footsteps heading out, the squeal of the door, and they are alone again.

"So, what happened to the baby?" Risa asks.

"By the time it landed on our doorstep again, it was sick. It was coughing like a seal and its skin and eyes were yellow."

"Jaundice," says Risa, gently. "A lot of babies show up at StaHo that way."

"My parents brought it to the hospital, but there was nothing they could do. I was there when it died. I *saw* it die." Connor closes his eyes, and grits his teeth, to keep tears back. He knows the others can't see them, but he doesn't want them to come anyway. "I remember thinking, if a baby was going to be so unloved, why would God want it brought into the world?"

He wonders if Lev will have some pronouncement on the topic—after all, when it comes to God, Lev claimed to have all the answers. But all Lev says is, "I didn't know you believed in God."

Connor takes a moment to push his emotions down, then continues. "Anyway, since it was legally ours, we paid for the funeral. It didn't even have a name, and my parents couldn't bear to give it one. It was just 'Baby Lassiter,' and even though no one had wanted it, the entire neighborhood came to the funeral. People were crying like it was their baby that had died. . . . And that's when I realized that the people who were crying—they were the ones who had passed that baby around. They were the ones, just like my own parents, who had a hand in killing it."

There's silence now. The leaky flush handle drizzles. Next door in the boys' bathroom a toilet flushes, and the sound echoes hollowly around them.

"People shouldn't give away babies that get left at their door," Lev finally says.

"People shouldn't stork their babies," Risa responds.

"People shouldn't do a lot of things," says Connor. He knows they're both right, but it doesn't make a difference. In a perfect world mothers would all want their babies, and strangers would open up their homes to the unloved. In a perfect world everything would be either black or white, right or wrong, and everyone would know the difference. But this isn't a perfect world. The problem is people who think it is.

"Anyway, I just wanted you to know."

In a few moments the bell rings, and there's commotion in the hall. The bathroom door creaks open. Girls laughing, talking about everything and nothing.

*"Next time wear a dress."*

*"Can I borrow your history book?"*

*"That test was impossible."*

Unending squeals from the door and constant tugs on Connor's locked stall door. No one's tall enough to look over, no one has any desire to look under. The late bell rings; the last girl hurries to class. They've made it to second period. If they're lucky, this school will have a midmorning break. Maybe they can sneak out then. In Risa's stall, the baby is making wakeful noises. Not crying but sort of clicking. On the verge of hungry tears.

"Should we change stalls?" asks Risa. "Repeat visitors might get suspicious if they see my feet in the same stall."

"Good idea." Listening closely to make sure he can't hear any footfalls in the hall, Connor pulls open his stall, switching places with Risa. Lev's door is open as well, but he's not coming out. Connor pushes Lev's door open all the way. He's not there.

"Lev?" He looks to Risa, who just shakes her head. They check every stall, then check the one Lev was in again, as if he might reappear—but he doesn't. Lev is gone. And the baby begins wailing for all it's worth.

# 15 · Lev

Lev is convinced his heart will explode in his chest.

It will explode, and he will die right here in a school hallway. Slipping out of the bathroom once the bell rang had been nerve-racking. He had unlocked his stall door, and had kept his hand on the handle for ten minutes waiting for the electronic buzz of the bell to mask the sound of its opening. Then he'd had to make it to the bathroom entrance without the others hearing his brand-new sneakers squeaking on the floor. (Why did they call them sneakers if it was so hard to sneak in them?) He couldn't open that squealing door, then walk out by himself. It would be too conspicuous. So he waited until a bathroom-bound girl did it for him. Since the bell had just rung, he only had to wait a few seconds. She pulled open the door and he pushed his way past her, hoping she didn't say anything that would give him away. If she commented about a boy being in the girl's bathroom, Connor and Risa would know.

"Next time, wear a dress," the girl said to him as he hurried away, and her friend laughed. Was that enough to alert Connor and Risa to his escape? He hadn't turned back to find out, he had just pressed forward.

Now he's lost in the hallways of the huge high school, his heart threatening to detonate at any second. A wild mob of kids hurrying to their next class surround him, bump him, disorient him. Most of the kids here are bigger than Lev. Imposing. Intimidating. This is how he always imagined high school—a dangerous place full of mystery and violent kids. He had never worried about it because he had always known he would never have to go. In fact, he only had to worry about getting partway through eighth grade.

"Excuse me, can you tell me where the office is?" he asks one of the slower-moving students.

The kid looks down at him as if Lev were from Mars. "How could you not know that?" And he just walks away shaking his head. Another, kinder kid points him in the right direction.

Lev knows that things must be put back on track. This is the best place to do it: a school. If there are any secret plans to kill Connor and Risa, it can't happen here with so many kids around, and if he does this right, it won't happen at all. If he does it right, all three of them will be safely on their way to their unwinding, as it ought to be. As it was *ordained* to be. The thought of it still frightens him, but these days of not knowing what the next hour will bring—that is truly terrifying. Being torn from his purpose was the most unnerving thing that had ever happened to Lev, but now he understands why God let it happen. It's a lesson. It's to show Lev what happens to children who shirk their destiny: They become lost in every possible way.

He enters the school's main office and stands at the counter, waiting to be noticed, but the secretary is too busy shuffling papers. "Excuse me . . ."

Finally, she looks up. "Can I help you, dear?"

He clears his throat. "My name is Levi Calder, and I've been kidnapped by two runaway Unwinds."

The woman, who really wasn't paying attention before, suddenly focuses her attention entirely on him. "What did you say?"

"I was kidnapped. We were hiding in a bathroom, but I got away. They're still there. They've got a baby, too."

The woman stands up and calls out, her voice shaky, like she's looking at a ghost. She calls in the principal, and the principal calls in a security guard.

A minute later, Lev sits in the nurse's office, with the nurse doting on him like he's got a fever.

"Don't you worry," she says. "Whatever happened to you, it's all over now."

From here in the nurse's office, Lev has no way of knowing if they've captured Connor and Risa. He hopes that, if they have, they don't bring them here. The thought of having to face them makes him feel ashamed. Doing the right thing shouldn't make you ashamed.

"The police have been called, everything's being taken care of," the nurse tells him. "You'll be going home soon."

"I'm not going home," he tells her. The nurse looks at him strangely, and he decides not to go into it. "Never mind. Can I call my parents?"

She looks at him, incredulous. "You mean, no one's done that for you?" She looks at the school phone in the corner, then fumbles for the cell phone in her pocket instead. "You call and let them know you're okay—and talk as long as you like."

She looks at him for a moment, then decides to give him

his privacy, stepping out of the room. "I'll be right here if you need me."

Lev begins to dial, but stops himself. It's not his parents he wants to talk to. He erases the numbers and keys in a different one, hesitates for a moment, then hits the send button.

It's picked up on the second ring.

"Hello?"

"Pastor Dan?"

There's only a split second of dead air, and then recognition. "Dear God, Lev? Lev, is that you? Where are you?"

"I don't know. Some school. Listen, you have to tell my parents to stop the police! I don't want them killed."

"Lev, slow down. Are you all right?"

"They kidnapped me—but they didn't hurt me, so I don't want them hurt. Tell my father to call off the police!"

"I don't know what you're talking about. We never told the police."

Lev is not expecting to hear this. "You never . . . what?"

"Your parents were going to. They were going to make a whole big deal about it—but I convinced them not to. I convinced them that your being kidnapped was somehow God's will."

Lev starts shaking his head like he can shake the thought away. "But . . . but why would you do that?"

Now Pastor Dan starts to sound desperate. "Lev, listen to me. Listen to me carefully. *No one else knows that you're gone.* As far as anyone knows, you've been tithed, and people don't ask questions about children who are tithed. Do you understand what I'm telling you?"

"But . . . I want to be tithed. I *need* to be. You have to call my parents and tell them. You have to get me to harvest camp."

Now Pastor Dan gets angry. *"Don't make me do that!*

*Please, don't make me do that!"* It's as if he's fighting a battle, but somehow it's not Lev he's battling. This is so far from Lev's image of Pastor Dan, he can't believe it's the same person he's known all these years. It's like an impostor has stolen the Pastor's voice, but none of his convictions.

"Don't you see, Lev? You can save yourself. You can be anyone you want to be now."

And all at once the truth comes to Lev. Pastor Dan wasn't telling him to run away from the kidnapper that day—he was telling Lev to run away from *him*. From his parents. From his tithing. After all of his sermons and lectures, after all that talk year after year about Lev's holy duty, it's all been a sham. Lev was born to be tithed—and the man who convinced him this was a glorious and honorable fate doesn't believe it.

"Lev? Lev, are you there?"

He's there, but he doesn't want to be. He doesn't want to answer this man who led him to a cliff only to turn away at the last minute. Now Lev's emotions spin like a wheel of fortune. One moment he's furious, the next, relieved. One instant he's filled with terror so extreme, he can smell it like acid in his nostrils, and the next, there's a spike of joy, like what he used to feel when he swung away and heard the crack of his bat against a ball. He is that ball now, soaring away. His life has been like a ballpark, hasn't it? All lines, structure, and rules, never changing. But now he's been hit over the wall into unknown territory.

"Lev?" says Pastor Dan. "You're scaring me. Talk to me."

Lev takes a slow, deep breath, then says, "Good-bye, sir." Then he hangs up without another word.

Lev sees police cars arrive outside. Connor and Risa will soon be caught, if they haven't been caught already. The nurse is no longer standing at the door—she's chiding the principal for how he's handling this situation. "Why didn't you call the poor boy's parents? Why haven't you put the school in lock-down?"

Lev knows what he has to do. It's something wrong. It's something bad. But suddenly he doesn't care. He slips out of the office right behind the nurse's and principal's backs, and goes out into the hallway. It only takes a second to find what he's looking for. He reaches for the little box on the wall.

*I am lost in every possible way.*

Then, feeling the coldness of the steel against his finger-tips, he pulls the fire alarm.

# 16 · Teacher

The fire alarm goes off during the teacher's prep period, and she silently curses the powers that be for their awful timing. Perhaps, she thinks, if she can just stay in her empty class-room until the false alarm—and it's always a false alarm—is dealt with. But then, what kind of example would she be set-ting if students passing by looked in to see her sitting there.

As she leaves the room, the hallways are already filling with students. Teachers try their best to keep them organized, but this is a high school; the organized lines of elementary school fire drills are long gone, having been replaced by the brazen hormonal zigzags of kids whose bodies are too big for their own good.

Then she sees something strange. Something troubling.

There are two policemen by the front office—they actually seem intimidated by the mob of kids flowing past them and out the front doors of the school. But why policemen? Why not firemen? And how could they have gotten here so quickly? They couldn't have—they must have been called before the alarm went off. But why?

The last time there were policemen in the school, some-one called in a clapper threat. The school was evacuated, and no one knew why until after the fact. Turns out, there was no clapper—the school was never in danger of being blown up. It was just some kid pulling a practical joke. Still, clapper threats are always taken seriously, because you never know when the threat might be real.

"Please, no pushing!" she says to a student who bumps her elbow. "I'm sure we'll all make it outside." Good thing she didn't take her coffee.

"Sorry, Ms. Steinberg."

As she passes one of the science labs, she notices the door ajar. Just to be thorough, she peeks in to make sure there are no stragglers, or kids trying to avoid the mass exodus. The stone-top tables are bare and the chairs are all in place. No one had been in the lab this period. She reaches to pull the door closed, more out of habit than anything else, when she hears a sound that is wholly out of place in the room.

A baby's cry.

At first she thinks it might be coming from the student mother nursery, but the nursery is way down the hall. This cry definitely came from the lab. She hears the cry again, only this time it sounds oddly muffled, and angrier. She knows that sound. Someone's trying to cover the baby's mouth to keep it from crying. These teen mothers always do that when they have their babies where they don't belong. They never seem to realize it only makes the baby cry louder.

"Party's over," she calls out. "C'mon, you and your baby have to leave with everyone else."

But they don't come out. There's that muffled cry again, followed by some intense whispering that she can't quite make out. Annoyed, she steps into the lab and storms down the cen-ter aisle looking left and right until she finds them crouched

82

behind one of the lab tables. It's not just a girl and a baby; there's a boy there too. There's a look of desperation about them. The boy looks as if he might bolt, but the girl grabs him firmly with her free hand. It keeps him in place. The baby wails.

The teacher might not know every name in school, but she's fairly certain she knows every face—and she certainly knows all the student mothers. This isn't one of them, and the boy is completely unfamiliar too.

The girl looks at her, eyes pleading. Too frightened to speak, she just shakes her head. It's the boy who speaks.

"If you turn us in, we'll die."

At the thought, the girl holds the baby closer to her. Its cries lessen, but don't go away entirely. Clearly these are the ones the police are looking for, for reasons she can only guess at.

"Please . . . ," says the boy.

*Please what?* the teacher thinks. *Please break the law? Please put myself and the school at risk?* But, no, that's not it at all. What he's really saying is: *Please be a human being.* With a life so full of rules and regiments, it's so easy to forget that's what they are. She knows—she *sees*—how often compassion takes a back seat to expediency.

Then a voice from behind her: "Hannah?"

She turns to see another teacher looking in from the door. He's a bit disheveled, having fought the raging rapids of kids still funneling out of the school. He obviously hears the baby's cries—how could he not?

"Is everything all right?" he asks.

"Yeah," says Hannah, with more calm in her voice than she actually feels. "I'm taking care of it."

The other teacher nods and leaves, probably glad not to share the burden of whatever this crying baby situation is.

Hannah now knows what the situation is, however—or at least she suspects. Kids only have this kind of desperation in their eyes when they're going to be unwound.

She holds out her hand to the frightened kids. "Come with me." The kids are hesitant, so she says, "If they're looking for you, they'll find you once the building is empty. You can't expect to hide here. If you want to get out, you have to leave with everyone else. C'mon, I'll help you."

Finally, they rise from behind the lab table, and she breathes a sigh of relief. She can tell they still don't trust her—but then, why should they? Unwinds exist in the constant shadow of betrayal. Well, they don't need to trust her now, they just need to go with her. In this case, necessity is the mother of compliance, and that's just fine.

"Don't tell me your names," she says to them. "Don't tell me anything, so if they question me afterward, I won't be lying when I say I don't know."

There are still crowds of kids pushing past in the hall, heading toward the nearest exit. She steps out of the room, making sure the two kids and their baby are right behind her. She will help them. Whoever they are, she will do her best to get them to safety. What kind of example would she be setting if she didn't?

# 17 · Risa

Police down the hall! Police at the exits! Risa knows this is Lev's doing. He didn't just run away, he turned them in. This teacher says she's helping them, but what if she's not? What if she's just leading them to the police?

*Don't think about that now! Keep your eyes on the baby.*

Policemen know panic when they see it. But if her eyes are

turned to the baby, her panic might be read as concern for the baby's tears.

"If I ever see Lev again," says Connor, "I'll tear him to pieces."

"Shh," says the teacher, leading them along with the crowd to the exit.

Risa can't blame Connor for his anger. She blames herself for not seeing through Lev's sham. How could she have been so naive to think he was truly on their side?

"We should have let the little creep be unwound," grumbles Connor.

"Shut up," says Risa. "Let's just get out of this."

As they near the door, another policeman comes into view standing just outside.

"Give me the baby," the teacher orders, and Risa does as she's told. She doesn't yet realize why the woman asked for the baby, but it doesn't matter. It's wonderful to have *someone* leading the way who seems to know what they're doing. Perhaps this woman isn't the enemy after all. Perhaps she truly will get them through this.

"Let me go ahead," the teacher says. "The two of you separate, and just walk out with the rest of the kids."

Without the baby to look at, Risa knows she can't hide the panic in her eyes, but suddenly she realizes that it might not matter—and now she understands why the woman took the baby. Yes, Lev turned them in. But if they're lucky, these local police may only have a description of them to go by: a scruffy-haired boy and a dark-haired girl with a baby. Take away the baby, and that could be half the kids in this school.

The teacher—Hannah— passes the policeman a few yards ahead of them, and he gives her only a momentary glance. But then he looks toward Risa, and his eyes lock on her. Risa knows she's just given herself away. Should she turn and race back into the school? Where's Connor now? Is he behind her, in front of her? She has no idea. She's completely alone.

And then salvation arrives in a most unlikely form.

"Hi, Didi!"

It's Alexis, the talkative girl from the school bus! She comes up beside her, with Chaz gnawing at her shoulder. "People pull the alarms all the time," she says. "Well, at least I got out of Math."

Suddenly the policeman's eyes shift to Alexis.

"Stop right there, miss."

Alexis looks stunned. "Who, me?"

"Step aside. We'd like to ask you a few questions."

Risa walks right on past, holding her breath for fear that her gasp of relief might draw the officer's attention again. Risa no longer fits the profile of what they're looking for . . . but Alexis does! Risa doesn't look back; she just continues down the steps to the street.

In a few moments Connor catches up with her. "I saw what happened back there. Your friend may have just saved your life."

"I'll have to thank her later."

Up ahead, Hannah reaches into her pocket with her free hand, pulls out her car keys, then turns left toward the faculty parking lot. *It's all going to be okay,* Risa thinks. *She's going to get us out of here.* Risa might just start believing in miracles, and angels. . . . And then she hears a familiar voice behind her.

"Wait! Stop!"

She turns to see Lev—he's spotted them—and although he's far away, he's quickly working his way through the crowd toward them.

"Risa! Connor! Wait!"

It wasn't enough to just turn them in, now he's leading the cops directly to them—and he's not the only one. Alexis still stands with the policeman at the school's side entrance. From where she stands she can easily see Risa, and she points Risa out to the cop. The cop instantly pulls out his radio to inform the other officers.

"Connor, we're in trouble."

"I know—I see it too."

"Wait!" screams Lev, still far away, but getting closer.

Risa looks for Hannah, but she's vanished into the crowd of kids in the parking lot.

Connor looks at Risa, fear overwhelming the fury in his eyes. "Run."

This time Risa doesn't hesitate. She runs with him, breaking toward the street just as a fire truck bursts onto the scene, siren blaring. The truck stops right in their path. There's nowhere to run. The fire alarm had mercifully been pulled at the perfect time, and it's gotten them this far, but the commotion is fading. Kids are milling instead of moving, and cops in every direction zero in on the two of them.

What they need is a fresh commotion. Something even worse than a fire alarm.

The answer comes even before Risa can formulate the entire idea in her mind. She speaks without even knowing what she's about to say.

"Start clapping!"

"What?"

"Start clapping. Trust me!"

A single nod from Connor makes it clear that he gets it, and he begins bringing his hands together, slowly at first, then more and more quickly. She does the same, both of them applauding as if they were at a concert cheering for their favorite band.

And beside them, a student drops his backpack and stares at them in utter horror.

"Clappers!" he screams.

In an instant the word is out.

*ClappersClappersClappers* . . .

It echoes in the kids around them. In an instant it reaches critical mass, and the entire crowd is in full-blown panic.

"Clappers!" everyone screams, and the crowd becomes a stampede. Kids bolt, but no one is sure where to go. All they know is that they must get away from the school as quickly as possible.

Risa and Connor continue to clap, their hands red from the force of their duet of applause. With the mob racing in blind terror, the cops can't get to them. Lev has vanished, trampled by the panicked mob, and everything is made worse by the fire siren, which blares like it's sounding out the end of the world.

They stop clapping and join the stampede, becoming a part of the running crowd.

That's when someone comes up beside them. It's Hannah. Her plans of driving them off campus are gone, so she quickly hands Risa the baby.

"There's an antique shop on Fleming Street," she tells them. "Ask for Sonia. She can help you."

"We're not clappers," is all Risa can think to say.

"I know you're not. Good luck."

There's no time to thank her. In a moment the wild crowd pulls them apart, taking Hannah in a different direction. Risa stumbles and realizes they're in the middle of the street. Traffic has come to a halt as hundreds of kids race in a mad frenzy to escape the terrorists, wherever they are. The baby in Risa's arms bawls, but its cries are nothing compared to the screams of the mob. In a moment they are across the street, and gone with the crowd.

# 18 · Lev

This is the true meaning of alone: Lev Calder beneath the trampling feet of a stampeding crowd.

"Risa! Connor! Help!"

He should never have called out their names, but it's too late to change that now. They ran from him when he called. They didn't wait—they ran. They hate him. They know what he did. Now hundreds of feet race over Lev like he's not there. His hand is stomped on, a boot comes down on his chest, and a kid springboards off of him to get greater speed.

Clappers. They're all screaming about clappers, just because he pulled the stupid alarm.

He has to catch up with Risa and Connor. He has to explain, to tell them that he's sorry—that he was wrong to turn them in and that he pulled the alarm to help them escape. He has to make them understand. They are his only friends now. They were. But not anymore. He's ruined everything.

Finally, the stampede thins out enough for Lev to pick himself up. A knee of his jeans is torn. He tastes blood—he must have bitten his tongue. He tries to assess the situation. Most of the mob is off campus, in the street and beyond, disappearing down side streets. Only stragglers are left.

"Don't just stand there," says a kid hurrying past. "There are clappers on the roof!"

"No," says another kid, "I heard they're in the cafeteria."

All around Lev, the bewildered cops pace with a false determination in their stride, as if they know exactly where to go, only to turn around and pace with the same determination in another direction.

Connor and Risa have left him.

He realizes that if he doesn't leave now with the last of the stragglers, he'll draw the attention of the police.

He runs away, feeling more helpless than a storked baby. He doesn't know who to blame for this: Pastor Dan for cutting him loose? Himself for betraying the only two kids willing to help him? Or should he blame God for allowing his life to reach this bitter moment? *You can be anyone you want to be now,* Pastor Dan had said. But right now, Lev feels like no one.

This is the true meaning of alone: Levi Jedediah Calder suddenly realizing he no longer exists.

# 19 · Connor

The antique shop is in an older part of town. Trees arch over the street, their branches cut into unnatural angular patterns by the profiles of passing trucks. The street is full of yellow and brown leaves, but enough diehards still cling to the branches to make a shady canopy.

The baby is inconsolable, and Connor wants to complain to Risa about it, but knows that he can't. If it hadn't been for him, the baby wouldn't even be part of the equation.

There aren't all that many people on the street, but there are enough. Mostly it's kids from the high school just knocking around, probably spreading more rumors about clappers trying to detonate themselves.

*"I hear they're anarchists."*

*"I hear it's some weird religion."*

*"I hear they just do it to do it."*

The threat of clappers is so effective because no one knows what they really stand for.

"That was smart back there," Connor tells Risa, as they

approach the antique shop. "Pretending to be clappers, I mean. I would never have thought of that."

"You thought quickly enough to take out that Juvey-cop the other day with his own tranq gun."

Connor grins. "I go by instinct, you go by brains. I guess we make a pretty decent team."

"Yeah. And we're a bit less dysfunctional without Lev."

At the mention of Lev, Connor feels a spike of anger. He rubs his sore arm where Lev bit him—but what Lev did today was much more painful than that. "Forget about him. He's history. We got away, so his squealing on us doesn't matter. Now he'll get unwound, just like he wants, and we won't have to deal with him again." And yet the thought of it brings Connor a pang of regret. He had risked his life for Lev. He had tried to save him, but had failed. Maybe if Connor were better with words, he could have said something that would have truly won him over. But who is he kidding? Lev was a tithe from the moment he was born. You don't undo thirteen years of brainwashing in two days.

The antique shop is old. White paint peels from the front door. Connor pushes open the door, and bells hanging high on the door jingle. Low-tech intruder alert. There's one customer: a sour-faced man in a tweed coat. He looks up at them, disinterested and maybe disgusted by the baby, because he wanders deeper into the recesses of the cluttered store to get away.

The shop has things from perhaps every point in American history. A display of iPods and other little gadgets from his grandfather's time cover an old chrome-rimmed dinner table. An old movie plays on an antique plasma-screen TV. The movie shows a crazy vision of a future that never came, with flying cars and a white-haired scientist.

"Can I help you?"

An old woman as hunched as a question mark comes out

from behind the cash register. She walks with a cane, but she seems pretty surefooted in spite of it.

Risa bounces the baby to get its volume down. "We're looking for Sonia."

"You found her. What do you want?"

"We . . . uh . . . we need some help," Risa says.

"Yeah," Connor chimes in, "Someone told us to come here."

The old woman looks at them suspiciously. "Does this have something to do with that fiasco over at the high school? Are you clappers?"

"Do we look like clappers to you?" says Connor.

The woman narrows her eyes at him. "Nobody *looks* like a clapper."

Connor narrows his gaze to match hers, then goes over to the wall. He holds up his hand and jabs it forward with all his might, punching the wall hard enough to bruise his knuckles. A little painting of a fruit bowl falls off the wall. Connor catches it before it hits the ground and sets it on the counter.

"See?" he says. "My blood isn't explosive. If I were a clapper, this whole shop would be gone."

The old woman stares at him, and it's a hard gaze for Connor to hold—there's some sort of fire in those weary eyes. But Connor doesn't look away. "See this hunch?" she asks them. "I got it from sticking my neck out for people like you."

Connor still won't break his gaze. "Guess we came to the wrong place, then." Glancing at Risa, he says, "Let's get out of here."

He turns to leave, and the old woman swings her cane sharply and painfully across his shins. "Not so fast. It just so happens that Hannah called me, so I knew you were coming."

Risa, still bouncing the baby, lets out a frustrated breath.

"You could have told us when we came in."

"What fun would that be?"

By now the sour-faced customer has made his way closer again, picking up item after item, his expression showing instant disapproval of everything in the shop.

"I have some lovely infant items in the back room," she tells them loud enough for the customer to hear. "Why don't you go back there, and wait for me?" Then she whispers, "And for God's sake, feed that baby!"

The back room is through a doorway covered by what looks like an old shower curtain. If the front room was cluttered, this place is a disaster area. Things like broken picture frames and rusty birdcages are piled all around—all the items that weren't good enough to be displayed out front. The junk of the junk.

"And you're telling me this old woman is going to help us?" says Connor. "It looks like she can't even help herself!"

"Hannah said she would. I believe her."

"How could you be raised in a state home and still trust people?"

Risa gives him a dirty look and says, "Hold this." She puts the baby in Connor's arms. It's the first time she's given it to him. It feels much lighter than he expected. Something so loud and demanding ought to be heavier. The baby's cries have weakened now—it's just about exhausted itself.

There's nothing keeping them tied to this baby anymore. They could stork it again first thing in the morning. . . . And yet the thought makes Connor uncomfortable. They don't owe this baby anything. It's theirs by stupidity, not biology. He doesn't want it, but he can't stand the thought of someone getting the baby who wants it even less than he does. His frustration begins to ferment into anger. It's the same kind of anger that always got him into trouble back home. It would cloud his judgment, making him lash out, getting into fights, cursing out teachers, or riding his skateboard wildly through busy intersections. "Why do you have to get wound so tight?" his father once asked, exasperated, and Connor had snapped back, "Maybe someone oughta unwind me." At the time, he thought he was just being funny.

Risa opens a refrigerator, which is as cluttered as the rest of the back room. She pulls out a container of milk, then finds a bowl, into which she pours the milk.

"It's not a cat," Connor says. "It won't lick milk out of a bowl."

"I know what I'm doing."

Connor watches as she rummages around in drawers until finding a clean spoon. Then she takes the baby from him. Sitting down, she cradles the baby a bit more skillfully than Connor, then she dips the spoon into the milk and spills the spoonful into the baby's mouth. The baby begins to gag on the milk, coughing and sputtering, but then Risa puts her index finger into its mouth. It sucks on her finger and closes its eyes, satisfied. In a few moments, she crooks her finger enough to leave a little space for her to spill in another spoonful of milk, then lets the baby suck on her finger again.

"Wow, that's impressive," says Connor.

"Sometimes I got to take care of babies at StaHo. You learn a few tricks. Let's just hope it's not lactose intolerant."

With the baby quieted, it's as if all the day's tension has been suddenly released. Connor's eyelids grow heavy, but he won't allow himself to fall asleep. They're not safe yet. They may never be, and he can't let his guard down now. Still, his mind begins to drift off. He wonders if his parents are still looking for him, or if it's just the police now. He thinks about Ariana. What would have happened to them if she had come along with him, as she had promised? They would have been caught on that first night—that's what would have happened. Ariana wasn't street-smart like Risa. She wasn't resourceful. Thoughts of Ariana bring a wave of sadness and longing, but it's not as powerful a feeling as Connor thought it would be. How soon until she forgets him? How soon until everyone forgets him? Not long. That's what happens with Unwinds. Connor had known other kids at school who disappeared over the past couple of years. One day they just didn't turn up. Teachers would say that they were "gone" or "no longer enrolled." Those were just code words, though. Everyone knew what they meant. The kids who knew them would talk about how terrible it was, and gripe about it for a day or two, and then it became old news. Unwinds didn't go out with a bang—they didn't even go out with a whimper. They went out with the silence of a candle flame pinched between two fingers.

The customer finally leaves, and Sonia joins them in the back room. "So, you're Unwinds and you want my help, is that it?"

"Maybe just some food," says Connor, "a place to rest for a few hours. Then we'll be on our way."

"We don't want to be any trouble," says Risa.

The old woman laughs at that. "Yes, you do! You want to be trouble to everyone you meet." She points her cane at Risa. "That's what you are now. TROUBLE in caps-lock." Then she puts her cane down, and softens a bit. "That's not your fault, though. You didn't ask to be born, and you didn't ask to be unwound, either." She looks back and forth between the two of them, then says to Risa just as bald-faced as can be: "If you really want to stay alive, honey, have him get you pregnant again. They won't unwind an expectant mother, so that will buy you nine whole months."

Risa drops her jaw, speechless, and Connor feels a flush

come to his face. "She . . . she wasn't pregnant the first time. It's not her baby. Or mine."

Sonia considers this and takes a closer look at the baby. "Not yours, hmm? Well, that explains why you're not breast-feeding." She laughs suddenly and sharply. It makes Connor and the baby jump.

Risa isn't startled, just annoyed. She gets the baby's attention again with another spoonful of milk and her index finger. "Are you going to help us or not?"

Sonia lifts her cane and raps it against Connor's arm, then points to a huge trunk covered with travel stickers. "Think you're boeuf enough to bring that over here?"

Connor gets up, wondering what could possibly be of use to them in the trunk. He grabs on to it and struggles to push it across the faded Persian rug.

"Not much of a boeuf, are ya?"

"I never said I was."

He inches the trunk across the floor until it's right in front of her. Instead of opening it, she sits on top of it and begins to massage her ankles.

"So what's in it?" Connor asks.

"Correspondence," she says. "But it's not what's in it that matters. It's what's underneath." Then with her cane she pushes away the rug where the trunk had been to reveal a trapdoor with a brass pull-ring.

"Go on," says Sonia, pointing again with her cane. Connor sighs and grabs the ring, pulling open the trapdoor to reveal steep stone steps leading down into darkness. Risa puts down her bowl and, holding the baby over her shoulder in burping position, approaches the trapdoor, kneeling beside Connor.

"This is an old building," Sonia tells them. "Way back in the early twentieth century, during the first Prohibition, they hid hooch down there."

"Hooch?" asks Connor.

"Alcohol! I swear, this whole generation's the same. Caps-lock IGNORANT!"

The steps down are steep and uneven. At first Connor thinks Sonia will send them down alone, but she insists on leading the way. She takes her time, and seems more surefooted on the steps than she does on level ground. Connor tries to hold her arm to give her support, but she shakes him off, and throws him a nasty gaze. "If I want your help, I'll ask. Do I look feeble to you?"

"Actually, yes."

"Looks are deceiving," she says. "After all, when I saw you, I thought you looked reasonably intelligent."

"Very funny."

At the bottom, Sonia reaches toward the wall and throws a light switch.

Risa gasps, and Connor follows her gaze until he see them. Three figures. A girl and two boys.

"Your little family has just grown," Sonia tells them.

The kids don't move. They appear to be close to Connor's and Risa's age. Fellow Unwinds, for sure. They look wary and exhausted. Connor wonders if he looks as bad.

"For God's sake, stop staring," she says to them. "You look like a pack of rats."

Sonia shuffles around the dusty cellar, pointing things out to Risa and Connor. "There are canned goods on these shelves, and a can opener around somewhere. Eat whatever you want, but don't leave anything over or you really will see rats. Bathroom's back there. Keep it clean. I'll go out in a bit and get some formula and a baby bottle." She glances at Connor. "Oh, and there's a first-aid kit around here somewhere for the bite on your arm, whatever *that's* all about."

Connor suppresses a grin. Sonia doesn't miss a thing.

"How much longer?" asks the oldest of the three cellar-rats, a muscular guy who looks at Connor with intense distrust, as if Connor might challenge his role as alpha male or something.

"What do you care?" says Sonia. "You got a pressing appointment?"

The kid doesn't respond; he just glares at Sonia and crosses his arms, displaying a shark tattooed on his forearm. *Ooh*, thinks Connor with a smirk. *Intimidating. Now I'm really scared.*

Sonia sighs. "Four more days until I'm rid of you for good."

"What happens in four days?" Risa asks.

"The ice cream man comes." And with that, Sonia climbs up the stairs faster than Connor thought she'd be able to. The trapdoor bangs closed.

"Dear, sweet Dragon Lady won't tell us what happens next," says the second boy, a lanky blond kid with a faint smirk that seems permanently fixed on his face. He has braces on teeth that don't appear to need them. Although his eyes tell of sleepless nights, his hair is perfect. Connor can tell that this kid, despite the rags he's wearing, comes from money.

"We get sent to harvest camp and they cut us apart, that's what happens next," says the girl. She's Asian, and looks almost as tough as the kid with the tattoo, with hair dyed a deep shade of pink and a spiked leather choker on her neck.

Shark Boy looks at her sharply. "Will you shut up with your end-of-the-world crap?" Connor notices that the kid has four parallel scratch marks on one side of his face, consistent with fingernails. The girl has a black eye.

"It's not the end of the world," she grumbles. "Just the end of us."

"You're beautiful when you're nihilistic," says the smirker.

"Shut up."

"You're only saying that because you don't know what nihilistic means."

Risa gives Connor a look, and he knows what she's thinking. *We have to suffer through four days with this crew?* Still, she's the first to hold out her hand to them and introduce herself. Reluctantly, Connor does the same.

Turns out, each of these kids, just like every Unwind, has a story that ranks a ten on the Kleenex scale.

The smirker is Hayden. As Connor predicted, he comes from a ridiculously wealthy family. When his parents got a divorce, there was a brutal custody battle over him. Two years and six court dates later, it still wasn't resolved. In the end the only thing his mother and father could agree on was that each would rather see Hayden unwound than allow the other parent to have custody.

"If you could harness the energy of my parents' spite," Hayden tells them, "you could power a small city for several years."

The girl is Mai. Her parents kept trying for a boy, until they finally got one—but not before having four girls first. Mai was the fourth. "It's nothing new," Mai tells them. "Back in China, in the days when they only allowed one kid per family, people were killing off their baby girls left and right."

The big kid is Roland. He had dreams of being a military boeuf but apparently had too much testosterone, or steroids, or a combination of both, leaving him a little too scary even for the military. Like Connor, Roland got into fights at school—although Connor suspected Roland's fights were much, much worse. That's not what did him in, though. Roland had beaten up his stepfather for beating his mom. The mother took her husband's side, and the stepfather got off with a warning. Roland, on the other hand, was sent to be unwound.

"That's so unfair," Risa tells him.

"Like what happened to you is any fairer?" says Connor.

Roland fixes his gaze on Connor. It's emotional stone. "You keep talking to her in that tone of voice, maybe she'll find herself a new boyfriend."

Connor smiles with mocking warmth at him, and glances at the tattoo on his wrist. "I like your dolphin."

Roland is not amused. "It's a tiger shark, idiot."

Connor makes a mental note never to turn his back on Roland.

Sharks, Connor once read, have a deadly form of claustrophobia. It's not so much a fear of enclosed spaces as it is an inability to exist in them. No one knows why. Some say it's the metal in aquariums that throws their equilibrium off. But whatever it is, big sharks don't last long in captivity.

After a day in Sonia's basement, Connor knows how they feel. Risa has the baby to keep her occupied. It requires a huge amount of attention, and although she gripes about the responsibility, Connor can tell she's thankful simply to have something to help pass the hours. There's a back room to the basement, and Roland insists that Risa have it for herself and the baby. He acts like he's doing it to be kind, but it's obvious that he's doing it because he can't stand the baby's crying.

Mai reads. There's a whole collection of dusty old books in the corner, and Mai always has one in her hand. Roland, having surrendered the back room to Risa, pulls out a shelving unit and sets up his own private residence behind it. He occupies the space like he's had experience with being in a cell. When he's not sitting in his little cell, he's reorganizing the food in the basement into rations. "I take care of the food," he announces. "Now that there's four of us, I'll redivide the rations, and decide who gets what and when."

"I can decide what I want and when for myself," Connor tells him.

"Not gonna work that way," Roland says. "I had things under control before you got here. It's gonna stay that way." Then he hands Connor a can of Spam. Connor looks at it in disgust. "You want better," Roland says, "then you get with the program."

Connor tries to weigh the wisdom of getting into a fight over this—but wisdom rarely arrives when Connor is ticked off. It's Hayden who defuses the situation before it can escalate. Hayden grabs the can from Connor and pulls open the top.

"You snooze, you lose," he says, and begins eating the Spam casually with his fingers. "Never had Spam till I came here—now I love it." Then he grins. "God help me, I'm turning into trailer trash."

Roland glares at Connor and Connor glares back. Then he says what he always says at moments like this.

"Nice socks."

Although Roland doesn't look down right away, it derails him just enough for him to back off. He doesn't check to see if his socks match until he thinks Connor isn't looking. And the moment he does, Connor snickers. Small victories are better than none.

Hayden is a bit of a riddle. Connor's not sure whether he's actually amused by everything that goes on around him or if it's all just an act—a way of defending himself against a situation too painful to allow himself to feel. Usually Connor disliked rich, affected kids like Hayden, but there's something about Hayden that simply makes it impossible not to like him.

Connor sits next to Hayden, who glances to make sure that Roland has gone behind his shelving unit.

"I like the 'nice socks' maneuver," says Hayden. "Mind if I use that sometime?"

"Be my guest."

Hayden pulls off a piece of Spam and offers it to Connor. Although it's the last thing Connor wants right now, he takes it, because he knows it's not about the meat—just as he knows Hayden didn't take it because he wanted it.

The chunk of processed ham passes from Hayden to Connor, and something between them relaxes. An understanding is reached. *I'm on your side,* that piece of Spam says. *I've got your back.*

"Did you mean to have the baby?" Hayden asks.

Connor considers how he might answer. He figures the truth is the best way to begin even a tentative friendship. "It's not mine."

Hayden nods. "It's cool that you're hanging with her even though the kid's not yours."

"It's not hers, either."

Hayden smirks. He doesn't ask how the baby came into their possession, because apparently the version he's come up with in his mind is far more entertaining than anything Connor can offer. "Don't tell Roland," he says. "The only reason he's being so nice to the two of you is because he believes in the sanctity of the nuclear family." Connor can't tell whether Hayden's being serious or sarcastic. He suspects he'll never figure that out.

Hayden chows down the last of the Spam, looks into the empty can, and sighs. "My life as a Morlock," he says.

"Am I supposed to know what that is?"

"Light-sensitive underground frogmen, often portrayed in bad green-rubber costumes. Sadly, this is what we've become. Except for the green-rubber costume part."

Connor glances at the food shelves. When he listens closely, he can hear the tinny beat of music coming from the antique MP3 player Roland must have stolen from upstairs when he first arrived.

"How long have you known Roland?"

"Three days longer than you," Hayden says. "Word to the unwise—which I suspect you are—Roland is fine as long as he thinks he's in charge. As long as you let him think that, we're all one big, happy family."

"What if I don't want him to think that?"

Hayden tosses his can of Spam into the trash a few feet away. "The thing about Morlocks is that they're known to be cannibals."

Connor can't sleep that first night. Between the discomfort of the basement and his distrust of Roland, all he can do is doze for moments at a time. He won't sleep in the side room with Risa because the space is small, and he and Risa would have to sleep right up against each other. He tells himself the real reason is that he's afraid of rolling over on the baby during the night. Mai and Hayden are also awake. It looks like Mai's trying to sleep, but her eyes are open and her mind is somewhere else.

Hayden has lit a candle he found in the debris, making the basement smell like cinnamon over mildew. Hayden passes his hand back and forth over the flame. He doesn't move slowly enough to burn himself, but he does move slowly enough to feel the heat. Hayden notices Connor watching him. "It's funny how a flame can only burn your hand if you move too slow," Hayden says. "You can tease it all you want and it never gets you, if you're quick enough."

"Are you a pyro?" Connor asks.

"You're confusing boredom with obsession."

Connor can sense, however, that there's more to it.

"I've been thinking about kids that get unwound," says Hayden.

"Why would you want to do that?" asks Connor.

"Because," says Mai from across the room, "he's a freak."

"I'm not the one wearing a dog collar."

Mai flips Hayden the finger, which he ignores. "I've been thinking about how harvest camps are like black holes. Nobody knows what goes on inside."

"Everybody knows what goes on," says Connor.

"No," says Hayden. "Everybody knows the result, but nobody knows how unwinding works. I want to know how it happens. Does it happen right away, or do they keep you waiting? Do they treat you kindly, or coldly?"

"Well," Mai sneers, "maybe if you're lucky, you'll get to find out firsthand."

"You know what," says Connor. "You think too much."

"Well, somebody has to make up for the collective lack of brainpower down here."

Now Connor finally begins to get it. Even though Hayden has put the candle down, all this talk of unwinding is just like passing his hand across the flame. He likes to linger at the edge of dangerous places. Dangerous thoughts. Connor thinks about his own favorite edge, behind the freeway road sign. In a way, they're both alike.

"Fine," Connor tells him. "Think about stuff until your head explodes. But the only thing I want to think about is surviving to eighteen."

"I find your shallowness both refreshing and disappointing at the same time. Do you think that means I need therapy?"

"No, I think your parents deciding to unwind you just to spite each other means you need therapy."

"Good point. You have a lot of insight for a Morlock." Then Hayden gets quiet for a moment. The smirk on his face fades.

"If I actually get unwound, I think it will bring my parents back together."

Connor doesn't have the heart to burst his fantasy, but Mai does. "Naah. If you get unwound, they'll just blame each other for it, and hate each other even more."

"Maybe," says Hayden. "Or maybe they'll finally see the light, and it will be Humphrey Dunfee all over again."

"Who?" says Mai.

They both turn toward her. Hayden cracks a wide smile. "You mean you've never heard of Humphrey Dunfee?"

Mai looks around suspiciously. "Should I have?"

The smile never leaves Hayden's face. "Mai, I'm truly amazed that you don't know this. It's *your* kind of story." He reaches for the candle and pushes it out so that it sits between the three of them. "It's not a campfire," he says, "but it will have to do." Hayden looks into the flame for a moment, then slowly, eerily turns his eyes toward Mai.

"Years ago there was this kid. His name wasn't really Humphrey—it was probably Hal or Harry or something like that—but Humphrey kind of fits, considering. Anyway, one day his parents sign the order to have him unwound."

"Why?" asks Mai.

"Why do any parents sign the order? They just did, and the Juvey-cops came for him bright and early one morning. They snatch him, ship him off, and it's over for him.—He's unwound without a hitch."

"So that's it?" asks Mai.

"No . . . because there *is* a hitch," says Connor, picking up where Hayden left off. "See, the Dunfees, they're not what you would call stable people. They were a little bit nuts to begin with, but after their kid is unwound, they lose it completely."

Now Mai's tough-girl exterior is all but gone. She truly is

like a little kid listening wide-eyed to a campfire story. "What did they do?"

"They decided they didn't want Humphrey unwound after all," says Hayden.

"Wait a second," says Mai. "You said they already unwound him."

Hayden's eyes look maniacal in the candlelight. "They did."

Mai shudders.

"Here's the thing," says Hayden. "Like I said, everything about harvest camp is secret—even the records of who receives what, once the unwinding is done."

"Yeah, so?"

"So the Dunfees found the records. The father, I think, worked for the government, so he was able to hack into the parts department."

"The what?"

Hayden sighs. "The National Unwind Database."

"Oh."

"And he gets a printout of every single person who received a piece of Humphrey. Then the Dunfees go traveling around the world to find them . . . so they can kill them, take back the parts, and bit by bit make Humphrey whole. . . ."

"No way."

"That's why people call him Humphrey," Connor adds. "'Cause 'all the king's horses and all the king's men . . . couldn't put Humphrey together again.'"

The thought hangs heavy in the air, until Hayden, leaning forward over the candle, suddenly throws his hands out toward Mai and shouts, "Boo!"

They all flinch in spite of themselves—Mai most of all.

Connor has to laugh. "Did you see that? She practically jumped out of her skin!"

"Better not do that, Mai," says Hayden. "Jump out of your skin, and they'll give it to someone else before you can get it back."

"You can both just take a flying leap." Mai tries to punch Hayden, but he easily evades her. That's when Roland appears from behind his bookshelves.

"What's going on here?"

"Nothing," says Hayden. "Just telling ghost stories."

Roland looks at the four of them, clearly irritated, and distrustful of any situation not involving him. "Yeah, well, get to bed. It's late."

Roland lumbers back to his corner, but Connor's sure he's monitoring the conversation now, probably paranoid that they're plotting against him.

"That Humphrey Dunfee thing," says Mai. "It's just a story, right?"

Connor keeps his opinion to himself, but Hayden says, "I knew a kid who used to tell people he had Humphrey's liver. Then one day he disappeared and was never seen again. People said he just got unwound, but then again . . . maybe the Dunfees got him." Then Hayden blows out the candle, leaving them in darkness.

On Connor and Risa's third day there, Sonia calls each of them upstairs—but one at a time, in the order they'd arrived.

"First the thieving ox," she says, pointing down the stairs at Roland. Apparently she knows about the stolen MP3 player.

"What do you suppose the Dragon Lady wants?" Hayden asks, after the trapdoor is closed.

"To drink your blood," says Mai. "Beat you with her cane for a while. Stuff like that."

"I wish you'd stop calling her the Dragon Lady," Risa says. "She's saving your ass—the least you could do is show some respect." She turns toward Connor. "You wanna take Didi? My arms are getting tired." Connor takes the baby, cradling it a bit more skillfully than he had before. Mai looks at him with mild interest. He wonders if Hayden told her that they're not really the baby's parents.

Roland comes back from his appointment with Sonia half an hour later, and says nothing about it. Neither does Mai when she comes back. Hayden takes the longest, and when he returns, he's closemouthed too—which is strange for him. It's unsettling.

Connor goes next. It's night outside when he goes upstairs. He has no idea what time of night. Sonia sits with him in her little back room, putting him in an uncomfortable chair that wobbles whenever he moves.

"You'll be leaving here tomorrow," she tells him.

"Going where?"

She ignores the question and reaches into the drawer of an old rolltop desk. "I'm hoping you're at least semiliterate."

"Why? What do you want me to read?"

"You don't have to read anything." Then she pulls out several sheets of blank paper. "I want you to write."

"What, my last will and testament? Is that it?"

"A will implies you have something to pass on—which you don't. What I want you to do is write a letter." She hands him the paper, a pen, and an envelope. "Write a letter to someone you love. Make it as long as you want, or as short as you want; I don't care. But fill it with everything you wished you could say, but never had the chance. Do you understand?"

"What if I don't love anybody?"

She purses her lips and shakes her head slowly. "You Unwinds are all the same. You think that because no one loves you, then you can't love anyone. All right, then, if there's no one you love, then pick someone who needs to hear what you have to say. Say everything that's in your heart—don't hold back. And when you're done, put it in the envelope and seal it. I'm not going to read it, so don't worry about that."

"What's the point? Are you going to mail it?"

"Just do it and stop asking questions." Then she takes a little ceramic dinner bell, and places it on the rolltop desk, next to the pen and paper. "Take all the time you need, and when you're done, ring the bell."

Then she leaves him alone.

It's an odd request, and Connor actually finds himself a bit frightened by it. There are places inside he simply doesn't want to go. He thinks he might write to Ariana. That would be easiest. He had cared about her. She was closer to him than any other girl had ever been. Every girl except Risa—but then, Risa doesn't really count. What he and Risa have isn't a relationship; it's just two people clinging to the same ledge hoping not to fall. After about three lines of his letter, Connor crumples the page. Writing to Ariana feels pointless. No matter how much he's resisted, he knows who he needs to address this letter to.

He presses his pen to a fresh page and writes, *Dear Mom and Dad.* . . .

It's five minutes before he can come up with another line, but once he does, the words start flowing—and in strange directions, too. At first it's angry, as he knew it would be. How could you? Why did you? What kind of people could do this to their kid? Yet by the third page it mellows. It becomes about all the good things that happened in their lives together. At first he does it to hurt them, and to remind them exactly what they've thrown away when they signed the order to unwind him. But then it becomes all about remembering—or more to the point, getting *them* to remember, so that when he's gone . . . *if* he's gone, there will be a record of all the things he felt were worth keeping alive. When he started, he knew how the letter would end. *I hate you for what you've done. And I'll never forgive you.* But when he finally reaches the tenth page, he finds himself writing, *I love you. Your one-time son, Connor.*

Even before he signs his name, he feels the tears welling up inside. They don't seem to come from his eyes but from deep in his gut. It's a heaving so powerful it hurts his stomach and his lungs. His eyes flood, and the pain inside is so great, he's certain it will kill him right here, right now. But he doesn't die, and in time the storm inside him passes, leaving him weak in every joint and muscle of his body. He feels like he needs Sonia's cane just to walk again.

His tears have soaked into the pages, warping little craters in the paper but not smudging the ink. He folds the pages and slips them into the envelope, then seals and addresses it. He takes a few more minutes to make sure the storm won't come back. Then he rings the little bell.

Sonia steps in moments later. She must have been waiting all this time just on the other side of that curtain. Connor knows she must have heard him bawling, but she doesn't say a thing. She looks at his letter, hefts it in her hand to feel its weight, and raises her eyebrows, impressed. "Had a lot to say, did you?"

Connor only shrugs. She puts the envelope facedown on the table again. "Now I want you to put a date on the back. Write down the date of your eighteenth birthday."

Connor doesn't question her anymore. He does as she asks. When he's done, she takes the envelope from him. "I'm going to hold this letter for you," she tells him. "If you survive to eighteen, you must promise that you'll come back here to get it. Will you make me that promise?"

Connor nods. "I promise."

She shakes the letter at him to help make her point. "I will keep this until a year after your eighteenth birthday. If you don't come back, I'll assume you didn't make it. That you were unwound. In that case I'll send the letter myself."

Then she hands the letter back to him, stands, and goes over to the old trunk that had covered the trapdoor. She opens the latch and, although it must be heavy, heaves open the lid to reveal envelopes—hundreds of them, filling the trunk almost up to the top.

"Leave it here," she says. "It will be safe. If I die before you come back, Hannah has promised to take care of the trunk."

Connor thinks of all the kids Sonia must have helped to have this many letters in her trunk, and he feels another wave of emotion taking hold of his gut. It doesn't quite bring him to tears, but it makes him feel all soft inside. Soft enough to say, "You've done something wonderful here."

Sonia waves her hand, swatting the thought away. "You think this makes me a saint? Let me tell you, I've had a considerably long life, and I've done some pretty awful things, too."

"Well, I don't care. No matter how many times you smack me with that cane, I think you're decent."

"Maybe, maybe not. One thing you learn when you've lived as long as I have—people aren't all good, and people aren't all bad. We move in and out of darkness and light all of our lives. Right now, I'm pleased to be in the light."

On his way downstairs, she makes sure to smack him on the butt with her cane hard enough to sting, but it only makes him laugh.

He doesn't tell Risa what's in store for her. Somehow telling her would be stealing something from her. Let this be between her, Sonia, the pen, and the page, as it had been for him.

She leaves the baby with him as she goes up to face the old

woman. It's asleep, and right now, in this place and at this moment, there's something so comforting about holding it in his arms, he's thankful he saved it. And he thinks that if his soul had a form, this is what it would be. A baby sleeping in his arms.

# 20 · Risa

The next time Sonia opens the trapdoor, Risa knows things are changing again. The time has come to leave the safety of Sonia's basement.

Risa's the first in line when Sonia calls them to come up. Roland would have been, but Connor threw an arm out like a turnstile to let Risa get to the stairs first.

With the sleeping baby crooked in her right arm, and her left hand on the rusty steel banister, Risa climbs the jagged stone steps. Risa assumes she'll be climbing into daylight, but it's night. The lights are out in the shop—just a few night-lights are on, carefully positioned so the kids can avoid the minefield of random antiques around them.

Sonia leads them to a back door that opens into an alley. There's a truck waiting for them there. It's a small delivery truck. On its side is a picture of an ice cream cone.

Sonia hadn't lied. It *is* the ice cream man.

The driver stands beside the open back door of the truck. He's a scruffy guy who looks like he'd more likely be delivering illegal drugs than kids. Roland, Hayden, and Mai head for the truck, but Sonia stops Risa and Connor.

"Not yet, you two."

Then Risa notices a figure standing in the shadows. Risa's neck hairs begin to bristle defensively, but when the figure steps forward, she realizes who it is. It's Hannah, the teacher who saved them at the high school.

"Honey, the baby can't go where you're going," Hannah says.

Reflexively, Risa holds the baby closer to her. She doesn't even know why. All she's wanted to do since getting stuck with the thing is to get rid of it.

"It's all right," says Hannah. "I've talked it over with my husband. We'll just say we were storked. It will be fine."

Risa looks in Hannah's eyes. She can't see all that well in the dim light, but she knows the woman means what she says.

Connor, however, steps between them. "Do you *want* this baby?"

"She's willing to take it," says Risa. "That's enough."

"But does she want it?"

"Did *you* want it?"

That seems to give Connor pause for thought. Risa knows he didn't want it, but he had been willing to take it when the alternative was a miserable life with a miserable family. Just as Hannah is willing to save it from an uncertain future right now. Finally Connor says, "It's not an *it*. It's a *she*." Then he heads off toward the truck.

"We'll give her a good home," Hannah says. She takes a step closer, and Risa transfers the baby to her.

The moment the baby is out of her arms Risa feels a tremendous sense of relief, but also an indefinable sense of emptiness. It's a feeling not quite intense enough to leave her in tears, but strong enough to leave her with a phantom sort of aching, the type of thing an amputee must feel after losing a limb. That is, before a new one is grafted on.

"You take care, now," says Sonia, giving Risa an awkward hug. "It's a long journey, but I know you can make it."

"Journey to where?"

Sonia doesn't answer.

"Hey," says the driver, "I don't got all night."

Risa says good-bye to Sonia, nods to Hannah, and turns to join Connor, who's waiting for her at the back of the truck. As Risa leaves, the baby starts to cry, but she doesn't look back.

She's surprised to find about a dozen other kids in the truck, all distrustful and scared. Roland's still the biggest, and he solidifies his position by making another kid move, even though there's plenty of other places to sit.

The delivery truck is a hard, cold, metal box. It once had a refrigeration unit to keep the ice cream cold, but that's gone along with the ice cream. Still, it's freezing in there, and it smells of spoiled dairy. The driver closes and locks the back doors, sealing out the sound of the baby, who Risa can still hear crying. Even after the door is closed, she thinks she can still hear it, although it's probably just her imagination.

The ice cream truck bounces along the uneven streets. The way the truck sways, their backs are constantly smacked against the wall behind them.

Risa closes her eyes. It makes her furious that she actually misses the baby. It was thrust upon her at the worst possible moment in her life—why should she have any regret about being rid of it? She thinks about the days before the Heartland War, when unwanted babies could just be unwanted pregnancies, quickly made to go away. Did the women who made that other choice feel the way she felt now? Relieved and freed from an unwelcome and often unfair responsibility . . . yet vaguely regretful?

In her days at the state home, when she was assigned to take care of the infants, she would often ponder such things. The infant wing had been massive and overflowing with identical cribs, each containing a baby that nobody had wanted, wards of a state that could barely feed them, much less nurture them.

"You can't change laws without first changing human nature," one of the nurses often said as she looked out over the crowd of crying infants. Her name was Greta. Whenever she said something like that, there was always another nurse within earshot who was far more accepting of the system and would counter with, "You can't change human nature without first changing the law." Nurse Greta wouldn't argue; she'd just grunt and walk away.

Which was worse, Risa often wondered—to have tens of thousands of babies that no one wanted, or to silently make them go away before they were even born? On different days Risa had different answers.

Nurse Greta was old enough to remember the days before the war, but she rarely spoke of them. All her attention was given to her job, which was a formidable one, since there was only one nurse for every fifty babies. "In a place like this you have to practice triage," she told Risa, referring to how, in an emergency, a nurse had to choose which patients would get medical attention. "Love the ones you can," Nurse Greta told her. "Pray for the rest." Risa took the advice to heart, and selected a handful of favorites to give extra attention. These were the ones Risa named herself, instead of letting the randomizing computer name them. Risa liked to think she had been named by a human being instead of by a computer. After all, her name wasn't all that common. "It's short for *sonrisa*," a Hispanic kid once told her. "That's Spanish for 'smile.'" Risa didn't know if she had any Hispanic blood in her, but she liked to think she did. It connected her to her name.

"What are you thinking about?" Connor asks, tearing her

115

out of her thoughts and bringing her back to the uneasy reality around them.

"None of your business."

Connor doesn't look at her—he seems to be focusing on a big rust spot on the wall, thinking. "You okay about the baby?" he asks.

"Of course." Her tone is intentionally indignant, as if the question itself offended her.

"Hannah will give her a good home," Connor says. "Better than us, that's for sure, and better than that beady-eyed cow who got storked." He hesitates for a moment, then says, "Taking that baby was a massive screwup, I know—but it ended okay for us, right? And it definitely ended better for the baby."

"Don't screw up like that again," is all Risa says.

Roland, sitting toward the front, turns to the driver and asks, "Where are we going?"

"You're asking the wrong guy," the driver answers. "They give me an address. I go there, I look the other way, and I get paid."

"This is how it works," says another kid who had already been in the truck when it arrived at Sonia's. "We get shuffled around. One safe house for a few days, then another, and then another. Each one is a little bit closer to where we're going."

"You gonna tell us where that is?" asks Roland.

The kid looks around, hoping someone else might answer for him, but no one comes to his aid. So he says, "Well, it's only what I hear, but they say we end up in a place called . . . 'the graveyard.'"

No response from the kids, just the rattling of the truck.

*The graveyard.* The thought of it makes Risa even colder. Even though she's curled up knees to chest, arms wrapped tight around her like a straitjacket, she's still freezing. Connor must hear the chattering of her teeth, because he puts his arm around her.

"I'm cold too," he says. "Body heat, right?"

And although she has an urge to push him away, she finds herself leaning into him until she can feel his heartbeat in her ears.

# Part Three

# Transit

## 2003: UKRAINIAN MATERNITY HOSPITAL #6

. . . *The BBC has spoken to mothers from the city of Kharkiv who say they gave birth to healthy babies, only to have them taken by maternity staff. In 2003 the authorities agreed to exhume around 30 bodies from a cemetery used by maternity hospital number 6. One campaigner was allowed into the autopsy to gather video evidence. She has given that footage to the BBC and Council of Europe.*

*In its report, the Council describes a general culture of trafficking of children snatched at birth, and a wall of silence from hospital staff upward over their fate. The pictures show organs, including brains, have been stripped—and some bodies dismembered. A senior British forensic pathologist says he is very concerned to see bodies in pieces—as that is not standard postmortem practice. It could possibly be a result of harvesting stem cells from bone marrow.*

*Hospital number 6 denies the allegations.*

Story by Matthew Hill, BBC Health Correspondent
From BBC NEWS: at BBC.com
http://news.bbc.co.uk/go/pr/fr/-/2/hi/europe/6171083.stm
Published: 2006/12/12 09:34:50 GMT © BBC MMVI

# 21 · Lev

"Ain't no one gonna tell you what's in your heart," he tells Lev. "You gotta find that out for yourself."

Lev and his new travel companion walk along train tracks, surrounded by thick, brushy terrain.

"You got it in your heart to run from unwinding, ain't no one can tell you it's the wrong thing to do, even if it *is* against the law. The good Lord wouldn't have put it in your heart if it wasn't right. You listenin', Fry? 'Cause this here is wisdom. Wisdom you can take to the grave, then dig it up again when you need some solace. Solace—that means 'comfort.'"

"I know what solace means," says Lev, peeved by the mention of "the good Lord," who hasn't done much for Lev lately, except confuse things.

The kid is fifteen, and his name is Cyrus Finch—although he doesn't go by that name. "No one calls me Cyrus," he had told Lev shortly after they met. "I go by CyFi."

And, since CyFi is partial to nicknames, he calls Lev "Fry"—short for small-fry. Since it has the same number of letters as "Lev," he says it's appropriate. Lev doesn't want to burst his bubble by pointing out that his full name is Levi.

CyFi enjoys hearing himself talk.

"I make my own roads in life," he tells Lev. "That's how come we're traveling the rails instead of some dumb old country road."

CyFi is umber. "They used to call us black—can you imagine? Then there was this artist dude—mixed-race himself, a

121

little bit of this, a little bit of that. He got famous, though, for painting people of African ancestry in the Deep South. The color he used most was umber. People liked that a whole lot better, so it stuck. Bet you didn't know where the word came from, did you, Fry? Following right along, they started calling so-called white people "sienna," after another paint color. Better words. Didn't have no value judgment to them. Of course, it's not like racism is gone completely, but as my dads like to say, the veneer of civilization got itself a second coat. You like that, Fry? 'The veneer of civilization?'" He slowly sweeps his hand in the air as he says it, like he's feeling the fine finish of a table. "My dads are always saying stuff like that."

CyFi's a runaway, although he claims not to be. "I ain't no runaway—I'm a run-to," he had told Lev when they first met, although he won't tell Lev where he's running to. When Lev asked, CyFi shook his head and said, "Information shall be given on a need-to-know basis."

Well, he can keep his secret, because Lev doesn't care where he's going. The simple fact that he has a destination is enough for Lev. It's more than Lev has. Destination implies a future. If this umber-skinned boy can lend Lev that much, it's worth it to travel with him.

They had met at a mall. Hunger had driven Lev there. He had hidden in dark lonely places for almost two days after he lost Connor and Risa. With no experience being a street rat, he went hungry—but eventually, hunger turns anyone into a master of survival.

The mall was a mecca for a newborn street rat. The food court was full of amazingly wasteful people. The trick, Lev discovered, was to find people who bought more food than they could possibly eat, and then wait until they were done. About half the time, they just left it on the table. Those were the ones Lev went after—because he might have been hungry enough to eat table scraps, but he was still too proud to rifle through the trash. While Lev was finishing off some cheerleader's pizza, he heard a voice in his ear.

"You ain't gotta be eatin' other folks' garbage, foo'!"

Lev froze, certain it was a security guard ready to haul him away, but it was only this tall umber kid with a funny grin, wearing attitude like it was a cologne. "Let me show you how it's done." Then he went to a pretty girl who was working at the Wicked Wok Chinese food concession, flirted with her for a few minutes, then left with nothing. No food, no drink, nothing.

"I think I'll stick to leftovers," Lev had told him.

"Patience, my man. See, it's gettin' on toward closing time. All these places, by law gotta get rid of all the food they made today. They can't keep it and reuse it tomorrow. So where do you think that food goes? I'll tell you where it goes. It goes home with the last shift. But the people who work these places ain't gonna eat that stuff on accounta they are sick to death of it. See that girl I was talkin' to? She likes me. I told her I worked at Shirt Bonanza, downstairs, and could get her some overstock maybe."

"*Do* you work there?"

"No! Are you even listenin' to me? So any-who, right before closing I'm gonna get myself over to the Wicked Wok again. I'll give her a smile, and I'll be all, like, 'Hey, whatcha gonna do with all that leftover food?' And she'll be all, like, 'Whatcha got in mind?' And five minutes later I'm walking away in orange chicken heaven, with enough to feed an army."

And sure enough, it happened exactly like he said it would. Lev was amazed.

"Stick with me," CyFi had said, putting his fist in the air, "and as God is my witness, you will never go hungry again." Then he added, "That's from *Gone with the Wind*."

"I know," said Lev. Which, in fact, he didn't.

Lev had agreed to go with him because he knew the two filled a need in each other. CyFi was like a preacher with no flock. He couldn't exist without an audience, and Lev needed someone who could fill his head with ideas, to replace the lifetime of ideas that had been taken from him.

A day later, Lev's shoes are worn and his muscles are sore. The memory of Risa and Connor is still a fresh wound, and it doesn't want to heal. Chances are, they were caught. Chances are, they've been unwound. All because of him. Does that make him an accomplice to murder?

*How could it, when Unwinds aren't really dead?*

He doesn't know whose voice is in his head anymore. His father's? Pastor Dan's? It just makes him angry. He'd rather hear CyFi's voice outside of his head than whatever voices were inside.

The terrain around them hasn't changed much since they left town. Eye-high shrubs and a smattering of trees. Some of the growth is evergreen, some of it yellow, turning brown. Weeds grow up between the train tracks, but not too tall.

"Any weed dumb enough to grow tall ain't got no chance. It gets decapitated by the next train that comes through. Decapitated—that means 'head cut off.'"

"I know what 'decapitated' means—and you can stop talking that way; all double negatives and stuff."

CyFi stops right there in the middle of the railroad tracks and stares at Lev like he's trying to melt him with his eyes.

"You got a problem with the way I talk? You got a problem with an Old World Umber patois?"

"I do when it's fake."

"Whachoo talkin' about, foo'!"

"It's obvious. I'll bet people never even said things like 'foo,' except on dumb prewar TV shows and stuff. You're speaking wrong on purpose."

"Wrong? What makes it wrong? It's classic, just like those TV shows—and I ain't appreciating you disrespecting my patois. Patois means—"

"I know what it means," Lev says even though he isn't entirely sure. "I ain't stupid!"

CyFi puts up an accusing finger like a lawyer. "A-HA! You said 'ain't.' Now who's talking wrong?"

"That doesn't count! I said it because it's all I hear from you! After a while I can't help but sound like you!"

At that, CyFi grins. "Yeah," he says. "Ain't that the truth. Old World Umber is contagious. It's *dominant*. And talkin' the talk don't make a person dumb. I'll have you know, I got the highest readin' and writin' score in my school, Fry. But I gotta respect my ancestors an' all they went through so I could be here. Sure, I can talk like you, but I *choose* not to. It's like art, you know? Picasso had to prove to the world he can paint the right way, before he goes putting both eyes on one side of a face, and noses stickin' outta kneecaps and stuff. See, if you paint wrong because that's the best you can do, you just a chump. But you do it because you want to? Then you're an artist." He smiles at Lev. "That's a bit of CyFi wisdom right there, Fry. You can take *that* to the grave, and dig it up when you need it!"

CyFi turns and spits out a piece of gum that hits a train rail and sticks there, then he shoves another piece in his mouth. "Anyway, my dads got no problem with it—and they're lily-sienna like you."

"They?" Cy had said "dads" before, but Lev had figured it was just some more Old Umber slang.

"Yeah," says CyFi, with a shrug. "I got two. Ain't no thang."

Lev tries his best to process this. Of course, he's heard of male parenting—or "yin families," as they're currently called—but in the sheltered structure of his life, such things always belonged to an alternate universe.

CyFi, however, doesn't even catch Lev's surprise. He's still on his brag jag.

"Yeah, I got myself an IQ of 155. Did you know that, Fry? A'course not—how would you know?" Then he hesitates. "It went down a few points, though, on account the accident. I was on my bike and got hit by some damfoo' in a Mercedes." He points to a scar on the side of his head. "What a mess. Splattered—y'know? I was nearly roadkill. It turned my right temporal lobe into Jell-O." He shivers as he thinks about it, then shrugs. "But brain damage ain't a problem like it used to be. They just replace the brain tissue and you're good as new. My dads even paid off the surgeon so I'd get an entire temporal lobe from an Unwind—no offense—rather than getting a buncha brain bits, like people are *supposed* to get."

Lev knows about that. His sister Cara has epilepsy, so they replaced a small part of her brain with a hundred tiny brain bits. It took care of the problem, and she didn't seem any worse for it. It had never occurred to Lev where those tiny pieces of brain tissue might have come from.

"See, brain bits work okay, but they don't work great," CyFi explains. "It's like puttin' spackle over a hole in a wall. No matter how well you do it, that wall ain't never gonna be as good. So my dads made sure I got an entire temporal lobe from a single donor. But that kid wasn't as smart as me. He wasn't no dummy, but he didn't have the 155. The last brain scan put me at 130. That's in the top 5 percent of the population, and still considered genius. Just not with a capital G. What's your IQ?" he asks Lev. "Are you a dim bulb or high-wattage?"

Lev sighs. "I don't know. My parents don't believe in intelligence scans. It's kind of a religious thing. Everyone's equal in God's eyes and all that."

"Oh—you come from one of *those* families." CyFi takes a

good look at him. "So if they all high and mighty, why they unwinding you?"

Although Lev doesn't want to get into it, he figures CyFi is the only friend he's got. Might as well tell him the truth. "I'm a tithe."

CyFi looks at him with eyes all wide, like Lev just told him he was God himself.

"Damn! So you all holy and stuff?"

"Not anymore."

CyFi nods and purses his lips, saying nothing for a while. They walk along the tracks. The railroad ties change from wood to stone, and the gravel on the side of the tracks now seems better maintained.

"We just crossed the state line," CyFi says.

Lev would ask him which state they've crossed into, but he doesn't want to sound stupid.

Any spot where multiple tracks merge or diverge, there's a little two-story shack standing there like a displaced lighthouse. A railroad switch house. There are plenty of them along this stretch of the line, and these are the places Lev and CyFi find shelter each night.

"Aren't you afraid someone from the railroads'll find us here?" Lev asks as they approach one of the sorry-looking structures.

"Nah—they ain't used anymore," CyFi tells him. "The whole system's automated—been that way for years, but it costs too much to tear all those switch houses down. Guess they figure nature will eventually tear them down for free."

The switch house is padlocked, but a padlock is only as strong as the door it's on—and this door had been routed by termites. A single kick rips the padlock hasp from the wood, and the door flies inward to a shower of dust and dead spiders.

Upstairs is an eight-by-eight room, windows on all four sides. It's freezing. CyFi has an expensive-looking winter coat that keeps him warm at night. Lev only has a puffy fiberfill jacket that he stole from a chair at the mall the other day.

CyFi had turned his nose up when he saw Lev take that jacket, just before they left the mall. "Stealing's for lowlifes," Cy had said. "If you got class, you don't steal what you need, you get other people to give it to you of their own free will—just like I did back at that Chinese place. It's all about being smart, and being smooth. You'll learn."

Lev's stolen jacket is white, and he hates it. All his life he'd worn white—a pristine absence of color that defined him—but now there was no comfort in wearing it.

They eat well that night—thanks to Lev, who finally had his own survivalist brainstorm. It involved small animals killed by passing trains.

"I ain't eatin' no track-kill!" CyFi insisted when Lev had suggested it. "Those things coulda been rottin' out here for weeks, for all we know."

"No," Lev told him. "Here's what we do: We walk a few miles down the tracks, marking each dead critter with a stick. Then, when the next train comes through, we backtrack. Anything we find that's not marked is fresh." Granted, it was a fairly disgusting idea on the surface, but it was really no different from hunting—if your weapon were a diesel engine.

They build a small fire beside the switch house and dine on roast rabbit and armadillo—which doesn't taste as bad as Lev thought it would. In the end, meat is meat, and barbecue does for armadillo exactly what it does for steak.

"Smorgas-bash!!" CyFi decides to call this hunting method as they eat. "That's what I call creative problem solving. Maybe you're a genius after all, Fry."

It feels good to have Cy's approval.

"Hey, is today Thursday?" says Lev, just realizing. "I think it's Thanksgiving!"

"Well, Fry, we're alive. That's plenty to be thankful for."

That night, up in the small room of the switch house, CyFi asks the big question. "Why'd your parents tithe you, Fry?"

One of the good things about being with CyFi is that he talks about himself a lot. It keeps Lev from having to think about his own life. Except, of course, when Cy asks. Lev answers him with silence, pretending to be asleep—and if there's one thing he knows CyFi can't stand, it's silence, so he fills it himself.

"Were you a storked baby? Is that it? They didn't want you in the first place, and couldn't wait to get rid of you?"

Lev keeps his eyes closed and doesn't move.

"Well, *I* was storked," Cy says. "My dads got me on the doorstep the first day of summer. No big deal—they were ready to have a family anyway. In fact, they were so pleased, they finally made it official and got themselves mmarried."

Lev opens his eyes, curious enough to admit he's still awake. "But . . . after the Heartland War, didn't they make it illegal for men to get married?"

"They didn't get married, they got *mmarried*."

"What's the difference?"

CyFi looks at him like he's a moron. "The letter *m*. Anyway, in case you're wondering, I'm not like my dads—my compass points to girls, if you know what I mean."

"Yeah. Yeah, mine does too." What he doesn't tell CyFi is that the closest he's ever been to a date or even kissing a girl was the slow dancing at his tithing party.

The thought of the party brings a sudden and sharp jolt of anxiety that makes him want to scream, so he squeezes his eyes tight and forces that explosive feeling to go away.

Everything from Lev's old life is like that now—a ticking time bomb in his head. *Forget that life,* he tells himself. *You're not that boy anymore.*

"What are your parents like?" CyFi asks.

"I hate them," Lev says, surprised that he's said it. Surprised that he means it.

"That's not what I asked."

This time Cy isn't taking silence for an answer, so Lev tells him as best he can. "My parents," he begins, "do everything they're supposed to. They pay their taxes. They go to church. They vote the way their friends expect them to vote, and think what they're supposed to think, and they send us to schools that raise us to think exactly like they do."

"Doesn't sound too terrible to me."

"It wasn't," says Lev, his discomfort building. "But they loved God more than they loved me, and I hate them for it. So I guess that means I'm going to Hell."

"Hmm. Tell you what. When you get there, save a room for me, okay?"

"Why? What makes you think you're going there?"

"I don't, but just in case. Gotta plan your contingencies, right?"

Two days later they find themselves in the town of Scottsburg, Indiana. Well, at least Lev finally knows what state they're in. He wonders if maybe this is CyFi's destination, but Cy hasn't said anything either way. They've left the railroad tracks, and CyFi tells Lev they have to go south on county roads until they can find tracks heading in that direction.

Cy hasn't been acting right.

It began the night before. Something in his voice. Something in his eyes, too. At first Lev thought it was his imagination, but now in the pale light of the autumn day it's

130

clear that CyFi isn't himself. He's lagging behind Lev instead of leading. His stride is all off—more like a shuffle than a strut. It makes Lev anxious in a way he hasn't been since before he met CyFi.

"Are you ever going to tell me where we're going?" Lev asks, figuring that maybe they're close, and maybe that's why Cy's acting weird.

CyFi hesitates, weighing the wisdom of saying anything. Finally he says, "We're going to Joplin. That's in southwest Missouri, so we've still got a long way to go."

In the back of his mind, Lev registers that CyFi has completely dropped his Old Umber way of talking. Now he sounds like any other kid Lev might have known back home. But there's also something dark and throaty about his voice now, too. Vaguely menacing, like the voice of a werewolf before it turns.

"What's in Joplin?" Lev asks.

"Nothing for you to worry about."

But Lev *is* beginning to worry—because when CyFi gets where he's going, Lev will be alone again. This journey was easier when he didn't know the destination.

As they walk, Lev can tell Cy's mind is somewhere else. Maybe it's in Joplin. What could be there? Maybe a girlfriend moved there? Maybe he had tracked down his birth mother. Lev has worked up a dozen reasons for CyFi to be on this trip, and there's probably a dozen more he hasn't even thought of.

There's a main street in Scottsburg trying to be quaint but just looking tired. It's late morning as they move through town. Restaurants are gearing up for the lunch crowd.

"So, are you gonna use your charms to get us a free meal, or is it my turn to try?" Lev asks. He turns to Cy, but he's not there. A quick scan of the shops behind him and Lev sees a door swinging closed. It's a Christmas store, its windows all done up in green and red decorations, plastic reindeer, and cotton snow. Lev can't imagine Cy has gone in there, but when he peers in the window, there he is, looking around like a customer. With the weird way CyFi has been acting, Lev has no choice but to go in as well.

It's warm in the store, and it smells of artificial pine. It's the kind of scent they put on cardboard air fresheners. There are fully trimmed aluminum Christmas trees all around, displaying all sorts of holiday decorations, each tree with a different theme. In another time and place, Lev would have loved wandering through a store like this.

A saleswoman eyes them suspiciously from behind the counter. Lev grabs Cy's shoulder. "C'mon, let's get out of here." But Cy shakes him off and goes over to a tree that's decorated all in glittering gold. He seems mesmerized by all the bulbs and tinsel. There's the slightest twitch right beneath his left eye.

"Cy," whispers Lev. "C'mon—we have to get to Joplin. Remember? Joplin."

But Cy's not moving. The saleswoman comes over. She wears a holiday sweater and a holiday smile. "Can I help you find something?"

"No," says Lev. "We were just leaving."

"A nutcracker," says Cy. "I'm looking for a nutcracker for my mom."

"Oh, they're on the back wall." The woman turns to look across the store, and the moment she does, Cy picks a dangling gold bauble from the glittering tree and slips it into his coat pocket.

Lev just stands there, stunned.

Cy doesn't even spare Lev a glance as he follows the woman to the back wall, where they discuss nutcrackers.

There's a panic brewing deep down in Lev now, slowly

fighting its way to the surface. Cy and the woman chat for a few moments more, then Cy thanks her and comes back to the front of the store. "I've gotta get more money from home," he says in his Cy/not-Cy voice. "I think my mom will like the blue one."

*You don't have a mom,* Lev wants to say, but he doesn't because all that matters now is getting out of the shop.

"All right then," says the saleswoman. "You have a nice day!"

Cy leaves, and Lev makes sure he's right behind him, just in case Cy suddenly has a phantom urge to go back into the store and take something else.

Then, the moment the door closes behind them, CyFi takes off. He doesn't just run, he ejects, like he's trying to burst out of his own skin. He bolts down the block, then into the street. Then back again. Cars honk, a truck nearly mows him down. He darts in random directions like a balloon losing air, and then he disappears into an alley far down the street.

This is not about a gold Christmas bulb. It can't be. It's a meltdown. It's a seizure, the nature of which Lev can't even begin to guess. *I should just let him go,* Lev thinks. *Let him go, then run in the opposite direction, and not look back.* Lev could survive on his own now. He's gotten street-smart enough. He could do it without CyFi.

But there was that look about Cy before he ran. Desperation. It was just like the look in Connor's face the moment he pulled Lev out of his father's comfortable sedan. Lev had turned on Connor. He will not turn on CyFi.

With a pace and stride far steadier than CyFi's, Lev crosses the street and makes his way down the alley.

"CyFi," he calls, loud enough to be heard but not loud enough to draw attention. "Cy!" He glances in Dumpsters and doorways. "Cyrus, where are you?" He comes to the end of the alley and looks left and right. No sign of him. Then, as he's about to lose hope, he hears, "Fry?"

He turns his head and listens again.

"Fry. Over here."

This time he can tell where it's coming from: a playground to his right. Green plastic and steel poles painted blue. There are no children playing—the only sign of life is the tip of CyFi's shoe poking out from behind the slide. Lev crosses through a hedge, steps down into the sand that surrounds the playground, and circles the apparatus until CyFi comes into view.

Lev almost wants to back away from what he sees.

Cy is curled, knees to chest, like a baby. The left side of his face is twitching, and his left hand quivers like gelatin. He grimaces as if he's in pain.

"What is it? What's wrong? Tell me. Maybe I can help you."

"Nothing," CyFi hisses. "I'll be all right."

But to Lev he looks like he's dying.

In his shaking left hand CyFi holds the ornament he stole. "I didn't steal this," he says.

"Cy . . ."

"I SAID, I DIDN'T STEAL THIS!" He smashes the heel of his right hand against the side of his head. "IT WASN'T ME!"

"Okay—whatever you say." Lev looks around to make sure they're unobserved.

Cy quiets down a bit. "Cyrus Finch doesn't steal. Never did, never will. It's not my style." He says it, even as he looks at the evidence right there in his hand. But in a second the evidence is gone. CyFi raises his right fist and smashes it into his left palm, shattering the bulb. Gold glass tinkles to the ground. Blood begins to ooze from his left palm and right knuckles.

"Cy, your hand . . ."

"Don't worry about that," he says. "I want you to do something for me, Fry. Do it before I change my mind."

Lev nods.

"See my coat over there? I want you to look in the pockets."

CyFi's heavy coat is a few yards away tossed over the seat of a swing. Lev goes to the swing set and picks up the coat. He reaches into an inside pocket and finds, of all things, a gold cigarette lighter. He pulls it out.

"Is that it, Cy? You want a cigarette?" If a cigarette would bring CyFi out of this, Lev would be the first to light it for him. There are things far more illegal than cigarettes, anyway.

"Check the other pockets."

Lev searches the other pockets for a pack of cigarettes, but there are none. Instead he finds a small treasure trove. Jeweled earrings, watches, a gold necklace, a diamond bracelet—things that shimmer and shine even in the dim daylight.

"Cy, what did you do . . . ?"

"I already told you, it wasn't me! Now go take all that stuff and get rid of it. Get rid of it and don't let me see where you put it." Then he covers his eyes like it's a game of hide-and-seek. "Go—before he changes my mind!"

Lev pulls everything out of the pocket and, cradling it in his arms, runs to the far end of the playground. He digs in the cold sand and drops it all in, kicking sand back over it. When he's done, he smoothes it over with the side of his shoe and drops a scattering of leaves above it. He goes back to CyFi, who's sitting there just like Lev left him, hands over his face.

"It's done," Lev says. "You can look now." When Cy takes his hands away, there's blood all over his face from the cuts on his hands. Cy stares at his hands, then looks at Lev helplessly, like . . . well, like a kid who just got hurt in a playground. Lev half expects him to cry.

"You wait here," Lev says. "I'll go get some bandages." He knows he'll have to steal them. He wonders what Pastor Dan would say about all the things he's been stealing lately.

"Thank you, Fry," Cy says. "You did good, and I ain't gonna forget it." The Old Umber lilt is back in his voice. The twitching has stopped.

"Sure thing," says Lev, with a comforting smile, and he heads off to find a pharmacy.

What CyFi doesn't know is that Lev has kept a single diamond bracelet, which he now hides in the inside pocket of his not-so-white jacket.

Lev finds them a place to sleep that night. It's the best they've had yet: a motel room. Finding it wasn't all that hard to do—he scouted out a run-down motel without many cars out front. Then it was just a matter of finding an unlocked bathroom window in an unoccupied room. As long as they kept the curtains drawn and the lights off, no one would know they were there.

"My genius keeps rubbin' off on you," CyFi tells him. Cy's back to his old self, like the incident that morning never happened. Only it *did* happen, and they both know it.

Outside they hear a car door open. Lev and Cy prepare to bolt if a key turns in the motel room lock, but it's another door they hear opening, a few rooms away. Cy shakes out his tension, but Lev doesn't relax. Not yet.

"I want to know about today," Lev says. It's not a question. It's a request.

Cy is unconcerned. "Ancient history," he says. "Leave the past in the past, and live for the moment. That's wisdom you can take to the grave, and dig up when you need it!"

"What if I dig it up right now?" Lev takes a moment to let it sink in, then he reaches into his pocket and pulls out the diamond bracelet. He holds it in front of him, making sure the streetlight spilling through a slit in the curtains catches the diamonds so they glisten.

"Where'd you get that?" CyFi's voice has lost all the playfulness it had only a second ago.

"I kept it," Lev says, calmly. "I thought it might come in handy."

"I told you to get rid of it."

"It wasn't yours to get rid of. After all, you said it yourself—*you* didn't steal it." Lev twists the bracelet so a diamond refracts a sparkle of light right into CyFi's eye. Without the room lights on Lev can't see much, but he can swear he sees CyFi's cheek starting to twitch.

Cy stands up, looming over Lev. Lev stands as well, a full head shorter than CyFi. "You take that outta my face," says CyFi, "or I swear I'm gonna pound you into pork rinds."

Lev thinks he might actually do it, too. CyFi clenches his fists; with the bandages he looks like a boxer, hands wrapped before putting on the gloves. Still, Lev doesn't back down. He just dangles the bracelet. It sends little twinkling lights flitting around the room like a lazy disco ball. "I'll put it away if you tell me why this bracelet and all those other things wound up in your pockets."

"Put it away first, then I'll tell you."

"Fair enough." Lev slips the bracelet back into his pocket and waits, but CyFi isn't talking. So Lev gives him a little prompt. "What's his name?" Lev asks. "Or is it a she?"

CyFi's shoulders slump in defeat. He crumples into a chair. Lev can't see his face at all now in the darkness, so Lev listens closely to his voice. As long as it still sounds like Cy's voice, he knows that Cy's okay. Lev sits himself on the edge of the bed a few feet away from Cy and listens.

"It's a he," Cy says. "I don't know his name. He musta kept

137

his name in another part of his brain. All I got was his right temporal lobe. That's only an eighth of the cerebral cortex, so I'm seven-eighths me, and one-eighth him."

"I figured that was it." Lev had realized what was going on with Cy even before he stole the bandages from the pharmacy. Cy gave him the clue himself. *Do it before he changes my mind,* Cy had said. "So . . . he was a shoplifter?"

"He had . . . problems. I guess those problems are why his parents had him unwound in the first place. And now one of his problems is mine."

"Wow. That sucks."

CyFi laughs bitterly at that. "Yeah, Fry, it does."

"It's kind of like what happened to my brother Ray," says Lev. "He went to this government auction thing—ended up with ten acres on a lake, and it cost next to nothing. Then he finds out that the land came with a bunker full of toxic chemicals seeping into the ground. Now he owned it, so now it was his problem. Cost him almost ten times the cost of the land to clean up the chemicals."

"Sucker," says Cy.

"Yeah. But then, those chemicals weren't in his brain."

Cy looks down for a moment. "He's not a bad kid. He's just hurting. Hurting real bad." The way Cy's talking, it's like the kid is still there, right in the room with them. "He's got this urge about him to grab things—like an addiction, y'know? Shiny things mostly. It's not like he really wants them, it's just that he kind of needs to snap 'em up. I figure he's a kleptomaniac. That means . . . ah, hell, you know what it means."

"So, he talks to you?"

"No, not really. I didn't get the part of him that uses words. I get feelings mostly. Sometimes images, but usually just feelings. Urges. When I get an urge and I don't know where it's coming from, I know it's from him. Like the time I saw this Irish

138

setter on the street and I wanted to go over and pet it. I'm not a dog person, see, but all of a sudden I just had to pet that pooch."

Now that Cy's talking about it, he can't stop. It's all spilling out like water over a dam. "Petting that dog was one thing, but the stealing is another. The stealing makes me mad. I mean, here I am, a law-abiding citizen, never took nothing that didn't belong to me my whole life, and now I'm stuck with this. There's people out there—like that lady in the Christmas store—they see an umber kid like me and they automatically assume I'm up to no good. And now, thanks to this kid in my head, they're right. And you wanna know what's funny? This kid was lily-sienna, like you. Blond hair, blue eyes."

Hearing that surprises Lev. Not the description, but the fact that Cy can describe him at all. "You know what he looked like?"

CyFi nods. "I can see him sometimes. It's hard, but sometimes I can. I close my eyes and imagine myself looking into a mirror. Usually I just see myself reflected, but once in a while I can see him. It's only for an instant. Kinda like trying to catch a bolt of lightning after you've already seen the flash. But other people—they don't see *him* when he steals. It's me they see. *My* hands grabbing."

"The people who matter know it's not you. Your dads . . ."

"They don't even know about this!" Cy says. "They think they did me a favor stickin' me with this brain chunk. If I told them about it, they'd feel guilty until the end of time, so I can't tell them."

Lev doesn't know what to say. He wishes he'd never brought it up. He wishes he hadn't insisted on knowing. But most of all, he wishes Cy didn't have to deal with this. He's a good guy. He deserves a better break.

"And this kid—he doesn't even understand he's a part of me," Cy says. "It's like those ghosts that don't know they're

139

dead. He keeps trying to be him, and can't understand why the rest of him ain't there."

All of a sudden Lev realizes something. "He lived in Joplin, didn't he!"

Cy doesn't answer for a long time. That's how Lev knows it's true. Finally Cy says, "There are things he's still got locked up in my brain that I can't get at. All I know is that he's got to get to Joplin, so I got to get there too. Once we're there, maybe he'll leave me alone."

CyFi shifts his shoulders—not in a shrug but in an uncomfortable roll, like when you get an itch in your back or a sudden shiver. "I don't want to talk about him no more. His one-eighth feels a whole lot bigger when I spend time hanging around in his gray matter."

Lev wants to put his arm around Cy's shoulder like an older brother to comfort him, but he just can't bring himself to do it. So instead he pulls the blanket from the bed and wraps it around Cy as he sits in the chair.

"What's this all about?"

"Just making sure you two stay warm." And then he says, "Don't worry about anything. I've got it all under control."

CyFi laughs. "You? You can't even take care of yourself and now you think you're gonna take care of me? If it weren't for me you'd still be chowing down on other folk's garbage back at the mall."

"That's right—but you helped me. Now it's my turn to do the same for you. And I'm going to get you to Joplin."

# 22 · Risa

Risa Megan Ward watches everything around her closely and carefully. She's seen enough at StaHo to know that

140

survival rests on how observant you are.

For three weeks she, Connor, and a mixed bag of Unwinds have been shuttled from one safe house to another. It's maddening, for there seems to be no end in sight to this relentless underground railroad of refugees.

There are dozens of kids being moved around, but there are never more than five or six at a time in any given safe house, and Risa rarely sees the same kids twice. The only reason she and Connor have been able to stay together is because they pose as a couple. It's practical, and it serves both their interests. What's that expression? The devil you know is better than the one you don't?

Finally, they're dumped in a huge, empty warehouse in a thundering air-traffic zone. Cheap realty for hiding unwanted kids. It's a spartan building with a corrugated steel roof that shakes so badly when a plane passes overhead, she half expects it to collapse.

There are almost thirty kids here when they arrive, many of them are kids Risa and Connor had come across over the past few weeks. This is a holding tank, she realizes, a place where all the kids are warehoused in preparation for some final journey. There are chains on the doors to keep anyone unwanted out, and to keep anyone too rebellious in. There are space heaters that are useless, since all the heat is lost to the high warehouse roof. There's only one bathroom with a broken lock and, unlike many of the safe houses, there's no shower, so personal hygiene is put on hold the moment they arrive. Put all that together with a gang of scared, angry kids, and you've got a powder keg waiting to explode. Perhaps that's why the people who run the show all carry guns.

There are four men and three women in charge, all of them militarized versions of the folks who, like Sonia, run the safe houses. Everyone calls them "the Fatigues"—not just because they have a penchant toward khaki military clothing, but also because they always seem exhausted. Even so, they have a high-tension determination about them that Risa admires.

A handful of new kids arrives almost every day. Risa watches each group of arrivals with interest, and notices that Connor does too. She knows why.

"You're looking for Lev too, aren't you?" She finally says to him.

He shrugs. "Maybe I'm just looking for the Akron AWOL, like everyone else."

That makes Risa chuckle. Even in the safe houses they had heard the inflated rumors of an AWOL from Akron who escaped from a Juvey-cop by turning his own tranq pistol against him. *"Maybe he's on his way here!"* kids would whisper around the warehouse, like they were talking about a celebrity. Risa has no idea how the rumor started, since it was never in the news. She's also a bit annoyed that she's not included in the rumor. It ought to be a Bonnie-and-Clyde kind of thing. The rumor mill is definitely sexist.

"So are you ever going to tell them you're the Akron AWOL?" she quietly asks Connor.

"I don't want that kind of attention. Besides, they wouldn't believe me anyway. They're all saying the Akron AWOL is this big boeuf superhero. I don't want to disappoint them."

Lev doesn't show up with any of the batches of new kids. The only thing that arrives with them is an increase of tension. Forty-three kids by the end of their first week, and there's still one bathroom, no shower, and no answer as to how long this will last. Restlessness hangs as heavy as body odor in the air.

The Fatigues do their best to keep them all fed and occupied, if only to minimize friction. There are a few crates of games, incomplete decks of cards, and dog-eared books that no library wanted. There are no electronics, no balls—nothing that would create or encourage noise.

"If people out there hear you, then you're all done for," the Fatigues remind them as often as they can. Risa wonders if the Fatigues have lives separate and apart from saving Unwinds, or if this endeavor is their life's work.

"Why are you doing this for us?" Risa asked one of them during their second week.

The Fatigue had been almost rote in her answer—like giving a sound bite to a reporter. "Saving you and others like you is an act of conscience," the woman had said. "Doing it is its own reward."

The Fatigues all talk like that. Big-Picture-speak, Risa calls it. Seeing the whole, and none of the parts. It's not just in their speech but in their eyes as well. When they look at Risa, she can tell they don't really see her. They seem to see the mob of Unwinds more as a concept rather than a collection of anxious kids, and so they miss all the subtle social tremors that shake things just as powerfully as the jets shake the roof.

By the end of the second week, Risa has a pretty good idea where trouble is brewing. It all revolves around one kid she hoped she'd never see again, but he had turned up shortly after she and Connor arrived.

Roland.

Of all the kids here, he is by far the most potentially dangerous. The troubling thing is that Connor hasn't exactly been the image of emotional stability himself this past week.

He'd been all right in the safe houses. He'd held his temper—he hadn't done anything too impulsive or irrational. Here, however, in the midst of so many kids, he's different. He's irritable and defiant. The slightest thing can set him off. He'd been in half a dozen fights already. She knows this must be why his parents chose to have him unwound—a firestorm temper can drive some parents to desperate measures.

Common sense tells Risa to distance herself from him. Their alliance has been one of necessity, but there's no reason to ally herself with him anymore. Yet, day after day, she keeps finding herself drawn to him . . . and worried about him.

She approaches him shortly after breakfast one day, determined to open his eyes to a clear and present danger. He's sitting by himself, etching a portrait into the concrete floor with a rusty nail. Risa wishes she could say it was good, but Connor's not much of an artist. It disappoints her, because she desperately wants to find something redeeming about him. If he were an artist they could relate on a creative level. She could talk to him about her passion for music, and he would get it. As it is, she doesn't think he even knows, or cares, that she plays piano.

"Who are you drawing?" she asks.

"Just a girl I knew back home," he says.

Risa silently suffocates her jealousy in a quick emotional vacuum. "Someone you cared about?"

"Sort of."

Risa takes a better look at the sketch. "Her eyes are too big for her face."

"I guess that's because it's her eyes that I remember most."

"And her forehead's too low. The way you've drawn it, she'd have no room for a brain."

"Yeah, well, she wasn't all that bright."

Risa laughs at that, and it makes Connor smile. When he smiles, it's hard to imagine he's the same guy who got into all those fights. She gauges whether or not he'd be open to hear what she has to tell him.

He looks away from her. "Is there something you want, or are you just an art critic today?"

"I . . . was wondering why you're sitting by yourself."

"Ah, so you're also my shrink."

"We're supposed to be a couple. If we're going to keep up the image, you can't be entirely antisocial."

Connor looks out over the groups of kids, busy in various morning activities. Risa follows his gaze. There's a group of kids who hate the world, and spend all day spewing venom. There's a mouth-breathing kid who does nothing but read the same comic book over and over again. Mai is paired off with a glum spike-haired boy named Vincent, who's all leather and body piercings. He must be her soul mate, because they make out all day long, drawing a cluster of other kids who sit there and watch.

"I don't want to be social," Connor says. "I don't like the kids here."

"Why?" asks Risa, "They're too much like you?"

"They're losers."

"Yeah, that's what I mean."

He gives her a halfhearted dirty look, then looks down at his drawing, but she can tell he's not thinking about the girl—his head is somewhere else. "If I'm off by myself, then I don't get into fights." He puts down the nail, giving up on his etching. "I don't know what gets into me. Maybe it's all the voices. Maybe it's all the bodies moving all around me. It makes me feel like I've got ants crawling inside my brain and I want to scream. I can stand it just so long, then I blow. It happened even at home, everyone was talking at once at the dinner table. One time, we had family over and the talk got me so crazy, I hurled a plate at the china hutch. Glass blew everywhere. Ruined the meal. My parents asked me what got into me, and I couldn't tell them."

That Connor is willing to share this with her makes her feel good. It makes her feel closer to him. Maybe now that he has opened up, he'll stay open long enough to hear what she has to tell him.

"There's something I want to talk about."

"Yeah?"

Risa sits beside him, keeping her voice low.

"I want you to watch the other kids. Where they go. Who they talk to."

"All of them?"

"Yeah, but one at a time. After a while you'll start to notice things."

"Like what?"

"Like the kids who eat first are the ones who spend the most time with Roland—but he never goes to the front of the line himself. Like the way his closest friends infiltrate the other cliques and get them arguing so they break apart. Like the way Roland is especially nice to the kids that everyone else feels sorry for—but only until nobody feels sorry for them anymore. Then he uses them."

"Sounds like you're doing a class project on him."

"I'm being serious. I've seen this before. He's power hungry, he's ruthless, and he's very, very smart."

Connor laughs at that. "Roland? He couldn't think himself out of a paper bag."

"No, but he could think everyone else *into* one, and then crush it." Clearly that gives Connor pause for thought. *Good*, thinks Risa. *He needs to think. He needs to strategize.*

"Why are you telling me this?"

"Because you're his biggest threat."

"Me?"

"You're a fighter—everyone knows that. And they also know that you don't take crap from anyone. Have you heard kids mumbling about how someone oughta do something about Roland?"

"Yeah."

"They only say that when you're close enough to hear. They're expecting *you* to do something about him—and Roland knows it."

He tries to wave her off, but she gets in his face.

"Listen to me, because I know what I'm talking about. Back at StaHo there were always dangerous kids who bullied their way into power. They were able to do it because they knew exactly who to take down, and when. And the kid they took down the hardest was the one with the greatest potential for taking *them* down."

She can see Connor curling his right hand into a fist. She knows she's not getting through to him. He's getting the wrong message.

"If he wants a fight, he'll get one."

"No! You can't take the bait! That's what he wants! He'll do everything within his power to pull you into a fight. But you can't do it."

Connor hardens his jaw. "You think I can't take him in a fight?"

Risa grabs his wrist and holds it tight. "A kid like Roland doesn't want to fight you. He wants to kill you."

# 23 · Connor

As much as Connor hates to admit it, Risa has been right about a lot of things. Her clarity of thought has saved them more than once, and now that he knows to look for it, her take on Roland's secret power structure is right on target. Roland is a master of structuring life around him for his own benefit. It's not the overt bullying that does it, either. It's the subtle manipulation of the situation. The bullying almost acts as cover for what's really going on. As long as people see him as a dumb, tough guy, they don't notice the more clever things he does . . . such as endearing himself to one of the Fatigues by making sure the man sees him giving his food to one of the younger kids. Like a master chess player, every move Roland makes has purpose, even if the purpose isn't immediately clear.

Risa wasn't just right about Roland, she was also right about Lev—or at least the way Connor feels about the kid. Connor hasn't been able to get Lev out of his mind. For the longest time he had convinced himself it was merely out of a desire for revenge, as if he couldn't wait to get even with him. But each time a new group of kids shows up and Lev isn't among them, a sense of despair worms its way through Connor's gut. It makes Connor angry that he feels this way, and he suspects this is part of the anger that fuels the fights he gets into.

The fact is, Lev hadn't just turned them in, he had turned himself in as well. Which means that Lev is probably gone. Unwound into nothing—his bones, his flesh, his mind, shredded and recycled. This is what Connor finds so hard to accept. Connor had risked his life to save Lev, just as Connor had done for the baby on the doorstep. Well, the baby had been saved, but Lev had not, and although he knows he can't be held responsible for Lev's unwinding, he feels as if it is his fault. So he stands there with secret anticipation each time there's a group of new arrivals, hoping beyond hope he'll find that self-righteous, self-important, pain-in-the-ass Lev still alive.

# 24 · Risa

The Fatigues arrive with Christmas dinner an hour late. It's the same old slop, but the Fatigues wear Santa hats.

Impatience rules the evening. Everyone's so hungry, they crowd noisily around, like it's a food delivery in a famine, and to make it worse, there are only two Fatigues there tonight to serve the meal instead of the usual four.

"Single line! Single line!" yell the Fatigues. "There's enough for everybody. Ho, ho, ho." But tonight it's not a matter of getting enough, it's a matter of getting it *now*.

Risa's just as hungry as the others, but she also knows that meals are the best time to have some privacy in the bathroom, without someone bursting in through the unlocked door or simply pounding repeatedly to get you out faster. Tonight, with everyone clamoring for their holiday hash, there's no one at the bathroom at all, so, putting her hunger on hold, she moves away from the crowd and across the warehouse toward the bathroom.

Once inside she hangs the makeshift OCCUPIED sign on the door knob, and pushes the door closed. She takes a moment to examine herself in the mirror, but she doesn't like the straggly-haired, ragged girl she's become, so she doesn't look at herself for long. She washes her face and, since there are no towels, dries it with her sleeve. Then, before she even turns for the toilet, she hears the door creak open behind her.

She turns and must stifle a gasp. It's Roland who has entered the bathroom. And now he closes the door gently behind him. Risa immediately realizes her mistake. She should never have come here alone.

"Get out!" she says. She wishes she could sound more forceful in the moment, but he's caught her by surprise.

"No need to be so harsh." Roland moves toward her in a slow, predatory stride. "We're all friends here, right? And since everyone's eating dinner, we've got some quality time to get to know each other."

"Stay away from me!" Now she's scanning her options, but

realizes in this tight a space, with only one door, and nothing she can use as a weapon, her options are limited.

Now he's dangerously close. "Sometimes I like having dessert before dinner. How about you?"

The second he's in range, she acts quickly to hit him, to knee him, to inflict any kind of pain that would distract him enough for her to fly out the door. His reflexes are simply too fast. He grabs her hands, pushes her back against the cold green tile wall, and presses his hip against her so that her knee can't reach its mark. And he grins, as if it was all so easy. His hand is on her cheek now. The shark tattooed on his forearm is inches away, and seems ready to attack.

"So, whaddaya say we have some fun and make sure you don't get unwound for nine months?"

Risa has never been a screamer. The way she always saw it, screaming was a show of weakness. A sign of defeat. Now she has to admit defeat, for although she has lots of experience warding off creeps, Roland has even more experience being one.

So she screams. She lets loose a bloodcurdler at the top of her lungs. But her timing is as bad as it could possibly be, because just then a jet roars by overhead, shaking the walls and completely swallowing her scream.

"Ya gotta learn to enjoy life," Roland says. "Let's call this lesson one."

That's when the door swings open, and over Roland's massive shoulder Risa sees Connor standing at the threshold, eyes blazing. She's never been happier to see anyone.

"Connor! Stop him!"

Roland sees him too, catching his reflection in the bathroom mirror, but he doesn't release Risa.

"Well," says Roland. "Isn't *this* awkward."

Connor makes no move to tear him away. He just stands there on the threshold. His eyes still rage, but his hands—

they're not even clenched into fists. They just hang there limply by his side. What's wrong with him?

Roland winks at Risa, then he calls over his shoulder to Connor. "Better get out if you know what's good for you."

Connor steps over the threshold, but he doesn't move toward them. Instead he goes to the sink. "Mind if I wash up for dinner?"

Risa waits for him to make a sharp and sudden move, catching Roland off guard, but he doesn't. He just washes his hands.

"Your girlfriend's had her eye on me since Sonia's basement," says Roland. "You know that, don't you?"

Connor dries his hands on his pants. "You two can do whatever you like. Risa and I broke up this morning. Should I turn off the light when I leave?"

The betrayal is so unexpected, so complete, Risa doesn't know who to hate more, Roland or Connor. But then Roland eases his grip on her. "Well, now the mood's ruined, isn't it." He lets her go. "Hell, I was just kidding, anyway. I wouldn't have done anything." He backs away and offers that smile of his again. "How's about we wait until you're ready." Then he struts out just as boldly as he had come in, bumping Connor's shoulder on the way out as a parting shot.

All of her confusion and frustration unleashes at Connor, and she pushes him back against the wall, shaking him. "What was that? You were just going to let him do it? You were just going to stand there and let it happen?"

Connor pushes her off of him. "Didn't you warn me not to take the bait?"

"What?"

"He didn't just follow you to the bathroom—he pushed past me first. *He made sure I knew he was following you here.* This whole thing wasn't about you, it was about me—just

151

like you said. He *wanted* me to catch him. He wanted to make me crazy, to get me fighting mad. So I didn't take the bait."

Risa shakes her head—not in disbelief, but reeling from the truth of it. "But . . . but what if . . . what if he . . ."

"But he didn't, did he? And now he won't. Because if he thinks you and I broke up, you're more useful to him if you're on his side. He might still be after you, but from now on, I'll bet he'll be killing you with kindness."

All the emotions rebounding madly through Risa finally come to rest in an unfamiliar place, and tears burst from her eyes. Connor steps forward to comfort her, but she pushes him away with the same force she would have used against Roland.

"Get out!" she yells. "Just get out!"

Connor throws up his hands, frustrated. "Fine. I guess I should have just gone to dinner and not come in here at all."

He leaves and she closes the door behind him, in spite of the line of kids now waiting for the bathroom. She sits down on the floor, her back against the door so no one can get in as she tries to get her emotions under control.

Connor had done the right thing. For once, he had seen the situation more clearly than she—and he had probably ensured that Roland wouldn't physically threaten her again, at least for a while. And yet there's a part of her that can't forgive him for just standing there. After all, heroes are supposed to behave in very specific ways. They're supposed to fight, even if it means risking their lives.

This is the moment Risa realizes that, even with all his troubles, she sees Connor as a hero.

# 25 · Connor

Holding his temper in that bathroom was perhaps the hardest thing Connor had ever had to do. Even now, as he storms away from Risa, he wants to lay into Roland—but blind rage is not what the moment needs, and Connor knows it. Risa's right—a brutal, all-out fight is exactly what Roland wants—and Connor's heard from some of the other kids that Roland has fashioned himself a knife out of some metal he found lying around the warehouse. If Connor launches at him with a rage of swinging fists, Roland will find a way to end it with a single deadly thrust—and he'll be able to get away with it, claiming it was self-defense.

Whether Connor can take him in a fight isn't the question. Even against a knife, Connor suspects he might be able to either turn the blade against him, or take Roland out in some other way before he has the chance to use it. The question is this: Is Connor willing to enter a battle that must end with one of them dead? Connor might be a lot of things, but he's no killer. So he holds his temper and plays it cool.

This is new territory for him. The fighter in him screams foul, but another side of him, a side that's growing steadily stronger, enjoys this exercise of silent power—and it *is* power, because Roland now behaves exactly the way he and Risa want him to. Connor sees Roland offer his dessert to Risa that night as an apology. She doesn't accept it, of course, but it doesn't change the fact that he offered it. It's as if Roland thinks his attack on her could be wiped away by feigning remorse—not because he's actually sorry for what he did, but because it serves Roland's needs to treat her well now. He has no idea that Risa and Connor have him on an invisible leash. Connor knows it will only be a matter of time, however, until he chews his way through it.

## Part Four

# Destinations

The following is a response from eBay with regard to a seller's attempt to auction his soul online in 2001.

*Thank you for taking the time to write eBay with your concerns. I'm happy to help you further.*

*If the soul does not exist, eBay could not allow the auctioning of the soul because there would be nothing to sell. However, if the soul does exist, then in accordance with eBay's policy on human parts and remains we would not allow the auctioning of human souls. The soul would be considered human remains; and although it is not specifically stated on the policy page, human souls are still not allowed to be listed on eBay. Your auction was removed appropriately and will not be reinstated. Please do not relist this item with us in the future.*

*You may review our policy at the following link: http://pages.ebay.com/help/policies/remains.html.*

*It is my pleasure to assist you. Thank you for choosing eBay.*

# 26 · Pawnbroker

The man inherited the pawnshop from his brother, who had died of a heart attack. He wouldn't have kept the place, but he inherited it while he was unemployed. He figured he could keep it and run it until he could find a better job. That was twenty years ago. Now he knows it's a life sentence.

A boy comes into his shop one evening before closing. Not his usual type of customer. Most folks come into a pawnshop down on their luck, ready to trade in everything they own, from TVs to family heirlooms, in exchange for a little quick cash. Some do it for drugs. Others have more legitimate reasons. Either way, the pawnbroker's success is based on the misery of others. It doesn't bother him anymore. He's grown used to it.

This boy is different, though. Sure, there are kids who come in, hoping to get a deal on items that were never claimed, but there's something about this kid that's markedly off. He looks more clean-cut than the kids that usually turn up in his store. And the way he moves, even the way he holds himself, is refined and graceful, deliberate and delicate, like he's lived his life as a prince and is now pretending to be the pauper. He wears a puffy white coat, but it's a bit dirty. Maybe he's the pauper after all.

The TV on the counter plays a football game, but the pawnbroker isn't watching the game anymore. His eyes are on it, but his mind is keeping track of the kid as he meanders through the shop, looking at things, like he might want to buy something.

After a few minutes, the kid approaches the counter.

"What can I do for you?" the pawnbroker asks, genuinely curious.

"This is a pawnshop isn't it?"

"Doesn't it says so on the door?"

"So that means you trade things for money, right?"

The pawnbroker sighs. The kid's just ordinary after all, just a little more naive than the other kids who show up here trying to hock their baseball card collections or whatever. Usually they want money for cigarettes or alcohol or something else they don't want their parents to know about. This kid doesn't look like the type for that, though.

"We *loan* money, and take objects of value as collateral," he tells the kid. "And we don't do business with minors. You wanna buy something, fine, but you can't pawn anything here, so take your baseball cards somewhere else."

"Who said I have baseball cards?"

Then the kid reaches into his pocket and pulls out a bracelet, all diamonds and gold.

The pawnbroker's eyes all but pop out of his skull as the kid dangles it from his fingers. Then the pawnbroker laughs. "Whad'ya do, steal that from your mommy, kid?"

The kid's expression stays diamond hard. "How much will you give me for it?"

"How about a nice boot out the door?"

Still, the kid shows no sign of fear or disappointment. He just lays the bracelet on the worn wooden counter with that same princely grace.

"Why don't you just put that thing away and go home?"

"I'm an Unwind."

"What?"

"You heard me."

This throws the pawnbroker for a loop for a whole lot of reasons. First of all, runaway Unwinds who show up at his shop never admit it. Secondly, they always appear desperate and angry, and the stuff they have to sell is shoddy at best. They're never this calm, and they never look this . . . angelic.

"You're an Unwind?"

The boy nods. "The necklace is stolen, but not from anywhere around here."

Unwinds also never admit that their items are stolen. Those other kids always come up with the most elaborate stories as to who they are, and why they're selling. The pawnbroker will usually listen to their stories for their entertainment value. If it's a good story, he'll just throw the kid out. If it's a lousy story, he'll call the police and have them picked up. This kid, however, doesn't have a story; he comes only with the truth. The pawnbroker doesn't quite know how to deal with the truth.

"So," says the kid. "Are you interested?"

The pawnbroker just shrugs. "Who you are is your business, and like I said, I don't deal with minors."

"Maybe you'll make an exception."

The pawnbroker considers the kid, considers the bracelet, then looks at the door to make sure no one else is coming in. "I'm listening."

"Here's what I want. Five hundred dollars, cash. Now. Then I leave like we never met, and you can keep the bracelet."

The pawnbroker puts on his well-practiced poker face. "Are you kidding me? This piece of junk? Gold plate, zircons instead of diamonds, poor workmanship—I'll give you a hundred bucks, not a penny more."

The kid never breaks eye contact. "You're lying."

159

Of course the pawnbroker is lying, but he resents the accusation. "How about if I turn you in to the Juvey-cops right now?"

The kid reaches down and takes the bracelet from the table. "You could," he says. "But then you won't get this—the police will."

The pawnbroker strokes his beard. Maybe this kid isn't as naive as he looks.

"If it were a piece of junk," the kid says, "you wouldn't have offered me a hundred. I'll bet you wouldn't have offered me anything." He looks at the necklace dangling from his fingers. "I really don't know what something like this is worth, but I'll bet it's worth thousands. All I'm asking is five hundred, which means, whatever it's worth, you're getting a great deal."

The pawnbroker's poker face is gone. He can't stop staring at the bracelet—it's all he can do not to drool over it. He knows what it's really worth, or at least he can guess. He knows where he can fence it himself for five times what the kid is asking. That would be a nice bit of change. Enough to take his wife on that long vacation she's always wanted.

"Two hundred fifty. That's my final offer."

"Five hundred. You have three seconds, and then I leave. One . . . two . . ."

"Deal." The pawnbroker sighs as if he's been beaten. "You drive a hard bargain, kid." That's the way these things are played. Make the kid think that he won, when all the while he's the one who's truly being robbed! The pawnbroker reaches for the bracelet, but the kid holds it out of reach.

"First the money."

"The safe's in the back room—I'll be back in a second."

"I'll come with you."

The pawnbroker doesn't argue. It's understandable that the kid doesn't trust him. If he trusted people, he'd have been

160

unwound by now. In the back room, the pawnbroker positions himself with the kid behind him, so the kid can't see the combination of the safe. He pulls open the door, and the second he does, he feels something hard and heavy connecting with his head. His thoughts are instantly scrambled. He loses consciousness before he hits the ground.

The pawnbroker comes to sometime later, with a headache and a faint memory that something had gone wrong. It takes a few seconds for him to pull himself together and realize exactly what happened. That little monster conned him! He got him to open the safe, and the moment he did, he knocked him out and cleaned out the safe.

Sure enough, the safe is open wide—but it's not entirely empty. Inside is the necklace, its gold and diamonds looking even brighter against the ugly gray steel of the empty safe. How much money had been in the safe? Fifteen hundred, tops. This necklace is worth at least three times that. Still a deal—and the kid knew it.

The pawnbroker rubs the painful knot on his head, furious at the kid for what he did and yet admiring him for the strangely honorable nature of the crime. If he himself had been this clever, this honorable, and had found this kind of nerve when he was a kid, perhaps he'd be more than just a pawnbroker.

# 27 · Connor

The morning after the bathroom incident, they are rousted awake by the Fatigues before dawn. "Everybody up! Now! Move it! Move it!" They're loud, they're on edge, and the first thing Connor notices is that the safeties on their weapons are off. Still bleary from sleep, he rises and looks for Risa. He sees her already being herded by two Fatigues toward a huge double door that has always been padlocked. Now the padlock is off.

"Leave your things! Go! Move it! Move it!"

To his right, a cranky kid pushes a Fatigue for tearing away his blanket. The Fatigue hits him on the shoulder with the butt of his rifle—not enough to seriously wound him, but enough to make it clear to the kid, and everyone else, that they mean business. The kid goes down on his knees, gripping his shoulder and cursing, and the Fatigue goes about the business of herding the others. Even in his pain, the kid looks ready for a fight. As Connor passes him, Connor grabs him by the arm and helps him up.

"Take it easy," Connor says. "Don't make it worse."

The kid pulls out of Connor's grip. "Get off me! I don't need your stinkin' help." The kid storms away. Connor shakes his head. Was he ever that belligerent?

Up ahead, the huge double doors are slid open to reveal another room of the warehouse that the Unwinds have never seen. This one is filled with crates—old airline packing crates, designed, both in shape and durability, to transport goods by air freight. Connor immediately realizes what they're for—and why he and the others have been warehoused so close to an airport. Wherever they're going, they're going as air cargo.

"Girls to the left, boys to the right. Move it! Move it!"

There's grumbling, but no direct defiance. Connor wonders how many kids get what's going on.

"Four to a crate! Boys with boys, girls with girls. Move it! Move it!"

Now everyone begins to scramble around, trying to team up with their preferred travel companions, but the Fatigues have neither patience nor time for it. They randomly create groups of four and push them toward the crates.

That's when Connor notices how dangerously close he is to Roland—and it's no accident. Roland moved close to him on purpose. Connor can just imagine it. Pitch black and close quarters. If he's in a crate with Roland, then he'll be dead before takeoff.

Connor tries to move away, but a Fatigue grabs Roland, Connor, and two of Roland's known collaborators. "You four. That crate over there!"

Connor tries not to let his panic show; he doesn't want Roland to see. He should have prepared his own weapon, like the one Roland certainly has concealed on him now. He should have prepared for the inevitability of a life-or-death confrontation, but he hadn't, and now his options are limited.

No time for thinking this through, so he lets impulse take over and gives in to his fighting instincts. He turns to one of Roland's henchmen and punches him in the face hard enough to draw blood, maybe even break his nose. The force of the punch spins the kid around, but before he can come back for a counterassault, a Fatigue grabs Connor and smashes him back against the concrete wall. The Fatigue doesn't know it, but this is *exactly* what Connor wanted.

"You picked the wrong day to do that, kid!" says the Fatigue, holding him against the wall with his rifle.

"What are you gonna do, kill me? I thought you were trying to save us."

That gives the Fatigue a moment's pause.

"Hey!" yells another Fatigue. "Forget him! We gotta load them up." Then he grabs another kid to complete the foursome with Roland and his henchmen, sending them toward a crate. They don't even care about the one kid's bleeding nose.

The Fatigue holding Connor against the wall sneers at him. "The sooner you're in a box, the sooner you're somebody else's problem."

"Nice socks," says Connor.

They put Connor in a four-by-eight crate that already has three kids waiting to complete their quartet. The crate is sealed even before he can see who's inside with him, but as long as it's not Roland, it will do.

"We're all gonna die in here," says a nasal voice, followed by a wet sniff that doesn't sound like it clears much of anything. Connor knows this kid by his mucous. He's not sure of his name—everyone just calls him "the Mouth Breather," since his nose is perpetually stuffed. Emby, for short. He's the one always obsessively reading his comic book, but he can't quite do that in here.

"Don't talk like that," says Connor. "If the Fatigues wanted to kill us, they would have done it a long time ago."

The Mouth Breather has foul breath that's filling up the whole crate. "Maybe they got found out. Maybe the Juvey-cops are on their way, and the only way to save themselves is to destroy the evidence!"

Connor has little patience for whiners. It reminds him too much of his younger brother. The one his parents chose to keep. "Shut up, Emby, or I swear I'm going to take off my sock, shove it in your stinky mouth, and you'll finally have to figure out a way to breathe through your nose!"

"Let me know if you need an extra sock," says a voice just across from him. "Hi, Connor. It's Hayden."

"Hey, Hayden." Connor reaches out and finds Hayden's shoe, squeezing it—the closest thing to a greeting in the claustrophobic darkness. "So, who's lucky number four?" No answer. "Sounds like we must be traveling with a mime." Another long pause, then Connor hears a deep, accented voice.

"Diego."

"Diego doesn't talk much," says Hayden.

"I figured."

They wait in silence, punctuated by the Mouth Breather's snorts.

"I gotta go to the bathroom," Emby mumbles.

"You should have thought of that before you left," says Hayden, putting on his best mother voice. "How many times do we have to tell you? Always use the potty before climbing into a shipping crate."

There's some sort of mechanical activity outside, then they feel the crate moving.

"I don't like this," whines Emby.

"We're being moved," says Hayden.

"By forklift, probably," says Connor. The Fatigues are probably long gone by now. What was it that one Fatigue had said? *Once you're in a box, you're somebody else's problem.* Whoever's been hired to ship them probably has no clue what's in the crates. Soon they'll be on board some aircraft, headed to an undisclosed destination. The thought of it makes him think about the rest of his family and their trip to the Bahamas—the one they'd planned to take once Connor was unwound. He wonders if they went—would they still take their vacation, even after Connor had kicked-AWOL? Sure they would. They were planning to take it once he got unwound, so why would his escape stop them? Hey, wouldn't it be funny if they were being shipped to the Bahamas too?

"We're gonna suffocate! I know it!" announces the Mouth Breather.

"Will you shut up?" says Connor. "I'm sure there's more than enough air in here for us."

"How do *you* know? I can barely breathe already—and I got asthma, too. I could have an asthma attack in here and die!"

"Good," says Connor. "One less person breathing the air."

That shuts Emby up, but Connor feels bad having said it. "No one's going to die," he says. "Just relax."

And then Hayden says, "At least dying's better than being unwound. Or is it? Let's take a poll—would you rather die, or be unwound?"

"Don't ask things like that!" snaps Connor. "I don't want to think about either." Somewhere outside of their little crated universe, Connor hears a metal hatch closing and can feel the vibration in his feet as they begin to taxi. Connor waits. Engines power up—he can feel the vibration in his feet. He's pushed back against the wall as they accelerate. Hayden tumbles into him, and he shifts over, giving Hayden room to get comfortable again.

"What's happening? What's happening?" cries Emby.

"Nothing. We're just taking off."

"What! We're on a *plane*?"

Connor rolls his eyes, but the gesture is lost in the darkness.

The box is like a coffin. The box is like a womb. Normal measures of time don't seem to apply, and the unpredictable turbulence of flight fills the dark space with an ever-present tension.

Once they're airborne, the four kids don't speak for a very long time. Half an hour, an hour maybe—it's hard to tell. Everyone's mind is trapped in the holding pattern of their own uneasy thoughts. The plane hits some rough air. Everything around them rattles. Connor wonders if there are kids in crates above them, below them, and on every side. He can't hear their voices if they are. From where he sits, it feels like the four of them are the only ones in the universe. Emby silently relieves himself. Connor knows because he can smell it—everyone can, but no one says anything. It could just as easily have been any one of them—and depending on how long this trip is, it still could be.

Finally, after what feels like forever, the quietest of them all speaks.

"Unwound," Diego says. "I'd rather be unwound."

Even though it's been a long time since Hayden posed the question, Connor knows immediately what it refers to. *Would you rather die or be unwound?* It's like the question has hung in the cramped darkness all this time, waiting to be answered.

"Not me," says Emby. "Because if you die, at least you go to Heaven."

*Heaven?* thinks Connor. More likely they'd go to the other place. Because if their own parents didn't care enough about them to keep them, who would want them in Heaven?

"What makes you think Unwinds don't go?" Diego asks Emby.

"Because Unwinds aren't really dead. They're still alive . . . sort of. I mean, they have to use every single part of us somewhere, right? That's the law."

Then Hayden asks the question. Not *a* question, *the* question. Asking it is the great taboo among those marked for unwinding. It's what everyone thinks about, but no one ever dares to ask out loud.

"So, then," says Hayden, "if every part of you is alive but inside someone else . . . are you alive or are you dead?"

This, Connor knows, is Hayden bringing his hand back and forth across the flame again. Close enough to feel it, but not close enough to burn. But it's not just his own hand now, it's everyone's, and it ticks Connor off.

"Talking wastes our oxygen," Connor says. "Let's just agree that unwinding sucks and leave it at that."

It shuts everyone up, but only for a minute. It's Emby who talks next.

"I don't think unwinding is bad," he says. "I just don't want it to happen to me."

Connor wants to ignore him but can't. If there's one thing that Connor can't abide, it's an Unwind who defends unwinding. "So it's all right if it happens to us but not if it happens to you?"

"I didn't say that."

"Yes, you did."

"Ooh," says Hayden. "This is getting good."

"They say it's painless," says Emby—as if that were any consolation.

"Yeah?" says Connor. "Well, why don't you go ask all the pieces of Humphrey Dunfee how painless it was?"

The name settles like a frost around them. The jolts and rattles of turbulence grow sharper.

"So . . . you heard that story too?" says Diego.

"Just because there are stories like that, doesn't mean unwinding is all bad," says Emby. "It helps people."

"You sound like a tithe," says Diego.

Connor finds himself personally insulted by that. "No, he doesn't. I know a tithe. His ideas might have been a little bit out there, but he wasn't stupid." The thought of Lev brings with it a wave of despair. Connor doesn't fight it—he just lets it wash through him, then drain away. He doesn't *know* a tithe; he *knew* one. One who has certainly met his destiny by now.

"Are you calling me stupid?" says Emby.

"I think I just did."

Hayden laughs. "Hey, the Mouth Breather is right—unwinding does help people. If it wasn't for unwinding, there'd be bald guys again—and wouldn't that be horrible?"

Diego snickers, but Connor is not the least bit amused. "Emby, why don't you do us all a favor and use your mouth for breathing instead of talking until we land, or crash, or whatever."

"You might think I'm stupid, but I got a good reason for the way I feel," Emby says. "When I was little, I was diagnosed with pulmonary fibrosis. Both my lungs were shutting down. I was gonna die. So they took out both my dying lungs and gave me a single lung from an Unwind. The only reason I'm alive is because that kid got unwound."

"So," says Connor, "your life is more important than his?"

"He was already unwound—it's not like I did it to him. If I didn't get that lung, someone else would have."

In his anger, Connor's voice begins to rise, even though Emby's only a couple of feet away at most. "If there wasn't unwinding, there'd be fewer surgeons, and more doctors. If there wasn't unwinding, they'd go back to trying to cure diseases instead of just replacing stuff with someone else's."

And suddenly the Mouth Breather's voice rings out with a ferocity that catches Connor by surprise.

"Wait till you're the one who's dying and see how you feel about it!"

"I'd rather die than get a piece of an Unwind!" Connor yells back.

The Mouth Breather tries to shout something else, but instead goes into a coughing fit that lasts for a whole minute. It gets so bad, it frightens even Connor. It's like he might actually cough up his transplanted lung.

"You okay?" asks Diego.

"Yeah," says Emby, trying to get it under control. "Like I said, the lung's got asthma. It was the best we could afford."

By the time his coughing fit is over, it seems there's nothing more to say. Except this:

"If your parents went to all that trouble," asks Hayden, "why were they having you unwound?"

Hayden and his questions. This one shuts Emby down for a few moments. It's clearly a tough topic for him—maybe even tougher than it is for most Unwinds.

"My *parents* didn't sign the order," Emby finally says. "My dad died when I was little, and my mom died two months ago. That's when my aunt took me in. The thing is, my mom left me some money, but my aunt's got three kids of her own to put through college, so . . ."

He doesn't have to finish. The others can connect the dots.

"Man, that stinks," says Diego.

"Yeah," says Connor, his anger at Emby now transferred to Emby's aunt.

"It's always about money," Hayden says. "When my parents were splitting up, they fought over money, until there was none left. Then they fought over me. So I got out before there was none of me left, either."

Silence falls again. There's nothing to hear but the drone of the engine, and the rattle of the crates. The air is humid and it's a struggle to breathe. Connor wonders if maybe the Fatigues miscalculated about how much air they had. *We're all gonna die in here.* That's what Emby said. Connor bangs his head back sharply against the wall, hoping to jar loose the bad thoughts clinging to his brain. This is not a good place to be alone with your thoughts. Perhaps that's why Hayden feels compelled to talk.

"No one ever answered my question," Hayden says. "Looks like no one has the guts."

"Which one?" asks Connor. "You've got questions coming out of you like farts on Thanksgiving."

"I was asking if unwinding kills you, or if it leaves you alive somehow. C'mon—it's not like we haven't thought about it."

Emby says nothing. He's clearly been weakened by coughing and conversation. Connor's not interested in volunteering either.

"It depends," says Diego. "Depends on where your soul is once you're unwound."

Normally Connor would walk away from a conversation like this. His life is about tangibles: things you can see, hear, and touch. God, souls, and all that has always been like a secret in a black box he couldn't see into, so it was easier to just leave it alone. Only now, he's inside the black box.

"What do you think, Connor?" asks Hayden. "What happens to your soul when you get unwound?"

"Who says I even got one?"

"For the sake of argument, let's say you do."

"Who says I want an argument?"

"*Ijolé!* Just give him an answer, man, or he won't leave you alone."

Connor squirms, but can't squirm his way out of the box. "How should I know what happens to it? Maybe it gets all broken up like the rest of us into a bunch of little pieces."

"But a soul isn't like that," says Diego. "It's indivisible."

"If it's indivisible," says Hayden, "maybe an Unwind's spirit stretches out, kind of like a giant balloon between all those parts of us in other places. Very poetic."

Hayden might find poetry in it, but to Connor the thought is terrifying. He tries to imagine himself stretched so thin and so wide that he can reach around the world. He imagines his spirit like a web strung between the thousand recipients of his hands, his eyes, the fragments of his brain—none of it under his control anymore, all absorbed by the bodies and wills of others. Could consciousness exist like that? He thinks about the trucker who performed a card trick for him with an Unwind's hand. Did the boy who once owned that hand still feel the satisfaction of performing the trick? Was his spirit still inexplicably whole, even though his flesh had been shuffled like that deck of cards, or was he shredded beyond all hope of

171

awareness—beyond Heaven, Hell, or anything eternal? Whether or not souls exist Connor doesn't know. But consciousness *does* exist—that's something he knows for sure. If every part of an Unwind is still alive, then that consciousness has to go somewhere, doesn't it? He silently curses Hayden for making him think about it . . . but Hayden isn't done done yet.

"Here's a little brain clot for you," says Hayden. "I knew this girl back home. There was something about her that made you want to listen to the things she had to say. I don't know whether she was really well-centered, or just psychotic. She believed that if someone actually gets unwound, then they never had a soul to begin with. She said God must know who's going to be unwound, and he doesn't give them souls."

Diego grunts his disapproval. "I don't like the sound of that."

"This girl had it all worked out in her head," continued Hayden. "She believed Unwinds are like the unborn."

"Wait a second," says Emby, finally breaking his silence. "The unborn have souls. They have souls from the moment they get made—the law says."

Connor doesn't want to get into it again with Emby, but he can't help himself. "Just because the law says it, that doesn't make it true."

"Yeah, well, just because the law says it, that doesn't make it false, either. It's only the law because a whole lot of people thought about it, and decided it made sense."

"Hmm," says Diego. "The Mouth Breather has a point."

Maybe so, but the way Connor sees it, a point ought to be sharper than that. "How can you pass laws about things that nobody knows?"

"They do it all the time," says Hayden. "That's what law is: educated guesses at right and wrong."

"And what the law says in fine with me," says Emby.

"But if it weren't for the law, would you still believe it?" asks Hayden. "Share with us a a personal opinion, Emby. Prove there's more than snot in that cranium of yours."

"You're wasting your time," says Connor. "There's not."

"Give our congested friend a chance," says Hayden.

They wait. The sound of the engine changes. Connor can feel them begin a slow descent, and wonders if the others can feel it too. Then Emby says, "Unborn babies . . . they suck their thumbs sometimes, right? And they kick. Maybe before that they're just like a bunch of cells or something, but once they kick and suck their thumbs—that's when they've got a soul."

"Good for you!" says Hayden. "An opinion! I knew you could do it."

Connor's head begins to spin. Was it the plane's banking, or a lack of oxygen?

"Connor, fair is fair—Emby found an opinion somewhere in his questionable gray matter. Now you have to give yours."

Connor sighs, not having the strength to fight anymore. He thinks about the baby he and Risa so briefly shared. "If there's such a thing as a soul—and I'm not saying that there is—then it comes when a baby's born into the world. Before that, it's just part of the mother."

"No, it's not!" says Emby.

"Hey—he wanted my opinion, I gave it."

"But it's wrong!"

"You see, Hayden? You see what you started?"

"Yes!" Hayden says excitedly. "It looks like we're about to have our own little Heartland War. Pity it's too dark for us to watch it."

"If you want my opinion, you're both wrong," says Diego. "The way I see it, it's got nothing to do with all of that. It has to do with love."

"Uh-oh," says Hayden. "Diego's getting romantic. I'm moving to the other end of the crate."

"No, I'm serious. A person don't got a soul until that person is loved. If a mother loves her baby—*wants* her baby—it's got a soul from the moment she knows it's there. The moment you're loved, that's when you got your soul. *Punto!*"

"Yeah?" says Connor. "Well, what about all those babies that get storked—or all those kids in state schools?"

"They just better hope somebody loves them some day."

Connor snorts dismissively, but in spite of himself, he can't dismiss it entirely, any more than he can dismiss the other things he's heard today. He thinks about his parents. Did they ever love him? Certainly they did when he was little. And just because they stopped, it didn't mean his soul was stolen away . . . although sometimes to admit that it felt like it was. Or at least, part of it died when his parents signed the order.

"Diego, that's really sweet," Hayden says in his best mocking voice. "Maybe you should write greeting cards."

"Maybe I should write them on your face."

Hayden just laughs.

"You always poke fun at other people's opinions," says Connor, "so how come you never give your own?"

"Yeah," says Emby.

"You're always playing people for your own entertainment. Now it's your turn. Entertain *us*."

"Yeah," says Emby.

"So tell us," says Connor, "in *The World According to Hayden*, when do we start to live?"

A long silence from Hayden, and then he says quietly, uneasily, "I don't know."

Emby razzes him. "That's not an answer."

But Connor reaches out and grabs Emby's arm, to shut

174

him up—because Emby's wrong. Even though Connor can't see Hayden's face, he can hear the truth of it in his voice. There was no hint of evasion in Hayden's words. This was raw honesty, void of Hayden's usual flip attitude. It was perhaps the first truly honest thing Connor had ever heard him say. "Yes, it is an answer," Connor says. "Maybe it's the best answer of all. If more people could admit they really don't know, maybe there never would have been a Heartland War."

There's a mechanical jolt beneath them. Emby gasps.

"Landing gear," says Connor.

"Oh, right."

In a few minutes they'll be there, wherever "there" is. Connor tries to guess how long they've been in the air. Ninety minutes? Two hours? There's no telling what direction they've been flying. They could be touching down anywhere. Or maybe Emby was right. Maybe it's piloted by remote control and they're just ditching the whole plane in the ocean to get rid of the evidence. Or what if it's worse than that? What if . . . what if . . .

"What if it's a harvest camp after all?" says Emby. Connor doesn't tell him to shut up this time, because he's thinking the same thing.

It's Diego who answers him. "If it is, then I want my fingers to go to a sculptor. So he can use them to craft something that will last forever."

They all think about that. Hayden is the next to speak.

"If I'm unwound," says Hayden, "I want my eyes to go to a photographer—one who shoots supermodels. That's what I want these eyes to see."

"My lips'll go to a rock star," says Connor.

"These legs are definitely going to the Olympics."

"My ears to an orchestra conductor."

"My stomach to a food critic."

175

"My biceps to a body builder."

"I wouldn't wish my sinuses on anybody."

And they're all laughing as the plane touches down.

# 28 · Risa

Risa doesn't know what went on in Connor's crate. She assumes guys talk about guy things, whatever those things are. She has no way of knowing that what occurred in his crate was a reenactment of what happened in her own, and in almost every other container on the plane. Fear, misgivings, questions rarely asked, and stories rarely told. The details are different, of course, as are the players, but the gist is the same. No one will discuss these things again, or even acknowledge having ever discussed them at all, but because of it, invisible bonds have been forged. Risa has gotten to know an overweight girl prone to tears, a girl wound up from a week of nicotine withdrawal, and a girl who was a ward of the state, just like her—and also just like Risa, an unwitting victim of budget cuts. Her name is Tina. The others told their names, but Tina's is the only one she remembers.

"We're exactly the same," Tina had said sometime during the flight. "We could be twins." Even though Tina is umber, Risa has to admit that it's true. It's comforting to know there are others in the same situation, but troubling to think her own life is just one of a thousand pirate copies. Sure, the Unwinds from state homes all have different faces, but otherwise, their stories are the same. They even all have the same last name, and she silently curses whoever it was who determined that they should all be named Ward—as if being one weren't enough of a stigma.

The plane touches down, and they wait.

"What's taking so long?" asks the nicotine girl, impatiently. "I can't stand this!"

"Maybe they're moving us to a truck, or another plane," suggests the pudgy girl.

"They'd better not be," says Risa. "There's not enough air in here for another trip."

There's noise—someone's outside the crate. "Shhh!" says Risa. "Listen." Footsteps. Banging. She hears voices, although she can't make out what the voices say. Then someone unlatches a side of the crate and pulls it open a crack. Hot, dry air spills in. The sliver of light from the plane's hold seems bright as sunlight after the hours of darkness.

"Is everyone all right in there?" It's not a Fatigue—Risa can tell right away. The voice is younger.

"We're okay," Risa says. "Can we get out of here?"

"Not yet. We gotta open all the other crates first and get everyone some fresh air." From what Risa can see, this is just a kid her age, maybe even younger. He wears a beige tank top and khaki pants. He's sweaty, and his cheeks are tan. No, not just tan: sunburned.

"Where are we?" Tina asks.

"The graveyard," says the kid, and moves on to the next crate.

In a few minutes the crate is opened all the way, and they're free. Risa takes a moment to look at her travel companions. The three girls look remarkably different from her memory of them when they first got in. Getting to know someone in blind darkness changes your impression of them. The large girl isn't as overweight as Risa had thought. Tina isn't as tall. The nicotine girl isn't nearly as ugly.

A ramp leads down from the hold, and Risa must wait her turn in a long line of kids leaving their crates. Rumors are already buzzing. Risa tries to listen, and sort the fact from fiction.

"A buncha kids died."

"No way."

"I heard half the kids died."

"No way!"

"Look around you, moron! Does it look like half of us died?"

"Well, I just heard."

"It was just one crateful that died."

"Yeah! Someone says they freaked out and ate each other—you know, like the Donner party."

"No, they just suffocated."

"How do you know?"

"'Cause I saw them, man. Right in the crate next to mine. There were five guys in there instead of four, and they all suffocated."

Risa turns to the kid who said that. "Is that really true, or are you just making it up?"

Risa can tell by the unsettled look on his face that he's sincere. "I wouldn't joke about something like that."

Risa looks for Connor, but her view is limited to the few kids around her in line. She quickly does the math. There were about sixty kids. Five kids suffocated. One-in-twelve chance it was Connor. No, because the boy who saw into the dead crate said there were *guys* in there. There were only thirty guys in all. One-in-six chance it was Connor. Had he been one of the last ones in? Had he been shoved into an overpacked crate? She didn't know. She had been so flustered when they were rousted that morning, it was hard enough to keep track of herself, much less anyone else. *Please, God, let it not be Connor.*

*Let it not be Connor.* Her last words to him had been angry ones. Even though he had saved her from Roland, she was furious at him. "Get out of here!" she had screamed. She couldn't bear the thought of his dying with those being her last words. She couldn't bear the thought of his dying, period.

She bangs her head on the low opening of the cargo hold on her way out.

"Watch your head," says one of the kids in charge.

"Yeah, thanks," says Risa. He smirks at her. This kid is also dressed in Army clothes, but he's too scrawny to be a military boeuf. "What's with the clothes?"

"Army surplus," he says. "Stolen clothes for stolen souls."

Outside the hold, the light of day is blinding, and the heat hits Risa like a furnace. The ramp beneath her slopes to the ground, and she has to stare at her feet, squinting to keep from stumbling. By the time she reaches the ground, her eyes have adjusted enough to take in their surroundings. All around them, *everywhere,* are airplanes, but there's no sign of an airport—just the planes, row after row, for as far as the eye can see. Many are from airlines that no longer exist. She turns to look at the jet they just arrived on. It carries the logo of FedEx, but this craft is a sorry specimen. It seems about ready for the junkyard. *Or,* thinks Risa, *the graveyard* . . .

"This is nuts," one kid beside Risa grumbles. "It's not like this plane is invisible. They're going to know exactly where the plane has gone. We're going to be tracked here!"

"Don't you get it?" says Risa. "That jet was just decommissioned. That's how they do it. They wait for a decommissioned plane, then load us in as cargo. The plane was coming here anyway, so no one's going to miss it."

The jets rest on a barren hardpan of maroon earth. Distant red mountains poke up from the ground. They are somewhere in the Southwest.

There's a row of port-o-potties that already have anxious lines. The kids shepherding them count heads and try to maintain order in the disoriented group. One of them has a megaphone.

"Please remain under the wing if you're not using the latrine," he announces. "You made it this far, we don't want you to die of sunstroke."

Now that everyone's out of the plane, Risa desperately searches the crowd until she finally finds Connor. Thank God! She wants to go to him, but remembers that they've officially ended their fake romance. With two dozen kids between them, they briefly make eye contact, and exchange a secret nod. That nod says everything. It says that what happened between them yesterday is history; today, everything starts fresh.

Then she sees Roland there as well. He meets her eye and gives her a grin. That grin says things too. She looks away, wishing he had been in the suffocation crate. She considers feeling guilty for such a nasty wish, then realizes that she doesn't feel guilty for wishing it at all.

A golf cart comes rolling down the rows of airliners, kicking up a plume of red dust in its wake. The driver is a kid. The passenger is clearly military. Not military surplus, either—he's the real thing. Instead of green or khaki, he's in navy blue. He seems accustomed to the heat—even in his hot uniform, he doesn't appear to sweat. The cart stops before the gathered hoard of juvenile refugees. The driver steps out first, and joins the four kids who had been leading them. The loud kid raises his megaphone. "May I have your attention! The Admiral is about to address you. If you know what's good for you, you'll listen."

The man steps out of the golf cart. The kid offers him the megaphone, but he waves it away. His voice needs no amplification. "I'd like to be the first to welcome you to the graveyard."

The Admiral is well into his sixties, and his face is full of scars. Only now does Risa realize that his uniform is one from the war. She can't recall whether these were the colors of the pro-life or pro-choice forces, but then, it doesn't really matter. Both sides lost.

"This will be your home until you turn eighteen or we procure a permanent sponsor willing to falsify your identification. Make no mistake about it: What we do here is highly illegal, but that does not mean we don't follow the rule of law. *My* law."

He pauses, making eye contact with as many kids as he can. Perhaps it's his goal to memorize each and every face before his speech is done. His eyes are sharp, his focus intense. Risa believes he can know each of them just by a single sustained glance. It's intimidating and reassuring at the same time. No one will fall between the cracks in the Admiral's world.

"All of you were marked for unwinding yet managed to escape, and, through the help of my many associates, you have found your way here. I don't care who you were. I don't care who you'll be when you leave here. All I care about is who you are while you're here—and while you're here, you will do what is expected of you."

A hand goes up in the crowd. It's Connor. Risa wishes it wasn't. The Admiral takes time to study Connor's face before saying, "Yes?"

"So . . . who are you, exactly?"

"My name is my business. Suffice it to say that I am a former admiral of the United States Navy." And then he grinned. "But now you could say I'm a fish out of water. The current political climate led to my resignation. The law said it was my job to look the other way, but I did not. I will not." Then he turns to the crowd and says loudly, "No one gets unwound on my watch."

Cheers from all those assembled, including the khaki kids that were already a part of his little army. The Admiral gives a wide grin. His smile shows a set of perfectly straight, perfectly white teeth. It's a strange disconnect, because, while his teeth are sparkling, the rest of him seems worn down to the nub.

"We are a community here. You will learn the rules and you will follow them, or you will face the consequences, as in any society. This is not a democracy; it is a dictatorship. I am your dictator. This is a matter of necessity. It is the most effective way to keep you hidden, healthy, and whole." Then he gives that smile again. "I like to believe I am a benevolent dictator, but you can make that judgment for yourselves."

By now, his gaze has traveled over the entire crowd. All of them feel as though they have been scanned like groceries at a checkout counter. Scanned and processed.

"Tonight you will all sleep in the newcomers' quarters. Tomorrow your skills will be assessed, and you'll be assigned to your permanent squads. Congratulations. You've arrived!"

He takes a moment to let that last thought sink in, then he returns to his golf cart and is spirited off, with the same cloud of red dust billowing behind him.

"Is there still time to get back into the crate?" some wiseguy says. A bunch of kids laugh.

"All right, listen up," yells the megaphone kid. "We're going to walk you to the supply jet, where you'll get clothes, rations, and everything else you'll need." They are quick to find out that the megaphone kid has earned the nickname "Amp." As for the Admiral's driver, he's been stuck with "Jeeves."

"It's a long walk," Amp says. "If anyone can't make it, let us know. Anyone who needs water now, raise your hand."

Nearly every hand goes up.

"All right, line up here."

Risa lines up along with the rest of them. There's buzzing

and whispering from the line of kids, but it's nowhere near as desperate as it had been in the weeks past. Now, it's more like the buzz of kids in a school lunch line.

As they're led off to be clothed and fed, the jet that brought them here is towed to its final resting place in the massive junkyard. Only now does Risa take a deep breath and release it, along with a month's worth of tension. Only now does she allow herself the wonderful luxury of hope.

# 29 · Lev

More than a thousand miles away, Lev is about to arrive as well. The destination, however, is not his own: It's Cyrus Finch's. Joplin, Missouri. "Home of the Joplin High Eagles— reigning state champions in girls' basketball," CyFi says.

"You know a lot about the place."

"I don't know anything about it," CyFi grumbles. "*He* knows. Or *knew*. Or whatever."

Their journey has gotten no easier. Sure, they have money now, thanks to Lev's "deal" at that pawnshop, but the money's only good for buying food. It can't get them train tickets, or even bus tickets, because there's nothing more suspicious than underage kids paying their own fare.

For all intents and purposes, things between Lev and CyFi are the same, with one major, unspoken exception. CyFi might still be playing the role of leader, but it's Lev who is now in charge. There's a guilty pleasure in knowing that CyFi would fall apart if Lev weren't there to hold him together.

With Joplin only twenty miles away, Cy's twitching gets bad enough that even walking is difficult for him. It's more than just twitching now—it's a shuddering that wracks his body like a seizure, leaving him shivering. Lev offers him his jacket, but Cy just swats him away. "I ain't cold! It's not about bein' cold! It's about being wrong. It's about there being oil and water in this brain of mine."

Exactly what Cy must do when he gets to Joplin is a mystery to Lev—and now he realizes that Cy doesn't know either. Whatever this kid—or this *bit* of kid—in his head is compelling him to do, it's completely beyond Cy's understanding. Lev can only hope that it's something purposeful, and not something destructive . . . although Lev can't help but suspect that whatever the kid wants, it's bad. Really bad.

"Why are you still with me, Fry?" CyFi asks after one of his body-shaking seizures. "Any sane dude woulda taken off days ago."

"Who says I'm sane?"

"Oh, you're sane, Fry. You're so sane, you scare me. You're so sane, it's *in*sane."

Lev thinks for a while. He wants to give Cyrus a real answer, not just something that chases away the question. "I'm staying," Lev says slowly, "because someone has to witness what happens in Joplin. Someone's got to understand why you did it. Whatever it is."

"Yeah," says CyFi. "I need a witness. That's it."

"You're like a salmon swimming upstream," Lev offers. "It's inside you to do it. And it's inside me to help you get there."

"Salmon." Cy looks thoughtful. "I once saw this poster about a salmon. It was jumping up this waterfall, see? But there was a bear at the top, and the fish, it was jumping right into the bear's mouth. The caption beneath— it was supposed to be funny—said, 'The journey of a thousand miles sometimes ends very, very badly.'"

"There's no bear in Joplin," Lev tells him. He doesn't try to cheer Cy up with any more analogies, because Cy's so smart, he can find a way to make anything sound bad. One hundred and thirty IQ points all focused on cooking up doom. Lev can't hope to compete with that.

The days go by, mile by mile, town by town, until the afternoon they pass a sign that says, NOW ENTERING JOPLIN. POPULATION 45,504.

# 30 · Cy-Ty

There is no peace in CyFi's his head. The Fry doesn't know how bad it is. The Fry doesn't know how the feelings crash over him like storm-driven waves pounding a failing seawall. The wall is going to collapse soon, and when it does, Cy will lose it. He'll lose everything. His mind will spill out of his ears and down the drains of the streets of Joplin. He knows it.

Then he sees the sign. NOW ENTERING JOPLIN. His heart is his own, but it pounds in his chest, threatening to burst—and wouldn't that be a fine thing? They'd rush him to a hospital, give him someone else's ticker, and he'd have *that* kid to deal with too.

This boy in the corner of his head doesn't talk to him in words. He *feels*. He *emotes*. He doesn't understand that he's only a part of another kid. It's like how in a dream you know some things, and other things you should know, but you don't. This kid—he knows where he is, but he doesn't know he's not all here. He doesn't know he's part of someone else now. He keeps looking for things in Cyrus's head that just aren't there. Memories. Connections. He keeps looking for words, but Cyrus's brain codes words differently. And so the kid hurls out anger. Terror. Grief. Waves pounding the wall, and beneath it all, there's a current tugging Cy forward. Something must be done here. Only the kid knows what it is.

"Would it help to have a map?" asks the Fry. The question

gets Cy mad. "Map won't help me," he says. "I need to see stuff. I need to *be* places. A map is just a map. It ain't *being* there."

They stand at a corner on the outskirts of Joplin. It's like divining for water. Nothing looks familiar. "He doesn't know this place," Cy says. "Let's try another street."

Block after block, intersection after intersection, it's the same. Nothing. Joplin is a small town, but not so small that a person could know all of it. Then, at last they get to a main street. There are shops and restaurants up and down the road. It's just like any other town this size, but—

"Wait!"

"What is it?"

"He knows this street," says Cy. "There! That ice cream shop. I can taste pumpkin ice cream. I hate pumpkin ice cream."

"I'll bet *he* didn't."

Cyrus nods. "It was his favorite. The loser." He points a finger at the ice cream shop and slowly swings his arm to the left. "He comes walking from that direction. . . ." He swings his arm to the right. "And when he's done, he goes that way."

"So, do we track where he comes from, or where he goes?"

Cy chooses to go left but finds himself at Joplin High, home of the Eagles. He gets an image of a sword, and instantly knows. "Fencing. The kid was on the fencing team here."

"Swords are shiny," the Fry notes. Cy would throw him a dirty look if he weren't right on target. Swords are, indeed, shiny. He wonders if the kid ever stole swords, and realizes that, yes, he probably did. Stealing the swords of opposing teams is a time-honored tradition of fencing.

"This way," says the Fry, taking the lead. "He must have gone from school, to the ice cream shop, to home. Home is where we're going, right?"

The answer comes to Cy as an urge deep in his brain that shoots straight to his gut. Salmon? More like a swordfish twisting on a line, and that line is pulling him relentlessly toward . . . "Home," says Cy. "Right."

It's twilight now. Kids are out in the street; half the cars have headlights on. As far as anyone knows, they're just two neighborhood kids, headed wherever neighborhood kids go. No one seems to notice them. But there's a police car a block away. It was parked, but now it begins moving.

They pass the ice cream parlor, and as they do, Cyrus can feel the change inside him. It's in his walk, and in the way he holds himself. It's in all the tension points of his face: They're changing. His eyebrows lower, his jaw opens slightly. *I'm not myself. That other kid is taking over.* Should Cy let it happen, or should he fight it? But he knows it's already past the point of fighting. The only way to finish this is to let it happen.

"Cy," says the kid next to him.

Cy looks at him, and although part of him knows it's just Lev, another part of him panics. He instantly knows why. He closes his eyes for a moment and tries to convince the kid in his head that the Fry is a friend, not a threat. The kid seems to get it, and his panic drops a notch.

Cy reaches a corner and turns left like he's done it a hundred times. The rest of him shudders as he tries to keep up with his determined temporal lobe. Now a feeling comes on him. Nervous, annoyed. He knows he must find a way to translate it into words.

"I'm gonna be late. They're gonna be so mad. They're always so mad."

"Late for what?"

"Dinner. They gotta eat it right on time, or I get hell for it. They could eat it without me, but they won't. They don't. They just stew. And the food goes cold. And it's my fault, my fault, always my fault. So I gotta sit there and they ask me how was my day? Fine. What did I learn? Nothing. What did I do wrong this time? Everything." It's not his voice. It's his vocal chords, but it's not his voice coming out of them. Same tones, but different inflections. A different accent. Like the way he might have talked if he came from Joplin, home of the Eagles.

As they turn another corner, Cy catches sight of that cop car again. It's behind them, following slowly. No mistake about it: It's following. And that's not all. There's another police car up ahead, but that one's just waiting in front of a house. His house. *My house.* Cy is the salmon after all, and that police car is the bear. But even so, he can't stop. He's got to get to that house or die trying.

As he nears the front walk, two men get out of a familiar Toyota parked across the street. It's the dads. They look at him, relief in their faces, but also pain. So they knew where he was coming. They must have known all along.

"Cyrus," one of them calls. He wants to run to them. He wants them to just take him home, but he stops himself. He can't go home. Not yet. They both stride toward him, getting in his path, but smart enough not to get in his face.

"I gotta do this," he says in a voice he knows isn't his at all.

That's when the police leap from their cars and grab him. They're too strong for him to fight them off, so he looks at the dads. "I gotta do this," he says again. "Don't be the bear."

They look at each other, not understanding what he means—but then, maybe they do, because they step aside and say to the cops, "Let him go."

"This is Lev," Cyrus says, amazed that the Fry is willing to risk his own safety to stand by Cy now. "Nobody bothers him, either." The dads take a brief moment to acknowledge the Fry, but quickly return their attention to Cyrus.

The cops frisk Cy to make sure he has no weapon, and,

satisfied, they let him go on toward the house. But there *is* a weapon. It's something sharp and heavy. Right now it's just in a corner of his mind, but in a few moments it won't be. And now Cy's scared, but he can't stop.

There's a police officer at the front door talking in hushed tones to a man and a woman standing at the threshold. They glance nervously at Cy.

The part of Cy that isn't Cy knows this middle-aged couple so well, he's hit by a lightning bolt of emotions so violent he feels like he'll incinerate.

As he walks toward the door, the flagstone path seems to undulate beneath his feet like a fun-house floor. Then finally he's standing before them. The couple look scared—horrified. Part of him is happy at that, part of him sad, and part of him wishes he could be anyplace else in the world, but he no longer knows which part is which.

He opens his mouth to speak, trying to translate the feelings into words.

"Give it!" he demands. "Give it to me, Mom. Give it to me, Dad."

The woman covers her mouth and turns away. She presses out tears like she's a sponge in a fist.

"Tyler?" says the man. "Tyler, is that you?"

It's the first time Cyrus has a name to go with that part of him. *Tyler. Yes. I'm Cyrus, but I'm also Tyler. I'm Cy-Ty.*

"Hurry!" Cy-Ty says. "Give it to me—I need it now!"

"What? Tyler," says the woman through her tears, "What do you want from us?"

Cy-Ty tries to say it, but he can't get the word. He can't even get the image straight. It's a thing. A weapon. Still the image won't come, but the action does. He's miming something. He leans forward, puts one arm in front of the other. He's holding something long, angling it down. He thrusts both arms lower. And now he knows it's not a weapon he seeks, it's a tool. Because he understands the action he's miming. He's digging.

"Shovel!" he says with a breath of relief. "I need the shovel."

The man and woman look at each other. The policeman beside them nods, and the man says, "It's out in the shed."

Cy-Ty makes a beeline through the house and out the back door with everyone following behind him: the couple, the cops, the dads, and the Fry. He heads straight for the shed, grabs the shovel—he knew exactly where it was—and heads toward a corner of the yard, where some twigs stick out of the ground.

The twigs have been tied to form lopsided crosses.

Cy-Ty knows this corner of the yard. He feels this place in his gut. This is where he buried his pets. He doesn't know their names, or even what kind of animals they were, but he suspects one of them was an Irish setter. He gets images of what happened to each of them. One met up with a pack of wild dogs. Another with a bus. The third, old age. He takes the shovel and thrusts it into the ground, but not near any of their graves. He'd never disturb them. Never. Instead, he presses his shovel into the soft earth two yards behind the graves.

He grunts with every thrust of the shovel, hurling the dirt wildly to the side. Then, at just about two feet down, the shovel hits something with a dull thud. He drops to all fours and begins scooping out the earth with his hands.

With the dirt cleared away, he reaches in, grabs a handle, and tugs, tugs, tugs until it comes up. He's holding a briefcase that's waterlogged and covered with mud. He puts it on the ground, flicks open the latches, and opens it.

The moment he sees what's inside, Cy-Ty's entire brain

seizes. He's frozen in a total system lockup. He can't move, can't think. Because it's all so bright, so shiny in the slanted red rays of the sun. There are so many pretty things to look at, he can't move. But he must move. He must finish this.

He digs both of his hands into the jewelry-filled briefcase, feeling the fine gold chains slide over his hands, hearing the rattle of metal against metal. There are diamonds and rubies, zircons and plastic. The priceless and the worthless, all mixed in together. He doesn't remember where or when he stole any of it, he only knows that he did. He stole it, hoarded it, and hid it. Put it in its own little grave, to dig up when he needed it. But if he can give it back, then maybe . . .

With hands tangled in gold chains more binding than the handcuffs on the policemen's belts, he stumbles toward the man and woman. Bits and pieces, rings and pins fall from the tangled bundle into the brush of the yard. They slip through his fingers, but still he holds on to what he can until he's there in front of the man and woman, who now hold each other as if cowering in the path of a tornado. Then he falls to his knees, drops the bundle of shiny things at their feet, and, rocking back and forth, makes a desperate plea.

"Please," he says. "I'm sorry. I'm sorry. I didn't mean it."

"Please," he says, "Take it. I don't need it. I don't want it."

"Please," he says. "Do anything. *But don't unwind me.*"

And all at once Cy realizes that Tyler doesn't know. The part of that boy which comprehends time and place isn't here, and never will be. Tyler can't understand that he's already gone, and nothing Cy can do will ever make him understand. So he goes on wailing.

"Please don't unwind me. I'll do anything. Please don't unwind me. *Pleeeeeeeease . . .*"

Then, behind him, he hears a voice.

# 31 · Lev

"Tell him what he needs to hear!" Lev says. He stands there with such wrath in him he feels the earth itself will split from his anger. He told Cy he'd witness this. But he can't witness it and not take action.

Tyler's parents still huddle together, comforting each other instead of comforting Cy. It makes Lev even more furious.

"TELL HIM YOU WON'T UNWIND HIM!" he screams.

The man and woman just look at him like stupid rabbits. So he grabs the shovel from the ground and swings it back over his shoulder like a baseball bat. "TELL HIM YOU WON'T UNWIND HIM, OR I SWEAR I'LL BASH YOUR WORTH-LESS HEADS IN!" He's never spoken like this to anyone. He's never threatened anyone. And he knows it's not just a threat—he'll do it. Today, he'll hit a grand slam if he has to.

The cops reach for their holsters and pull out their guns, but Lev doesn't care.

"Drop the shovel!" one of them yells. His gun is trained at Lev's chest, but Lev won't drop it. *Let him shoot. If he does, I'll still get in one good swing at Tyler's parents before I go down. I might die, but at least I'll take one of them with me.* In his whole life, he's never felt like this before. He's never felt this close to exploding.

"TELL HIM! TELL HIM NOW!"

Everything freezes in the stand-off: the cops and their guns, Lev and his shovel. Then finally the man and woman end it. They look down at the boy rocking back and forth, sob-bing over the random pieces of tangled jewelry he's spread at their feet.

"We won't unwind you, Tyler."

"PROMISE HIM!"

"We won't unwind you, Tyler. We promise. We promise."

Cy's shoulders relax, and although he still cries, they're no longer sobs of desperation. They're sobs of relief.

"Thank you," Cy says. "Thank you . . ."

Lev drops the shovel, the cops lower their guns, and the tearful couple escape toward the safety of their home. Cyrus's dads are there to fill the void. They help Cyrus up and hold him tight.

"It's all right, Cyrus. Everything's going to be okay."

And through his sobs, Cy says, "I know. It's all good now. It's all good."

That's when Lev takes off. He knows he's the only variable in this equation left to resolve, and in a moment the cops are going to realize that. So he backs into the shadows while the officers are still distracted by the scurrying couple, and the crying kid, and the two dads, and the shiny things on the ground. Then, once he's in the shadows, he turns and runs. In a few moments they'll know he's gone, but a few moments is all he needs. Because he's fast. He's always been fast. He's through the bushes, into the next yard, and onto another street in ten seconds.

The look on Cy's face as he dropped the jewelry at the feet of those horrible, horrible people, and the way they acted, as if *they* were the ones being victimized—these things will stay with Lev for the rest of his life. He knows he's been changed by this moment, transformed in some deep and frightening way. Wherever his journey now takes him, it doesn't matter, because he has already arrived there in his heart. He's become like that briefcase in the ground— full of gems yet void of light, so nothing sparkles, nothing shines.

The last bit of daylight is gone from the sky now; the only color left is dark blue fading to black. The streetlights have not yet come on, so Lev dodges through endless shades of pitch. The better to run. The better to hide. The better to lose himself now that darkness is his friend.

# Part Five

# Graveyard

*[Southwest Arizona] serves as an ideal graveyard for airplanes. It has a dry, clear and virtually smog-free climate that helps minimize corrosion. It has an alkaline soil so firm that airplanes can be towed and parked on the surface without sinking. . . .*

*An airplane graveyard is not just a fence around airplane carcasses and piles of scrap metal. Rather, many millions of dollars' worth of surplus parts are salvaged to keep active aircraft flying. . . .*

—JOE ZENTNER, *"Airplane Graveyards," desertusa.com*

# 32 · The Admiral

The blazing sun bakes the Arizona hardpan by day, and the temperature plunges at night. More than four thousand planes from every era of aviation history shine in the heat of that sun. From cruising altitude, the rows of planes look like crop lines, a harvest of abandoned technology.

#1) YOU ARRIVED HERE BY NECESSITY. YOU STAY HERE BY CHOICE.

From way up there you can't see that some of those grounded jets are occupied. Thirty-three, to be exact. Spy satellites can catch the activity, but catching it and noticing it are two different things. CIA data analysts have far more pressing things to look for than a band of refugee Unwinds. This is what the Admiral's counting on—but just in case, the rules in the Graveyard are strict. All activity takes place in the fuselage or under the wings, unless it's absolutely necessary to go out into the open. The heat helps enforce the edict.

#2) SURVIVING HAS EARNED YOU THE RIGHT TO BE RESPECTED.

The Admiral doesn't exactly own the Graveyard, but his management is undisputed, and he answers to no one but himself. A combination of business sense, favors owed, and a military willing to do anything to get rid of him are what made such a sweet deal possible.

#3) MY WAY IS THE ONLY WAY.

The Graveyard is a thriving business. The Admiral buys decommissioned airplanes and sells the parts, or even resells them whole. Most business is done online; the Admiral is able to acquire about one retired jet a month. Of course, each one arrives loaded with a secret cargo of Unwinds. That's the real business of the Graveyard, and business has been good.

#4) YOUR LIFE IS MY GIFT TO YOU. TREAT IT LIKE ONE.

Buyers do, on occasion, come to inspect or to pick up merchandise, but there's always plenty of warning. From the time they enter the gate, it's five miles to the yard itself. It gives the kids more than enough time to disappear like gremlins into the machinery. These types of business-related visitors come only about once a week. There are people who wonder what the Admiral does with all the rest of his time. He tells them he's building a wildlife preserve.

#5) YOU ARE BETTER THAN THOSE WHO WOULD UNWIND YOU. RISE TO THE OCCASION.

There are only three adults in the Admiral's employ; two office workers stationed in a trailer far from the Unwinds, and a helicopter pilot. The pilot goes by the name of Cleaver, and he has two jobs. The first is to tour important buyers around the lot in style. The second is to take the Admiral on trips around the Graveyard once a week. Cleaver is the only employee who knows about the hoard of Unwinds sequestered in the far reaches of the lot. He knows, but he's paid more than enough to keep quiet; and besides, the Admiral trusts Cleaver implicitly. One must trust one's personal pilot.

#6) EVERYONE IN THE GRAVEYARD CONTRIBUTES. NO EXCEPTIONS.

The real work in the yard is done by the Unwinds. There are whole teams specially designated to strip the jets, sort parts, and get them ready for sale. It's just like any other junkyard, but on a larger scale. Not all the jets get stripped. Some remain untouched, if the Admiral thinks he can resell them whole. Some are retooled as living quarters for the kids who are, both literally and figuratively, under his wing.

#7) TEENAGE REBELLION IS FOR SUBURBAN SCHOOLCHILDREN. GET OVER IT.

The kids are grouped in teams best suited for their jobs, their ages, and their personal needs. A lifetime of experience molding military boeufs into a coherent fighting force has prepared the Admiral for creating a functional society out of angry, troubled kids.

#8) HORMONES WILL NOT RULE MY DESERT.

Girls are never grouped with boys.

#9) AT EIGHTEEN YOU CEASE TO BE MY CONCERN.

The Admiral has a list of his ten supreme rules, posted in each and every plane where kids live and work. The kids call them "The Ten Demandments." He doesn't care what they call them, as long as each and every one of them knows the list by heart.

#10) MAKE SOMETHING OF YOURSELF. THIS IS AN ORDER.

It's a challenge keeping almost four hundred kids healthy, hidden, and whole. But the Admiral has never walked away from a challenge. And his motivation for doing this, like his name, is something he prefers to keep to himself.

# 33 · Risa

For Risa, the first days in the Graveyard are harsh and seem to last forever. Her residency begins with an exercise in humility.

Every new arrival is required to face a tribunal: three seventeen-year-olds sitting behind a desk in the gutted shell of a wide-bodied jet. Two boys and a girl. These three, together with Amp and Jeeves, who Risa met when she first stepped off the plane, make up the elite group of five everyone calls "the Goldens." They're the Admiral's five most trusted kids—and therefore the ones in charge.

By the time they get to Risa, they've already processed forty kids.

"Tell us about yourself," says the boy on the right. Starboard Boy, she calls him, since, after all, they're in a vessel. "What do you know, and what can you do?"

The last tribunal Risa faced was back at StaHo, when she was sentenced to be unwound. She can tell these three are bored and don't care what she says, just as long as they can get on to the next one. She finds herself hating them, just as she hated the headmaster that day he tried to explain why her membership in the human race had been revoked.

The girl, who sits in the middle, must read her feelings, because she smiles and says, "Don't worry, this isn't a test—we just want to help you find where you'll fit in here." It's an odd thing to say, since not fitting in is every Unwind's problem.

Risa takes a deep breath. "I was a music student at StaHo," she says, then immediately regrets telling them she's from a state home. Even among Unwinds there's prejudice and pecking orders. Sure enough, Starboard leans back, crossing his arms in clear disapproval, but the port-side boy says: "I'm a Ward too. Florida StaHo 18."

"Ohio 23."

"What instrument do you play?" the girl asks.

"Classical piano."

"Sorry," says Starboard. "We've got enough musicians, and none of the planes came with a piano."

"'Survival has earned me the right to be respected,'" Risa says. "Isn't that one of the Admiral's rules? I don't think he'd like your attitude."

Starboard squirms. "Can we just get on with this?"

The girl offers an apologetic grin. "As much as I hate to admit it, in the here and now, there are other things we need before a virtuoso. What else can you do?"

"Just give me a job and I'll do it," Risa says, trying to get this over with. "That's what you're going to do anyway, right?"

"Well, they always need help in the galley," says Starboard. "Especially after meals."

The girl gives Risa a long, pleading look, perhaps hoping that Risa will come up with something better for herself, but all Risa says is "Fine. Dishwasher. Am I done here?"

She turns to leave, doing her best to douse her disgust. The next kid comes in as she's heading out. He looks awful. His nose is swollen and purple. His shirt is caked with dried blood, and both his nostrils have started bleeding fresh.

"What happened to you?"

He looks at her, sees who it is, and says, "Your boyfriend—that's what happened to me. And he's gonna pay."

Risa could ask him a dozen questions about that, but the kid's bleeding all over his shirt, and the first priority is to stop it. He tips his head back.

"No," Risa tells him. "Lean forward, otherwise you'll gag on your own blood."

The kid listens. The tribunal of three come out from behind their desk to see what they can do, but Risa has it under control.

"Pinch it like this," she tells him. "You need to be patient with this kind of thing." She shows the kid exactly how to pinch his nose to stem the flow of blood. Then, once the bleeding stops, Port-side comes over to her and says, "Nice work."

She's immediately promoted from dishwasher to medic. Funny, but it's indirectly Connor's doing, since he's the one who broke that kid's nose in the first place.

As for the kid with the bloody nose, he gets assigned to dish washing.

The first few days, actually trying to act like a medic without any real training is terrifying. There are other kids in the medical jet who seem to know a lot more, but she quickly comes to realize they were thrown into this just like she was, when they first arrived.

"You'll do fine. You're a natural," the senior medic, who is all of seventeen, tells her. He's right. Once she gets used to the idea, handling first aid, standard illnesses, and even suturing simple wounds becomes as familiar to her as playing the piano. The days begin to pass quickly, and before she realizes it, she's been there a month. Each day that goes by adds to her sense of security. The Admiral was an odd bird, but he'd done something no one else had been able to do for her since she'd left StaHo. He'd given her back her right to exist.

# 34 · Connor

Like Risa, Connor finds his niche by accident. Connor never considered himself mechanically capable, but there are few things he can stand less than a bunch of morons standing around looking at something that doesn't work and wondering who's going to fix it. During that first week, while Risa's off learning how to be an exceptionally good fake doctor, Connor decides to figure out the workings of a fried air-conditioning unit, then find replacement parts from one of the junk piles and get it working again.

He soon comes to realize it's the same way with every other broken thing he comes across. Sure, it began with trial and error, but the errors become fewer and fewer as the days go by. There are plenty of other kids who claim to be mechanics, and are really good at explaining why things won't work.

Connor, on the other hand, actually fixes them.

It quickly gets him reassigned from trash duty to the repair crew, and since there are endless things to repair, it keeps his mind off of other things . . . such as how little he gets to see Risa in the Admiral's tightly structured world . . . and how quickly Roland is advancing through the social ranks of the place.

Roland has managed to get himself one of the best assignments in the Graveyard. By working the angles and applying plenty of flattery, he's been taken on as the pilot's assistant. Mostly, he just keeps the helicopter cleaned and fueled, but the assignment reeks of an apprenticeship.

"He's teaching me how to fly it," he overhears Roland tell a bunch of other kids one day. Connor shudders to think of Roland behind the controls of a helicopter, but many kids are impressed by Roland. His age gives him seniority, and his manipulations gain him either fear or respect from a surprising number of others. Roland draws his negative energy from the kids around him, and there are a lot of kids here for him to draw from.

Social manipulation is not one of Connor's strengths. Even among his own team, he's a bit of a mystery. Kids know not to tread on him, because he has a low tolerance for irritation and idiocy. But there's no one they'd rather have on their side than Connor.

"People like you because you've got integrity," Hayden tells him. "Even when you're being an ass."

Connor has to laugh at that. Him? Integrity? There have been plenty of people in Connor's life who would think differently. But on the other hand, he's changing. He's been getting into fewer fights. Maybe it's because there's more room to breathe here than in the warehouse. Or maybe he's been working out his brain enough for it to successfully muscle his impulses into line. A lot of that has to do with Risa, because every time he forces himself to think before acting, it's her voice in his head telling him to slow down. He wants to tell her, but she's always so busy in the medical jet—and you don't just go to somebody and say, "I'm a better person because you're in my head."

She's also still in Roland's head, and that worries Connor. At first Risa had been a tool to provoke Connor into a fight, but now Roland sees her as a prize. Now, instead of using brute strength against her he tries to charm her at every turn.

"You're not actually falling for him, are you?" he asks her one day, on one of the rare occasions he can get her alone.

"I'll pretend you didn't just ask that," she tells him in disgust. But Connor has reasons to wonder.

"On that first night here, he offered you his blanket, and you accepted it," he points out.

"Only because I knew it would make him cold."

"And when he offers you his food, you take it."

"Because it means he goes hungry."

It's coolly logical. Connor finds it amazing that she can put her emotions aside and be as calculating as Roland, beating him at his own game. Another reason for Connor to admire her.

"Work call!"

It happens about once a week beneath the meeting canopy—the only structure in the entire graveyard that isn't part of a plane, and the only place large enough to gather all 423 kids. Work call. A chance to get out into the real world. A chance to have a life. Sort of.

The Admiral never attends, but there are video feeds from the meeting canopy, just as there are feeds all over the yard, so everyone knows he's watching. Whether or not every camera is constantly monitored, no one knows, but the potential for being seen is always there. Connor did not care for the Admiral the first day he met him. The sight of all those video cameras shortly thereafter made Connor like him even less. It seems each day there's something to add to his general feeling of disgust with the man.

Amp leads the work call meeting with his megaphone and clipboard. "A man in Oregon needs a team of five to clear cut a few acres of forest," Amp announces. "You'll be given room and board, and taught to use the tools of the trade. The job should take a few months, and at the end you'll get new identities. Eighteen-year-old identities."

Amp doesn't let them know the salary, because there is none. The Admiral gets paid, though. He gets paid a purchase price.

"Any takers?"

There are always takers. Sure enough, more than a dozen hands go up. Sixteen-year-olds, mostly. Seventeens are too close to eighteen to make it worth their while, and younger kids are too intimidated by the prospect.

"Report to the Admiral after this meeting. He'll make the final decision as to who goes."

Work call infuriates Connor. He never puts his hand up, even if it's something he might actually want to do. "The Admiral's using us," he says to the kids around him. "Don't you see that?"

Most of the kids just shrug, but Hayden's there, and he never misses an opportunity to add his peculiar wisdom to a situation. "I'd rather be used whole than in pieces," Hayden says.

Amp looks at his clipboard and holds up the megaphone again. "Housecleaning services," he says. "Three are needed, female preferred. No false IDs, but the location is secure and remote—which means you'll be safe from the Juvey-cops until you turn eighteen."

Connor won't even look. "Please tell me no one raised their hand."

"About six girls—all seventeen years old, it looks like," says Hayden. "I guess no one wants to be a house-girl for more than a year."

"This place isn't a refuge, it's a slave market. Why doesn't anyone see that?"

"Who says they don't see it? It's just that unwinding makes slavery look good. It's always the lesser of two evils."

"I don't see why there have to be any evils at all."

As the meeting breaks up, Connor feels a hand on his shoulder. He thinks it must be a friend, but it's not. It's Roland. It's such a surprise, it takes Connor a moment before he reacts. He shakes Roland's hand off. "Something you want?"

"Just to talk."

"Don't you have a helicopter to wash?"

Roland smiles at that. "Less washing, more flying. Cleaver made me his unofficial copilot."

"Cleaver must have a death wish." Connor doesn't know who he's more disgusted with: Roland, or the pilot for being suckered in by him.

Roland looks around at the thinning crowd. "The Admiral's got some racket going here, doesn't he?" he says. "Most of the losers here don't care. But it bothers you, doesn't it?"

"Your point?"

"Just that you're not the only one who thinks the Admiral needs some . . . retraining."

Connor doesn't like where this is going. "What I think of the Admiral is my business."

206

"Of course it is. Have you seen his teeth, by the way?"

"What about them?"

"Pretty obvious that they're not his. I hear he keeps a picture of the kid he got them from in his office. An Unwind like us, who, thanks to him, never made it to eighteen. Makes you wonder how much more of him comes from us. Makes you wonder if there's anything left of the original Admiral at all."

This is too much information to process here and now—and considering the source, Connor doesn't want to process it at all. But he knows he will.

"Roland, let me make this as clear to you as I can. I don't trust you. I don't like you. I don't want to have anything to do with you."

"I can't stand you, either," Roland says, then he points to the Admiral's jet. "But right now, we've got the same enemy."

Roland strolls off before anyone else can take notice of their conversation, leaving Connor with a heaviness in his stomach. The very idea that he and Roland could in any way be on the same side makes him feel like he swallowed something rancid.

For a week the seed that Roland planted in Connor's brain grows. It's fertile ground, because Connor already distrusted the Admiral. Now, every time he sees the man, Connor notices something. His teeth *are* perfect. They're not the teeth of an aging war veteran. The way he looks at people—looking into their eyes—it's as if he were sizing those eyes up, looking for a pair that might suit him. And those kids that disappear on work calls—since they never come back, who's to know where they really go? Who's to say they don't all get sent off to be unwound? The Admiral says his goal is to save Unwinds, but what if he's got an entirely different agenda? These thoughts keep Connor awake at night, but he won't share them with anyone, because once he does, it aligns him with Roland. And that's an alliance he never wants to make.

During their fourth week in the Graveyard, while Connor is still building his case against the Admiral in his own mind, a plane arrives. It's the first one since the old FedEx jet that brought them here, and like that jet, this one is packed full of live cargo. While the five Goldens march the new arrivals from their jet, Connor works on a faulty generator. He watches them with mild interest as they pass, wondering if any of them would be more mechanically skilled than him and bump him into a less enviable position.

Then, toward the back of the line of kids is a face he thinks he recognizes. Someone from home? No. Someone else. All at once it comes to him who this is. It's the boy he was sure had been unwound weeks ago. It's the kid he kidnapped for his own good. It's Lev!

Connor drops his wrench and runs toward him, but gains control before he gets there, burying his mixed flood of feelings beneath a calm saunter. This is the kid who betrayed him. This is the kid he once swore he'd never forgive. And yet the thought of him unwound had been too much to bear. But Lev hasn't been unwound—he's right here, marching off to the supply jet. Connor is thrilled. Connor is furious.

Lev doesn't see him yet—and that's fine, because it gives Connor some time to take in what he sees. This is no longer the clean-cut tithe he pulled out of his parents' car more than two months before. This kid has long, unkempt hair and a hardened look about him. This kid isn't in tithing whites but wears torn jeans and a dirty red T-shirt. Connor wants to let him pass, just so he can have time to process this new image, but Lev sees him, and gives him a grin right away. This is also different—because during that brief time they knew each other, Lev had never been pleased by Connor's presence.

Lev steps toward him.

"Stay in line!" orders Amp. "The supply jet's this way."

But Connor waves Amp off. "It's okay—I know this one."

Amp reluctantly gives in. "Make sure he gets to the supply jet." Then he returns to herding the others.

"So, how are things?" says Lev. Just like that. How are things. You'd think they were buds back from summer vacation.

Connor knows what he has to do. It's the only thing that will ever make things right between him and Lev. Once again, it's instinctive action without time for thought. Instinctive, not irrational. Impassioned, but not impulsive. Connor has come to know the difference.

He hauls off and punches Lev in the eye. Not hard enough to knock him down, but hard enough to snap his head halfway around and give him a nasty shiner. Before Lev can react, Connor says, *"That's* for what you did to us." Then, before Lev can respond, he does something else sudden and unexpected. He pulls Lev toward him and hugs him tightly—the way he hugged his own little brother last year when he took first place in the district pentathlon. "I'm really, *really* glad you're alive, Lev."

"Yeah. Me, too."

He lets Lev go before it starts feeling awkward, and when he does, he can see Lev's eye is already beginning to swell. And an idea occurs to him. "C'mon—I'll take you over to the medical jet. I know someone who'll take care of that eye."

It isn't until later that night that Connor gets an inkling of how much Lev has truly changed. Connor is shaken awake sometime during the night. He opens his eyes to a flashlight shining in his face, so close the light hurts.

"Hey! What is this?"

"Shhh," says a voice behind the flashlight. "It's Lev."

Lev should have been in the newcomers' jet—that's where all the kids go until they get sorted into their teams. There are strict orders that no one is to be out at night. Apparently Lev is no longer a boy bound by rules.

"What are you doing here?" Connor says. "Do you know the trouble you could be in?" He still can't see Lev's face behind that flashlight.

"You hit me this afternoon," says Lev.

"I hit you because I owed that to you."

"I know. I deserved it, and so it's okay," says Lev. "But don't you *ever* hit me again, or you'll regret it."

Although Connor has no intention of ever punching Lev out again, he does not respond well to ultimatums.

"I'll hit you," says Connor, "if you deserve it."

Silence from behind the flashlight. Then Lev says, "Fair enough. But you better make sure that I do."

The light goes off. Lev leaves, but Connor can't sleep. Every Unwind has a story you don't want to know. He supposes that Lev now has his.

The Admiral calls for Connor two days later. Apparently he has something in need of repair. His residence is an old 747 that was used as Air Force One years before any of the kids here were born. The engines had been removed and the presidential seal painted over, but you could still see a shadow of the emblem beneath the paint.

Connor climbs the stairs with a bag of tools, hoping that whatever it is, he can get in and out quickly. Like everyone else, he has a morbid curiosity about the man, and he wonders what an old presidential jet looks like on the inside. But being under the Admiral's scrutiny scares the hell out of him.

He steps through the hatch to find a couple of kids tidying up. They're younger kids that Connor doesn't know; he thought the Goldens might be in here, but they're nowhere to be seen. As for the jet, it's not nearly as luxurious as Connor had expected. The leather seats have tears, the carpet is almost worn through. It looks more like an old motor home than Air Force One.

"Where's the Admiral?"

The Admiral steps out from the deeper recesses of the jet. Although Connor's eyes are still adjusting to the light, he can see the Admiral is holding a weapon. "Connor! I'm glad you could make it." Connor winces at the sight of the gun—and at the realization the Admiral knows him by name.

"What do you need that for?" Connor asks, pointing at the gun.

"Just cleaning it," says the Admiral. Connor wonders why he would still have a clip in a gun he was cleaning, but decides it's best not to ask. The Admiral puts the gun into a drawer and locks it. Then he sends the two kids off and seals the hatch behind them. This is exactly the kind of situation Connor feared most, and he can feel a rush of adrenaline begin to tingle in his fingers and toes. His awareness becomes heightened.

"You need me to fix something sir?"

"Yes, I do. My coffeemaker."

"Why don't you just take one from the other planes?"

"Because," says the Admiral calmly, "I prefer to have this one repaired."

He leads Connor through the jet, which seems even larger on the inside than out, filled with cabins, conference rooms, and studies.

"You know, your name comes up quite often," the Admiral says.

This is news to him, and not welcome news, either. "Why?"

"First, for the things you repair. Then for the fighting."

Connor senses a reprimand on the way. Yes, he's had fewer fights here than usual, but the Admiral is a man of zero tolerance. "Sorry about the fighting."

"Don't be. Oh, there's no question that you're a loose cannon, but more often than not you're aimed in the right direction."

"I don't know what you mean, sir."

"From what I can see, each fight you've engaged in has resolved one problem or another. Even the fights you lose. So, even then, you're fixing things." He offers Connor that white-toothed smile. Connor shudders. He tries to hide it, but he's sure the Admiral sees it.

They come to a small dining room and galley. "Here we are," says the Admiral. The old coffeemaker sits on a counter. It's a simple device. Connor's about to pull out a screwdriver to open up the back when he notices that it's not plugged in. When he plugs it in, the light comes on, and it starts to gurgle out coffee into the little glass pot.

"Well, how about that," says the Admiral, with another of his terrible grins.

"I'm not here for the coffeemaker, am I?"

"Have a seat," the Admiral says.

"I'd rather not."

"Have one anyway."

That's when Connor sees the picture. There are several photos up on the wall, but the one that captures Connor's attention is of a smiling kid about his age. The smile looks familiar. In fact, it looks *exactly* like the Admiral's smile. It's just like Roland had said!

Now Connor wants to bolt, but Risa's voice is in his head

again, telling him to scan his options. Sure, he can run. Chances are, he can get to the hatch before the Admiral can stop him—but opening the hatch won't be easy. He could hit the Admiral with one of his tools. That might give him enough time to get away. But where would he go? Beyond the Graveyard there's just desert, desert, and more desert. In the end, he realizes his best choice is to do as the Admiral says. He sits down.

"You don't like me, do you?" asks the Admiral.

Connor won't meet his gaze. "You saved my life by bringing me here. . . ."

"You will not avoid answering this question. You don't like me, do you?"

Connor shudders once more, and this time doesn't even try to hide it. "No, sir, I don't."

"I want to know your reasons."

Connor lets out a single rueful chuckle as his answer.

"You think I'm a slave dealer," says the Admiral. "And that I'm using these Unwinds for my own profit?"

"If you know what I'm going to say, why ask me?"

"I want you to look at me."

But Connor doesn't want to see the man's eyes—or, more accurately, doesn't want the Admiral seeing his.

"I said look at me!"

Reluctantly, Connor lifts his eyes and fixes them on the Admiral's. "I'm looking."

"I believe you are a smart kid. Now I want you to think. *Think!* I am a decorated Admiral of the United States Navy. Do you think I need to be selling children to earn money?"

"I don't know."

"*Think!* Do I care about money and lavish things? I do not live in a mansion. I do not vacation on a tropical island. I spend my time in the stinking desert living in a rotting plane 365 days a year. Why do you think that is?"

"I don't know!"

"I think you do."

Connor stands up now. In spite of the Admiral's tone of voice, he feels less and less intimidated by him. Whether it's wise or whether it's foolhardy, Connor decides to give the Admiral what he's asking for. "You do it because of the power. You do it because it lets you keep hundreds of helpless kids in the palm of your hand. And you do it because you can pick and choose who gets unwound—and which parts you'll get."

The Admiral is caught off guard by this. Suddenly, he's on the defensive. "What did you say?"

"It's obvious! All the scars. And those teeth! They're not the ones you were born with, are they? So, what is it you want from me? Is it my eyes, or my ears? Or maybe it's my hands that can fix things so well. Is that why I'm here? Is it?"

The Admiral's voice is a predatory growl. "You've gone too far."

"No, *you've* gone too far." The fury in the Admiral's eyes should terrify Connor, but his cannon has come loose, and it's beyond locking down. "We come to you in desperation! What you do to us is . . . is . . . obscene!"

"So I'm a monster, then!"

"Yes!"

"And my teeth are the proof."

"Yes!"

"Then you can have them!"

Then the Admiral does something beyond imagining. He reaches into his mouth, grabs onto his own jaw, and rips the teeth out of his mouth. His eyes blazing at Connor, he hurls the hard pink clump in his hand down on the table, where it clatters in two horrible pieces.

Connor screams in shock. It's all there. Two rows of white

teeth. Two sets of pink gums. But there's no blood. Why is there no blood? There's no blood in the Admiral's mouth, either. His face seems to have collapsed onto itself—his mouth is just a floppy, puckered hole. Connor doesn't know which is worse—the Admiral's face, or the bloodless teeth.

"They're called dentures," the Admiral says. "They used to be common in the days before unwinding. But who wants false teeth when, for half the price, you can get real ones straight from a healthy Unwind? I had to get these made in Thailand—no one does it here anymore."

"I . . . I don't understand. . . ." Connor looks at the false teeth, and jerks his head almost involuntarily toward the picture of the smiling boy.

The Admiral follows his gaze. "That," says the Admiral, "was my son. His teeth looked very much like my own at that age, so they designed my dentures using his dental records."

It's a relief to hear an explanation other than the one Roland gave. "I'm sorry."

The Admiral neither accepts nor rejects Connor's apology. "The money I get for placing Unwinds into service positions is used to feed the ones who remain, and to pay for the safe houses and warehouses that get runaway Unwinds off the street. It pays for the aircraft that get them here, and pays off anyone who needs bribery to look the other way. After that, the money that remains goes into the pockets of each Unwind on the day they turn eighteen and are sent out into this unforgiving world. So you see, I may still be, by your definition of the word, a slave dealer—but I am not quite the monster you think I am."

Connor looks to the dentures that still sit there, glistening, on the table. He thinks to grab them and hand them back to the Admiral as a peace offering, but decides the prospect is simply too disgusting. He lets the Admiral do it himself.

"Do you believe the things I've told you today?" the Admiral asks.

Connor considers it, but finds his compass is out of whack. Truth and rumors, facts and lies are all spinning in his head so wildly he still can't say what is what. "I think so," says Connor.

"*Know* so," says the Admiral. "Because you will see things today more awful than an old man's false teeth. I need to know that my trust in you is not misplaced."

Half a mile away, in aisle fourteen, space thirty-two, sits a FedEx jet that has not moved since it was towed here more than a month ago.

The Admiral has Connor drive him to the jet in his golf cart—but not before retrieving the pistol from his cabinet as "a precaution."

Beneath the starboard wing of the FedEx jet are five mounds of dirt marked by crude headstones. These are the five who suffocated in transit. Their presence here makes this truly a graveyard.

The hatch to the hold is open. Once they've stopped, the Admiral says, "Climb inside and find crate number 2933. Then come out again, and we'll talk."

"You're not coming?"

"I've already been." The Admiral hands him a flashlight. "You'll need this."

Connor stands on the roof of the cart, climbs through the cargo hatch, and turns on the flashlight. The moment he does, he has a shiver of memory. It looks exactly same as it did a month ago. Open crates, and overtones of urine. The after-birth of their arrival. He works his way deeper into the jet, passing the crate that he, Hayden, Emby, and Diego had occupied. Finally, he finds number 2933. It was one of the first crates to be loaded. Its hatch is open just a crack. Connor pulls it all the way open, and shines his light in.

When he catches sight of what's inside, he screams and reflexively lurches back, banging his head on the crate behind him. The Admiral could have warned him, but he hadn't. *Okay. Okay. I know what I saw. There's nothing I can do about it. And nothing in there can hurt me.* Still, he takes time to prepare himself before he looks in again.

There are five dead kids in the crate.

All seventeen-year-olds. There's Amp, and Jeeves. Beside them are Kevin, Melinda, and Raul, the three kids who gave out jobs his first day there. All five of the Goldens. There are no signs of blood, no wounds. They could all be asleep except for the fact that Amp's eyes are open and staring at nothing. Connor's mind reels. Did the Admiral do this? Is he mad after all? But why would he? No, it has to have been someone else.

When Connor comes out into the light, the Admiral is paying his respects to the five kids already buried beneath the wing. He straightens the markers and evens out the mounds.

"They disappeared last night. I found them sealed in the crate this morning," the Admiral tells him. "They suffocated, just like the first five did. It's the same crate."

"Who would do this?"

"Who, indeed," says the Admiral. Satisfied with the graves, he turns to Connor. "Whoever it is took out the five most powerful kids . . . which means, whoever did this wants to systematically dismantle the power structure here, so that they can rise to the top of it more quickly."

There's only one Unwind Connor knows of who might be capable of this—but even so, he has a hard time believing Roland would do something this horrible.

"I was meant to discover them," the Admiral says. "They

left my golf cart here this morning so that I would. Make no mistake about it, Connor, this is an act of war. They have made a surgical strike. These five were my eyes and ears among the kids here. Now I have none."

The Admiral takes a moment to look at the dark hole of the hold. "Tonight, you and I will come back here to bury them."

Connor swallows hard at the prospect. He wonders who he pissed off in Heaven to get singled out to be the Admiral's new lieutenant.

"We'll bury them far away," says the Admiral, "and we will tell no one that they're dead. Because if word of it gets out, the culprits will have their first victory. If someone does start talking—and they will—we'll track the rumors down to the guilty party."

"And then what?" Connor asks.

"And then justice will be served. Until then, this must be our secret."

As Connor chauffeurs him back to his plane, the Admiral makes his business with Connor clear. "I need a new set of eyes and ears. Someone to keep me abreast of the state of things among the Unwinds. And someone to ferret out the wolf in the herd. I'm asking you to do this for me."

"So you want me to be a spy?"

"Whose side are you on? Are you on my side, or the side of whoever did this?"

Connor now knows why the Admiral brought him here and forced him to see this for himself. It's one thing to be told, and another one entirely to discover the bodies. It makes it brutally clear to Connor where his allegiance must lie.

"Why me?" Connor has to ask.

The Admiral gives him his white-dentured smile. "Because you, my friend, are the least of all evils."

The next morning, the Admiral makes an announcement that the Goldens were sent off to organize new safe houses. Connor watches Roland for a reaction—perhaps a grin, or a glance at one of his buddies. But there's nothing. Roland gives no telltale sign that he knows what really happened to them. In fact, throughout the morning announcements he seems disinterested and distracted, like he can't wait to get on with his day. There's a good reason for that. Roland's apprenticeship with Cleaver, the helicopter pilot, has been paying off. Over the past weeks Roland has learned to fly the helicopter like a pro, and when Cleaver isn't around he offers free rides to those kids he feels deserve it. He says Cleaver doesn't care, but more likely he just doesn't know.

Connor had assumed that Roland would offer rides to his own inner circle of kids, but that's not the case. Roland rewards work well done—even by kids he doesn't know. He rewards loyalty to one's team. He lets other kids vote on who should get a chance to do a flyby of the yard in the helicopter. In short, Roland acts as if he's the one in charge, and not the Admiral.

When the Admiral is present, he feigns obedience, but when others are gathered around him—and there are always others gathered around Roland—he takes every opportunity to cut the man down. "The Admiral's out of touch," he would say. "He doesn't know what it's like to be one of us. He can't possibly understand who we are and what we need." And in groups of kids he's already won over, he whispers his theories about the Admiral's teeth, and his scars, and his diabolical plans for all of them. He spreads fear and distrust, using it to unite as many kids as he can.

Connor has to bite his lip to keep himself quiet when he

hears Roland mouth off—because if he speaks out in defense of the Admiral, then Roland will know which side of the line he's on.

There's a recreation jet at the Graveyard, near the meeting tent. Inside there are TVs and electronics, and under its wings are pool tables, a pinball machine, and reasonably comfortable furniture. Connor proposed setting up a water mister, so that the area beneath the wings will stay at least a little bit cooler during the heat of the day. But even more importantly, Connor figures the project will allow him to be a fly on the wall, hearing conversations, cataloguing cliques, and performing general espionage. The problem is, Connor is never a fly on the wall. Instead, his work becomes the center of attention. Kids offer to help him like he's Tom Sawyer painting a fence. They all keep seeing him as a leader when all he wants is to be ignored. He's glad that he never told anyone he's the so-called "Akron AWOL." According to the current rumors, the Akron AWOL took on an entire legion of Juvey-cops, outsmarted the national guard, and liberated half a dozen harvest camps. He has enough attention from other kids without having to contend with that kind of reputation.

While Connor works to install the mister line, Roland keeps an eye on him from the pool table. He finally puts down the cue and comes over.

"You're just a busy little worker bee, ain't ya," Roland says, loud enough for all the kids around to hear. Connor's up on a stepladder, attaching mist piping to the underside of the wing. It allows him the satisfaction of carrying on this conversation while looking down on Roland. "I'm just trying to make life a little easier," Connor says. "We need a mister down here— wouldn't want anyone to *suffocate* in this heat."

Roland keeps a cool poker face. "It looks like you're the

Admiral's new golden boy, now that the others have left." He looks around to make sure he has everyone's attention. "I've seen you go up to his jet."

"He needs things fixed, so I fix them," says Connor. "That's all."

Then, before Roland can push his interrogation, Hayden speaks up from the pool table.

"Connor's not the only one going up there," Hayden says. "There's kids going in and out all the time. Kids with food. Kids cleaning—and I hear he's taken an interest in a certain mouth breather we all know and love."

All eyes turn toward Emby, who has become a fixture at the pinball machine since he arrived. "What?"

"You've been up to the Admiral's, haven't you," Hayden says. "Don't deny it!"

"So?"

"So, what does he want? I'm sure we'd all like to know."

Emby squirms, uncomfortable at the center of anyone's attention. "He just wanted to know about my family and stuff."

This is news to Connor. Perhaps the Admiral's looking for someone else to help him ferret out the killer. True, Emby's much less visible than Connor, but a fly on the wall shouldn't actually be a fly on the wall.

"I know what it is," says Roland. "He wants your hair."

"Does not!"

"Yeah—his own hair is thinning, right? You got yourself a nice mop up there. The old man wants to scalp you, and send the rest of you to be unwound!"

"Shut up!"

Most of the kids laugh. Sure, it's a joke, but Connor wonders how many think Roland might be right. Emby must suspect it himself, because he looks kind of sick. It makes Connor furious.

"That's right, pick on Emby," says Connor. "Show everyone just how low you are." He climbs down off the ladder, facing Roland eye to eye. "Hey—did you notice Amp left his megaphone? Why don't you take his place? You're such a loudmouth, you'd be perfect for it."

Roland's response comes without the slightest smile. "I wasn't asked."

That night Connor and the Admiral have a secret meeting in his quarters, drinking coffee made by a machine rumored to be broken. They speak of Roland and Connor's suspicions about him, but the Admiral is not satisfied.

"I don't want suspicion, I want proof. I don't want your feelings, I want evidence." The Admiral adds some whiskey from a flask to his own coffee.

When Connor is done with his report, he gets up to leave, but the Admiral won't let him. He pours Connor a second cup of coffee, which will surely keep him up all night—but then, he doubts he'll be sleeping well tonight anyway.

"Very few people know what I'm about to tell you," says the Admiral.

"So why tell me?"

"Because it serves my purposes for you to know."

It's an honest answer, but one that still keeps his motives hidden. Connor imagines he must have been very good in a war.

"When I was much younger," begins the Admiral, "I fought in the Heartland War. The scars you so impertinently assumed were transplant scars came from a grenade."

"Which side were you on?"

The Admiral gives Connor that scrutinizing look he's so good at. "How much do you know about the Heartland War?"

Connor shrugs. "It was the last chapter in our history text-

222

book, but we had state testing, so we never got to it."

The Admiral waves his hand in disgust. "Textbooks sugarcoat it anyway. No one wants to remember how it really was. You asked which side I was on. The truth is, there were three sides in the war, not two. There was the Life Army, the Choice Brigade, and the remains of the American military, whose job it was to keep the other two sides from killing each other. That's the side I was on. Unfortunately, we weren't very successful. You see, a conflict always begins with an issue—a difference of opinion, an argument. But by the time it turns into a war, the issue doesn't matter anymore, because now it's about one thing and one thing only: how much each side hates the other."

The Admiral pours a little more whiskey into his mug before he continues. "There were dark days leading up to the war. Everything that we think defines right and wrong was being turned upside down. On one side, people were murdering abortion doctors to protect the right to life, while on the other side people were getting pregnant just to sell their fetal tissue. And everyone was selecting their leaders not by their ability to lead, but by where they stood on this single issue. It was beyond madness! Then the military fractured, both sides got hold of weapons of war, and two opinions became two armies determined to destroy each other. And then came the Bill of Life."

The mention of it sends ice water down Connor's spine. It never used to bother him, but things change once you become an Unwind.

"I was right there in the room when they came up with the idea that a pregnancy could be terminated retroactively once a child reaches the age of reason," says the Admiral. "At first it was a joke—no one intended it to be taken seriously. But that same year the Nobel Prize went to a scientist who perfected neurografting—the technique that allows every part of a donor to be used in transplant."

The Admiral takes a deep gulp of his coffee. Connor hasn't had a bit of his second cup. The thought of swallowing anything right now is out of the question. It's all he can do to keep the first cup down.

"With the war getting worse," says the Admiral, "we brokered a peace by bringing both sides to the table. Then we proposed the idea of unwinding, which would terminate unwanteds without actually ending their lives. We thought it would shock both sides into seeing reason—that they would stare at each other across the table and someone would blink. But nobody blinked. The choice to terminate without ending life—it satisfied the needs of both sides. The Bill of Life was signed, the Unwind Accord went into effect, and the war was over. Everyone was so happy to end the war, no one cared about the consequences."

The Admiral's thoughts go far away for a moment, then he waves his hand. "I'm sure you know the rest."

Connor might not know all the particulars, but he knows the gist. "People wanted parts."

"Demanded is more like it. A cancerous colon could be replaced with a healthy new one. An accident victim who would have died from internal injuries could get fresh organs. A wrinkled arthritic hand could be replaced by one fifty years younger. And all those new parts had to come from some-where." The Admiral paused for a moment to consider it. "Of course, if more people had been organ donors, unwinding never would have happened . . . but people like to keep what's theirs, even after they're dead. It didn't take long for ethics to be crushed by greed. Unwinding became big business, and people let it happen."

The Admiral glances over at the picture of his son. Even without the Admiral telling him, Connor realizes why—but he allows the Admiral the dignity of his confession.

"My son, Harlan, was a great kid. Smart. But he was troubled—you know the type."

"I *am* the type," says Connor, offering a slight grin.

The Admiral nods. "It was just about ten years ago. He got in with the wrong group of friends, got caught stealing. Hell, I was the same at his age—that's why my parents first sent me to military school, to straighten me out. Only, for Harlan there was a different option. A more . . . *efficient* option."

"You had him unwound."

"As one of the fathers of the Unwind Accord, I was expected to set an example." He presses his thumb and forefinger against his eyes, stemming off tears before they can flow. "We signed the order, then changed our minds. But it was already too late. They had taken Harlan right out of school to the harvest camp, and rushed him through. It had already been done."

It had never occurred to Connor to consider the toll unwinding had on the ones who signed the order. He never thought he could have sympathy for a parent who could do that—or sympathy for one of the men who had made unwinding possible.

"I'm sorry," Connor says, and means it.

The Admiral stiffens up—sobers up—almost instantly. "You shouldn't be. It's only because of his unwinding that you're all here. Afterward, my wife left me and formed a foundation in Harlan's memory. I left the military, spent several years more drunk than I am now, and then, three years ago, I had The Big Idea. This place, these kids, are the result of it. To date I've saved more than a thousand kids from unwinding."

Connor now understands why the Admiral was telling him these things. It was more than just a confession. It was a way of securing Connor's loyalty—and it worked. The

Admiral was a darkly obsessed man, but his obsession saved lives. Hayden once said that Connor had integrity. That same integrity locks him firmly on the Admiral's side, and so Connor holds up his mug. "To Harlan!" he says.

"To Harlan!" echoes the Admiral, and together they drink to his name. "Bit by bit I am making things right, Connor," the Admiral says. "Bit by bit, and in more ways than one."

# 35 · Lev

Where Lev was between the time he left CyFi and his arrival at the Graveyard is less important than where his thoughts resided. They resided in places colder and darker than the many places he hid.

He had survived the month through a string of unpleasant compromises and crimes of convenience—whatever was necessary to keep himself alive. Lev quickly became street-smart, and survival-wise. They say it takes complete immersion in a culture to learn its language and its ways. It didn't take him very long to learn the language of the lost.

Once he landed in the safe-house network, he quickly made it known that he was not a guy to be trifled with. He didn't tell people he was a tithe. Instead, he told them his parents signed the order to have him unwound after he was arrested for armed robbery. It was funny to him, because he had never even touched a gun. It amazed him that the other kids couldn't read the lie in his face—he had always been such a bad liar. But then, when he looked in the mirror, what he saw in his own eyes scared him.

By the time he reached the Graveyard, most kids knew enough to stay away from him. Which is exactly what he wanted.

The same night that the Admiral and Connor have their secret conference, Lev heads out into the oil-slick dark of the moonless night, keeping his flashlight off. His first night there he had successfully slipped out to find Connor, in order to set him straight about a few things. Since then, the bruise from Connor's punch has faded, and they haven't spoken of it again. He hasn't spoken much to Connor at all, because Lev has other things on his mind.

Each night since then he's tried to sneak away, but every time, he's been caught and sent back. Now that the Admiral's five watchdogs have left, though, the kids on sentry duty are getting lax. As Lev sneaks between the jets, he finds that a few of them are even asleep on the job. Stupid of the Admiral to send those other kids away without having anyone to replace them.

Once he's far enough away he turns on his flashlight and tries to find his destination. It's a destination told to him by a girl he had encountered a few weeks before. She was very much like him. He suspects he'll meet others tonight who are very much like him as well.

Aisle thirty, space twelve. It's about as far from the Admiral as you can get and still be in the Graveyard. The space is occupied by an ancient DC-10, crumbling to pieces in its final resting place. When Lev swings open the hatch and climbs in, he finds two kids inside, both of whom bolt upright at the sight of him and take defensive postures.

"My name's Lev," he says. "I was told to come here."

He doesn't know these kids, but that's no surprise—he hasn't been in the Graveyard long enough to know that many kids here. One is an Asian girl with pink hair. The other kid has a shaved head and is covered in tattoos.

"And who told you to come here?" asks the flesh-head.

"This girl I met in Colorado. Her name's Julie-Ann."

Then a third figure comes out from the shadows. It's not a kid but an adult—midtwenties, maybe. He's smiling. The guy has greasy red hair, a straggly goatee to match, and a boney face with sunken cheeks. It's Cleaver, the helicopter pilot.

"So Julie-Ann sent you!" he says. "Cool! How is she?"

Lev takes a moment to think about his answer. "She did her job," Lev tells him.

Cleaver nods. "Well, it is what it is."

The other two kids introduce themselves. The flesh-head is Blaine, the girl is Mai.

"What about that boeuf who flies the helicopter with you?" Lev asks Cleaver. "Is he part of this too?"

Mai gives a disgusted laugh. "Roland? Not on your life!"

"Roland isn't exactly . . . the material for our little group," Cleaver says. "So, did you come here to give us the good news about Julie-Ann, or are you here for another reason?"

"I'm here because I want to be here."

"You say it," says Cleaver, "but we still don't know you're for real."

"Tell us about yourself," says Mai.

Lev prepares to give them the armed-robbery version, but before he opens his mouth, he changes his mind. The moment calls for honesty. This must begin with the truth. So he tells them everything, from the moment he was kidnapped by Connor to his time with CyFi and the weeks after that. When he's done, Cleaver seems very, very pleased.

"So, you're a tithe! That's great. You don't even know how great that is!"

"What now?" asks Lev. "Am I in, or not?"

The others become quiet. Serious. He feels some sort of ritual is about to begin.

"Tell me, Lev," says Cleaver. "How much do you hate the

228

people who were going to unwind you?"

"A lot."

"Sorry, that's not good enough."

Lev closes his eyes, digs down, and thinks about his parents. He thinks about what they planned to do to him, and how they made him actually want it.

"How much do you hate them?" Cleaver asks again.

"Totally and completely," answers Lev.

"And how much do you hate the people who would take parts of you and make them parts of themselves?"

"Totally and completely."

"And how much do you want to make them, and everyone else in the world, pay?"

"Totally and completely." Someone has to pay for the unfairness of it all. *Everyone* has to pay. He'll make them.

"Good," says Cleaver.

Lev is amazed by the depth of his own fury—but he's becoming less and less frightened of it. He tells himself that's a good thing.

"Maybe he's for real," says Blaine.

If Lev makes this commitment, he knows there's no turning back. "One thing I need to know," Lev asks, "because Julie-Ann . . . she wasn't very clear about it. I want to know what you believe."

"What we believe?" says Mai. She looks at Blaine, and Blaine laughs. Cleaver, however, puts his hand up to quiet him. "No—no, it's a good question. A real question. It deserves a real answer. If you're asking if we have a cause, we don't, so get that out of your head." Cleaver gestures broadly, his hands and arms filling the space around him. "Causes are old news. We believe in randomness. Earthquakes! Tornados! We believe in forces of nature—and *we* are forces of nature. We are havoc. We're chaos. We mess with the world."

"And we messed pretty good with the Admiral, didn't we," says Blaine slyly. Cleaver throws him a sharp gaze, and Mai actually looks scared. It's almost enough to give Lev second thoughts.

"How did you mess with the Admiral?"

"It's done," says Mai, her body language both anxious and angry. "We messed, and now it's done. We don't talk about things that are done. Right?"

Cleaver gives her a nod, and she seems to relax a bit. "The point is," says Cleaver, "it doesn't matter who or what we mess with, just as long as we mess. The way we see it, the world doesn't *move* if things don't get shaken up—am I right?"

"I guess."

"Well, then, *we* are the movers and shakers." Cleaver smiles and points a finger at Lev. "The question is, are you one too? Do you have what it takes to be one of us?"

Lev takes a long look at these three. These are the kinds of people his parents would hate. He could join them just out of spite, but that's not enough—not this time. There must be more. Yet, as he stands there, Lev realizes that there *is* more. It's invisible, but it's there, like the deadly charge lurking in a downed power line. Anger, but not just anger: a will to act on it as well.

"All right, I'm in." Back at home Lev always felt part of something larger than himself. Until now, he hadn't realized how much he missed that feeling.

"Welcome to the family," says Cleaver, and gives him a slap on the back so painful, he sees stars.

# 36 · Risa

Risa is the first to notice something's wrong with Connor. Risa is the first to care that something's wrong with Lev.

In a moment of selfishness, she finds herself aggravated by it, because things are going so well for her now. She finally has a place to be. She wishes this could remain her sanctuary beyond her eighteenth birthday, because in the outside world she'd never be able to do the things she's doing now. It would be practicing medicine without a license—fine when you're in survival mode, but not in the civilized world. Perhaps, after she turned eighteen, she could go to college, and medical school— but that takes money, connections, and she'd have to face even more competition than in her music classes. She wonders if maybe she could join the military and become an Army medic. You don't have to be a boeuf to be in a medical unit. Whatever her choice ends up being, the important thing is that there could *be* a choice. For the first time in a long time she can see a future for herself. With all these good thoughts in her life, the last thing she wants is something that will shoot it all down.

This is what fills Risa's mind as she makes her way to one of the study jets. The Admiral has three of his most accessible and well-appointed jets set aside as study spaces, complete with libraries, computers, and the resources to learn anything you want to learn. "This is not a school," the Admiral told them shortly after they arrived. "There are no teachers, there are no exams." Oddly, it's precisely that lack of expectation that keeps the study jets full most of the time.

Risa's duties start shortly after dawn, and it has become her habit to begin her day at one of the study jets, since at that time of the morning she's usually the only one there. She likes it that way, because the things she wants to learn make other kids uncomfortable. It's not the subject matter that bothers them, it's the fact that Risa's the one studying it. Anatomy and medical texts, mostly. Kids assume that just because she works in the medical jet, she knows all there is to know. It disturbs them to see her actually having to learn it.

When she arrives today, however, she discovers Connor already there. She stops at the hatch, surprised. He's so absorbed in whatever he's reading that he doesn't hear her come in. She takes a moment to look at him. She's never seen him so tired—not even when they were on the run. Still, she's thrilled to see him. They have both been so busy, there hasn't been much time to spend together.

"Hi, Connor."

Startled, he looks up quickly and slams his book closed. When he realizes who it is, he relaxes. "Hi, Risa." By the time she sits down beside him, he's smiling, and doesn't seem quite so tired. She's glad she can have that kind of effect on him.

"You're up early."

"No, I'm up late," he says. "I couldn't sleep, so I came here. He glances out one of the little round windows. "Is it morning already?"

"Just about. What are you reading?"

He tries to push it out of view, but it's too late for that. He has two books out. The bottom volume is a book on engineering. That's no surprise, considering the interest he's taken in the way things work. It's the book on top—the one his nose was in when she arrived—that catches her by surprise, almost making her laugh.

*"Criminology for Morons?"*

"Yeah, well, everyone needs a hobby."

She tries to take a long look into him, but he looks away. "There's something wrong, isn't there?" she asks. "I don't need to read *Connor for Morons* to know that you're in some kind of trouble."

He looks everywhere but into her eyes. "It isn't trouble. At least not for me. Or maybe it is in some ways, I don't know."

"Want to talk about it?"

"That," says Connor, "is the *last* thing I want to do." He takes a deep breath and shifts in his chair. "Don't worry, everything will be fine."

"You don't sound too sure."

He looks at Risa, then looks at the hatch, making sure they're still alone. Then he leans in close to her and says, "Now that the Goldens are . . . no longer around, the Admiral's going to be looking for replacements. I want you to promise me that if he asks you to help him, you'll turn him down."

"The Admiral doesn't even know I exist. Why would he ask me for anything?"

"Because he asked me," Connor says in an intense whisper. "And I think he's asked Emby, too."

"Emby?"

"All I'm saying is that I don't want you to be a target!"

"A target for what? For whom?"

"Shhh! Keep your voice down!"

She looks again at that book he was reading, trying to piece it all together, but there just aren't enough pieces. She gets close to him, forcing him to look at her. "I want to help you," she says. "I'm worried about you. Please let me help you."

He darts his eyes back and forth, trying to find an escape from her gaze, but he can't. Suddenly, he bridges the small distance between them and kisses her. She did not expect it, and when he breaks off the kiss she realizes from the look on his face that he hadn't expected it either.

"What was that for?"

It takes a moment for him to get his brain functioning

again. "That," he says, "is in case something happens and I don't see you again."

"Fine," she says, and she pulls him into another kiss—this one longer than the first. When she breaks it off, she says, "That's in case I *do* see you again."

He leaves, awkwardly stumbling out and nearly falling down the steel steps to the ground. In spite of all that just went on between them, Risa has to smile. It's amazing that something as simple as a kiss can overpower the worst of worries.

Lev's troubles appear to be of a different nature, and Risa finds herself frightened by him. He comes to infirmary call that morning with a bad sunburn. Since he's a fast runner, he's been assigned messenger duty. Mostly, it involves running back and forth between the jets carrying notes. It's one of the Admiral's rules that all messengers wear sunscreen, but it seems Lev is no longer bound by anyone's rules.

They make small talk for a bit, but it's awkward, so she quickly gets down to business. "Well, now that your hair is longer, at least your forehead and neck seem to have been spared. Take off your shirt."

"I kept my shirt on most of the time," he says.

"Let's have a look anyway."

Reluctantly, he removes his shirt. He's burned there as well, but not as badly as on his arms and cheeks. What catches her attention, however, is a welt on his back in the faint shape of a hand. She brushes her fingers across it.

"Who did this to you?" she asks.

"Nobody," he says, grabbing the shirt back from her and slipping it on. "Just some guy."

"Is someone on your team giving you trouble?"

"I told you, it's nothing—what are you, my mother?"

"No," says Risa. "If I were your mother, I'd be rushing you off to the nearest harvest camp."

She means it as a joke, but Lev doesn't find it funny. "Just give me something to put on the burns."

There's a deadness to his voice that's haunting. She goes to the cabinet and finds a tube of aloe cream, but she doesn't hand it to him just yet. "I miss the old Lev," she says.

That makes him look at her. "No offense, but you didn't even know me."

"Maybe not, but at least back then I wanted to."

"And you don't want to anymore?"

"I don't know," says Risa. "The kid I'm looking at now is a little too creepy for my taste." She can tell that gets to him. She doesn't know why it should, because he seems proud of his new creep factor.

"The old Lev," he says, "tricked you into trusting him, then turned you in to the police the first chance he got."

"And the new Lev wouldn't do that?"

He thinks about it, then says, "The new Lev has better things to do."

She puts the tube of burn cream in his hand. "Yeah, well, if you see the old one—the one who always thought about God and his purpose and stuff—tell him we want him back."

There's an uneasy silence and he looks down at the tube in his hand. For a moment she thinks he might say something that brings a hint of that other kid back into the room, but all he says is, "How often do I put this on?"

There's a work call the following day.

Risa hates them, because she knows there isn't going to be anything for her, but everyone must attend work call. Today, the gathering isn't run by an Unwind, it's run by Cleaver. Apparently he's temporarily taken over the job, since no one's been found to fulfill Amp's duties. Risa doesn't like him. He's got an unpleasant, slimy look about him.

There are only a few calls for work today. Someone wants a plumber's assistant in some godforsaken town named Beaver's Breath; there's some farm work out in California; and the third job is just plain weird.

"Prudhoe Bay, Alaska," Cleaver says. "You'll be working on an oil pipeline until you're eighteen. From what I hear, it's one of the coldest, most brutal places on Earth. But, hey, it's a way out, right? I need three volunteers."

The first hand up belongs to an older kid who looks like punishment is his middle name—like he was born for brutal work, right down to his shaved head. The second hand raised catches Risa by surprise. It's Mai. What is Mai doing volunteering for work on a pipeline? Why would she leave the boy she was so attached to back in the warehouse? But then, come to think of it, Risa hasn't seen that boy around the Graveyard at all. While she tries to process this, a third hand goes up. It's a younger kid. A smaller kid. A kid with a bad sunburn. Lev's hand is held high, and he gets chosen for the pipeline job.

Risa just stands there in disbelief, then she searches for Connor in the crowd. He's seen it too. He looks at Risa and shrugs. Well, maybe this is just a shrug to Connor, but it's not to her.

When the meeting breaks up, she makes a beeline for Lev, but he's already vanished into the mob. So the instant Risa gets back to the infirmary, she calls for a messenger, and another and another, sending them each off with redundant notes reminding kids to take their medications. Finally, after her fourth call, the messenger they send is Lev.

He must see the look on her face, because he just stands there at the hatch not coming in. One of the other medics is there, so Risa glares at Lev, pointing toward the back. "That way. Now!"

"I don't take orders," he says.

"That way!" she says again, even more forcefully. "NOW!"

Apparently he does take orders after all, because he steps in and marches toward the back of the plane. Once they reach the storage room at the back, she closes the bulkhead door behind them and lays into him.

"What the hell are you thinking?"

His face is steel. It's the door of a safe she can't get into. "I've never been to Alaska," he says. "I might as well go now."

"You've barely been here a week! Why are you in such a hurry to leave—and for a job like that?"

"I don't have to explain anything to you or to anyone else. I raised my hand, I got chosen, and that's all."

Risa crosses her arms in defiance of his defiance. "You don't go anywhere if I don't give you a clean bill of health. I could tell the Admiral you've got . . . you've got . . . infectious hepatitis."

"You wouldn't!"

"Just watch me."

He storms away from her, kicking the wall in fury, then storms back. "He won't believe you! And even if he does, you can't keep me sick forever!"

"Why are you so determined to go?"

"There are things I have to do," Lev says. "I don't expect you to understand. I'm sorry I'm not who you want me to be, but I've changed. I'm not that same stupid, naive kid you guys kidnapped two months ago. Nothing you can do will keep me from leaving here and doing what I've got to do."

Risa says nothing, because she knows he's right. She can stall him at best, but she can't stop him.

"So," says Lev, a bit more calmly now. "Do I have infectious hepatitis or not?"

She sighs. "No. You don't."

He turns to leave, opening the bulkhead door. He's so determined to move on, he doesn't even think to offer her a good-bye.

"You're wrong about one thing," she says before he's out the door. "You're just as naive as you were before. And maybe twice as stupid."

Then he's gone. That same afternoon, an unmarked white van comes to take him, Mai, and the flesh-head away. Once again, Risa thinks she'll never see Lev again. Once again, she'll be wrong.

# 37 · Emby and the Admiral

Emby has no idea of all the gears turning in the Graveyard—or even that he's one of them. His world is contained within the square panels of his comic books and the well-defined borders of a pinball machine. Staying within those borders has been a successful defense against the injustice and cruelty of life outside of them.

He does not question the oddness of the trio that just left for Alaska; it's not his business. He does not sense the tension in Connor; Connor can take care of himself. He does not spend time wondering about Roland; he just stays out of Roland's way.

But keeping his head down does not keep him in the safe zone. Emby is, in fact, the central bumper on the pinball board, and every single ball in play is about to rebound off of him.

The Admiral has called for him.

Emby now stands nervously at the entrance to what was

once the mobile command center for a president of the United States. There are two other men here. They are in white shirts and dark ties. The black sedan that waits at the bottom of the stairs must be theirs. The Admiral sits at his desk. Emby tries to decide whether he should enter, or turn around and run away. But the Admiral sees him, and his gaze freezes Emby's feet in place.

"You wanted me, sir?"

"Yes. Have a seat, Zachary."

He forces his feet to move toward the chair across from the Admiral. "Emby," he says. "Everyone just calls me Emby."

"Is that your choice, or theirs?" asks the Admiral.

"Well . . . theirs, mostly—but I got used to it."

"Never let anyone else name you," says the Admiral. He leafs through a file with Emby's picture clipped to the cover. It's a full file, and Emby can't imagine how there could be enough interesting things in his life to fill a file that thick. "You may not realize this, but you're a very special boy," says the Admiral.

Emby can only look down at his shoelaces, which are, as always, moments away from coming untied. "Is that why I'm here, sir? Because I'm special?"

"Yes, Zachary. And because of it, you're going to be leaving us today."

Emby looks up. "What?"

"There's someone who wants to meet you. In fact, it's someone who has been looking for you for a very long time."

"Really?"

"These men will take you there."

"Who is it?" Emby has a longstanding fantasy that one of his parents is actually still alive. If not his mother, then his father. He has always dreamed that his father was actually a spy—that his death all those years ago was just the official story, and he's been off in the untamed corners of the world fighting evil, like a real-life comic-book hero.

"It's no one you know," says the Admiral, dashing Emby's hopes. "She's a good woman, though. Actually, she's my ex-wife."

"I . . . I don't understand."

"It will be clear to you soon enough. Don't worry."

Which, to Emby, is an open invitation to worry without end. It makes him start to hyperventilate, which makes his bronchial tubes begin to constrict. He starts to wheeze. The Admiral looks at him with concern.

"Are you all right?"

"Asthma," Emby says between wheezes. He pulls out an inhaler from his pocket and takes a puff.

"Yes," says the Admiral. "My son had asthma—he responded very well to Xolair." He looks up at one of the men behind Emby. "Please make sure you get some Xolair for that lung."

"Yes, Admiral Dunfee."

It takes a moment for this to bounce around on the pegs and pins in Emby's mind before hitting his mental flippers.

"Dunfee? Your last name is *Dunfee*?"

"We have no last names in the Graveyard," says the Admiral, then he stands and grabs Emby's hand, shaking it. "Good-bye, Zachary. When you see my ex-wife, give her my regards."

Emby can only squeak a wordless response as the men take him by the arms and lead him out and down toward the waiting sedan.

Once the boy is gone, Admiral Dunfee leans back in his chair. With all the things threatening his domain, here's one thing he can be pleased with. He allows himself a brief moment of satisfaction, glancing over at the smiling picture of his son Harlan—better known as Humphrey in modern folklore, but those who loved him know his real name. Yes, the Admiral is redeeming himself, and setting things right, bit by bit by bit.

# 38 · Mob

Emby's disappearance goes undiscovered for almost two days, until someone takes a look at the pinball machine and notices that something is missing.

"Where's the mouth breather?" people begin to ask. It's not until nightfall that people start asking seriously, and by morning it's clear that he's gone.

Some people claim they saw him wandering off into the desert. Some people claim there was a mysterious car that took him away. Ralphy Sherman claims he saw Emby beamed up to the mother ship to be with his own kind. Every suggestion is mulled over. Every theory is entertained. A search is mounted by Emby's team. It turns up nothing.

Through all of this, the Admiral is silent.

Now Emby, the kid at the bottom of the pecking order, has suddenly become everyone's best friend, and his disappearance fuel for everyone's fire. Roland uses it to further his own agenda of fear—after all, he was the one who very publicly predicted that Emby would vanish. He didn't believe it for an instant, but now that his prediction has come true, he has everyone's attention.

"You watch," Roland tells all those who will listen. "The Admiral's going to show up one of these days with a nice, thick head of Emby-hair hidden beneath his hat—and any one of us could be next. Has he been looking at your eyes? Has he been listening to the sound of your voice? If he wants a part of you, you'll end up just like Emby!"

He's so convincing, he almost believes it himself.

Connor has a completely different view of the situation. He's certain that Roland did away with Emby so he could use his disappearance to gather support. For Connor, it's more proof that Roland killed the Goldens—that he'll stop at nothing to get what he wants.

Connor brings his suspicions to the Admiral. He listens, but still says nothing. The Admiral knows that claiming responsibility for Emby's absence would play right into the mania that Roland is creating. The Admiral could tell Connor that he was the one who sent the boy away, but that would beg questions that he has no desire to answer. He decides to let Connor think that Roland did it—it would motivate Connor even more to find that crucial link connecting Roland to the murders. Because now the Admiral has come to believe in Roland's guilt as well.

"Forget the missing boy," he tells Connor. "Concentrate on proving Roland killed the others. Someone must have helped him—someone must know. Right now Roland has too many supporters. We can't take him down without hard evidence."

"Then somehow I'll get you evidence," Connor tells him. "I'll do it for Emby."

After Connor leaves the Admiral's jet, the Admiral sits alone, pondering the ins and outs of the situation. Things in the Graveyard have gotten dicey before, but dicey situations have always been the Admiral's specialty. He's sure he can play this one to a successful conclusion, and get everything back under his control. As he sits there in his jet, he gets an ache in his shoulder that spreads down to his arm. No doubt it's another manifestation of his various war wounds. He calls for a medic to bring him some aspirin.

# 39 · Roland

Roland opens the envelope that Hayden has just handed him, and reads the note inside:

> I KNOW WHAT YOU DID. I'LL MAKE YOU A DEAL.
> MEET ME AT THE FEDEX JET.

The note isn't signed, but it doesn't have to be. Roland knows who sent it. Connor's the only one with nerve enough to blackmail him. The only one stupid enough. The note sets Roland's mind spinning. *I know what you did.* There are quite a lot of activities Connor could be talking about. He might know that Roland has been sabotaging the generators so he can blame the Admiral for outrageous living conditions. Or he might know about the bottle of ipecac he stole from the infirmary while pretending to flirt with Risa. He was planning to use the stuff to spike the drinks, create a puke-fest, and then blame the Admiral for giving them all food poisoning. Yes, there are plenty of things Connor could have found out about. Roland puts the note in his pocket, showing no emotion, and glares at Hayden. "So you're Connor's messenger boy now?"

"Hey," says Hayden, "I'm Switzerland: neutral as can be, and also good with chocolate."

"Get lost," Roland tells him.

"Already am." And Hayden strolls away.

It burns Roland that he might have to bargain with Connor, but there are worse things. And after all, bargains and subterfuge are a way of life for him. So he heads off toward the FedEx jet, making sure he takes a knife with him—in case there's no deal to be made.

# 40 · Connor

"I'm here," Roland calls from outside the FedEx jet. "What do you want?"

Connor remains hidden inside the hold. He knows he's only going to get one chance at this, so he's got to do it right. "Come inside, and we'll talk about it."

"No, you come out."

*Nice try,* Connor thinks, *but this is going to be on my terms.* "If you don't come in, I'll tell everyone what I know. I'll show everyone what I *found.*"

Silence for a moment, then he sees Roland's silhouette as he climbs into the hold. Connor has the advantage now. His eyes have adjusted to the dim light of the hold, and Roland's have not. He leaps forward and firmly plants the muzzle of the Admiral's gun against Roland's back. "Don't move."

Instinctively, Roland's hands go up, as if he's been in this position many times before. "Is this your deal?"

"Shut up." Connor uses one hand to frisk him, finds the concealed knife, and hurls it out of the cargo hold. Satisfied, he pushes the gun harder against Roland. "Move."

"Where am I supposed to go?"

"You know where to go. Crate 2933. Move!"

Roland begins to walk forward, squeezing between the narrow rows of crates. Connor is conscious of every movement of Roland's body. Even with a gun to his back, Roland is arrogant and sure of himself. "You don't want to kill me," he says. "Everyone here likes me. If you do anything to me, they'll tear you apart."

They reach crate 2933. "Get in," Connor says.

That's when Roland makes his move. He spins, knocks Connor back, and grabs for the gun. Connor expected this.

He holds the gun out of reach and, using the crate behind him for leverage, places his foot firmly in Roland's gut and pushes him back. Roland falls backward into crate 2933. The second he does, Connor lurches forward, slams the hatch, and seals it. While Roland rages inside, Connor takes aim at the crate and fires the gun once, twice, three times.

The blasts echo, blending with the terrified screams from within the crate, and then Roland shouts, "What are you doing? Are you *insane*?"

Connor's shots had been very precise; they were low, and directed at a corner of the crate. "I've given you something your victims never had," Connor tells him. "I've given you air-holes." Then he sits down. "Now we talk."

# 41 · Mob

Half a mile away, a search party returns from the desert. They didn't find Emby. Instead, they found five unmarked graves behind a distant outcropping of rocks. In a few short minutes, word spreads through the ranks like flames in a steady wind. The Goldens have been found, and apparently they weren't so golden after all. Someone suggests that the Admiral did it himself. The suggestion becomes a rumor, and the rumor quickly becomes accepted as fact. The Admiral killed his own! He's everything Roland says he is—and, hey, where *is* Roland? He's missing too? So is Connor! What has the Admiral done to them?!

A mob of Unwinds with a hundred reasons to be angry have all simultaneously found one more, and that's all it takes to push them over the edge. The mob storms toward the Admiral's jet, picking up more and more kids along the way.

# 42 · Risa

A few minutes earlier, Risa had responded to the Admiral's request and showed up at his jet with some aspirin. She was greeted by the Admiral, who, as she had told Connor, didn't even know her name. Now he chats with her, telling her that the experience she's getting here is better than what anyone her age gets in the outside world. She tells him of her thoughts of becoming an Army medic, and he seems pleased. He complains of shoulder pain, and asks her for the aspirin. She gives it to him, but just to be on the safe side, she checks his blood pressure, and he applauds her for being so thorough.

There's some sort of commotion outside that makes it hard for her to focus on taking the Admiral's blood pressure. Commotion is not unusual here. Whatever it is, Risa suspects it will end with bandages and ice packs for someone. Her work is never done.

# 43 · Mob

Furious kids begin to arrive at the Admiral's jet.

"Get him! Get him! Pull him out!"

They climb the steel steps. The hatch is open, but just a crack. Risa looks out at the wave of mayhem, like a human tsunami pounding toward her.

"He's got a girl in there with him!"

The first of the kids reaches the top of the stairs and heaves the hatch open, only to be met by Risa, and a brutal punch to the jaw. It sends him tumbling over the side and to the ground—but there's more where he came from.

"Don't let her close that door!"

The second kid is met by an aerosol burst of bactine right to his eyes. The pain is excruciating. He stumbles backward into the other kids coming up the stairs, and they tumble like dominos. Risa grabs the hatch, swings it closed, and seals it from the inside.

Kids are on the wings now, finding every piece of loose metal and prying it up. It's amazing how much of a plane can be shredded by bare-handed fury.

"Break the windows! Pull them out!"

Kids on the ground throw rocks that hit their comrades as often as they hit the jet. On the inside it sounds like a hailstorm. The Admiral blanches at the scene outside the windows. His heart races. His shoulder and arm ache. "How did this happen? How did I let this happen?"

The barrage of stones batters the fuselage, but nothing breaks the armored steel, nothing cracks the bulletproof glass of the former Air Force One. Then someone tears out the power line connecting the jet to its generator. The lights go out, the air-conditioning shuts down, and the entire jet quickly begins to bake in the broiling sun.

# 44 · Connor

"You murdered Amp, Jeeves, and the rest of the Goldens."

"You're crazy!"

Connor sits outside crate 2933, wiping his brow in the heat. Roland's voice comes from inside, muffled, but loud enough to hear.

"You got rid of them so you could take their place," Connor says.

"I swear, when I get out of here, I'll—"

"You'll what? You'll kill me like you killed them? Like you killed Emby?"

No response from Roland.

"I said I'd make you a deal," says Connor, "and I will. If you confess, I'll make sure the Admiral spares your life."

In response, Roland suggests Connor perform a physical impossibility.

"Confess, Roland. It's the only way I'm letting you out of there." Connor is sure that, if put under enough pressure, Roland will confess to what he's done. The Admiral needs evidence, and what better evidence than a full confession.

"I have nothing to confess to!"

"Fine," says Connor. "I can wait. I have all day."

# 45 · Mob

The fortress of the Admiral's jet is impenetrable. The temperature inside is soaring past one hundred. Risa's handling the heat, but the Admiral doesn't look too good. She still can't open the door, because the mob is relentlessly trying to get in.

Outside, whatever kids aren't swarming over the Admiral's jet are spreading out. If they can't get to the Admiral, then they'll destroy everything else. The study jets, the dormitory jets, even the recreation jet—everything is being torn apart, and whatever can burn is set aflame. They are filled with an insatiable fury, and beneath it is a strange joy that the anger can finally be released. And beneath the joy is more fury.

From halfway across the Graveyard, Cleaver sees the smoke rising in the distance, beckoning him. Cleaver is drawn to mayhem. He must be a witness to it! He gets into his helicopter and flies toward the angry mob.

He sets down as close to the chaos as he dares to get. Have his deeds in any way led to this? He hopes so. He turns off the engine, letting the blades slow, so he can hear the wonderful sounds of havoc. . . . Then the angry Unwinds turn toward him.

"It's Cleaver! He works for the Admiral."

Suddenly, Cleaver is the center of attention. He can't help but feel this is a good thing.

# 46 · Connor

Roland is slowly breaking. He confesses to many things, petty acts of vandalism and theft, that Connor couldn't care less about. But this is going to work. It has to work. Connor has no other plan to bring him to justice—it *has* to work.

"I've done a lot of things," Roland tells him through the three bullet holes in the crate. "But I never killed anybody!"

Connor just listens. He barely speaks to him anymore. Connor finds the less he speaks, the more Roland does.

"How do you know they're even dead?"

"Because I buried them. Me and the Admiral."

"Then *you* did it!" says Roland. "You did it, and you're trying to make me take the blame!"

Now Connor begins to see the flaw in his plan. If he lets Roland out without a confession, then he's a dead man. But he can't keep him in there forever. His options are now narrower than the spaces between the crates.

Then a voice calls to them from outside. "Is anyone there? Connor? Roland? Anybody?" It's Hayden.

"Help!" screams Roland at the top of his lungs. "Help, he's

crazy! Come in here and let me out!" But his screams don't make it out of the hold. Connor gets up and makes his way to the entrance. Hayden looks up at him. He's not his usual cool self, and there's a nasty bruise on his forehead, like he was hit by something.

"Thank God! Connor, you've got to get back there! It's nuts—you've gotta stop it—they'll listen to you!"

"What are you talking about?"

"The Admiral killed the Goldens—and then everyone thought he'd killed you. . . ."

"The Admiral didn't kill anybody!"

"Well, try telling *them* that!"

"Them *who*?"

"Everybody! They're tearing the place apart!"

Connor sees the far-off smoke, and he takes a quick glance back into the hold, deciding that, for the moment, Roland can wait. He hops down to the ground and races off with Hayden. "Tell me everything, from the beginning."

When Connor arrives at the scene, his mind keeps trying to reject what his eyes are telling him. He stares, part of him hoping the vision will go away. It's like the aftermath of some natural disaster. Broken bits of metal, glass, and wood are everywhere. Pages torn from books flutter past smashed electronics. Bonfires burn, and kids hurl in more wreckage to feed the flames.

"My God!"

There's a group of jeering kids near the helicopter, gathered like a rugby scrum, kicking something in the center. Then Connor realizes it's not some*thing*, it's some*one*. He races in, pulling the kids apart. The kids who know Connor immediately back off, and the others follow suit. The man on the ground is battered and bloody. It's Cleaver. Connor kneels down and props up his head.

"It's okay. You're going to be okay." But even as he says it, Connor knows it's not true: He's been beaten to a pulp.

Cleaver grimaces, his mouth bloody. Then Connor realizes that this isn't a grimace at all. It's a smile. "Chaos, man," Cleaver says weakly. "Chaos. It's beautiful. Beautiful."

Connor doesn't know what to say to this. The man's delirious. He has to be.

"It's okay," Cleaver says. "This is an okay way to die. Better than suffocating, right?"

Connor can only stare at him. "What . . . what did you say?" No one but Connor and the Admiral knew about the suffocations. Connor, the Admiral, and the one who did it . . .

"*You* killed the Goldens! You and Roland!"

"Roland?" says Cleaver. In spite of his pain, he actually seems insulted. "Roland's not one of us. He doesn't even know." Cleaver catches the look on Connor's face and begins to laugh. Then the laugh becomes a rattle that resolves into a long, slow exhale. The grin never entirely leaves his face. His eyes stay open, but there's nothing in them. Just like his victim, Amp.

"Oh, crap, he's dead, isn't he," says Hayden. "They killed him! Holy crap, they killed him!"

Connor leaves the dead pilot in the dust and storms toward the Admiral's plane. He passes the infirmary along the way. Everything's been torn out of there as well. *Risa! Where's Risa?* There are still kids all over the Admiral's jet. The tires have been slashed; wing flaps lean at jagged angles, like broken feathers. The entire jet lists to one side.

"Stop it!" screams Connor. "Stop it now! What are you doing? What have you done?"

He reaches up to the wing, grabs a kid's ankle, and pulls him off onto the ground, but he can't do that to every single one of them. So he grabs a metal pole and smashes it against the wing over and over, the sound ringing out like a church bell, until their attention turns his way.

"Look at you!" he screams. "You've destroyed everything! How could you have done this? You should all be unwound, every single one of you! YOU SHOULD ALL BE UNWOUND!"

It stops everyone. The kids on the wings, the kids at the bonfires. The shock of hearing such words from one of their own snaps them back to sanity. The shock of hearing his own words—and knowing that he meant them—frightens Connor almost as much as the scene before him.

The rolling staircase leading to the Admiral's jet has fallen on its side. "Over here!" says Connor. "Help me with this!"

A dozen kids, their fury spent, come running obediently. Together, they right the stairs, and Connor climbs up to the hatch. He peers in the window. Connor can't see much. The Admiral's there on the floor, but he's not moving. If the Admiral can't get to the door, they'll never be able to get in. Wait—is that someone else in there with him?

Suddenly a lever is thrown on the inside, and the hatch begins to swing open. The heat hits him instantly—a blast furnace of heat—and the face at the door is so red and puffy, it takes a moment for him to realize who it is.

"Risa?"

She coughs and almost collapses into his arms, but manages to keep herself up. "I'm okay," she says. "I'm okay. But the Admiral . . ."

Together they go in and kneel beside him. He's breathing, but it's shallow and strained. "It's the heat!" says Connor, and orders the kids lingering at the door to swing open every hatch.

"It's not just the heat," says Risa. "Look at his lips—they're cyanotic. And his pressure is down to nothing."

Connor just stares at her, not comprehending.

252

"He's having a heart attack! I've been giving him CPR, but I'm not a doctor. There's only so much I can do!"

"M . . . m. . . my fault," says the Admiral. "My fault . . ."

"Shh," says Connor. "You're going to be okay." But Connor knows, just as he knew when he said it to Cleaver, the chances of that are slim.

They carry the Admiral down the stairs, and as they do, the kids waiting outside back away, making room for him, as if it's already a coffin they're carrying. They set him down in the shade of the wing.

Then kids around them begin to murmur.

"He killed the Goldens," someone says. "The old man deserves what he gets."

Connor boils, but he's gotten much better at keeping his anger in check. "Cleaver did it," Connor says forcefully enough for everyone to hear. That starts a murmur through the crowd, until someone says, "Yeah? Well, what about Emby?"

The Admiral's hand flutters up. "My . . . my son . . ."

"Emby's his *son*?" says one kid, and the rumor begins to spread through the crowd.

Whatever the Admiral meant, it's lost now in incoherence as he slips in and out of consciousness.

"If we don't get him to a hospital, he'll die," says Risa, giving him chest compressions once more.

Connor looks around, but the closest thing to a car on the Graveyard is the golf cart.

"There's the helicopter," says Hayden, "but considering the fact that the pilot's dead, I think we're screwed."

Risa looks at Connor. He doesn't need to read *Risa for Morons* to know what she's thinking. The pilot is dead—but Cleaver was training another one. "I know what to do," says Connor. "I'll take care of it."

Connor stands up and looks around him—the smoke-stained faces, the smoldering bonfires. After today nothing will be the same. "Hayden," he says, "you're in charge. Get everything under control."

"You're kidding me, right?"

Connor leaves Hayden to grapple with authority and finds three of the largest kids in his field of vision. "You, you and you," Connor says. "I need you to come with me to the FedEx jet."

The three kids step forward and Connor leads the way to Crate 2399, and Roland. This, Connor knows, will not be an easy conversation.

# 47 · First-Year Residents

In her six months working in the emergency room, the young doctor has seen enough strange things to fill her own medical school textbook, but this is the first time someone has crashlanded a helicopter in the hospital parking lot.

She races out with a team of nurses, orderlies, and other doctors. It's a small private craft—four-seater, maybe. It's in one piece, and its blades are still spinning. It missed hitting a parked car by half a yard. Someone's losing their flying license.

Two kids get out, carrying an older man in bad shape. There's already a gurney rolling out to meet them.

"We have a rooftop helipad, you know,"

"He didn't think he'd be able to land on it," says the girl.

When the doctor looks at the pilot, still sitting behind the controls, she realizes that losing his license is not an issue. The kid at the controls can't be any older than seventeen. She hurries to the old man. A stethoscope brings barely a sound from his chest cavity. Turning to the medical staff around her, she says, "Stabilize him, and prep him for transplant." Then she turns back to the kids. "You're lucky you landed at a hospital with a heart bank, or we'd end up having to medevac him across town."

Then the man's hand rises from the gurney. He grabs her sleeve, tugging with more strength than a man in his condition should have.

"No transplant," he says.

*No, don't do this to me,* thinks the doctor. The orderlies hesitate. "Sir, it's a routine operation."

"He doesn't want a transplant," says the boy.

"You brought him in from God-knows-where with an underage pilot to save his life, and he won't let us do it? We have an entire tissue locker full of healthy young hearts—"

"No transplant!" says the man.

"It's . . . uh . . . against his religion," says the girl.

"Tell you what," says the boy. "Why don't you do whatever they did *before* you had a tissue locker full of healthy young hearts."

The doctor sighs. At least she's still close enough to medical school to remember what that is. "It drastically lowers his chances of survival—you know that, don't you?"

"He knows."

She gives the man a moment more to change his mind, then gives up. The orderlies and other staff rush the man back toward the ER, and the two kids follow.

Once they're gone, she takes a moment to catch her breath. Someone grabs her arm, and she turns to see the young pilot, who had been silent through all of it. The look on his face is pleading, yet determined. She thinks she knows what it's about. She glances at the helicopter, then at the kid. "Take it up with the FAA," she says. "If he lives, I'm sure you'll be off the hook. They might even call you a hero."

"I need you to call the Juvey-cops," he says, his grip getting a little stronger.

"Excuse me?"

"Those two are runaway Unwinds. As soon as the old man is admitted, they'll try to sneak away. Don't let them. Call the Juvey-cops now!"

She pulls out of his grip. "All right. Fine. I'll see what I can do."

"And when they come," he says, "make sure they talk to me first."

She turns from him and heads back into the hospital, pulling out her cell phone on the way. If he wants the Juvey-cops, fine, he'll get them. The sooner they come, the sooner this whole thing can fall into the category of "not my problem."

# 48 · Risa

Juvey-cops always look the same. They look tired, they look angry—they look a lot like the Unwinds they capture. The cop who now guards Risa and Connor is no exception. He sits blocking the door of the doctor's office they're being held in, with two more guards on the other side of the door just in case. He's content to stay silent, while another cop questions Roland in an adjacent room. Risa doesn't even want to guess at the topics of conversation in there.

"The man we brought in," Risa says. "How is he?"

"Don't know," says the cop. "You know hospitals—they only tell those things to next of kin, and I guess that's not you."

Risa won't dignify that with a response. She hates this Juvey-cop instinctively, just because of who he is, and what he represents.

"Nice socks," Connor says.

The cop does not glance down at his socks. No show of weakness here. "Nice ears," he says to Connor. "Mind if I try them on sometime?"

The way Risa sees it, there are two types of people who become Juvey-cops. Type one: bullies who want to spend their lives reliving their glory days of high school bullying. Type two: the former victims of type ones, who see every Unwind as the kid who tormented them all those years ago. Type twos are endlessly shoveling vengeance into a pit that will never be full. Amazing that the bullies and victims can now work together to bring misery to others.

"How does it feel to do what you do?" she asks him. "Sending kids to a place that ends their lives."

Obviously he's heard all this before. "How does it feel to live a life no one else feels is worth living?"

It's a harsh blow designed to get her to shut up. It works.

"I feel her life is worth living," says Connor, and he takes her hand. "Anyone feel that way about you?"

It gets to the man—although he tries not to show it. "You both had more than fifteen years to prove yourselves, and you didn't. Don't blame the world for your own lousy choices."

Risa can sense Connor's rage, and she squeezes his hand until she hears him take a deep breath and release it, keeping his anger under control.

"Doesn't it ever occur to you Unwinds that you might be better off—*happier* even—in a divided state?"

"Is that how you rationalize it?" says Risa, "Making yourself believe we'll be happier?"

"Hey, if that's the case," says Connor, "maybe everyone should get unwound. Why don't you go first?"

The cop glares at Connor, then takes a quick glance down at his socks. Connor snickers.

Risa closes her eyes for a moment, trying to see some ray of light in this situation, but she can't. She had known getting caught was a possibility when they came here. She knew that being out in the world was a risk. What surprised her was how quickly the Juvey-cops had descended on them. Even with their unorthodox entrance, they should have had enough time to slip away in the confusion. Whether the Admiral lives or dies, it won't change things for her or for Connor now. They are going to be unwound. All her hopes of a future have been torn away from her again—and having those hopes, even briefly, makes this far more painful than not having had them at all.

# 49 · Roland

The Juvey-cop questioning Roland has eyes that don't exactly match, and a sour smell, like his deodorant soap hadn't quite worked. Like his partner in the other room, the man is not easily impressed, and Roland, unlike Connor, doesn't have the wits to rattle him. That's all right, though, because rattling him is not what Roland has in mind.

Roland's plan began to take shape shortly after Connor released him from the crate. He could have torn Connor limb from limb at the time, but Connor had three kids equal in size and strength to Roland to back him up. They were kids who should have been on Roland's side. *Should* have been. It was his first indication that everything had drastically changed.

Connor told him about the riot, and about Cleaver. He offered a lame apology for accusing him of killing the Goldens—an apology that Roland refused to accept. Had Roland been at the riot, it would have been organized and successful. If he had been there, it would have been a revolt, not a riot. By locking Roland away, Connor had robbed him of the chance to lead.

When they had arrived back at the scene of the riot, all focus was on Connor; all questions were directed to him. He was telling everyone what to do, and they were all listening. Even Roland's closest friends cast their eyes down when they saw him. He instinctively knew that all his support was gone. His absence from the disaster had made him an outsider, and he would never regain what he had lost here—which meant it was time to devise a new plan of action.

Roland agreed to fly the helicopter to save the Admiral's life, not because he had any desire to see the man live, but because taking that flight provided a new door of opportunity. . . .

"I'm curious," says the sour-smelling cop. "Why would you turn in the other two kids when it means turning yourself in as well?"

"There's a reward of five hundred dollars for turning in a runaway Unwind, right?"

He smirks. "Well, that's fifteen hundred, if you're including yourself."

Roland looks the Juvey-cop in the eye—no shame, no fear—and boldly presents his offer. "What if I told you I know where there are more than four hundred AWOL Unwinds? What if I helped you take down a whole smuggling operation? What would that be worth?"

The cop seems to freeze in place, and he regards Roland closely. "All right," he says. "You have my attention."

# 50 · Connor

He's lasted longer than anyone expected. This is the consolation Connor must hold on to as the cop and two armed guards escort him and Risa into the room where Roland is being interrogated. By the smug look on Roland's face, however, Connor suspects it wasn't so much an interrogation as a negotiation.

"Please, sit down," says the cop sitting on the edge of a desk near Roland. Roland won't look at them. He won't even acknowledge their presence in the room. He just leans back in his chair. He'd fold his arms if the handcuffs allowed it.

The cop wastes no time in getting right to business. "Your friend here had quite a lot to say—and offered us a very interesting deal. His freedom, in exchange for four hundred Unwinds. He's volunteered to tell us exactly where they are."

Connor knew Roland would give him and Risa up, but giving up all of them—that's a new low for Roland. He still won't look at them, but his smug expression seems to have grown a little harder.

"Four hundred, huh?" says the second cop.

"He's lying," says Risa, her voice remarkably convincing. "He's trying to trick you. It's just the three of us."

"Actually," says the cop on the desk, "he's telling the truth—although we're surprised the number's at four hundred. We thought there'd be at least six hundred by now, but I guess they keep on turning eighteen."

Roland regards him, uncertain. "What?"

"Sorry to tell you this, but we know all about the Admiral and the Graveyard," the cop says. "We've known about it for more than a year."

The second cop chuckles, amused by the dumbfounded look on Roland's face. "But . . . but . . ."

"But why don't we round them up?" says the cop, anticipating Roland's question. "Look at it this way. The Admiral— he's like that neighborhood stray cat that nobody likes but no one wants to get rid of because he takes care of the rats. See, runaway Unwinds on the street—that's a problem for us. But the

Admiral gets them off the street and keeps them in that little desert ghetto of his. He doesn't know it, but he's doing us a favor. No more rats."

"Of course," says the second cop, "if the old man dies, we may have to go in there and clean the place out after all."

"No!" says Risa. "Someone else can take over!"

The second cop shrugs as if it's nothing to him. "Better be a good mouser."

While Roland can only stare incredulously as his plan crumbles, Connor feels relief, and maybe even a bit of hope. "So, then you'll let us go back?"

The cop on the desk picks up a file. "I'm afraid I can't do that. It's one thing to look the other way, but quite another to release a criminal." Then he begins to read. "Connor Lassiter. Scheduled to be unwound the 21st of November—until you went AWOL. You caused an accident that killed a bus driver, left dozens of others injured, and shut down an interstate highway for hours. Then, on top of it, you took a hostage *and* shot a Juvey-cop with his own tranq gun."

Roland looks at the cop in awe. "*He's* the Akron AWOL?!"

Connor glances at Risa, then back at the cop. "Fine. I admit it. But she had nothing to do with it! Let her go!"

The cop shakes his head, scanning the file. "Witnesses say she was an accomplice. I'm afraid there's only one place she's going. Same place as you: the nearest harvest camp."

"But what about me?" asks Roland. "I had nothing to do with any of that!"

The cop closes the file. "Ever hear of 'guilt by association'?" he asks Roland. "You should be more careful with the company you keep." Then he signals for the guards to take all three of them away.

# Part Six

# Unwound

For your ease and peace of mind, there are a variety of harvest camps to choose from. Each facility is privately owned, state licensed, and federally funded by your tax dollars. Regardless of the site you choose, you can feel confident that your Unwind will receive the finest possible care from our board-certified staff as they make their transition to a divided state.

—From *The Parents' Unwinding Handbook*

# 51 · Camp

On the existence of a soul, whether unwound or unborn, people are likely to debate for hours on end, but no one questions whether an unwinding facility has a soul. It does not. Perhaps that's why those who build these massive medical factories try so hard to make them kid-conscious and user-friendly, in a number of ways.

First of all, they are no longer called unwinding facilities, as they were when they were first conceived. They are now called harvest camps.

Secondly, every single one of them is located in a spectacularly scenic location, perhaps to remind its guests of the big picture, and the reassuring majesty of a larger plan.

Third, the grounds are as well maintained as a resort, filled with bright pastel colors and as little red as possible, since red is psychologically associated with anger, aggression, and, not coincidentally, blood.

Happy Jack Harvest Camp, in beautiful Happy Jack, Arizona, is the perfect model of what a harvest camp should be. Nestled on a pine-covered ridge in northern Arizona, the sedating forest views give way to the breathtaking red mountains of Sedona to the west. No doubt it was the view that made happy men of the twentieth century lumberjacks who founded the town. Hence the name.

The boys' dormitory is painted light blue, with green accents. The girls' is lavender, with pink. The staff have uniforms that consist of comfortable shorts and Hawaiian shirts, except for the surgeons in the medical unit. Their scrubs are sunshine yellow.

There's a barbed-wire fence, but it's hidden behind a

towering hibiscus hedge—and although the Unwinds in residence see the crowded buses arriving at the front gate each day, they are spared the sight of departing trucks. Those leave the back way.

The average stay for an Unwind is three weeks, although it varies depending on blood type and supply and demand. Much like life in the outside world, no one knows when it's their time.

Occasionally, in spite of the professional and positive attitude of the staff, outbursts do occur. This week's rebellion is in the form of graffiti on the side of the medical clinic that reads, YOU'RE NOT FOOLING ANYONE.

On the fourth of February, three kids arrive by police escort. Two are brought unceremoniously into the welcome center, just like any other arriving Unwinds. The third is singled out to take the longer route that passes by the dormitories, the sports fields, and all the various places where Unwinds are gathered.

Hobbled by leg shackles, constricted by handcuffs, Connor's strides are short, his posture hunched. Armed Juvey-cops are on either side, in front of and behind him.

All things at Happy Jack are serene and gracious—but this moment is the exception to the rule. Once in a while, a particularly troublesome Unwind is singled out and publicly humbled for all to see before being set loose into the general population. Invariably, that Unwind will try to rebel and, invariably, that Unwind will be taken to the clinic and unwound within just a few days of his or her arrival.

It stands as an unspoken warning to every Unwind there. You will get with the program, or your stay here will be very, very short. The lesson is always learned.

However, this time, what the Happy Jack staff doesn't

know is that Connor Lassiter's reputation has preceded him. The staff's own announcement that they've taken down the Akron AWOL does not deflate the spirits of the Unwinds there. Instead, it takes a boy who was only a rumor and turns him into a legend.

# 52 · Risa

*"Before we begin our session, I feel it's important to remind you that although you've developed a friendship with the so-called Akron AWOL, it's in your best interests to dissociate yourself from him."*

The first thing they did was to separate the three of them. Divide and conquer, isn't that the term? Risa has no problem being separated from Roland, but seeing what they did to Connor makes her long to see him even more. Physically, he was not harmed in any way. It would not do to damage the merchandise. Psychologically, however, that's a different story. They paraded him through the grounds for nearly twenty minutes. Then they took off his shackles and just left him there by the flagpole. No trip to the "welcome center," no orientation, nothing. He was left to figure everything out for himself. Risa knew the point wasn't to challenge him, or even to punish him. It was to give him every opportunity to do the wrong thing. That way, they could justify any punishment they gave. It had worried Risa, but only for a moment—because she knows Connor all to well. He will only do the wrong thing when it's the right thing to do.

*"It looks like you did very well on the aptitude tests, Risa— above average, actually. Good for you!"*

After being there for half a day, Risa is still shell-shocked by the general appearance of Happy Jack Harvest Camp. In her mind's eye she always pictured harvest camps as human cattle stockades: dead-eyed crowds of malnourished kids in small gray cells—a nightmare of dehumanization. Yet somehow this picturesque nightmare is worse. Just as the airplane graveyard was Heaven disguised as Hell, harvest camp is Hell masquerading as Heaven.

*"You seem to be in good physical condition. You've been getting a lot of exercise, yes? Running, perhaps?"*

Exercise seems to be a principal component of the Unwind's day. At first she assumed the various activities were designed to keep the Unwinds occupied until their number came up. Then, as she passed a basketball game on the way to the welcome center, she noticed a totem pole by the court. In the eyes of each of the five totems were cameras. Ten players, ten cameras. It meant that someone, somewhere, was studying each of the Unwinds in that game, taking notes on eye-hand coordination, gauging the strengths of various muscle groups. Risa had quickly realized that the basketball game wasn't to keep the Unwinds entertained, but to help put a cash value on their parts.

*"Over the next few weeks you'll be involved in a program of diverse activities. Risa, dear, are you listening? Is any of this going over your head—would you like me to slow down?"*

The harvest counselor who interviews her seems to assume that, in spite of aptitude scores, every Unwind must be an imbecile. The woman wears a floral print blouse with lots of leaves and pink flowers. Risa would like to attack her with a weed whacker.

"Do you have any questions or concerns, dear? If you do, there's no better time to ask."

"What happens to the bad parts?"

The question seems to throw the woman off stride. "Excuse me?"

"You know—the bad parts. What do you do with the club feet, and the deaf ears? Do you use those in transplants?"

"You don't have either of those, do you?"

"No—but I do have an appendix. What happens to that?"

"Well," says the counselor with near infinite patience, "a deaf ear is better than no ear at all, and sometimes it's all people can afford. And as for your appendix, nobody really needs that anyway."

"Then, aren't you breaking the law? Doesn't the law specify that you have to keep 100 percent of an Unwind alive?"

The smile has begun to fade from the counselor's face. "Well, actually it's 99.44 percent, which takes into account things like the appendix."

"I see."

"Our next bit of business is your preadmission questionnaire. Due to your unorthodox arrival, you never had the opportunity to fill one out." She flips through the pages of the questionnaire. "Most of the questions don't matter at this point . . . but if you have any special skills you'd like to let us know about—you know, things that could be of use to the community during your stay here . . ."

Risa wishes she could just get up and leave. Even now, at the end of her life, she still has to face that inevitable question, *What good are you?*

"I have some medical experience," Risa tells her flatly. "First aid, CPR."

The woman smiles apologetically. "Well, if there's one thing we have too many of here, it's medical staff." If the woman says "well" one more time, Risa may just drop her down a nice deep one. "Anything else?"

"I helped in the infant nursery back at StaHo."

Again that slim smile. "Sorry. No babies here. Is that all?"

Risa sighs. "I also studied classical piano."

The woman's eyebrows raise about an inch. "Really? You play piano? Well, well, well!"

# 53 · Connor

Connor wants to fight. He wants to mistreat the staff and disobey every rule, because he knows if he does, it will get this over with faster. But he won't give in to the urge for two reasons. One: It's exactly what they want him to do. And two: Risa. He knows how it will devastate her to see him led to the Chop Shop. That's what the kids call it, "the Chop Shop"—although they never say it in front of the staff.

Connor is a celebrity in his dormitory. He finds it absurd and surreal that the kids here see him as some sort of symbol, when all he did was survive.

"It can't be all true, right?" the kid who sleeps in the bed next to his asks the first night. "I mean, you didn't *really* take on an entire squad of Juvey-cops with their own tranq guns."

"No! It's not true," Connor tells him, but denying it just makes the kid believe it even more.

"They didn't *really* shut down entire freeways looking for you," another kid says.

"It was just one freeway—and they didn't shut it down. I did. Sort of."

"So, then it is true!"

It's no use—no amount of downplaying the story can convince the others that the Akron AWOL is not some larger-than-life action figure.

And then there's Roland, who as much as he despises Connor, is now riding Connor's fame wave for all it's worth. Although Roland's in another unit, wild stories are already getting back to Connor about how he and Roland stole a helicopter and liberated a hundred Unwinds being held in a Tucson hospital. Connor considers telling them that all Roland did was turn them in, but decides life is literally too short to start things up with Roland again.

There's one kid Connor speaks to who actually listens and can tell the truth from the fabrications. His name is Dalton. He's seventeen but short and stocky, with hair that has a mind of its own. Connor tells him exactly what happened on that day he went AWOL. It's a relief to have someone believe the truth. Dalton, however, has his own perspective on it.

"Even if that's all that happened," Dalton says, "it's still pretty impressive. It's what the rest of us *wish* we could have done."

Connor has to admit that he's right.

"You're, like, king of the Unwinds here," Dalton tells him, "but guys like you get unwound real quick—so watch yourself." Then Dalton takes a long look at him. "You scared?" he asks.

Connor wishes he could tell him different, but he won't lie. "Yeah."

He seems almost relieved that Connor's scared too. "In group they tell us that the fear will pass and we'll get to a place of acceptance. I've been here almost six months, and I'm just as scared as the day I got here."

"Six months? I thought everyone goes down in just a few weeks."

Dalton leans in close and whispers, as if it's dangerous information. "Not if you're in the band."

A band? The thought of there being music at a place where lives are silenced doesn't sit well with Connor.

"They set us up on the roof of the Chop Shop and have us play while they're bringing kids in," Dalton says. "We play everything—classics, pop, Old World rock. I'm the best bass player this place has ever seen." And then he grins. "You should come listen to us tomorrow. We just got a new keyboard player. She's hot."

Volleyball in the morning. Connor's first official activity. Several staffers in their rainbow of flowered shirts stand on the sidelines with clipboards, because apparently the volleyball court isn't equipped with twelve individual cameras. From behind them, on the roof of the chop shop, music plays. Dalton's band. It's their sound track for the morning.

The opposing team completely deflates when they see Connor, as if his mere presence will ensure their loss. Never mind that Connor stinks at volleyball; to them the Akron AWOL is a star in every sport. Roland's on the opposing team as well. He doesn't wilt like the others—he just glares, holding the volleyball, ready to serve it down Connor's throat.

The game begins. The intensity of play can only be matched by an undercurrent of fear that runs beneath every tap of the ball. Both teams play as if the losers will be immediately unwound. Dalton had told Connor that it doesn't work that way, but losing can't help, either. It reminds Connor of the Mayan game of pokatok—something he learned about in history class. The game was a lot like basketball, except that the losers were sacrificed to the Mayan gods. At the time Connor thought it was cool.

Roland spikes the ball, and it hits one of the staffers in the face. Roland grins before he apologizes and the man glares at him, making a note on his clipboard. Connor wonders if it will cost Roland a few days.

Then suddenly, the game pauses, because everyone's attention begins to shift to a group of kids in white, passing the far side of the court.

"Those are tithes," a kid tells Connor. "You know what those are, right?"

Connor nods. "I know."

"Look at them. They think they're so much better than everyone else."

Connor has already heard how tithes are treated differently than the regular population. "Tithes" and "Terribles," that's how the staff refers to the two kinds of Unwinds. Tithes don't participate in the same activities as the terribles. They don't wear the same blue and pink uniforms the terribles wear. Their white silk outfits are so bright in the Arizona sun, you have to squint your eyes when you look at them, like they were adolescent versions of God himself—although to Connor they look more like a little squad of aliens. The terribles hate the tithes the way peasants despise royalty. Connor might have once felt the same way, but having known one, he feels more sorry for them than anything else.

"I hear they know the exact date and time of their unwinding," one kid says.

"I hear they actually make their own *appointment*!" says another.

The ref blows his whistle, "All right, back to the game."

They turn away from the bright white uniforms of the chosen few, and add one more layer of frustration to the match.

For a moment, as the tithes disappear over a hillside, Connor thinks that he recognizes a face among them, but he knows it's just his imagination.

# 54 · Lev

It's not Connor's imagination.

Levi Jedediah Calder is one of the very special guests of

Happy Jack Harvest Camp, and he is wearing his tithing whites once more. He does not see Connor on the volleyball court because the tithes are strictly instructed not to look at the terribles. Why should they? They have been told from birth they are of a different caste and have a higher calling.

Lev may still have the remnants of a sunburn, but his hair is cut short and neat, just as it used to be, and his manner is sensitive and mild. At least on the outside.

He has an appointment for unwinding in thirteen days.

# 55 · Risa

She plays on the roof of the Chop Shop, and her music carries across the fields to the ears of more than a thousand souls waiting to go under the knife. The joy of having her fingers on the keys again can only be matched by the horror of knowing what's going on beneath her feet.

From her vantage point on the roof she sees them brought down the maroon flagstone path that all the kids call "the red carpet." Kids who walk the red carpet have guards flanking them on either side, with firm grips on their upper arms—firm enough to restrain them, but not enough to bruise them.

Yet in spite of this, Dalton and the rest of his band play like it doesn't matter at all.

"How can you do this?" she asks during one of their breaks. "How can you watch them day after day, going in and never coming out?"

"You get used to it," the drummer tells her, taking a swig of water. "You'll see."

"I won't! I can't!" She thinks about Connor. He doesn't have this same reprieve from unwinding. He doesn't stand a chance. "I can't be an accomplice to what they're doing!"

"Hey," says Dalton, getting annoyed. "This is survival here, and we do what we have to do to survive! You got chosen because you can play, and you're good. Don't throw it away. Either you get used to kids walking down the red carpet or you'll be on it yourself, and we'll have to play for *you*."

Risa gets the message, but it doesn't mean she has to like it. "Is that what happened to your last keyboard player?" Risa asks. She can tell it's a subject they'd rather not think about. They look at one another. No one wants to take on the question. Then the lead singer answers with a nonchalant toss of her hair, like it doesn't matter. "Jack was about to turn eighteen, so they took him a week before his birthday."

"He was not a very happy Jack," says the drummer, and hits a rim shot.

"That's it?" says Risa. "They just took him?"

"Business is business," says the lead singer. "They lose a ton of money if one of us turns eighteen, because then they've got to let us go."

"I've got a plan, though," says Dalton, winking at the others, who have obviously heard this before. "When I'm getting close to eighteen, and they're ready to come for me, I'm jumping right off this roof."

"You're going to kill yourself?"

"I hope not—it's only two stories, but I'll sure get busted up real bad. See, they can't unwind you like that; they have to wait until you heal. By then I'll be eighteen and they will be *screwed*!" He high-fives the drummer, and they laugh. Risa can only stare in disbelief.

"Personally," says the lead singer, "I'm counting on them lowering the legal age of adulthood to seventeen. If they do, I'll go to the staffers and counselors, and the friggin' doctors. I'll spit right in their faces—and they won't be able to do anything but let me walk right out that gate on my own two legs."

Then the guitar player, who hasn't said a word all morning, picks up his instrument.

"This one's for Jack," he says, and begins playing the opening chords to the prewar classic "Don't Fear the Reaper."

The rest of them join in, playing from the heart, and Risa does her best to keep her eyes away from the red carpet.

# 56 · Connor

The dormitories are divided into units. There are thirty kids per unit—thirty beds in a long, thin room with large shatter-proof windows to bring in the cheerful light of day. As Connor prepares for dinner he notices that two beds in his unit have been stripped, and the kids who slept in them are nowhere to be seen. Everyone notices but no one talks about it, except one kid who takes one of the bunks because his mattress has broken springs.

"Let a newbie have the broken one," he says. "I'm gonna be comfortable my last week."

Conner can't remember either the names or the faces of the missing kids, and that haunts him. The whole day weighs heavily on him—the way the kids think he can somehow save them, when he knows he can't even save himself. The way the staff keeps waiting for him to make a mistake. His one joy is knowing that Risa is safe, at least for now.

He had seen her after lunch when he stopped to watch the band. He had been searching for her everywhere, and all that time she was right there in plain view, playing her heart out. She had told him she played piano, but he never gave it much thought. She's amazing, and now he wishes he had taken more time to get to know who she was before she escaped from that bus. When she saw him watching that afternoon, she smiled—

something she rarely did. But the smile was quickly replaced by a look that registered the reality. She was up there, and he was down here.

Connor spends so much time with his thoughts in the dormitory that, when he looks up, he realizes that everyone in the unit has already left for dinner. As he gets up to leave, he sees someone lurking at the door and stops short. It's Roland.

"You're not supposed to be here," Connor says.

"No, I'm not," says Roland, "but thanks to you, I am."

"That's not what I mean. If you get caught out of your unit, it's a mark against you. They'll unwind you sooner."

"Nice of you to care."

Connor heads for the doorway, but Roland blocks his path. For the first time Connor notices that in spite of Roland's muscular build, they're not all that different in height. Connor always thought Roland towered over him. He doesn't. Connor prepares himself for whatever Roland might have up his sleeve and says, "If you're here for a reason, get on with it. Otherwise, step aside so I can get to dinner."

The look on Roland's face is so toxic it could take out an entire unit. "I could have killed you a dozen times. I should have—because then we wouldn't be here."

"You turned us in at the hospital," Connor reminds him. "If *you* hadn't done *that*, we wouldn't be here. We all would've made it safely back to the Graveyard!"

"What Graveyard? There's nothing left. You locked me in that crate and let them all destroy it! I would have stopped it, but you never gave me the chance!"

"If you were there, you would have found a way to kill the Admiral yourself. Hell, you would have killed the Goldens if they weren't already dead! That's what you are! That's *who* you are!"

Roland suddenly gets very quiet, and Connor knows he's gone too far.

"Well, if I'm a killer, I'm running out of time," says Roland. "I better get to it." He begins swinging, and Connor is quick to defend, but soon it's more than just defending himself. Connor taps into his own wellspring of fury, and he lets loose a brutal offensive of his own.

It's the fight they never had in the warehouse. It's the fight Roland wanted when he had cornered Risa in the bathroom. Both of them fuel their fists with a world's worth of anger. They smash against walls and bedframes, relentlessly pummeling each other. Connor knows this is not like any fight he's ever had before, and although Roland doesn't have a weapon, he doesn't need one. He's his own weapon.

As well as Connor fights, Roland is simply stronger, and as Connor's strength begins to fade, Roland grabs him by the throat and slams him against the wall, his hand pressed against Connor's windpipe. Connor struggles, but Roland's grip is way too strong. He slams Connor against the wall over and over, never loosening that grip on his neck.

"You call me a killer, but you're the only criminal here!" screams Roland. "I didn't take a hostage! I didn't shoot a Juvey-cop! And I never killed anyone! Until now!" Then he squeezes his fingers together and shuts off Connor's windpipe completely.

Connor's struggles become weaker without oxygen to feed his muscles. His chest heaves against the absence of air, and his vision begins to darken until all he can see is Roland's furious grimace. *Would you rather die, or be unwound?* Now he finally knows the answer. Maybe this is what he wanted. Maybe it's why he stood there and taunted Roland. Because he'd rather be killed with a furious hand than dismembered with cool indifference.

Connor's eyesight fills with frantic squiggles, the darkness closes in, and his consciousness fails.

But only for an instant.

Because in a moment his head hits the ground, startling him conscious again—and when his vision starts to clear he sees Roland looking down on him. He's just standing there, staring. To Connor's amazement, there are tears in Roland's eyes that he tries to hide behind his anger, but they're still there. Roland looks at the hand that came so close to taking Connor's life. He wasn't able to go through with it—and he seems just as surprised as Connor.

"Consider yourself lucky," Roland says. Then he leaves without another word.

Connor can't tell whether Roland is disappointed or relieved that he's not the killer he thought he was, but Connor suspects it's a little bit of both.

# 57 · Lev

The tithes at Happy Jack are like first-class passengers on the *Titanic*. There's plush furniture throughout the tithing house. There's a theater, a pool, and the food is better than home-made. Sure, their fate is the same as the "terribles," but at least they're getting there in style.

It's after dinner, and Lev is alone in the tithing house workout room. He stands on a treadmill that isn't moving, because he hasn't turned it on. On his feet are thickly padded running shoes. He wears a double pair of socks to cushion his feet even more. However, his feet are not his concern at the moment—it's his hands. He stands there staring at his hands, lost in the prospect of them. Never before has he been so intrigued by the lines across his palms. Isn't one of them supposed to be a life line? Shouldn't the life line of a tithe divide out like the branches of a tree? Lev looks at the swirls of his fingerprints. What a nightmare of identification it must be when other people get an Unwind's hands. What can fingerprints mean when they're not necessarily yours?

No one will be getting Lev's fingerprints. He knows this for a fact.

There are tons of activities for the tithes, but unlike the terribles, no one is forced to participate. Part of preparation for tithing is a monthlong regimen of mental and physical assessments even before one's tithing party, so all the hard work is done at home, before they get here. True, this isn't the harvest camp he and his parents had chosen, but he's a tithe— it's a lifetime pass that's good anywhere.

Most of the other tithes are in the rec room at this time of the evening, or in any number of prayer groups. There are pastors of all faiths in the tithing house—ministers, priests, rabbis, and clerics—because that notion of giving the finest of the flock back to God is a tradition as old as religion itself.

Lev attends as often as necessary, and in Bible study he says just enough of the right things so as not to look suspect. He also keeps his silence when Bible passages become shredded to justify unwinding, and kids start to see the face of God in the fragments.

"My uncle got the heart of a tithe and now people say he can perform miracles."

"I know this woman who got a tithe's ear. She heard a baby crying a block away, and rescued it from a fire!"

"We are Holy Communion."

"We are manna from Heaven."

"We are the piece of God in everyone."

Amen.

Lev recites prayers, trying to let them transform him and lift him up like they used to, but his heart has been hardened. He wishes it could be hard enough to be diamond instead of crumbling jade—maybe then he'd have chosen a different path. But for who he is now, for what he feels and what he doesn't feel, the path is right. And if it's not right, well, he doesn't care enough to change it.

The other tithes know Lev is different. They've never seen a fallen tithe before, much less one who, like the prodigal son, has renounced his sins and returned to the fold. But then, tithes don't generally know many other tithes. Being surrounded by so many kids just like them feeds that sense of being a chosen group. Still, Lev is outside of that circle.

He turns the treadmill on, making sure his strides are steady and his footfalls as gentle as can be. The treadmill is state-of-the-art. It has a screen with a programmable vista: You can jog through the woods, or run the New York Marathon. You can even walk on water. Lev was prescribed extra exercise when he arrived a week ago. That first day, his blood tests showed high triglyceride levels. He's sure that Mai's and Blaine's blood tests showed the same problem as well—although the three of them were "captured" independently and arrived a few days apart from one another, so no connection among the three of them could be made.

"Either it runs in your family or you've had a diet high in fats," the doctor had said. He prescribed a low-fat diet during his stay at Happy Jack, and suggested additional exercise. Lev knows there's another reason for the high triglyceride level. It's not actually triglyceride in his bloodstream at all, but a similar compound. One that's a little less stable.

Another boy enters the workout room. He has fine hair so blond it's practically white, and eyes so green, there must have been some genetic manipulation involved. Those eyes will go for a high price. "Hi, Lev." He gets on the treadmill next to Lev and begins running. "What's up?"

"Nothing. Just running."

Lev knows the kid didn't come here of his own accord. Tithes are never supposed to be left alone. He was sent here to be Lev's buddy.

"Candlelighting will be starting soon. Are you coming?"

Every evening, a candle is lit for each tithe being unwound the next day. The honored kids each give a speech. Everyone applauds. Lev finds it disgusting.

"I'll be there," Lev tells the kid.

"Have you started working on your speech yet?" he asks. "I'm almost done with mine."

"Mine's still in bits and pieces," Lev says. The joke goes over the kid's head. Lev turns off the machine. This kid will not leave him alone as long as he's here, and Lev really doesn't want to talk to him about the glory of being a chosen one. He'd rather think about those who aren't chosen, and are lucky enough to be far from the harvest camp—like Risa and Connor, who to the best of his knowledge are still in the sanctuary of the Graveyard. It's a big comfort to know that their lives will continue even after he's gone.

There's an old trash shed behind the dining room that's no longer in use. Lev found it last week, and decided it was the perfect place for secret meetings. When he arrives that evening, Mai is pacing in the small space. She's been getting more and more nervous each day. "How long are we going to wait?" she asks.

"Why are you in such a hurry?" Lev asks. "We'll wait until the time is right."

Blaine pulls out six small paper packets from his sock, tears one open, and pulls out a little round Band-Aid.

"What's that for?" Mai asks.

"For me to know and for you to find out."

"You're so immature!"

Mai always has a short fuse, especially when it comes to Blaine, but tonight there seems to be more rumbling beneath the surface of her attitude. "What's wrong, Mai?" Lev asks.

Mai takes a moment before answering. "I saw this girl today playing piano on the Chop Shop roof. I know her from the Graveyard—and she knows me."

"That's impossible. If she's from the Graveyard, why would she be here?" asks Blaine.

"I know what I saw—and I think there are other kids here I know from the Graveyard too. What if they recognize us?"

Blaine and Mai look to Lev as if he can explain it. Actually, he can. "They must be kids who were sent out on a job and got caught, that's all."

Mai relaxes. "Yeah. Yeah, that must be it."

"If they recognize us," says Blaine, "we can say the same thing happened to us."

"There," says Lev. "Problem solved."

"Good," says Blaine. "Back to business. So . . . I'm thinking we go for the day after tomorrow, on account of I'm scheduled for a game of football the day after that, and I don't think it'll go very well."

Then he hands two of the little Band-Aids to Mai and two to Lev.

"What do we need Band-Aids for?" Mai asks.

"I was told to give these to you after we got here." Blaine dangles one from his fingers, like a little flesh-colored leaf. "They're not Band-Aids," he says. "They're detonators."

There was never a job on an Alaskan pipeline. After all, what Unwind would volunteer for such a job? The whole point was to make sure no one but Lev, Mai, and Blaine volunteered. Their van had taken them from the Graveyard to a run-down house, in a run-down neighborhood where people who had been run down by life plotted unthinkable deeds.

Lev was terrified of these people, and yet he felt a kinship with them. They understood the misery of being betrayed by life. They understood what it felt like to have less than nothing inside you. And when they told Lev how important he was in the scheme of things, Lev felt, for the first time in a long time, truly important.

The word "evil" was never used by these people—except to describe the evils of what the world had done to them. What they were asking Lev, Mai, and Blaine to do wasn't evil—no, no, no, not at all. It was an expression of all the things they felt inside. It was the spirit, and the nature, and the manifestation of all they had become. They weren't just messengers, they were the message. This is what they filled Lev's mind with, and it was no different than the deadly stuff they filled his blood with. It was twisted. It was wrong. And yet it suited Lev just fine.

"We have no cause but chaos," Cleaver, their recruiter, was always so fond of saying. What Cleaver never realized, even at the end of his life, is that chaos is as compelling a cause as any other. It can even become a religion to those unlucky enough to be baptized into it, those whose consolation can only be found in its foul waters.

Lev does not know of Cleaver's fate. He does not know, or care, that he himself is being used. All Lev knows is that someday soon the world will suffer a small part of the loss and the emptiness and the utter disillusionment he feels inside. And they will know the moment he raises his hands in applause.

# 58 · Connor

Connor eats his breakfast as quickly as he can. It's not because he's hungry but because he has somewhere else he wants to be. Risa's breakfast hour is right before his. If she's slow, and he's quick, they can force their paths to cross without attracting the attention of the Happy Jack staff.

They meet in the girls' bathroom. The last time they were forced to meet in a place like this, they took separate, isolated stalls. Now they share one. They hold each other in the tight space, making no excuses for it. There's no time left in their lives for games, or for awkwardness, or for pretending they don't care about each other, and so they kiss as if they've done it forever. As if it is as crucial as the need for oxygen.

She touches the bruises on his face and neck, the ones he got from his fight with Roland. She asks what happened. He tells her it's not important. She tells him she can't stay much longer, that Dalton and the other band members will be waiting for her on the Chop Shop roof.

"I heard you play," Connor tells her. "You're amazing."

He kisses her again. They don't speak of unwinding. In this moment none of that exists. Connor knows they would take this further if they could—but not here, not in a place like this. It will never happen for them, but somehow he's content in knowing that in some other place and time it would have. He holds her for ten seconds, twenty. Thirty. Then she slips away, and he returns to the dining hall. In a few minutes he hears her playing, the strains of her music pouring forth, filling Happy Jack with the upbeat, pulse-pounding sound track of the damned.

# 59 · Roland

They come for Roland that same morning, right after breakfast. A harvest counselor and two guards corner him in the
dormitory hallway, isolating him from the others.

"You don't want me," Roland says desperately. "I'm not the
Akron AWOL; Connor's the one you want."

"I'm afraid not," says the counselor.

"But . . . but I've only been here a few days. . . ." He knows
why this happened. It's because he hit that guy with the volleyball, that must be it. Or it's because of his fight with Connor.
Connor turned him in! He knew Connor would turn him in!

"It's your blood type," the counselor says. "AB negative—
it's rare and in very high demand." He smiles. "Think of it this
way, you're worth more than any other kid in your unit."

"Lucky you," says one of the guards as he grabs Roland by
the arm.

"If it's any consolation," says the counselor, "your friend
Connor is scheduled for unwinding this afternoon."

Roland's legs feel weak as they bring him out into the light of
day. The red carpet stretches out before him, the color of dried
blood. Any time kids cross that terrible stone path, they always
jump over it as if touching it were bad luck. Now they won't
let Roland step off of it.

"I want a priest," says Roland. "They give people priests,
right? I want a priest!"

"Priests give last rites," says the counselor, putting a gentle
hand on his shoulder. "That's for people who are dying. You're
not dying—you'll still be alive, just in a different way."

"I still want a priest."

"Okay, I'll see what I can do."

The band on the roof of the Chop Shop has begun their morning set. They play a familiar dance tune, as if to mock the dirge playing inside his head. He knows Risa is in the band now. He sees her up there playing the keyboard. He knows she hates him but still he waves to her, trying get her attention. Even an acknowledgment from someone who hates him is better than having no one but strangers watch him perish.

She doesn't turn her eyes toward the red carpet. She doesn't see him. She doesn't know. Perhaps someone will tell her he was unwound today. He wonders what she'll feel.

They've reached the end of the red carpet. There are five stone steps leading to the doors of the Chop Shop. Roland stops at the bottom of the steps. The guards try to pull him along, but he shakes them off.

"I need more time. Another day. That's all. One more day. I'll be ready tomorrow. I promise!"

And still, above him, the band plays. He wants to scream, but here, so close to the Chop Shop, his screams will be drowned out by the band. The counselor signals to the guards. They grab him more firmly just beneath the armpits, forcing him to take those five steps. In a moment he's through the doors, which slide closed behind him, shutting out the world. He can't even hear the band anymore. The Chop Shop is soundproof. Somehow he knew it would be.

# 60 · Harvest

No one knows how it happens. No one knows how it's done. The harvesting of Unwinds is a secret medical ritual that stays within the walls of each harvesting clinic in the nation. In this way it is not unlike death itself, for no one knows what mysteries lie beyond those secret doors, either.

What does it take to unwind the unwanted? It takes twelve surgeons, in teams of two, rotating in and out as their medical specialty is needed. It takes nine surgical assistants and four nurses. It takes three hours.

# 61 · Roland

Roland is fifteen minutes in.

The medical staff that buzz around him wear scrubs the color of a happy-face.

His arms and legs have been secured to the operating table with bonds that are strong but padded so he won't hurt himself if he struggles.

A nurse blots sweat from his forehead. "Relax, I'm here to help you through this."

He feels a sharp pinprick in the right side of his neck, and then in the left side.

"What's that?"

"That," says the nurse, "is the only pain you'll be feeling today."

"This is it, then," Roland says. "You're putting me under?"

Although he can't see her mouth beneath her surgical mask, he can see the smile in her eyes.

"Not at all," she says. "By law, we're required to keep you conscious through the entire procedure." The nurse takes his hand. "You have a right to know everything that's happening to you, every step of the way."

"What if I don't want to?"

"You will," says one of the surgical assistants, wiping Roland's legs down with brown surgical scrub. "Everybody does."

"We've just inserted catheters into your carotid artery and

jugular vein," says the nurse. "Right now your blood is being replaced with a synthetic oxygen-rich solution."

"We send the real stuff straight to the blood bank," says the assistant at his feet. "Not a bit gets wasted. You can bet, you'll be saving lives!"

"The oxygen solution also contains an anaesthetic that deadens pain receptors." The nurse pats his hand. "You'll be fully conscious, but you won't feel a thing."

Already Roland feels his limbs starting to go numb. He swallows hard. "I hate this. I hate you. I hate all of you."

"I understand."

Twenty-eight minutes in.

The first set of surgeons has arrived.

"Don't mind them," says the nurse. "Talk to me."

"What do we talk about?"

"Anything you want."

Someone drops an instrument. It clatters on the table and falls to the floor. Roland flinches. The nurse holds his hand tighter.

"You may feel a tugging sensation near your ankles," says one of the surgeons at the foot of the table. "It's nothing to worry about."

Forty-five minutes in.

So many surgeons, so much activity. Roland couldn't remember ever having so much attention directed at him. He wants to look, but the nurse holds his focus. She's read his file. She knows everything about him. The good and the bad. The things he never talks about. The things he can't stop talking about now.

"I think it's horrible what your stepfather did."

"I was just protecting my mother."

"Scalpel," says a surgeon.

"She should have been grateful."

"She had me unwound."

"I'm sure it wasn't easy for her."

"All right, clamp it off."

An hour and fifteen.

Surgeons leave, new ones arrive. The new ones take an intense interest in his abdomen. He looks toward his toes but can't see them. Instead he sees a surgical assistant cleaning the lower half of the table.

"I almost killed a kid yesterday."

"That doesn't matter now."

"I wanted to do it, but I got scared. I don't know why, but I got scared."

"Just let it go." The nurse was holding his hand before. She's not anymore.

"Strong abdominal muscles," says a doctor. "Do you work out?"

A clanging of metal. The lower half of the table is unhooked and pulled away. It makes him think of when he was twelve and his mom took him to Las Vegas. She had dropped him off at a magic show while she played the slots. The magician had cut a woman in half. Her toes were still wiggling, her face still smiling. The audience gave him thunderous applause.

Now Roland feels discomfort in his gut. Discomfort, a tickling sensation, but no pain. The surgeons lift things away. He tries not to look, but he can't help it. There's no blood, just the oxygen-rich solution, which is flourescent green, like antifreeze.

"I'm scared," he says.

"I know," says the nurse.

"I want you all to go to Hell."

"That's natural."

One team leaves; another comes in. They take an intense interest in his chest.

An hour forty-five.

"I'm afraid we need to stop talking now."

"Don't go away."

"I'll be here, but we won't be able to talk anymore."

The fear surrounds him, threatening to take him under. He tries to replace it with anger, but the fear is too strong. He tries to replace it with the satisfaction that Connor will be taken very soon, but not even that makes him feel better.

"You'll feel a tingling in your chest," says a surgeon. "It's nothing to worry about."

Two hours, five minutes.

"Blink twice if you can hear me."

*Blink, blink.*

"You're being very brave."

He tries to think of other things, other places, but his mind keeps being drawn back to this place. Everyone's so close around him now. Yellow figures lean all around him like flower petals closing in. Another section of the table is taken away. The petals move in closer. He does not deserve this. He has done many things, not all good, but he does not deserve this. And he never did get his priest.

Two hours, twenty minutes.

"You'll feel a tingling in your jaw. It's nothing to worry about."

"Blink twice if you can hear me."

*Blink, blink.*

291

"Good."

He locks his eyes on the nurse, whose eyes still smile. They always smile. Someone made her have eternally smiling eyes.

"I'm afraid you're going to have to stop blinking now."

"Where's the clock?" says one of the surgeons.

"Two hours, thirty-three minutes."

"We're running late."

Not quite darkness, just an absence of light. He hears everything around him but can no longer communicate. Another team has entered.

"I'm still here," the nurse tells him, but then she falls silent. A few moments later he hears footsteps, and he knows she's left.

"You'll feel a tingling in your scalp," says a surgeon. "It's nothing to worry about." It's the last time they talk to him. After that, the doctors talk like Roland is no longer there.

"Did you see yesterday's game?"

"Heartbreaker."

"Splitting the corpus callosum."

"Nice technique."

"Well, it's not brain surgery." Laughter all around.

Memories tweak and spark. Faces. Dreamlike pulses of light deep in his mind. Feelings. Things he hasn't thought about in years. The memories bloom, then they're gone. When Roland was ten, he broke his arm. The doctor told his mom he could have a new arm, or a cast. The cast was cheaper. He drew a shark on it. When the cast came off he got a tattoo to make the shark permanent.

"If they had just made that three-pointer."

"It'll be the Bulls again. Or the Lakers."

"Starting on the left cerebral cortex."

Another memory tweaks.

*When I was six, my father went to jail for something he did before I got born. I never knew what he did, but Mom says I'm just the same.*

"The Suns don't stand a chance."

"Well, if they had a decent coaching staff . . ."

"Left temporal lobe."

*When I was three, I had a babysitter. She was beautiful. She shook my sister. Real hard. My sister got wrong. Never got right again. Beautiful is dangerous. Better get them first.*

"Well, maybe they'll make the playoffs next year."

"Or the year after that."

"Did we get the auditory nerves?"

"Not yet. Getting them right n—"

*I'm alone. And I'm crying. And no one's coming to the crib. And the nightlight burned out. And I'm mad. I'm so mad.*

Left frontal lobe.

*I . . . I . . . I don't feel so good.*

Left occipital lobe.

*I . . . I . . . I don't remember where . . .*

Left parietal lobe.

*I . . . I . . . I can't remember my name, but . . . but . . .*

Right temporal.

*. . . but I'm still here.*

Right frontal.

*I'm still here . . .*

Right occipital.

*I'm still . . .*

Right parietal.

*I'm . . .*

Cerebellum.

*I'm . . .*

Thalamus.

*I . . .*

**Hypothalamus.**

*I . . .*

**Hippocampus.**

. . .

**Medulla.**

. . .

. . .

. . .

"Where's the clock?"

"Three hours, nineteen minutes."

"All right, I'm on break. Prep for the next one."

# 62 · Lev

The detonators are hidden in a sock in the back of his cubby. Anyone who finds them will think they're Band-Aids. He tries not to think about it. It's Blaine's job to think about it, and to tell him when it's time.

Today Lev's unit of tithes are taking a nature walk to commune with creation. The pastor who leads them is one of the more self-important ones. He speaks as if every word out of his mouth were a pearl of wisdom, pausing after each thought as if he expects someone to write it down.

He leads them to an odd winter-bare tree. Lev, who is used to winters with ice and snow, finds it odd that trees in Arizona still lose their leaves. This tree has a multitude of branches that don't quite match, each with different bark and a different texture.

"I wanted you to see this," the pastor says to the crew. "It's not much to see now, but, oh, you should see it in the spring.

Over the years many of us have grafted branches from our favorite trees to the trunk." He points to the various limbs. "This branch sprouts pink cherry blossoms, and this one fills with huge sycamore leaves. This one fills with purple jacaranda flowers, and this one grows heavy with peaches."

The tithes examine it, touching its branches cautiously, as if it might at any moment turn into the burning bush. "What kind of tree was it to begin with?" asks one of the tithes.

The pastor can't answer him. "I'm not sure, but it really doesn't matter—what matters is what it's become. We call it our little 'tree of life.' Isn't it wonderful?"

"There's nothing wonderful about it." The words are out of Lev's mouth before he realizes he's spoken them, like a sudden, unexpected belch. All eyes turn toward him. He quickly covers. "It's the work of man, and we shouldn't be prideful," he says. "'When pride comes, then comes disgrace; but with humility comes wisdom.'"

"Yes," says the pastor. "Proverbs—eleven, isn't it?"

"Proverbs 11:2."

"Very good." He appears suitably humbled. "Well, it *is* pretty in the spring."

Their path back to the tithing house takes them by fields and courts where the terribles are being observed and brought to the best possible physical condition before their unwinding. The tithes endure the occasional jeers and hisses from the terribles, like martyrs.

It's as they pass one of the dormitories that Lev finds himself face-to-face with someone he never expected to see again. He finds himself standing in front of Connor.

Each was heading in a different direction. Each sees the other at the same instant and stops short, staring in absolute shock.

"Lev?"

Suddenly the pompous pastor is there, grabbing Lev by both shoulders. "Get away from him!" the pastor snarls at Connor. "Haven't you done enough damage already?" Then he spirits Lev away, leaving Connor standing there.

"It's all right," says the pastor, his protective grip on Lev's shoulders still firm as they stride away. "We're all aware of who he is and what he did to you. We were hoping you wouldn't find out he was at the same harvest camp. But I promise you, Lev, he will never harm you again." And then he says quietly, "He's being unwound this afternoon."

"What?"

"And good riddance, too!"

It's not unusual to see tithes unsupervised on the grounds of Happy Jack, although they're usually in clusters—or at the very least, groups of two. It's rare to see one hurrying alone, almost running across the fields.

Lev hadn't lingered long once he got back to the tithing house—he took the first opportunity to slip out. Now he searches everywhere for Blaine and Mai.

*Connor is being unwound this afternoon.* How could this have happened? How did he get here? Connor was safe at the Graveyard. Did the Admiral throw him out, or did he leave on his own? Either way, Connor must have been caught and brought here. The one thing Lev had taken comfort in—the safety of his friends—has now been torn away. Connor's unwinding must not be allowed . . . and it's in Lev's power to stop it.

He finds Blaine in the grassy commons between the dining hall and the dormitories, being put through a regimen of calisthenics with his unit. Blaine does them oddly, putting as little force into them as possible, making all his moves low-impact.

"I need to talk to you."

Blaine looks at him, surprised and furious. "What, are you crazy? What are you doing here?"

A staffer sees him and makes a beeline toward them—after all, everyone knows tithes and terribles do not mix.

"It's all right," Lev tells the staffer, "I know him from home. I just wanted to say good-bye."

The staffer reluctantly nods his approval. "All right, but make it quick."

Lev pulls Blaine aside, making sure they're far enough away that nobody can hear. "We're doing it today," Lev tells him. "No more waiting."

"Hey," says Blaine, "*I* decide when we do it, and I say not yet."

"The longer we wait, the longer we risk going off by accident."

"So? Randomness works too."

He wants to hit Blaine but knows if he does they'll probably leave a crater in the field fifty yards wide, so he tells Blaine the only thing he knows for sure will get him to give in.

"They know about us," whispers Lev.

"What?"

"They don't know who it is, but they know there are clappers here—I'm sure they're reviewing the blood tests right now, looking for anything unusual. It won't be long until they find us."

Blaine grits his teeth and curses. He thinks for a moment, then starts shaking his head. "No. No, I'm not ready."

"It doesn't matter if you're ready. You want chaos? Well, it's coming today, whether you want it or not—because if they find us, what do you think they'll do?"

Blaine looks even sicker at the prospect. "They'll detonate us in the forest?"

"Or out in the desert where no one will ever know."

Blaine considers it for a moment more, then takes a deep, shuddering breath. "I'll find Mai at lunch and tell her. We'll go at two o'clock sharp."

"Make it one."

Lev rummages through his cubby, getting more and more frantic. Those socks have to be here! They have to be—but he can't find them. The detonators aren't crucial, but they're cleaner. Lev wants it to be clean. Clean and quick.

"That's mine."

Lev turns to see the towheaded kid with the emerald-green eyes standing behind him. "That's my cubby. Yours is over there."

Lev looks around and realizes he's off by one bed. There's nothing in the unit to identify one bed, or one cubby, from another.

"If you need socks, I can lend you."

"No, I've got enough of my own, thanks." He takes a deep breath, closes his eyes to get his panic under control, and goes to the right cubby. The sock with the detonators is there. He slips it in his pocket.

"You okay, Lev? You look kinda funny."

"I'm fine. I've just been running, that's all. Running on the treadmill."

"No, you haven't," says the kid. "I was just in the gym."

"Listen, mind your own business, okay? I'm not your buddy, I'm not your friend."

"But we oughta be friends."

"No. You don't know me. I'm not like you, okay, so just leave me alone!"

Then he hears a deeper voice behind him. "That's enough, Lev."

He turns to see a man in a suit. It's not one of the pastors but the counselor who admitted him a week ago. This can't be good.

The counselor nods to the towheaded kid. "Thank you, Sterling." The boy casts his eyes down and hurries out. "We assigned Sterling to keep an eye on you and make sure you're adjusting. We are, to say the least, concerned."

Lev sits in a room with the counselor, and two pastors. The sock bulges in his pocket. He bounces his knees nervously, then remembers he's not supposed to make any jarring motions, or he might detonate. He forces himself to stop.

"You seem troubled, Lev," says the counselor. "We'd like to understand why."

Lev looks at the clock. It's 12:48. Twelve minutes until he, Mai, and Blaine are supposed to meet and take care of business.

"I'm being tithed," Lev says. "Isn't that enough of a reason?"

The younger of the two pastors leans forward. "We try to make sure every tithe enters the divided state in the proper frame of mind."

"We wouldn't be doing our job if we didn't try to make things right for you," says the elder pastor, then offers a smile so forced, it's more like a grimace.

Lev wants to scream at them, but he knows that won't get him out of here any faster. "I just don't like being around other kids right now. I'd rather prepare for this alone, okay?"

"But it's not okay," says the older pastor. "That's not the way we do things here. Everyone supports one another."

The junior pastor leans forward. "You need to give the other boys a chance. They're all good kids."

"Well maybe I'm not!" Lev can't help but look at the clock

299

again. Twelve fifty. Mai and Blaine will be in place in ten minutes, and what if he's still here in this stinking office? Won't that be just great.

"Have somewhere you need to be?" the counselor asks. "You keep checking the time."

Lev knows his answer needs to make sense or they truly will become suspicious of him. "I . . . I heard the kid who kidnapped me was being unwound today. I was just wondering if it had happened yet."

The pastors look at one another and at the counselor, who leans back in his chair, as calm as can be. "If he hasn't been, he will be shortly. Lev, I think it would be healthy for you to discuss what happened to you while you were held hostage. I'm sure it was horrible, but talking about it can take away the power of the memory. I'd like to hold a special group tonight with your unit. It will be a time for you to share with the others what you've been holding inside. I think you'll find they'll be very understanding."

"Tonight," says Lev. "Okay. Fine. I'll talk about everything tonight. Maybe you're right and it will make me feel better."

"We just want to ease your mind," says one of the pastors.

"So, can I go now?"

The counselor studies him for a moment more. "You seem so tense. I'd like to talk you through some guided relaxation exercises. . . ."

# 63 · Guard

He hates his job, he hates the heat, he hates that he has to stand in front of the Chop Shop for hours guarding the doors, making sure no one unauthorized enters or leaves. He had dreams back in StaHo of starting a business with his buddies, but no one loans start-up money to StaHo kids. Even after he changed his last name from Ward to Mullard—the name of the richest family in town—he couldn't fool anyone. Turns out half the kids from his state home took on that name when they left, figuring they could outsmart the world. In the end, he outsmarted no one but himself. The best he could do was find a series of unfulfilling jobs in the year he's been out of StaHo—the most recent of which is being a harvest camp guard.

On the roof, the band has started its afternoon set. At least that helps the time to pass a little more quickly.

Two Unwinds approach, and climb the steps toward him. They're not being escorted by guards and both carry plates covered with aluminum foil. The guard doesn't like the look of them. The boy's a flesh-head. The girl is Asian.

"What do you want? You're not supposed to be here."

"We were told to give this to the band." They both look nervous and shifty. This is nothing new. All Unwinds get nervous near the Chop Shop—and to the guard, all Unwinds look shifty.

The guard peeks under the aluminum foil. Roast chicken. Mashed potatoes. They do send food up to the band once in a while, but usually it's staff that carries the food, not Unwinds. "I thought they just had lunch."

"Guess not," says the flesh-head. He looks like he'd rather be anywhere in the world but standing in front of the Chop Shop, so the guard decides to draw it out, making them stand there even longer.

"I'll have to call this in," he says. He pulls out his phone and calls the front office. He gets a busy signal. Typical. The guard wonders which he'd get in more trouble for—letting them bring the food in, or turning them away if they really were sent by administration. He considers the plate in the girl's hands. "Let me see that." He peels back the foil and takes the largest chicken breast. "Go in through the glass doors, and the stairs are to your left. If I see you go anywhere but up the stairs, I'll come in there and tranq you so fast, you won't know what hit you."

Once they're inside, they're out of sight, out of mind. He doesn't know that although they went into the stairwell, they never brought the food to the band—they just ditched the plates. And he never noticed the little round Band-Aids on their palms.

# 64 · Connor

Connor looks out of the dormitory window, devastated. Lev is here at Happy Jack. How he got here doesn't matter; all that matters is that Lev will now be unwound. It's all been for nothing. Connor's sense of futility makes him feel like a part of himself has already been cut out and taken to market.

"Connor Lassiter?"

He turns to see two guards at the entrance. Around him, most of the kids have left the unit for their afternoon activity. The ones that remain take a quick glance at the guards, and at Connor, then look away, busying themselves in anything that will keep them out of this business.

"Yeah. What do you want?"

"Your presence is requested at the harvest clinic," says the first guard. The other guard doesn't talk. He just chomps on chewing gum.

Connor's first reaction is that this can't be what it sounds like. Maybe Risa sent them. Maybe she wants to play something for him. After all, now that she's in the band, she has more influence than the average Unwind, doesn't she?

"The harvest clinic," echoes Connor. "What for?"

"Well, let's just say you're leaving Happy Jack today."

*Chomp, chomp,* goes the other guard.

"Leaving?"

"C'mon, son, do we have to spell it out for you? You're a problem here. Too many of the other kids look up to you, and that's never a good thing at a harvest camp. So the administration decided to take care of the problem."

They advance on Connor, lifting him up by the arms.

"No! No! You can't do this."

"We can, and we are. It's our job—and whether you make it hard, or easy, it doesn't matter. Our job gets done either way."

Connor looks to the other kids as if they might help him, but they don't. "Good-bye, Connor," says one, but he won't even look in Connor's direction.

The gum-chewing guard looks more sympathetic, which means there might be a way to get through to him. Connor looks at him pleadingly. It makes him stop chewing for an instant. The guard thinks for a moment and says, "I got a buddy looking for brown eyes, on account of his girlfriend don't like the ones he got. He's a decent guy—you could do a lot worse."

"What!"

"We sometimes get dibs on parts and stuff," he says. "One of the perks of the job. Anyways, all I'm saying is I can give you some peace of mind. You'll know your eyes won't go to some lowlife or nothin'."

The other guard snickers. "Piece of mind. Good one. Okay, time to go." They pull Connor forward, and he tries to prepare himself, but how do you prepare yourself for something like this? *Maybe what they say is right. Maybe it's not dying. Maybe it's just passing into a new form of living. It could be all right, couldn't it? Couldn't it?*

He tries to imagine what it must be like for an inmate to be led to his execution. Do they fight it? Connor tries to imagine himself kicking and screaming his way to the Chop Shop, but what would be the use of that? If his time on Earth as Connor Lassiter is ending, then maybe he should use the time well. He should allow himself to spend his final moments appreciating who he was. No! Who he still *is*! He should appreciate the last breaths moving in and out of his lungs while those lungs are still under his control. He should feel the tension and release in his muscles as he moves, and see the many sights of Happy Jack with *his* eyes and store them in *his* brain.

"Hands off me, I'll walk by myself," he orders the guards, and they instantly release him, perhaps surprised by the authority in his voice. He rolls his shoulders, cracks his neck, and strides forward. The first step is the hardest, but from that moment on he decides that he will neither run nor dawdle. He will neither quiver nor fight. He will take this last walk of his life in steady strides—and in a few weeks from now, someone, somewhere, will hold in their mind the memory that this young man, whoever he was, faced his unwinding with dignity and pride.

# 65 · Clappers

Who can say what goes through the mind of a clapper in the moments before carrying out that evil deed? No doubt whatever those thoughts are, they are lies. However, like all dangerous deceptions, the lies that clappers tell themselves wear seductive disguises.

For clappers who have been led to believe their acts are smiled upon by God, their lie is clothed in holy robes and has outstretched arms promising a reward that will never come.

For clappers who believe their act will somehow bring about change in the world, their lie is disguised as a crowd looking back at them from the future, smiling in appreciation for what they've done.

For clappers who seek only to share their personal misery with the world, their lie is an image of themselves freed from their pain by witnessing the pain of others.

And for clappers who are driven by vengeance, their lie is a scale of justice, weighted evenly on both sides, finally in balance.

It is only when a clapper brings his hands together that the lie reveals itself, abandoning the clapper in that final instant so that he exits this world utterly alone, without so much as a lie to accompany him into oblivion.

Or her.

The path that brought Mai to this place in her life was full of fury and disappointment. Her breaking point was Vincent. He was a boy no one knew. He was a boy she met and fell in love with in the warehouse more than a month ago. He was a boy who died in midair, crammed into a crate with four other kids who choked on their own carbon dioxide. No one seemed to notice his disappearance, and certainly no one cared. No one but Mai, who had found her soul mate, and had lost him that day she arrived in the Graveyard.

The world was to blame, but when she secretly witnessed the Admiral's golden five burying Vincent and the others, she was able to give faces to her fury. The Goldens buried Vincent not with respect, but with profanities. They cracked jokes and laughed. They covered the five dead boys carelessly with dirt like cats cover their turds. Mai had never felt such rage.

Once Cleaver befriended her, she told him what she had seen, and he agreed that revenge was in order. It was Cleaver's idea to kill the Goldens. It was Blaine who drugged them and brought them to the FedEx jet—but it was Mai who sealed the hatch of the crate. It was amazing to her that killing could be as easy as closing a door.

After that, there was no turning back for Mai. Her bed had been made; all that remained was for her to lie in it. She knows that today will be the day she climbs in and goes to her rest.

Once inside the Chop Shop she finds a storage room full of surgical gloves, syringes, and shiny instruments she cannot identify. She knows Blaine is somewhere in the north wing of the building. She expects Lev is in position too, standing on the loading dock at the back of the Chop Shop—at least that's the plan. It is now one o'clock on the nose. Time to do this.

Mai enters the storage room and closes the door. And waits. She will do this, but not quite yet. Let one of the others go. She refuses to be the first.

Blaine waits in a deserted hallway on the second floor. This area of the Chop Shop doesn't appear to be in use. He has decided not to use his detonators. Detonators are for wimps. For a hardcore clapper, a single, powerful clap is enough to bring it on, even without detonators—and Blaine wants to believe he's hardcore, like his brother was. He stands at the end of the hallway, legs spread to shoulder width, bouncing on the balls of his feet like a tennis player awaiting a serve. His hands are held apart. But he waits. He's hardcore, yes—but he's not going first.

Lev has convinced the psychologist that he's suitably relaxed. It's the best acting performance of his life, because his heart is racing and there's so much adrenaline flooding his blood, he's afraid he'll spontaneously combust.

"Why don't you go back to the tithing house?" the doctor suggests. "Spend some time getting to know the other kids. Make an effort, Lev—you'll be glad you did."

"Yes. Yes, I'll do that. Thank you. I feel better now."

"Good."

The counselor motions to the pastors and everyone rises. It is 1:04. Lev wants to race out the door, but he knows that will just get him another therapy session. He leaves the office with the pastors, who babble about his place in the scheme of things and the joys of tithing. It's only as Lev gets outside that he becomes aware of the commotion. Kids are all running from their activities and into the commons between the dormitories and the Chop Shop. Have Blaine and Mai gone off already? He didn't hear any explosions. No, this is something else.

"It's the Akron AWOL," he hears one of the kids shout. "He's being unwound!"

That's when Lev spots Connor. He's halfway down the red carpet, marching with two guards right behind him. Kids have gathered in the grassy commons, but they keep their distance as more kids arrive. They're spilling out of the dormitories, the dining hall—everywhere.

The band has stopped playing in the middle of a tune. The keyboardist—a girl—wails at the sight of Connor on the red stone path. Connor looks up at her, halts for a second, and blows her a kiss before continuing on. Lev can hear her crying.

Now guards, staffers, and counselors converge on the quad in panic, trying to herd this volatile gathering of kids back to their places, but no one will leave. The kids just stand there—maybe they can't stop this, but they can witness it. They can be there as Connor strides out of this life.

"Let's hear it for the Akron AWOL!" one boy shouts. "Let's

hear it for Connor!" and he starts to applaud. Soon the entire crowd of kids is applauding and cheering Connor as he marches down the red carpet.

*Applause.*

*Clapping.*

*Mai and Blaine!*

Suddenly Lev realizes what's about to happen. He can't let Connor go in there! Not now! He's got to stop him.

Lev breaks away from the pastors. Connor is almost to the steps of the Chop Shop. Lev races between the kids, but he can't push his way through them. If he does, he knows he'll detonate. He must be quick, but he must be careful—and being careful slows him down.

"Connor!" He screams, but the cheers all around him are too loud. And now the band has begun to play again. They're playing the national anthem, just like they do at the funerals of great Americans. The guards and the staff can't stop this. They try but they can't—and they're so busy trying to control the crowd, they let Lev slip right past onto the red carpet.

Now he has a clear path to Connor, who has begun climbing the steps. Lev screams his name again, but Connor still can't hear. Although Lev races down the path, he's still twenty yards away when the glass doors open and Connor steps inside with the guards.

"No! Connor! No!"

But the doors close. Connor is inside the Chop Shop. But he won't be unwound. He's going to die just like everyone else inside . . . and as if to complete Lev's failure, he finally takes a look up at the roof to catch the gaze of the keyboard player looking down at him.

It's Risa.

How could he have been so stupid? He should have known

it was her from the way she wailed, and from the kiss that Connor blew her. Lev stands there, petrified with disbelief . . . And then the world comes to an end.

Blaine still stands at the end of the hall, waiting for someone else to go first.

"Hey! Who are you? What are you doing here?" a guard shouts at Blaine.

"Stay back!" Blaine says. "Stay back, or else!"

The guard pulls out his tranq pistol and speaks into his radio. "I got an Unwind loose up hear. I need backup!"

"I'm warning you," says Blaine. But the guard knows exactly how to deal with an Unwind loose in the Chop Shop. He aims his tranq gun at Blaine's left thigh, and fires.

"No!"

But it's too late. The impact of a tranq bullet is more effective than any detonator. Blaine and the guard are instantly incinerated as the six quarts of liquid explosive coursing through Blaine's body ignites.

Mai hears the explosion. It shakes the entire storage room like an earthquake. She doesn't think about it. She can't. Not anymore. She looks at the detonators on her palm. This is for Vincent. This is for her parents, who signed the Unwind order. This is for the whole world.

She claps once.

Nothing.

She claps twice.

Nothing.

She claps a third time.

The third time is the charm.

The moment Risa sees Lev standing below, on the red carpet,

an explosion rips through the north wing of the Chop Shop. She turns to see the entire wing crumble. "Oh, my God! Oh, my God!"

"We gotta get out of here!" yells Dalton, but before he can make a move, a second explosion roars beneath them, sending the air-vent caps shooting skyward like rockets. The roof beneath their feet cracks like thin ice, and the entire roof gives way. Risa plunges with the rest of the band into the smoky abyss, and in that instant all she can think of is Connor, and how the band never got to finish playing his farewell anthem.

Lev stands there as the glass blows past him. He sees the band fall as the roof collapses. A howl builds up inside him, escaping his mouth, an inhuman sound born of an agony he can't describe. His world has truly ended. Now he must finish the job.

Standing there before the ruined building, he pulls out the sock in his pocket. He fumbles with it until he finds the detonators. He peels the backs, revealing the adhesive, and sticks them to his palms. They look like stigmata, the nail wounds in the hands of Christ. Still wailing his agony, he holds his hands up before him, preparing to make the pain go away. He holds his hands up before him. He holds his hands up before him. He holds his hands up before him.

And he cannot bring them together.

He wants to. He needs to. But he can't.

*Make this go away. Please, somebody make this all go away.*

No matter how hard he tries, no matter how much his mind wants to end this here and now, another part of him—a *stronger* part of him—refuses to let him clap his hands together. Now he is even a failure as a failure.

*God, dear God, what am I doing? What have I done? How did I get here?*

The crowd, which had run at the sound of the blasts, has come back. They ignore Lev, because there's something else they see.

"Look!" someone shouts. "*Look!*"

Lev turns to see where the kid is pointing. Coming out of the ruined glass doors of the Chop Shop is Connor. He's stumbling. His face is a shredded, bloody mess. He's lost an eye. His right arm is crushed and mangled. But he's alive!

"Connor blew up the Chop Shop!" someone yells. "He blew it up and saved us all!"

And then a guard bursts onto the scene. "Get back to your dormitories. All of you! Now!"

No one moves.

"Didn't you hear me?"

Then a kid slams the guard with a right hook that practically spins his whole body around. The guard responds by pulling out his tranq gun and shooting the kid in the offending arm. The kid goes to dreamland, but there are other kids, and they tear the gun out of the guard's hand, using it against him. Just like Connor once had.

The word that the Akron AWOL blew up the Chop Shop zigs like lightning through every Unwind in Happy Jack, and in seconds, disobedience erupts into a full-scale revolt. Every terrible is now a terror. The guards fire, but there are simply too many kids, and not enough tranq bullets. For every kid that goes down, there's another kid that doesn't. The guards are quickly overwhelmed, and once they are, the mob starts storming the front gate.

Connor has no understanding of this event. All he knows is that he was led into the building, then something happened. And now he's not in the building anymore. His face is wrong.

It hurts. It hurts bad. He can't move his arm. The ground feels strange beneath his feet. His lungs hurt. He coughs and they hurt more.

He's stumbling down steps now. There are kids here. Lots of kids. Unwinds. That's right, he's an Unwind. They're all Unwinds. But the meaning of that is slipping from him fast. The kids are running. They're fighting. Then Connor's legs give out, and suddenly he's on the ground. Looking up at the sun.

He wants to sleep. He knows this isn't a good place, but he wants to anyway. He feels wet. He feels sticky. Is his nose running?

Then there's an angel hovering above him, all in white.

"Don't move," the angel says. Connor recognizes the voice.

"Hi, Lev. How are things . . . ?"

"Shh."

"My arm hurts," Connor says lazily. "Did you bite me again?"

Then Lev does something funny. He takes off his shirt. Then he tears his shirt in half. He presses half the torn shirt to Connor's face. That makes his face hurt more. He groans. Then Lev takes the other half of his shirt and ties it around Connor's arm. He ties it tight. That hurts too.

"Hey . . . what . . ."

"Don't try to talk. Just relax."

There are others around him now. He doesn't know who. A kid holding a tranq pistol looks at Lev, and Lev nods. Then the kid kneels down next to Connor.

"This is going to hurt a little," says the kid with the tranq gun. "But I think you need it."

He aims uncertainly at various parts of Connor's body, then settles on Connor's hip. Connor hears the gunshot, feels

312

a sharp pain in his hip, and as his vision begins to darken he sees Lev hurrying shirtless toward a building that's pouring out black smoke.

"Weird," says Connor. Then his mind goes to a quiet place where none of this matters.

## Part 7

# Consciousness

"A human being is part of a whole, called by us the Universe, a part limited in time and space. He experiences himself, his thoughts and feelings, as something separated from the rest—a kind of optical delusion of his consciousness. This delusion is a kind of prison for us . . . Our task must be to free ourselves from this prison by widening our circles of compassion to embrace all living creatures and the whole of nature in its beauty."

—*ALBERT EINSTEIN*

"Two things are infinite: the universe and human stupidity; and I'm not sure about the universe."

—*ALBERT EINSTEIN*

# 66 · Connor

Connor regains consciousness with nothing but hazy confusion where his thoughts ought to be. His face aches, and he can see out of only one eye. He feels pressure over his other eye.

He's in a white room. There's a window through which he can see daylight. This is unquestionably a hospital room, and that pressure over his eye must be a bandage. He tries to lift his right arm but there's an ache in his shoulder, so he decides it's not worth the effort just yet.

Only now does he begin to piece together the events that landed him here. He was about to be unwound. There was an explosion. There was a revolt. Then Lev was standing over him. That's all he can remember.

A nurse comes into the room. "So you're finally awake! How are you feeling?"

"Good," he says, his voice little more than a croak. He clears his throat. "How long?"

"You've been in a medically induced coma for a little over two weeks," says the nurse.

Two weeks? With a life that has been lived day to day for so long, two weeks sounds like an eternity. And Risa . . . what about Risa? "There was a girl," he says. "She was on the roof of the Chop—of the harvest clinic. Does anyone know what happened to her?"

The nurse's expression doesn't give anything away. "That can all be sorted out later."

"But—"

"No buts. Right now you need time to heal—and I have to

say, you're doing better than anyone expected, Mr. Mullard."

His first thought is that he hasn't heard her right. He shifts uncomfortably. "Excuse me?"

She fluffs his pillows. "Just relax now, Mr. Mullard. Let us handle everything."

His second thought is that he's been unwound after all. He's been unwound, and somehow, someone got his entire brain. He's inside someone else now. But as he thinks about it, he knows that can't be it. His voice still sounds like his voice. When he rubs his tongue against his teeth, those teeth are still the ones he remembers.

"My name is Connor," he tells her. "Connor Lassiter."

The nurse studies him with an expression that's kind, but calculated—almost disturbingly so. "Well," she says, "as it so happens, an ID with the picture charred off was found in the wreckage. It belonged to a nineteen-year-old guard by the name of Elvis Mullard. With all the confusion after the blast there really was no telling who was who, and many of us agreed that it would be a shame to let that ID go to waste, don't you agree?" She reaches over and adjusts the angle of Connor's bed until he's sitting up more comfortably. "Now tell me," she asks, "What was your name again?"

Connor gets it. He closes his eye, takes a deep breath, and opens it again. "Do I have a middle name?"

The nurse checks the chart. "Robert."

"Then my name is E. Robert Mullard."

The nurse smiles and holds out her hand to shake his. "A pleasure to meet you, Robert."

As a reflex, Connor reaches out his right hand toward hers, and gets that dull ache in his shoulder again.

"Sorry," says the nurse. "My fault." She shakes his left hand instead. "Your shoulder will feel a bit sore until the graft is completely healed."

"What did you just say?"

The nurse sighs. "Me and my big mouth. The doctors always want to be the ones to tell you, but the cat's out of the bag now, isn't it? Well, the bad news is that we weren't able to save your arm, or your right eye. The good news is that, as E. Robert Mullard, you qualified for emergency transplants. I've seen the eye—don't worry, it's a decent match. As for the arm, well, the new one is a little more muscular than your left one, but some good physical therapy can even that out in no time."

Connor lets it sink in, playing it over in his mind. *Eye. Arm. Physical therapy.*

"I know it's a lot to get used to," says the nurse.

For the first time Connor looks at his new hand. There are bandages padding his shoulder, and his arm is in a sling. He flexes the fingers. They flex. He twists his wrist. It twists. The fingernails need clipping, and the knuckles are thicker than his own. He runs his thumb across the pads of his fingertips. The sense of touch is just as it ever was. Then he rotates his wrist a bit farther, and stops. He feels a wave of panic surge through him, one that resolves into a knot deep in his gut.

The nurse grins as she looks at the arm. "Parts often come with their own personalities," she says. "Nothing to worry about. You must be hungry. I'll get you some lunch."

"Yeah," says Connor. "Lunch. That's good."

She leaves him alone with the arm. His arm. An arm that bears the unmistakable tattoo of a tiger shark.

# 67 · Risa

Risa's life as she knew it ended the day the clappers blew up the Chop Shop—and everyone eventually did learn that it was clappers, not Connor. The evidence was indisputable.

Especially after the confession of the clapper who survived.

Unlike Connor, Risa never lost consciousness. Even though she was pinned beneath a steel I beam, she stayed wide awake. As she lay there in the wreckage, some of the pain she felt when the I beam came down on her was gone. She didn't know whether that was a good sign, or bad. Dalton was in lots of pain though. He was terrified. Risa calmed him down. She talked to him, telling him it was all right—that everything would be fine. She kept telling him that right up until the moment he died. The guitar player had been luckier. He was able to wrestle himself out from under the debris, but he couldn't free Risa, so he left, promising her he'd send back help. He must have kept his promise, because help finally did come. It took three people to lift the beam, but only one to carry her out.

Now she rests in a hospital room, trussed up in a contraption that looks more like a torture device than a bed. She is riddled with steel pins like a human voodoo doll. The pins are held in precise place by rigid scaffolding. She can see her toes, but she can't feel them. From now on, seeing them will have to be enough.

"You have a visitor."

A nurse stands at the door, and when she steps aside, Connor is standing in the doorway. He's bruised and bandaged, but very much alive. Her eyes instantly fill with tears, but she knows she can't let herself sob. It still hurts too much to sob. "I knew they were lying," she says. "They said you died in the explosion—that you were trapped in the building—but I saw you outside. I knew they were lying."

"I probably would have died," Connor said, "but Lev stopped the bleeding. He saved me."

"He saved me, too," Risa tells him. "He carried me out of the building."

Connor smiles. "Not bad for a lousy little tithe."

By the look on his face, Risa can tell he doesn't know that Lev was one of the clappers—the one who didn't go off. She decides not to tell him. It's still all over the news; he'll know soon enough.

Connor tells her of his coma, and about his new identity. Risa tells him how few of Happy Jack's AWOLs have been caught—how the kids stormed the gates and escaped. She glances at his sling as they speak. The fingers sticking out of that arm sling are definitely not Connor's. She knows what must have happened, and she can tell he's self-conscious about it.

"So, what do they say?" Connor asks. "About your injuries, I mean. You're going to be okay, right?"

Risa considers how she might tell him, then just decides to be quick about it. "They tell me I'm paralyzed from the waist down."

Connor waits for more, but that's all she has to give him. "Well . . . that's not so bad, right? They can fix that—they're always fixing that."

"Yes," says Risa. "They fix it by replacing a severed spine with the spine of an Unwind. That's why I refused the operation."

He looks at her in disbelief, and she in turn points at his arm. "You would have done the same thing if they'd given you a choice. Well, I had a choice, and I made it."

"I'm so sorry, Risa."

"Don't be!" The one thing she doesn't want from Connor is pity. "They can't unwind me now—there are laws against unwinding the disabled—but if I got the operation, they'd unwind me the moment I was healed. This way I get to stay whole." She smiles at him triumphantly. "So you're not the only one who beat the system!"

He smiles at her and rolls his bandaged shoulder. The sling shifts, exposing more of his new arm—enough to reveal the tattoo. He tries to hide it, but it's too late. She sees it. She knows it. And when she meets Connor's eye, he looks away in shame.

"Connor . . . ?"

"I promise," he says. "I promise I will never touch you with this hand."

Risa knows this is a crucial moment for both of them. That arm—the same one that held her back against a bathroom wall. How could she look at it now with anything but disgust? Those fingers that threatened unspeakable things. How can they make her feel anything but revulsion? But when she looks at Connor, all that fades away. There's only him.

"Let me see it," she says.

Connor hesitates, so she reaches out and gently slips it from the sling. "Does it hurt?"

"A little."

She brushes her fingers across the back of his hand. "Can you feel that?"

Connor nods.

Then she gently lifts the hand to her face, pressing the palm to her cheek. She holds it there for a moment, then lets go, letting Connor take over. He moves his hand across her cheek, wiping away a tear with his finger. He softly strokes her neck, and she closes her eyes. She feels as he moves his fingertips across her lips before he takes his hand away. Risa opens her eyes and takes the hand in hers, clasping it tightly.

"I *know* this is your hand now," she tells him. "Roland would never have touched me like that." Connor smiles, and Risa takes a moment to look down at the shark on his wrist. It holds no fear for her now, because the shark has been tamed by the soul of a boy. No—the soul of a man.

# 68 · Lev

Not far away, in a high-security federal detention center, Levi Jedediah Calder is held in a cell designed for his very specific needs. The cell is padded. There is a steel blast door three inches thick. The room is kept at a constant forty-five degrees Fahrenheit to keep Lev's body temperature from rising too high. Lev is not cold, though—in fact he's hot. He's hot because he's wrapped in layer after layer of fire-resistant insulation. He looks like a mummy, suspended in midair—but unlike a mummy, his hands aren't crossed over his chest, they're held out to each side and lashed to a crossbeam so he cannot bring his hands together. The way Lev sees it, they didn't know whether to crucify him or mummify him, so they did both. This way, he can't clap, he can't fall, he can't inadvertently detonate himself—and if for some reason he does, the cell is designed to withstand the blast.

They've given him four transfusions. They won't tell him how many more he'll need until the explosive is out of his system. They won't tell him anything. The federal agents who come visit him are only interested in what he can tell them. They've given him a lawyer who talks about insanity like it's a good thing. Lev keeps telling him that he isn't insane, although he's not even sure himself anymore.

The door to his cell opens. He expects another interrogation, but his visitor is someone new. It takes a moment for Lev to recognize him—mainly because he's not wearing his modest pastor's vestments. He wears jeans and a striped buttondown shirt.

"Good morning, Lev."

"Pastor Dan?"

The door slams closed behind him, but it doesn't echo.

323

The soft walls absorb the sound. Pastor Dan rubs his arms against the cold. They should have told him to bring a jacket.

"Are they treating you okay?" he asks.

"Yeah," says Lev. "The good thing about being explosive is that no one can beat you."

Pastor Dan gives an obligatory chuckle, then awkwardness takes over. He forces himself to meet Lev's eyes. "I understand they'll only keep you wrapped up like this for a few weeks, until you're out of the woods."

Lev wonders which particular woods he means. Certainly his life will now be one dark forest within another, within another. Lev doesn't even know why the pastor is here, or what he hopes to prove. Should Lev be happy to see him, or should he be mad? This is the man who always told him that tithing was a holy thing from the time he was a small boy—and then told him to run from it. Is Pastor Dan here to reprimand him? To congratulate him? Did Lev's parents send him because he's so untouchable now, they won't come themselves? Or maybe Lev's about to be executed and he's here to give last rites.

"Why don't you just get it over with?" Lev says.

"Get what over with?"

"Whatever you're here to do. Do it, and go."

There are no chairs in the room, so Pastor Dan leans back against the padded wall. "How much have they told you about what's going on out there?"

"All I know is what goes on in here. Which isn't much."

Pastor Dan sighs, rubs his eyes, and takes his time to consider where to begin. "First of all, do you know a boy by the name of Cyrus Finch?"

The mention of his name makes Lev begin to panic. Lev knew his background would be checked and rechecked. That's what happens to clappers—their whole life becomes pages pasted on a wall to be examined, and the people in their lives become suspects. Of course, that usually happens after the clapper has applauded his way into the next world.

"CyFi had nothing to do with this!" says Lev. "Nothing at all. They can't pull him into this!"

"Calm down. He's fine. It just so happens that he's come forward and is making a big stink—and since he knew you, people are listening."

"A stink about me?"

"About unwinding," says Pastor Dan, for the first time moving closer to Lev. "What happened at Happy Jack Harvest Camp—it got a whole lot of people talking, people who had just been burying their heads in the sand. There have been protests in Washington against unwinding—Cyrus even testified before Congress."

Lev tries to imagine CyFi in front of a congressional committee, trash-talking them in prewar sitcom Umber. The thought of it makes Lev smile. It's the first time he's smiled in a long time.

"There's talk that they might even lower the legal age of adulthood from eighteen to seventeen. That'll save a full fifth of all the kids marked for unwinding."

"That's good," says Lev.

Pastor Dan reaches into his pocket and pulls out a folded piece of paper. "I wasn't going to show you this, but I think you need to see it. I think you need to understand where things have gone."

It's the cover of a magazine.

Lev's on it.

Not just on it, Lev *is* the cover. It's his seventh-grade baseball picture—mitt in hand, smiling at the camera. The headline reads, WHY, LEV, WHY? In all the time he's had here alone to think and rethink his actions, it never occurred to him that the outside world had been doing the same thing. He doesn't want this attention, but now he's apparently on a first-name basis with the world.

"You've been on the cover of just about every magazine."

He didn't need to know that. He hopes that Pastor Dan doesn't have a whole collection of them in his pocket. "So what," Lev says, trying to act as if it doesn't matter. "Clappers always make the news."

"Their *actions* make the news—the destruction they've caused—but nobody ever cares who a clapper is. To the public all clappers are the same. But you're different from those others, Lev. You're a clapper who didn't clap."

"I wanted to."

"If you wanted to, you would have. But instead you ran into the wreckage and pulled out four people."

"Three."

"Three—but you probably would have gone in for more if you could have. The other tithes, they all stayed back. They protected their own precious parts. But you basically led that rescue effort, because there were 'terribles' who followed you in to bring out survivors."

Lev remembers that. Even as the mob was crashing down the gate, there were dozens of Unwinds going back into the wreckage with him. And Pastor Dan is right—Lev would have kept going back in, but then it occurred to him that one false move would have set him off and brought the rest of the Chop Shop down around them. So he went back out to the red carpet and sat with Risa and Connor until ambulances took them away. Then he stood in the midst of the chaos and confessed to being a clapper. He confessed over and over again to anyone willing to listen, until finally a police officer kindly offered to arrest him. The officer was afraid to even handcuff Lev for fear of detonating him, but that was all right—he had no intention of resisting arrest.

"What you did, Lev—it confused people. No one knows whether you're a monster or a hero."

Lev thinks about that. "Is there a third choice?"

Pastor Dan doesn't answer him. Maybe he doesn't know the answer. "I have to believe that things happen for a reason. Your kidnapping, your becoming a clapper, your refusing to clap"—he glances at the magazine cover in his hand—"it's all led to this. For years, Unwinds were just faceless kids that no one wanted—but now you've put a face on unwinding."

"Can they put my face on someone else?"

Pastor Dan chuckles again, and this time it's not as forced as before. He looks at Lev like he's just a kid, and not something inhuman. It makes him feel, if only for a moment, like a normal thirteen-year-old. It's a strange feeling, because even in his old life he never really was a normal kid. Tithes never are.

"So, what happens now?" Lev asks.

"The way I understand it, they'll clear the worst of the explosive out of your bloodstream in a few weeks. You'll still be volatile, but not as bad as before. You can clap all you want and you won't explode—but I wouldn't play any contact sports for a while."

"And then they'll unwind me?"

Pastor Dan shakes his head. "They won't unwind a clapper—that stuff never entirely gets out of your system. I've been talking to your lawyer. He has a feeling they're going to offer you a deal—after all, you did help them catch that group who gave you the transfusion to begin with. Those people who used you, they'll get what they deserve. But the courts are likely to see you as a victim."

"I knew what I was doing," Lev tells him.

"Then tell me why you did it."

Lev opens his mouth to speak but he can't put it into words. Anger. Betrayal. Fury at a universe pretending to be fair and just. But was that really a reason? Was that justification?

"You may be responsible for your actions," Pastor Dan says, "but it's not your fault you weren't emotionally prepared for life out there in the real world. That was *my* fault—and the fault of everyone who raised you to be a tithe. We're as guilty as the people who pumped that poison into your blood." He looks away in shame, curbing his own growing anger, but Lev can tell it's not anger aimed at him. He takes a deep breath and continues. "The way the winds are blowing, you'll probably serve a few years of juvenile detention, then a few more years of house arrest."

Lev knows he should be relieved by this, but the feeling is slow in coming. He considers the idea of house arrest. "Whose house?" he asks.

He can tell Pastor Dan reads everything between the lines of that question. "You have to understand, Lev, your parents are the kind of people who can't bend without breaking."

"Whose house?"

Pastor Dan sighs. "When your parents signed the unwind order, you became a ward of the state. After what happened at the harvest camp, the state offered to return custody to your parents, but they refused it. I'm sorry."

Lev is not surprised. He's horrified, but not surprised. Thoughts of his parents bring up the old feelings that drove him crazy enough to become a clapper. But now he finds that sense of despair is no longer bottomless. "So is my last name 'Ward' now?"

"Not necessarily. Your brother Marcus is petitioning for guardianship. If he gets it, you'll be in his care whenever they let you go. So you'll still be a Calder . . . that is, if you want to be."

Lev nods his approval, thinking back to his tithing party and how Marcus was the only one to stand up for him. Lev hadn't understood it at the time. "My parents disowned Marcus, too." At least he knows he'll be in good company.

Pastor Dan straightens out his shirt and shivers a bit from the cold. He doesn't really look like himself today. This is the first time Lev has seen him without his pastor's clothes. "Why are you dressed like that, anyway?"

He takes a moment before he answers. "I resigned my position. I left the church."

The thought of Pastor Dan being anything but Pastor Dan throws Lev for a loop. "You . . . you lost your faith?"

"No," he says, "just my convictions. I still very much believe in God—just not a god who condones human tithing."

Lev begins to feel himself choking up with an unexpected flood of feeling, all the emotions that had been building up throughout their talk—throughout the weeks—arriving all at once, like a sonic boom. "I never knew that was a choice."

All his life there was only one thing Lev was allowed to believe. It had surrounded him, cocooned him, constricted him with the same stifling softness as the layers of insulation around him now. For the first time in his life, Lev feels those bonds around his soul begin to loosen.

"You think maybe I can believe in that God, too?"

# 69 · Unwinds

There's a sprawling ranch in west Texas.

The money to build it came from oil that had long since dried up, but the money remained and multiplied. Now there's a whole compound, an oasis as green as a golf course in the middle of the flat, wild plains. This is where Harlan Dunfee grew to the age of sixteen, finding trouble along the way. He was arrested for disorderly behavior twice in Odessa, but his father, a big-shot admiral, got him off both times. The third time, his parents came up with a different solution.

Today is Harlan Dunfee's twenty-sixth birthday. He's having a party. Of sorts.

There are hundreds of guests at Harlan's party. One of them is a boy by the name of Zachary, though his friends know him as Emby. He's been living here at the ranch for some time now, waiting for this day. He has Harlan's right lung. Today, he gives it back to Harlan.

At the same time, six hundred miles to the west a wide-bodied jet lands in an airplane graveyard. The jet is full of crates, and each crate contains four Unwinds. As the crates are opened, a teenage boy peers out of one, not sure what to expect. He's faced by a flashlight, and when the flashlight lowers he can see that it's not an adult who opened the crate but another kid. He wears khaki clothes and he smiles at them, showing braces on a set of teeth that don't seem to need them. "Hi, my name's Hayden, and I'll be your rescuer today," he announces. "Is everyone safe and sound in there?"

"We're fine," says the young Unwind. "Where are we?"

"Purgatory," says Hayden. "Also known as Arizona."

The young Unwind steps out of the crate, terrified of what might be in store for him. He stands in the processional of kids being herded along, and, against Hayden's warning, bangs his head on the door of the cargo hold as he steps out. The harsh light of day and the blistering heat assault him as he walks down a ramp to the ground. He can tell this isn't an airport, and yet there are planes everywhere.

In the distance a golf cart rolls toward them, kicking up a plume of red dust. The crowd falls silent as it approaches. As it comes to a stop, the driver steps out. He's a man with serious scars over half of his face. The man speaks quietly for a moment with Hayden, then addresses the crowd.

It's then that the young Unwind realizes this is not a man but just another kid, one not much older than himself. Perhaps it's the scars on his face that make him look older—or maybe it's just the way he carries himself.

"Let me be the first to welcome you all to the Graveyard," he says. "Officially, my name is E. Robert Mullard. . . ." He smiles. "But everyone calls me Connor."


The Admiral never returned to the Graveyard. His health would not allow it. Instead, he's at his family's Texas ranch, in the care of a wife who left him years before. Although he's weak and can't get around well anymore, he hasn't changed much. "The doctors say only 25 percent of my heart is still alive," he tells anyone who asks. "It'll do."

What has kept him alive more than anything else is the prospect of Harlan's big party. You could say that those terrifying stories about "Humphrey Dunfee" are true. At last, all his parts have been found, all the recipients have been gathered. But there will be no surgeries here—in spite of the rumors, rebuilding Harlan piece by piece was never the plan. But the Dunfees *are* putting their son together in the only meaningful way they can.

He's here even now, as the Admiral and his wife step into their garden. He's in the voices of their many party guests, talking and laughing. There are men and women of all ages. Each wears a name tag, but there are no names on those tags. Today, names are unimportant.

RIGHT HAND reads the sticker on one young man's lapel. He couldn't be any older than twenty-five.

"Let me see," says the Admiral.

331

The man holds out his hand. The Admiral looks it over until he finds a scar between the thumb and forefinger. "I took Harlan fishing when he was nine. He got that scar trying to gut a trout."

And then there's a voice from behind him—another man, a little bit older than the first.

"I remember!" he says. The Admiral smiles. Perhaps the memories are spread out, but they're here—every one of them.

He catches that boy who insists on calling himself Emby milling around at the edge of the garden by himself, wheezing less now that he's finally been put on the proper asthma medication. "What are you doing over here?" the Admiral asks. "You should be over with the others."

"I don't know anybody."

"Yes, you do," says the Admiral. "You just don't realize it yet." And he leads Emby toward the crowd.

Meanwhile, in the airplane graveyard, Connor speaks to the new arrivals as they stand outside the jet that brought them here. Connor is amazed that they listen to him. He's amazed that he actually commands their respect. He'll never get used to that.

"You're all here because you were marked for unwinding but managed to escape, and, thanks to the efforts of many people, you've found your way here. This will be your home until you turn seventeen and become a legal adult. That's the good news. The bad news is that they know all about us. They know where we are and what we're doing. They let us stay here because they don't see us as a threat."

And then Connor smiles.

"Well, we're going to change that."

As Connor talks, he makes eye contact with every one of them, making sure he remembers each of their faces. Making sure each of them feels recognized. Unique. Important.

"Some of you have been through enough and just want to survive to seventeen," he tells them. "I don't blame you. But I know that some of you are ready to risk everything to end unwinding once and for all."

"Yeah," screams a kid from the back, and pumping his fist in the air he begins chanting, "Happy Jack! Happy Jack!" A few kids join in, until everyone realizes this is not what Connor wants. The chants quickly die down.

"We will not be blowing up chop shops," he says. "We're not going to feed into their image of us as violent kids who are better off unwound. We will *think* before we act—and that's going to make it difficult for them. We'll infiltrate harvest camps and unite Unwinds across the country. We'll free kids from buses, before they even arrive. We will have a voice, and we will use it. We will make ourselves heard." Now the crowd can't hold back their cheers, and this time Connor allows it. These kids have been beaten down by life, but there's an energy now in the Graveyard that's beginning to fill each and every one of them. Connor remembers that feeling. He had it when he first arrived here.

"I don't know what happens to our consciousness when we're unwound," says Connor. "I don't even know when that consciousness starts. But I do know this." He pauses to make sure all of them are listening. "We have a right to our lives!"

The kids go wild.

"We have a right to choose what happens to our bodies!"

The cheers reach fever pitch.

"We deserve a world where both those things are possible— and it's our job to help make that world."

Meanwhile, excitement is also building at the Dunfee ranch. The buzz of conversations around the garden grows to a roar

333

as more and more people connect. Emby shares his experiences with a girl who has the left match to his right lung. A woman talks about a movie she never saw, with a man who remembers the friends he never saw it with. And as the Admiral and his wife watch, something amazing happens.

The conversations begin to converge!

Like water vapor crystalizing into the magnificent, unique form of a snowflake, the babble of voices coalesces into a single conversation.

"Look over there! He fell off that wall when he was—"

"—six! Yes—I remember!"

"He had to wear a wrist brace for months."

"The wrist still hurts when it rains."

"He shouldn't have climbed the wall."

"I had to—I was being chased by a bull."

"I was so scared!"

"The flowers in that field—do you smell them?"

"They remind me of that one summer—"

"—when my asthma wasn't so bad—"

"—and I felt like I could do anything."

"Anything!"

"And the world was just waiting for me!"

The Admiral grips his wife's arm. Neither can hold back their tears—not tears of sorrow but of awe. If the rest of his heart were to stop now, in this moment, the Admiral would die more content than any man on Earth.

He looks at the crowd and says weakly, "H-Harlan?"

Every eye in the garden turns toward him. A man raises his hand to his throat, touching it gently, and says in a voice that is most definitely Harlan Dunfee's, just a bit older, "Dad?"

The Admiral is so overwhelmed by emotion he cannot speak, and so his wife looks at the man before her, at the people beside her, at the crowd all around her, and she says:

"Welcome home."

Six hundred miles away, in the airplane graveyard, a girl plays a grand piano sheltered beneath the wing of a battered jet that was once Air Force One. She plays with a rare sort of joy in defiance of her wheelchair, and her sonata lifts the spirits of all the new arrivals. She smiles at them as they go by and continues to play, making it clear that this furnace of a place, full of planes that cannot fly, is more than it seems. It is a womb of redemption for every Unwind, and for all those who fought the Heartland War and lost—which was everybody.

Connor lets Risa's music fill him as he watches the new arrivals being greeted by the thousands of kids already here. The sun has begun to set, taking the edge off the heat, and the rows of jets at this time of day create pleasing patterns of shadow on the hard earth. Connor has to smile. Even a place as harsh as this can be beautiful in a certain light.

Connor takes it all in—the music, the voices, the desert, and the sky. He has his work cut out for him, changing the world and all, but things are already in motion; all he has to do is keep up the momentum. And he doesn't have to do it alone. He has Risa, Hayden, and every Unwind here. Connor takes a deep breath and releases it along with his tension. At last, he allows himself the wonderful luxury of hope.

# About the Author

**Neal Shusterman** is the author of many novels for young adults, including *Everlost* and *Downsiders*, which was nominated for twelve state reading awards and was an ALA Best Book for Young Adults and a Quick Pick for Reluctant Young Adult Readers. He also writes screenplays for motion pictures and television shows such as *Animorphs* and *Goosebumps*. The father of four children, Neal lives in southern California.

# Praise for UNWIND

"Gripping, brilliantly imagined futuristic thriller ... The issues raised could not be more provocative – the sanctity of life, the meaning of being human – while the delivery could hardly be more engrossing or better aimed to teens." *Publishers Weekly*, starred review

"Well-written, this draws the readers into a world that is both familiar and strangely foreign, and generates feelings of horror, disturbance, disgust, and fear. As with classics such as *1984* and *Fahrenheit 451*, one can only hope that this vision of the future never becomes reality." *Kirkus Reviews*

"A thought-provoking, well-paced read that will appeal widely." *School Library Journal*, starred review

"a powerful, shocking, and intelligent novel ... It's wonderful, wonderful stuff." thebookbag.co.uk

"This is the kind of rare book that makes the hairs on your neck rise up. It is written with a sense of drama that should get it instantly snapped up for film." *Times*

"A breathless tale turning pages for teenage boys, as it challenges not just where life begins and ends, but what it means to be alive." *Educ8 magazine*

"Poignant, compelling, and ultimately terrifying, this book will enjoy popularity with a wide range of readers." *Voya*

"Hundreds of thousands of today's teens are reading future-as-a-nightmare novels – and not just the *1984* and *Brave New World* classics required by their teachers ... Led by Suzanne

Collin's *The Hunger Games*, end-of-the-world novels are selling briskly ... What's the appeal? Kids love 'what ifs' ... What if, as in Neal Shusterman's Unwind, the organs of healthy teens were transplanted into other people?" *Publishers Weekly*

"This is a fantastic book, both thought-provoking and comprehensible. Like all great writers who envisage a new world, Shusterman manages to humanise the reality of it, as Huxley did with *Brave New World* and Atwood with *The Handmaid's Tale*, the author creates a convincing environment that creates this change ... I was truly disappointed when it ended. The mark of a great book." *Armadillo*

"This book challenges ones ideas about life, about morality, about religion, about fanatics. It is not a comfortable read but it is thought-provoking." *Carousel*

Turn the page for an extract from

# UNWHOLLY

## NEAL SHUSTERMAN

# 1 · Starkey

He's fighting a nightmare when they come for him.

A great flood is swallowing the world, and in the middle of it all, he's being mauled by a bear. He's more annoyed than terrified. As if the flood isn't enough, his deep, dark mind has to send an angry grizzly to tear into him.

Then he's dragged feetfirst out of the jaws of death and drowning Armageddon.

"Up! Now! Let's go!"

He opens his eyes to a brightly lit bedroom that ought to be dark. Two Juvey-cops manhandle him, grabbing his arms, preventing him from fighting back long before he's awake enough to try.

"No! Stop! What is this?"

Handcuffs. First his right wrist, then his left.

"On your feet!"

They yank him to his feet as if he's resisting—which he would, if he were more awake.

"Leave me alone! What's going on?"

But in an instant he's awake enough to know exactly what's going on. It's a kidnapping. But you can't call it kidnapping when transfer papers have been signed in triplicate.

"Verbally confirm that you are Mason Michael Starkey."

There are two officers. One is short and muscular, the other tall and muscular. Probably military boeufs before they took jobs as Juvey-rounders. It takes a special heartless breed to be a Juvey-cop, but to specialize as a rounder you probably need to be soulless as well. The fact that he's being rounded for unwinding shocks and terrifies Starkey, but he refuses to show it, because he knows Juvey-rounders get off on other people's fear.

The short one, who is clearly the mouthpiece of this duo, gets in his face and repeats, "Verbally confirm that you are Mason Michael Starkey!"

"And why should I do that?"

"Kid," says the other rounder, "this can go down easy or hard, but either way it's going down." The second cop is more soft spoken with a pair of lips that clearly aren't his. In fact, they look like they came from a girl. "The drill's not so hard, so just get with the program."

He talks as if Starkey should have known they were coming, but what Unwind ever really knows? Every Unwind believes in their heart of hearts that it won't happen to them—that their parents, no matter how strained things get, will be smart enough not to fall for the net ads, TV commercials, and billboards that say things like "Unwinding: the sensible solution." But who is he kidding? Even without the constant media blitz, Starkey's been a potential candidate for unwinding since the moment he arrived on the doorstep. Perhaps he should be surprised that his parents waited so long.

Now the mouthpiece gets deep in his personal space. "For the last time, verbally confirm that you are—"

"Yeah, yeah, Mason Michael Starkey. Now get out of my face, your breath stinks."

With his identity verbally confirmed, Lady-Lips pulls out a form in triplicate: white, yellow, and pink.

"So is this how you do it?" Starkey asks, his voice beginning to quaver. "You arrest me? What's my crime? Being sixteen? Or maybe it's just being here at all."

"Quiet-or-we-tranq-you," says Mouthpiece, like it's all one word.

A part of Starkey wants to be tranq'd—just go to sleep and if he's lucky, never wake up. That way he won't have to face the utter humiliation of being torn from his life in the middle of the night. But no, he wants to see his parents' faces. Or, more to the point, he wants *them* to see *his* face, and if he's tranq'd, they get off easy. They won't have to look him in the eye.

Lady-Lips holds the unwind order in front of him and begins to read the infamous Paragraph Nine, the "Negation Clause."

"Mason Michael Starkey, by the signing of this order, your parents and/or legal guardians have retroactively terminated your tenure, backdated to six days postconception, leaving you in violation of Existential Code 390. In light of this, you are hereby remanded to the California Juvenile Authority for summary division, also known as unwinding."

"Blah, blah, blah."

"Any rights previously granted to you by the county, state, or federal government as a citizen thereof are now officially and permanently revoked." He folds the unwind order and shoves it into his pocket.

"Congratulations, Mr. Starkey," says Mouthpiece. "You no longer exist."

"Then why are you talking to me?"

"We won't be for much longer." They tug him toward the door.

"Can I at least put on shoes?"

They let him go but stay on their guard.

Starkey takes his sweet time tying his shoes. Then they pull him out of his room and down the stairs. The Juvey-cops have heavy boots that intimidate the wood of the steps. The three of them sound like a herd of cattle as they go down.

His parents wait in the foyer. It's three in the morning, but they're still fully dressed. They've been awake all night antici-pating this. Starkey sees anguish on their faces, or maybe it's relief, it's hard to tell. He hardens his own emotions, hiding them behind a mock smile.

"Hi, Mom! Hi, Dad!" he says brightly. "Guess what just happened to me? I'll give you twenty guesses to figure it out!"

His father takes a deep breath, preparing to launch into the Great Unwinding Speech that every parent prepares for a way-ward child. Even if they never use it, they still prepare it, run-ning the words through their minds while on lunch break, or while sitting in traffic, or while listening to some moronic boss blather on about price points and distribution, and whatever other crap that people in office buildings have meetings about.

What were the statistics? Starkey saw it on the news once. Every year the thought of unwinding passes through the mind of one in ten parents. Of those, one in ten seriously consid-ers it, and of those, one in twenty actually goes through with it—and the statistic doubles with every additional kid a family has. Crunch those juicy numbers, and one out of every two thousand kids between the ages of thirteen and seventeen will be unwound each year. Better odds than the lottery—and that doesn't even include the kids in state homes.

His father, keeping his distance, begins the speech. "Mason, can't you see that you left us no choice?"

The Juvey-cops hold him firm at the bottom of the stairs, but they make no move to get him outside. They know they must allow the parental rite of passage; the verbal boot out the door.

"The fights, the drugs, the stolen car—and now being expelled from yet another school. What's next, Mason?"

"Gee, I don't know, Dad. There are so many bad choices I can make."

"Not anymore. We care enough about you to end your bad choices before they end you."

That just makes him laugh out loud.

And then there's a voice from the top of the stairs.

"No! You can't do this!"

His sister, Jenna—his parents' biological daughter—stands at the top of the stairs in teddy bear pajamas that seem too old for her thirteen years.

"Go back to bed, Jenna," their mother says.

"You're unwinding him just because he was storked, and that's unfair! And right before Christmas, too! What if I had come storked? Would you unwind me also?"

"We are not having this discussion!" yells their father, as their mother begins to cry. "Go back to bed!"

But she doesn't. She folds her arms and sits at the top of the stairs in defiance, witnessing the whole thing. Good for her.

His mother's tears are genuine, but he's unsure whether she's crying for him or for the rest of the family. "All these things you do, everyone told us they were a cry for help," she says. "So why didn't you let us help you?"

He wants to scream. How could he possibly explain it to them if they can't see? They don't know what it's like to go through sixteen years of life knowing you weren't wanted; a mystery baby of uncertain race storked on the doorstep of a couple so sienna-pale, they could have been vampires. Or to still remember that day when you were three years old and your mom, all doped up on pain medication from your sister's cesarean delivery, took you to a fire station and begged them to take you away and make you a ward of the state. Or how about knowing every Christmas morning that your gift is not a joy, but an obligation? And that your birthday isn't even real because they can't pinpoint when you were born, just the day you were left on a welcome mat that some new mother took too literally?

And what about the taunts from the other kids at school?

In fourth grade Mason's parents were called into the principal's office. He had flipped a boy off the top platform of the jungle gym. The kid had suffered a concussion and a broken arm.

"Why, Mason?" his parents had asked, right there in front of the principal. "Why did you do it?"

He told them that the other kids were calling him "Storky" instead of Starkey, and that this was the boy who had started it. He naively thought they'd rise to his defense, but they just dismissed it as if it didn't matter.

"You could have killed that boy," his father had reprimanded. "And why? Because of words? Words don't hurt you." Which is one of the hugest criminal lies perpetrated by adults against children in this world. Because words hurt more than any physical pain. He would have gladly taken a concussion and a broken arm if he never had to be singled out as a storked child ever again.

In the end, he got sent to a different school and was ordered to have mandatory counseling.

"You think about what you did," his old principal had told him.

And he did what he was told, like a good little boy. He gave it plenty of thought and decided he should have found a higher platform.

So how do you even begin to explain that? How do you explain a lifetime of injustice in the time it takes the Juvey-cops to herd you out the door? The answer is easy: You don't even try.

"I'm sorry, Mason," his father says, tears in his eyes as well. "But it's better for everyone this way. Including you."

Starkey knows he'll never make his parents understand, but if nothing else, he'll have the last word.

"Hey, Mom, by the way . . . Dad's late nights at the office

aren't really at the office. They're with your friend Nancy."

But before he can begin to relish his parents' shocked expressions, it occurs to him that this secret knowledge could have been a bargaining chip. If he had told his father he knew, it could have been ironclad protection from unwinding! How could he be so stupid not to have thought of that when it mattered?

So in the end he can't even enjoy his bitter little victory as the Juvey-cops push him out into a cool December night.

---

---

The Juvey squad car leaves the driveway with Starkey locked in the backseat behind a bulletproof barrier. Mouthpiece drives while Lady-Lips flips through a fat file folder. Starkey can't imagine his life could have that much data.

"It says here you scored in the top ten percentile in your early childhood exams."

The mouthpiece shakes his head in disgust. "What a waste."

"Not really," says Lady-Lips. "Plenty of folks will get the benefit of your smarts, Mr. Starkey."

The suggestion gives him an unpleasant chill, but he tries not to show it. "Love the lip graft, dude," Starkey says. "What's the deal? Did your wife tell you she'd rather be kissed by a woman?"

Mouthpiece smirks, and Lady-Lips says nothing.

"But enough lip service," says Starkey. "You boys hungry? Because I could go for a midnight snack right about now. Some In-N-Out? Whaddaya say?"

No answer from the front seat. Not that he expects one, but it's always fun to mess with law enforcement and see how much it takes to irritate them. Because if they get ticked off, he wins. What's that story about the Akron AWOL? What did he always say? Oh yeah. "Nice socks." Simple, elegant, but it always undermined the confidence of any figure of false authority.

The Akron AWOL—now *there* was an Unwind! Sure, he died in the attack on Happy Jack Harvest Camp almost a year ago, but his legend lives on. Starkey longs for the kind of notoriety that Connor Lassiter has. In fact, Starkey imagines Connor Lassiter's ghost sitting by his side, appreciating his thoughts and his every action—not just approving, but guiding Starkey's hands as he wriggles his handcuffs down to his left shoe—just low enough to fish out the knife from the lining. The knife he's saved for special occasions like this.

"Come to think about it, In-N-Out Burger does sound good right about now," says Lady-Lips.

"Excellent," says Starkey. "There's one up ahead on the left. Order me a Double-Double, Animal Style, and Animal fries, too, because, hey—I'm an animal."

He is amazed that they actually pull into the all-night drive-through. Starkey feels like the master of subliminal suggestion, even though his suggestion was not all that subliminal. Still, he is in control of the Juvey-cops . . . or at least he thinks he is until they order meals for themselves and nothing for him.

"Hey! What's the deal?" He pounds his shoulder against the glass that separates their world from his.

"They'll feed you at harvest camp," says Lady-Lips.

Only now does it hit home that the bulletproof glass doesn't just separate him from the cops—it's a barrier between him and any part of the outside world. He will never taste his favorite foods again. Never visit his favorite places. At least not as Mason Starkey. Suddenly he feels like hurling up everything he's eaten, backdated to six days postconception.

The night shift cashier at the drive-through window is a girl Starkey knows from his last school. As he sees her, a whole mess of emotions toy with his brain. He could just lurk in the shadows of the backseat, hoping not to be seen, but that would make him feel pathetic. No, he will not be pathetic. If he's going down, then it will be in flames that everyone must see.

"Hey, Amanda, will you go to the prom with me?" He shouts loud enough to be heard through the thick glass barrier.

Amanda squints in his direction, and when she realizes who it is, she turns up her nose as if she's smelled something rancid on the grill.

"Not in this life, Starkey."

"Why not?"

"A, you're a sophomore, and B, you're a loser in the back of a police car. And anyway, don't they have their own prom at the alternative school?"

Could she possibly be any denser? "Uh, as you can see, I've graduated."

"Pipe down," says Mouthpiece, "or I'll unwind you right into the burgers."

Finally Amanda gets it, and suddenly she becomes a little sheepish. "Oh! Oh, I'm sorry, Starkey. I'm really sorry. . . ."

Pity is something Mason Starkey can't stand. "Sorry for what? You and your friends wouldn't give me the time of day before, but now you're sorry for me? Save it."

"I'm sorry. I mean—I'm sorry that I'm sorry—I mean . . ." She sighs in exasperation and gives up, handing Lady-Lips a bag of food. "Do you need ketchup?"

"No, we're good."

"Hey, Amanda!" Starkey shouts as they drive away. "If you really want to do something for me, tell everyone I went down fighting, will you? Tell them I'm just like the Akron AWOL."

"I will, Starkey," she says. "I promise."

But he knows she'll forget by morning.

Twenty minutes later they're turning into the back alley of county lockup. No one goes in the front way, least of all the Unwinds. The county jail has a juvenile wing, and in the back of the juvey wing is a special box within a box where they hold Unwinds awaiting transport. Starkey's been in regular juvey enough to know that once you're in the Unwind holding cell, that's it. End of story. Even death row inmates don't have such tight security.

But he's not there yet. He's still here, in the car, waiting to be transferred inside. Right here is where the hull of this little ship of fools is thinnest, and if he's going to sink their plans, it has to happen between the car and the back door of the county jail. As they prepare for his "perp walk," he thinks about his chances of breaking free—because as much as his parents may have imagined this night, so has he, and he's made up a dozen valiant escape plans. The thing is, even his day-dreams are fatalistic; in every anxiety-filled fantasy, he always loses, gets tranq'd, and wakes up on an operating table. Sure, they say they don't unwind you right away, but Starkey doesn't believe it. No one really knows what goes on in the harvest camps, and those who find out aren't exactly around to share the experience.

They pull him out of the car and flank him on either side, grasping his upper arms tightly. They are practiced in this walk. Lady-Lips grips Starkey's fat file in his other hand.

"So," says Starkey, "does that file show my hobbies?"

"Probably," says Lady-Lips, not really caring either way.

"Maybe you should have read it a little more closely, because then we'd have something to talk about." He grins. "You know, I'm pretty good with magic."

"That so?" says Mouthpiece, with a twisted sneer. "Too bad you can't make yourself disappear."

"Who says I can't?"

Then, in his finest Houdini fashion, he raises his right hand, revealing the cuff no longer on it. Instead, it dangles free from his left hand. Before they can even react, Starkey slides the penknife he used to pick the lock out of his sleeve, grips it in his hand, and slashes it across Lady-Lips's face.

The man screams, and blood flows from a four-inch wound. Mouthpiece, for once in his miserable life of public disservice, is speechless. He reaches for his weapon, but Starkey is already on the run, zigzagging in the shadowy alley.

"Hey!" yells Mouthpiece. "You're only making it worse for yourself."

But what are they going to do? Reprimand him before they unwind him? The Mouthpiece can talk all he wants, but he's got no bargaining position.

The alley turns to the left and then to the right like a maze, and all the while beside him is the tall, imposing brick wall of the county jail.

Finally he turns another corner and sees a street up ahead. He charges forward, but just as he emerges into that street, he's grabbed by Mouthpiece. Somehow he made it there before Starkey. He's surprised, but he shouldn't be, because doesn't every Unwind try to run? And couldn't they build a twisting alley specifically designed to waste your time and give the Juvey-cops an advantage that they never really lost?

"You're through, Starkey!" He crushes Starkey's wrist enough to dislodge the knife and brandishes a tranq gun with trigger-happy fury. "Down on the ground, or this goes in your eye!"

But Starkey does not go down. He will not humble himself before this legalized thug.

"Do it!" says Starkey. "Tranq me in the eye and explain to the harvest camp why the goods are damaged."

Mouthpiece turns him around and pushes him against the brick wall, hard enough to scrape and bruise his face.

"I've had enough of you, Starkey. Or maybe I should call you *Storky*." Then Mouthpiece laughs, like he's a genius. Like every moron in the world hasn't already called him that. "Storky!" he snorts. "That's a better name for you, isn't it? How do you like that, Storky?"

Blood boils hotter than water. Starkey can vouch for that, because with adrenaline-pumped fury, he elbows Mouthpiece in the gut and spins around, grabbing the gun.

"Oh no, you don't."

Mouthpiece is stronger—but maybe animal-style beats strength.

The gun is between them. It points at Starkey's cheek, then his chest, then to Mouthpiece's ear, then under his chin. They both grapple for the trigger and—*Blam!*

The concussive shock of the blast knocks Starkey back against the wall. Blood! Blood everywhere! The ferrous taste of it in his mouth, and the acrid smell of gun smoke and—

*That was no tranq bullet! That was the real thing!*

And he thinks he's microseconds away from death, but he suddenly realizes that the blood isn't his. In front of him, Mouthpiece's face is a red, pulpy mess. The man goes down, dead before he hits the pavement and—

*My God, that was a real bullet. Why does a Juvey-cop have real bullets? That's illegal!*

He can hear footsteps around the bend, and the dead cop is still dead, and he knows the whole world heard the gunshot, and everything hinges on his next action.

He is partners with the Akron AWOL now. The patron saint of runaway Unwinds is watching over his shoulder, waiting for Starkey to make a move, and he thinks, *What would Connor do?*

Just then another Juvey-cop comes around the bend—a cop he has never seen and is determined to never see again. Starkey raises Mouthpiece's gun and shoots, turning what was just an accident into murder.

As he escapes—truly escapes—all he can think about is the bloody taste of victory, and how pleased the ghost of Connor Lassiter would be.

---

---

To be an AWOL Unwind is one thing, but to be a cop killer is another. The manhunt for Starkey becomes more than just your typical Unwind chase. It seems the whole world is put on alert. First Starkey changes his look, dying his straggly brown hair red, cutting it bookworm-short, and shaving off the little victory garden goatee that he's been cultivating since middle school. Now when people see him, they might get a feeling they've seen him before, but not know from where, because now he looks less like a face from a wanted poster and more like someone you'd see on a Wheaties box. The red hair is a bit of a disconnect with his olive complexion, but then, being a genetic hodgepodge has served him well all his life. He's always been a chameleon who could pass for any ethnicity. The red hair just adds one more level of misdirection.

He skips town and never stays anywhere for more than a day or two. Word is that the Pacific Northwest is more sympathetic to AWOL Unwinds than Southern California, so that's where he's headed.

Starkey is prepared for life as a fugitive, because he has always lived in a kind of protective paranoia. Don't trust anyone, not even your own shadow, and look out for your own best interests. His friends appreciated his clear-cut approach to life, because they always knew where they stood. He would fight to the end for his friends . . . as long as it was in his own interest to do so.

"You have the soul of a corporation," a teacher once told

him. It was meant as an insult, but he took it as a compliment. Corporations have great power and do fine things in this world when they choose to. She was a glacier-hugging math teacher who got laid off the following year, because who needs math teachers when you can just get a NeuroWeave? Just goes to show you, hugging a chunk of ice gets you nothing but cold.

Now, however, Starkey's one with the huggers, because they're the kind of people who run the Anti-Divisional Resistance, harboring runaway Unwinds. Once he's in the hands of the ADR, he knows he'll be safe, but finding them is the hard part.

"I've been AWOL for almost four months now and haven't seen no sign of the resistance," says an ugly kid with a bulldog face. Starkey met him while hanging out behind a KFC on Christmas Eve, waiting for them to throw out the leftover chicken. He's not the kind of kid Starkey would hang with in real life, but now that real life has flipped into borrowed time, his priorities have changed.

"I've survived because I don't fall for no traps," Dogface tells him.

Starkey knows all about the traps. If a hiding place seems too good to be true, it probably is. An abandoned house with a comfortable mattress; an unlocked truck that happens to be full of canned food. They're traps set by Juvey-cops for AWOL Unwinds. There are even Juvies pretending to be part of the Anti-Divisional Resistance.

"The Juvies are offering rewards now for people who turn in AWOLs," Dogface says, as they stuff themselves sick with chicken. "And there are bounty hunters, too. *Parts pirates*, they call 'em. They don't bother with collecting rewards—they sell the AWOLs they catch on the black market—and if you think regular harvest camps are bad, you don't wanna know about the illegal ones."

Connor, Lev and Risa uncover shocking secrets about Proactive Citizenry and the future plans for Unwinding teens in the gripping final instalment of Neal Shusterman's acclaimed **Unwind** Dystology.

"Perfectly poised to catch the **Hunger Games** wave, and based von an even more plausible dystopian scenario" Booklist